Entangled

A
Collection of Dark Tales
by
Travis Little

Published by

MELROSE BOOKS

An Imprint of Melrose Press Limited
St Thomas Place, Ely
Cambridgeshire
CB7 4GG, UK
www.melrosebooks.com

FIRST EDITION

Cover designed by Hannah Belcher

ISBN 978-1-907040-92-4

Printed and bound in Great Britain by:
CPI Antony Rowe. Chippenham, Wiltshire

For my parents,
who taught me to see.

Acknowledgements

Thank you for taking the time to read the following acknowledgements. Without these people and others, I doubt this journey would ever have started.

My thanks go to Julie for her love and patience, her support and ideas in the time that I write.

Thanks to my parents for their love and understanding over the years and for giving me the gift of imagination. Thanks to Bob and Liz, brother and sister and true friends to be proud of.

Thanks to Natasha Mostert for her friendship and confidence given throughout the last few years.

Thanks to my reading circle for their views, thoughts and suggestions.

To Bonita who has always read with an open heart.

To Rachel and Maribel who, across the Atlantic, waited patiently for the silver bird to deliver.

To Louise who saw the healing within the stories.

To Sabine and Vanessa for knowing what beautiful really means.

Thanks to Kyle Vallis for believing and your support.

A final thank you goes to close friends who, aside from reading my work whenever I pester them, continue to give their own forms of love, support, and friendship.

Here we go…

Contents

The Gift

For
Natasha

He was unsure what had woken him. Normally, even at his age, he had no problem sleeping through the night, but something had stirred him from his sleep.

Looking across at his bedside clock he saw it was 4.03am. With his sleep now lost, he stepped out of bed and wandered out onto the landing. Looking down the stairway, he heard no sound of movement or noise from below. The house was silent. Yet the uneasy sensation he had awoken with remained. He switched on the landing light and descended the steps.

By the time he entered the kitchen, he decided to make himself a drink.

He ran some water to fill the kettle; as he did, his eyes were drawn to the calendar on the far wall. Upon it, an angel of silver and white shimmered in the sky above the silhouetted outline of figures on a hillside. Christmas is almost upon us, he thought.

Clicking the kettle on, he took a mug from a cupboard and waited for the kettle to boil.

With his drink made, he stood a while in the small hallway listening for any sound.

Outside the closed lounge door, he stopped and listened with his ear pressed against the door, but no sound came. With his drink made, he returned to his bedroom and stood for a while looking out of the window. Steam rose from his drink and formed moisture on the inside of the pane which glowed pale yellow in the light of the streetlamp outside. Returning to his bed, the man lay awake for a while before sleep found him again.

All this time the uneasy feeling stayed with him. A feeling not felt for a long time but one he knew well. Someone was coming.

As Sarah Reynolds neared the end of her journey, there had been no bright star in the east to guide her to her destination; no angel had appeared in the sky to announce her arrival.

She looked out of the train window as the rain fell across the town. Dark banks of grey clouds had rolled in during the early hours of the day

3

and, though now just after ten in the morning, it appeared much later. She had noticed many changes on the train ride in; surprised somehow how the town seemed to have moved on without her. Sarah looked away from the window in the direction of the other passengers and, although she had taken a 6am train, no seat was unoccupied. It was oppressively hot inside the carriage and she noticed she was the only person wearing a coat. Since quitting her most recent job, she had been sleeping rough for the last week and appreciated the warmth and comfort that the train provided.

For the last two months Sarah had worked in a pub, mainly covering the daytime shifts. But as Christmas had approached and trade had steadily increased, she had worked there most evenings as well; the long hours leaving her shattered by the time she had finished. The landlord paid her cash-in-hand which suited her fine, especially as she had no bank account. She cared little as to how he ran his business; he was either on the fiddle or had been just too keen on her. She always thought the latter and those thoughts had later been proven right.

Most of the shifts she hated. Aside from the lecherous landlord there was a stream of men and, surprisingly to her, women basically trying to get into her jeans. Sarah had spent a long while away from regular contact with people and found the adjustment hard.

Late afternoon was her favourite part of the shifts. The pub sat on a main road and had several legal offices alongside and although these supplied regular trade, it was the people from a nearby small trading estate that she preferred. Most days quite a few of the employees came in for a drink before making their way home.

They were genuine down-to-earth people who thankfully didn't pry into her affairs. It was on one of these afternoon shifts that she met Jenny.

Jenny worked as a receptionist for an engineering company based on the estate and, having made out she needed to find somewhere to stay for a while as her flat was being renovated, Sarah had lived with her for the last few weeks. Jenny had never suspected anything untoward and offered straight away. Besides, Jenny said the extra money would help with the rent and it would be really appreciated. Sarah had offered this before she asked her, which seemed to swing it.

Not that Sarah actually paid her herself. The cash came from the solicitors and legal people who pawed her each evening, too interested in the smiling long-haired barmaid to notice their coats being searched and wallets being lifted. Having removed the cash, Sarah simply slipped the wallets back and smiled as she brushed quickly past them.

The train slowed as it approached the station. Being Christmas Eve, the train was packed with people making their way to friends and family, even at such an early hour. Several rose from their seats and began to collect their belongings as the train ground to a halt, but Sarah stayed seated, uncertain and cautious of her next move. An elderly woman collecting bags smiled at her. Sarah didn't return this though, feeling uncomfortable with the attention, so she looked away back out of the window. Condensation had formed on the glass inside the carriage and she wiped it away with the back of her hand. The sleeve of her jumper had a hole at the bottom where Sarah usually hooked her thumb in; she had done this on the sleeves of both of her two jumpers, bought along with her coat from a charity shop last month as the weather became colder. This helped her hide the bruises and needle marks, which had faded, though they remained still visible in places to her. The scars within always take longer to heal, she thought.

When she had worked behind the bar she had tended to wear long-sleeved blouses or a jacket Jenny had thrown out. It was a little big on her, especially on the sleeves, but this she preferred. Sarah had been clean now for two years, yet her arms still showed evidence of her past lifestyle.

It had been eight months since being found lying face down in the street and Sarah had never seen Liam since that night. The same Liam who had been with her when she had left home, amid the shouts and screams. How she ever thought she would find her way with him she never knew, but as their money began to run out and their habits increased, Liam always seemed to find the cash they needed from somewhere. At the time she cared little how her next hit was financed. She shut her mind to the household misery hers and countless thousands of other addictions caused.

They made their home in a flat alongside a railway station. Often, during the evenings, Sarah would sit and watch the trains heading off into the night, sometimes wishing she was on one going somewhere; anywhere other than there with Liam. If he had ever known kindness he had long forgotten it, putting her down at every opportunity. He was never violent physically with her, but the mind games and mental abuse he inflicted on her had, in a way, been worse. When love and hope is taken from you, quite easily you wonder if they ever existed in the first place.

One spring morning, having fallen behind with the rent, the landlord had kicked them both out. Liam had used every excuse for not paying and had managed to avoid the man until he eventually caught them in one night. During another row, Liam had even offered Sarah to make up for the back rent.

This had so horrified Sarah that she flew at them both in such a rage, scratching the landlord's face and hands as she spurned his advances. Eventually he pushed her away and told them to leave. Their belongings had been thrown out into the street, some being run over by the passing traffic. The humiliation Sarah had felt picking up her clothes on her hands and knees almost broke her then, yet she stayed with the worthless Liam and lived on the streets with him for the next six months. During this time she lived life in a daze, still following Liam and doing all that he asked. Maybe it was the thought of being totally alone in the world that made her stay with him, but either way, by now she had more than one habit to kick.

Her life took another turn one night as they waited in a queue at a food shelter. A local charity offered the service each Friday; they had both used it many times. The food was always good, and occasionally there was some good company. On this particular night, whilst in the queue, Liam got into an argument with two other men. A fight suddenly broke out and Liam laid several punches on the men before he realised that they had several friends on hand to help. He and Sarah had no choice but to make a run for it. For a while the men gave chase, but eventually they managed to lose them near the back of a row of garages. Sarah was more annoyed that she had lost the chance of food, than of any danger they were in. She was so cold and weak; all she wanted was some warm food which was small comfort in an ever-depressing life. Their lack of money had made her fixes harder and harder to come by recently; her whole body ached and the endless feeling of desperation was almost unbearable.

Another row ensued and Liam pushed her away, causing her to overbalance on the edge of the kerb where she spun round and fell face down in the street. Lying there on the wet pavement, her weakness so intense, she just about managed to turn her head to the side to see Liam walking off. Sarah lay there for what seemed like hours, until daylight finally came, and through misty eyes she could make out flashing lights approaching and she found herself being lifted inside the back of an ambulance. Whilst she could hear voices as the paramedics tried to talk to her, their voices were too faint for her to understand. She tried to rise from the stretcher as they lifted her, but her body was too weak. As they shut the rear doors, no-one joined her. Liam had gone.

Sarah spent nearly a week in hospital. She had no means of identification. No visitors came to see her. No-one knew she was there. Eventually, she gave the staff at the hospital her personal details but asked that no family members be informed that she was there. She responded well to the treatment administered to her, surprised how none of the staff judged her or made any comment on her lifestyle. The care and kindness she was shown was a world away from her time with Liam. She answered all their questions on what substances she had taken but, aside from this, rarely spoke. When her time eventually came to leave, she was placed in the care of a local charity who dealt with rehabilitation cases. Home then became The Willows, a residential treatment centre, where she stayed for several months. She had her own room and though there were plenty of people there in similar circumstances, she rarely mixed with the others.

Night times were the worst for her. Though her body was now clean, she felt so hollow inside and curled herself up tightly each night, and though her body and mind ached badly, no tears came. Every night her thoughts turned more and more to home and her family.

Then one morning, without warning or even a simple plan, she packed her few belongings into a rucksack which the centre had provided, and left.

An immense feeling of guilt went with her, as she had left without as much as a thank you. She wandered the streets of the city for the next few days, keeping warm by wandering around the big department stores. What sleep she got was mainly in the main bus station where the buses came and went all through the night, so no-one tended to notice her. Or if they did, they didn't care.

On the fourth day away from the centre, she crossed a busy main road and had to wait while a crowd of people in a bus queue waited to board. Heavy rain was falling, accompanied by a strong wind. As the crowd passed she noticed an elderly lady stumble and fall to the ground. A man helped her to her feet and, as they stood, his hat blew off in a gust of wind. It swirled in the air a couple of times before landing in front of Sarah. The crowd had thinned now and Sarah managed to rescue the hat. Handing it to him, her eye was drawn to a noticeboard outside a pub. The sign said that the pub was looking for staff behind the bar. For some strange reason, which she never knew or understood, she walked into the pub; ten minutes later she had the job.

The train had nearly emptied now and Sarah picked up her rucksack, pulling her knitted woollen hat over her long brown hair, and made her way out onto the platform. The concourse of the station was a mass of people, many looking up at the destination boards above, whilst below people milled around café bars or waited patiently for their journey times. Aside from the crowd, the concourse was dominated by a large

Christmas tree, next to which a Salvation Army band played traditional carols. To the top of the boards and around the tree, decorated angels with wings of silver and gold hung from the ceiling, gently swaying as they circled around in the warmth of the station. Sarah weaved her way through the crowds, almost colliding with a small child who had stopped suddenly to pick up a dropped toy. She handed the small bear back and made her way to the exit.

The rain that had been falling for most of the day fell heavier as she left the cover of the station. Several cars and taxis were parked by the entrance but she continued her journey by foot. Most of her remaining money had gone on her train ticket, so she didn't have enough money to take one even if she felt like it.

When she had finished her last evening shift a week ago, she had already decided it was time to leave. With the pub now empty, she cleared the final glasses and wiped the last of the tables before returning to the bar. Normally she would shoot off as soon as her shift was done, but tonight she was hanging back to collect her wages. She placed the final glass in the dishwasher just as the landlord appeared. As ever, he stood far too close to Sarah, almost rubbing against her as he handed her the wage packet. He had an annoying habit of dangling the packet in front of her face, almost as if she had to beg for it. Sarah was tired of his advances and endless innuendos; even the smell of him disgusted her. She took the envelope from him, tucking it in the back pocket of her jeans. As she did, the landlord leant against her, the scent of cheap scotch reeked from him. He had tried on several occasions to kiss her and this time it provided the situation she needed. She looked at him and smiled. This had the desired effect on the landlord who leant back away from her in surprise. At the same time she swiftly raised her right knee up hard between his legs. She felt a great satisfaction as she connected, his breath quickly taken from him as the pain overcame him. He doubled over, clutching himself between his legs. 'Take that as my resignation,' she told him as she stepped over him. As she passed the till, she tipped the contents of the tip jar out, tucking the money into her other pocket. The landlord remained on the floor as she pulled on her coat. Opening the till, she removed most of the notes taken that evening and stuffed them in the charity box at the end of the bar. The landlord would hardly think to look in there for his money. She wished she could have seen the collector's face when he opened it though. She then took two bottles of Jack Daniels from the stock room near the cellar door, before she slid back the front door bolts and left.

That night at Jenny's, she lay on her bed thinking about how she had ended up here. She hated being dishonest to Jenny about her life and dreaded another Christmas feeling unloved.

Earlier when she had got back to the flat, Jenny had greeted her with a smile as ever and a cup of tea. She told Sarah she was packing a case for a visit to her parents in the South West. From her bedroom and the midst of her packing, Jenny asked Sarah whether she was going home too. She had lied 'yes'. It seemed the easiest thing to say at the time but now, as she stood cradling her tea in her hands, her mind had drifted to home and she thought instead of lying, she could actually just do it. Later that evening Jenny booked their train tickets online. Sarah gave her the cash courtesy of a married solicitor. The photo of his wife and children had smiled back at Sarah when she had lifted his wallet earlier that evening while he was telling her what absolutely fabulous hair she had.

Sarah had been walking for over half an hour now, following roads she knew from her childhood. Some new properties had gone up since she had left and a couple of times she had to check her bearings. The rain seemed to be stopping and, as she looked up, she could see breaks in the clouds as clearer weather approached. At a road junction she passed St. Stephen's Church where she remembered going as a child to a carol concert with an aunt. Inside she could hear a choir practising, their voices sounding soothing as they were carried in the air.

The barking of a dog drew her attention to the other side of the road; turning back she barely had time to notice the figure moving quickly towards her. She was about to step back when her bag was jerked from her body. About a year ago, Sarah had fallen asleep on a bus in London and wakened to find her bag gone. Ever since, she had tied one of the rucksack straps to her jeans' belt. This had prevented her from losing it this time, but the force of the snatch caused her to lose her balance and fall to the pavement. The wet surface soaked into her jeans, all but removing the warmth she had gained on her train journey. She put down a hand to steady herself when another attempt to steal her bag was made. Again the tied-on Sarah came with it. Her assailant struck out at her. Sarah felt her bottom lip split under the contact of the blow; the taste of blood seeped into her mouth. The next strike caught the side of her head, the impact making her feel dizzy. Her eyes closed and white stars danced madly behind her eyes as she tried desperately to regain her composure, fear for her safety now creeping in. No further blows came and suddenly she became aware of the presence of another person beside her.

Her vision was still poor from the blows to her head and her hearing was muffled. She could make out that there were two figures now that seemed to be struggling with each other. Raised voices tried in vain to come to Sarah's ears, but she felt too weak when she tried to stand and fell back onto the pavement, the rucksack on her back softening the impact. The sounds of scuffling abated and her vision returned enough for her to see a tall man standing over her. There appeared to be a distinctive brightness in the light around the top of his figure, which seemed to fade as the clarity of her vision returned fully. He appeared to be alone.

'Are you okay?' the stranger asked softly. But Sarah felt unable to answer, still gripped by fear. The man knelt down beside her and spoke again.

'It's okay, you are quite safe. He's gone.'

Sarah felt her arm being lifted as the man tried to help her to her feet.

'There is a seat just here,' he gestured to his side. 'You should try to sit; you have had quite a fright.'

11

She slowly made it to her feet and managed to find the seat the man had indicated.

Sitting on the bench, she was at last able to see that she and the man were, as he had mentioned, alone. Her head throbbed along with her lip. As she ran her tongue over the cut, she could feel it was still bleeding. 'Thank you,' Sarah said looking up as the man stood over her.

She ran her eyes over him and could see that he stood at over six feet. He appeared to be in his early sixties; silver hair stuck out from the side of a dark Panama-style hat he wore. Rain glistened on his long raincoat from which he produced a white handkerchief. 'You should hold this against your lip for the bleeding,' he told her before smiling at her. And, despite the shadow that was across his face, Sarah noticed the warmth in his eyes.

'I'm Lewis, Lewis Harwood,' he said. 'Your lip looks very sore. You could do with some ice on that.' Sarah raised the handkerchief and pressed it to her lip, wincing at her own heavy touch.

The rain had cleared now, though the clouds still hung heavy in places. Some brightness shone as the afternoon light slowly faded.

Sarah was noticeably cold now. Her wet clothes, accompanied by the shock of her attack, all helped to lower her spirits even further. If it really was the season of goodwill, never had it seemed so far away. Lost in her own thoughts, Sarah almost jumped when Lewis spoke again.

'Not the best way to spend a Christmas Eve?'

'I can remember better,' she said weakly.

Lewis looked at the young girl who he guessed was in her early twenties. Her skin was quite pale with dark shadows clinging under her eyes. Though she wore a woollen hat and long hair covered part of her face, the girl's high cheekbones were still quite striking.

'Have you far to go?' he asked. 'I don't want to appear nosey, just that you look like you could do with a rest, at least a while to warm yourself up.' He smiled to try to reassure her, and then added, 'I live just across the road there. You could at least clean yourself up.'

Lewis had pointed to a row of houses which stood on the opposite side of the road.

When Sarah tried to stand, her legs felt like jelly and she was forced to sit back down again. The man sat beside her and again she saw the kindness in his eyes; he didn't repeat his offer, just let her collect herself and rest for a minute.

'Thank you,' she said again. 'I think I'll take you up on that offer.'

He helped her to stand, which was easier with his support, and they made their way across the road and Sarah soon found herself looking up at the house.

The property was a three-storey end terrace. The small front garden was somewhat overgrown, with tall bushes edging the property and obscuring the view to an open area of wasteland alongside. The gate opened onto a small path, which led to a set of four steps with black rail- ings on either side. As Lewis helped her slowly up the stairs, he brought out a set of keys from his pocket and opened the door, switching on the hallway light as he helped her inside.

The hallway was quite small. What it lacked in width was more than made up for with the depth of the house, and to the rear Sarah could see a doorway which she presumed led to the kitchen. A stairway stood in front of them.

Lewis led them through a doorway to the left, which opened up into a large sitting room.

'Please come in and make yourself at home,' he said, as he removed his hat and coat.

He laid them on the back of a large sofa, one of two which surrounded a low table which stood in front of a tall fireplace. The stone fireplace had a strength and beauty that dominated the room. On its top stood an elegant clock, which she noticed appeared not to be working as the time was several hours out. She glanced down at her watch and saw it was almost four o'clock. She turned her attention to the man Lewis as he spoke.

'Sit yourself down. I'll get you some ice for your mouth.' Apart from Jenny, kindness had not approached Sarah for so long that Lewis's actions seemed almost alien to her. He had warmth which you could almost feel radiate from him and she felt a safety here for a reason she couldn't fathom. Taking off her hat, her hair spilled across her face. She brushed it aside and, as Lewis reached the door, he motioned for her to sit down.

'Sarah,' she said faintly as she kneaded the hat between her hands.

'Sorry?' Lewis replied.

'My name is Sarah. I hadn't told you, I'm sorry.'

She smiled back at Lewis, and for the first time some of the cloud seemed to lift from her. Lewis noticed how her face became almost enchanting as the smile spread across it, though it never reached her eyes. He detected moisture in those eyes, as old ghosts walked the corridors of her mind. He disappeared into the kitchen and Sarah turned her attention back to the room.

At the far end stood a large bookcase, the width of which covered half of the wall, while it reached almost to the height of the ceiling. It towered over her. She looked at Lewis's collection of books. They were everywhere in the room, not just in the bookcase; even behind one of the sofas there were two tea chests crammed with books. She looked up at those in the bookcase. Most of the authors were unknown to her, but there were popular novelists and the odd topic she knew amongst them. On the lower shelves the books gave way to a large glass bowl which was filled with letters. Alongside were various framed photographs. The central photograph was of Lewis and a woman. He appeared somewhat younger in the photograph, his hair still as grey as now but somewhat shorter. He wore a white shirt with the sleeves rolled up. Standing behind the woman with his arms around her shoulders, they were both laughing. Sarah's eyes were drawn to the woman, whose beauty radiated from the scene; her elegant features were surrounded by long auburn, almost red, hair.

Sarah let her finger trace the outline of the frame, just as Lewis returned carrying a small tray with two mugs on it. He placed the tray down on the table, beside a pile of assorted papers. Also from the tray he lifted a small bag which he passed to her, along with a small hand towel.

'There's ice inside. It should reduce the swelling on your lip,' he told her.

Motioning down at the table Lewis added, 'Somewhat silly of me to be offering you a hot drink when your mouth is so sore!'

Sarah had replaced the photograph and sat down on the sofa to the side of Lewis as she wiped her face with the cloth and patted it against her damp jeans.

The ice felt soothing to her lip. The bleeding had stopped and, though her head and the back of her neck ached, she did feel her strength slowly returning.

Lewis passed Sarah her drink; she held it between her hands, enjoying the warmth. When she spoke, her voice was slightly stronger than before.

'This is a wonderful room. I like the high ceilings,' she looked up as she spoke.

Lewis sipped his drink slowly. As he did, Sarah placed down her untouched drink and stood. When she removed her coat, her legs still felt weak as she placed it on a chair to the side of the door.

'Guess you like reading,' she continued. 'You have enough to have your own library.'

Turning back to Lewis, she added, 'This room would look beautiful decorated for Christmas. Why don't you?'

When Lewis didn't respond, she thought she had been too blunt and intrusive. Before she could speak again, Lewis stood up and walked over to the bookcase where he picked up the photograph that Sarah had been looking at before his return.

'I didn't mean to sound rude, I...' she let the words trail off.

Lewis sat down again on the sofa and a reassuring smile fell across his face. He seemed lost in his memories and, when he spoke, he did so without looking up from the frame.

'My wife always did the Christmas decorating. This is her.' He turned the photograph toward Sarah and continued,

'She had a real skill for it; such thought and detail went into every last thing. I never thought I could match her.'

'She's very beautiful,' Sarah told him.

'She was. She still is,' Lewis replied. 'How's the lip?' he then enquired, subtly changing the conversation.

'Much better, thank you. I think I'll try that tea now,' she replied.

Lewis returned the frame to the bookcase, but stayed alongside it. He put his hands deep in his pockets and rocked gently on his heels. 'My wife died several years ago,' he told her. 'I miss her always. I remember the day of that picture as if it was yesterday. It was taken in Regent's Park in London on her birthday. We had just had dinner at the hotel where we were staying and went out for a walk there afterwards.' He turned and, looking at Sarah, continued, 'It's funny how we remember the slightest detail even after years have passed. We forget everyday things yet memories from years back we remember in such detail. The mind is a powerful thing; the way we store memories is incredible. You should never underestimate it.'

Sarah sipped from her mug, wincing from the heat. The tea tasted good though, it had been several days since her last hot drink and she found the warmth comforting.

Lewis smiled at her and said, 'Don't be worrying you have done or said the wrong thing. My wife loved guests and loved Christmas. She would have been pleased to have you as a guest, possibly under better circumstances though. Some people hate unannounced guests, but Evelyn, that was her name, she always welcomed everyone.'

For a minute neither of them spoke, each of them continuing with their drink.

It was Lewis who broke the silence.

'Sarah, it's Christmas Eve. You must have somewhere you should be.'

Sarah leant back and ran her hands through her hair, feeling the side of her head. There was a slight swelling where she had been hit; it was tender to her touch.

'I was planning to go somewhere, but now I'm not sure.' She picked up the ice pack again, pressing it to her mouth. The pain and swelling on her mouth had eased immeasurably.

'I was going home to see my parents.'

Putting the ice pack back on the table, she leant back against the sofa and ran her hands through her hair again. This time when they reached the base of her neck, she kept them there and closed her eyes.

'How long since you last saw them?' he enquired.

Opening her eyes, he saw moisture in them. She bit gently on her bottom lip, despite the cut and the swelling, and looked away from him toward the fireplace. He saw her swallow as if keeping back the tears.

'Six years,' she finally said. 'We had a fall-out back then and ever since I've kept away. A couple of times I thought about returning but I needed to sort myself out first, get some kind of order in my life again.'

'Why go back now?' he asked.

If she was offended by this, she didn't show it. She was not used to talking openly about herself and though Lewis was a complete stranger to her, she felt his honesty in his voice and found his way so very comforting.

Sarah held her hands together, with her elbows on her knees. She played with her thumbs as she spoke. 'I guess I just got tired. I was tired of running, tired of feeling scared all the time, tired of being alone. The truth is, I was never the daughter that they hoped for and I am not sure if I'll be welcome.'

She could have continued and, had Lewis asked, she might have told him more, but sometimes the silence between people speaks more than words can ever say.

For a while Lewis was quiet and returned to his tea. When he had finished he put his mug down. Sarah looked at him and smiled a weak, tight smile as if to reassure him, but the sadness lingered deep in her eyes.

'Sometimes, Sarah, things are not as bad as they seem. Earlier you asked me why I haven't decorated the room for Christmas. I do decorate and celebrate this time of year, not though in the way you might expect.'

He again stood up and returned to the bookcase where he lingered for a moment. This time, without looking back at her, he said, 'I have something to show you that you may find interesting.'

At the side of the bookcase there was a small space, from which Lewis pulled out a small set of metal steps. Placing them in front of the bookcase, he used them to reach high up onto one of the top shelves and brought down a cardboard box. He returned to the table and placed it down in front of them. Sarah moved back alongside him, curious at what he wanted to show her. Lewis turned his attention to the box in front of him. It was about twice the size of a shoe box and, when he pulled back the flaps, it appeared to be full of tissues. He pushed these to the side and, putting in both hands, brought out another box, which he placed down in front of her.

Putting down the ice pack, Sarah studied the box. It was rectangular in shape, about ten inches by six. The top was dome-shaped, while the base was flat. The remainder of the box was decorated in what appeared to be holly and ivy, small berries and, upon closer inspection, tiny flowers. It appeared to be a combination of both wood and metal.

It was mainly silver in colour, though in parts, especially around the carvings, it appeared almost black. When Sarah picked it up she was surprised by its weight. It was a stunning piece of work, the craftsman-ship was superb. Strangely, she noticed that there were no clasps or locks, nor were there any sign of hinges. The dome-shaped top suggested it had a lid but it looked almost solid.

'It's beautiful, Lewis.'

He watched her expression closely, and could see how fascinated she was by it. Only when she put it down, Lewis began to speak. 'Evelyn and I were married for only twelve years. Before we met she travelled extensively across Europe, North Africa and Indonesia. She was an avid collector of unusual artefacts, most of which I packed away after her death. A few remain about the place, but I only came across this a few years ago when I was looking for something else.'

He continued, 'I had never seen it before and, like yourself just now, I was fascinated by it. It was wrapped in an old cloth, which had a silk ribbon tied around it. When I removed the cloth, I found on the top there was a note in Evelyn's handwriting.'

'What did it say?' asked Sarah, her curiosity evident on her face.

Lewis thought for a while and stood up, he crossed over to the fireplace where he rested a hand on the top and, turning back to her, replied,

'It said: For Christmas.'

'Does the box contain anything?' Sarah asked, looking puzzled.

Lewis acted as if he hadn't heard her question and continued with his story. 'That Christmas I put the box on the fireplace where the clock is now. When I came home that evening, the box was on the table there. I couldn't remember moving it and put it back on the fireplace. Later that evening, it was Christmas Eve; I was making a drink in the kitchen when I heard a noise coming from the lounge here. When I came to investigate, I could find nothing untoward and sat down with my drink, then noticed that the box was back on the table. This time I was concerned and began to believe that someone was in the house playing tricks. To put my mind at rest, I searched the entire house. I found no-one.'

Sarah listened eagerly as Lewis carried on.

'It was then that I tried to open it, but found it quite impossible. As you see there is no lock or any way it can be opened that is visible. You can imagine how frustrated I was.'

Only a few hours ago Sarah could never have believed how her day was to change so much. The attack on her had led her now to this scene with Lewis. She also had a curious feeling deep within her, that this was all leading somewhere.

His manner and the soft way he spoke seemed very reassuring, making her feel almost as if she was being enchanted.

'It was later that evening that I discovered how to open it.

'We all miss people who have left us, especially at times like Christmas. The feeling of being alone can be unbearable. I so missed Evelyn that year. Why so much that particular year, I couldn't say. I intended to put the box away again, but as I picked it up the lid came loose.'

'How did you open it?' Sarah asked. 'What had you done?'

'I didn't know then. I do now, of course.'

Lewis looked at Sarah; she noted that he was more serious now. He held his chin in his hands as if thinking and, looking straight at Sarah, said, 'Would you like me to show you?'

Sarah was so eager to know what the box contained, forcing Lewis to try and calm her down before he could add, 'What is in this box is something you could never imagine, Sarah.'

It seemed to her a strange thing to say, almost as if he was pre-warning her somehow. She really didn't know how to react and waited for him to continue.

Lewis pushed the tray and papers back along the table. A box of pens tipped off the edge, spilling its contents on the floor. Lewis ignored this and placed the box in the centre. He seemed to be settling himself and focusing solely on the box before him.

He closed his eyes. She noticed his breathing became soft and light, and for a while he just sat there holding the top of the box. Then slowly, lifting his hand, he removed the lid. Sarah wasn't quite sure how he had achieved this, what was about to happen or what she was about to see. Lewis lifted the lid about ten inches then placed it down alongside the box. Sarah leant forward and looked down into the box. She saw to her surprise that it was empty; only what appeared to be a black silk lining was visible.

Lewis had opened his eyes and was still looking at the box, but before Sarah could speak, he said, 'Wait.' Sarah wanted Lewis to explain but she became aware that the temperature in the room was dropping, not in a way that you felt a slight chill, but dropping significantly. Sarah shuddered as the cold crept over her. She could see her breath when she breathed out. Aside from the drop in temperature, she also noticed it had become quite difficult to breathe. She felt her chest and throat tighten and, when she tried to stand, it was as though the pressure in the room was so low that she felt weighed down.

Lewis though didn't seem to have been affected in the same way. As he stood up, she saw him stretch his arms out just as a light shone out of the box. The light was of such intensity that Sarah was momentarily blinded. Slowly her eyes adjusted to the light, to find that the room had become a mass of colour.

The entire room seemed to be swirling around her at great speed. She thought her dizziness had returned at first, but as the temperature lifted she felt the pressure in the room returning and her breathing ease. As the storm of colour slowed, so the room came back into focus. But the room had changed. It was still the same room she and Lewis had been sitting in, but now it had been transformed into a scene of colour and decoration.

The furniture in the room had changed and she found herself sitting at a large dining table. Alongside the bookcase, there now stood a large Christmas tree filled with a mass of decorations. Various sized baubles covered most of the branches, among which were beautifully wrapped presents of gold and crimson paper. Wooden reindeer, snowmen, toy soldiers, hand-carved figures and multi-coloured glass angels seemed to dance from the branches. All around the tree lights flickered and sparkled, and from the tree top a large silver-coloured star shone down upon them both. Around the rest of the room were other decorations. A huge garland circled around the ceiling edges; this too was covered in an array of lights, which were more red and gold than the tree lights. Small beautifully-wrapped presents hung down towards the room.

The table, on which the box now lay, had also been transformed. It had been set for dinner, with two place settings. A white tablecloth covered the table, on which lay an ornately decorated table runner, which hung over each end of the table. The runner tapered to a point from which a silver tassel hung at each end.

21

On each setting were two different-sized plates, each with a small bowl on top. Inside there lay a small decorated box surrounded by small golden pine cones. At the side of each plate, crisp white napkins were rolled softly inside silver napkin rings, next to gleaming silver cutlery. A black candelabra stood in the centre with five tall candles, all alight; their light reflected and sparkled in the champagne flutes and wine glasses on the table. Tea lights also shone from two gold mantleholders, which slightly wrapped themselves around two red pillar candles, standing on small wreaths. These were at each end of the table, while the box lay alongside the nearest to where Sarah looked on in bewilderment.

She looked across to the fireplace, where the previously dark interior had been replaced by a roaring fire in which the wood crackled and hissed. On top she noticed that the clock was now working again. Either side of it were other garlands. These were what looked like layers of chocolate leaves, covered in gold berries. So animated was her sight that she saw the golden berries sparkle as they also reflected in the candlelight; so vivid was the colour in the room, that she felt as though she was discovering new shades of colour as she sat there. The light of dozens of candles shone in the eyes of Lewis, who still stood there, arms outstretched. Sarah seemed unable to move, as if she was merely an observer to this spectacle.

Lewis then lowered one of his arms, the other he turned toward Sarah as if he was asking for her hand. Sarah though, could see he was in fact looking past her towards the doorway behind her which, although she didn't hear it open, she felt as though it had. More colours burst from behind her into the room. Still she could not move, but from behind her she felt something or someone approach. As Lewis moved slowly towards her, out of the corner of her eye she saw something pass. As her eyes focused she could see it was a woman's arm, the hand was down-turned elegantly as it moved towards Lewis's hand. The crimson sleeve of a dress came into view, swaying gracefully from her arm, as did the long, radiant auburn hair Sarah had seen earlier, which had also now come into view from the side of her vision.

Sarah could not believe what was happening; she felt her heart pounding against her chest. The scream or shout she was trying to release seemed locked deep in her throat. Just as their hands were about to touch, Sarah could see the look of joy etched upon Lewis's face, and for some reason deep inside her she knew what the look meant. Lewis turned his eyes to Sarah, who was still looking up at him. In doing so, he withdrew his hand and leant across towards the table, Sarah's eyes following it down to the opened box. As Lewis picked up the lid, the room began to swirl again and the image Sarah had seen receded. Such was the rush of colour and light it almost made her pass out; they seemed to race all around her into the box as Lewis slowly placed the box lid back on. Immediately the room darkened and the intense swirling and movement stopped. The room had returned to the way it had been moments before.

Sarah sat there shaking, her mouth agape. All sanity and reason seemed to have deserted her as she tried to comprehend what had happened. Lewis had collapsed back onto the other sofa, a warm smile on his face. Sarah, however, was – not surprisingly – having difficulty believing what she had just seen. She felt as if she had to leave, to put some space between what she had just seen. Frantically looking for her coat, she looked at Lewis, her mind swirling.

'What the hell happened there?' she screamed at him. 'Tell me I imagined that.'

'Imagined what?' Lewis asked.

Sarah remembered where she had put her coat and as she hurriedly slipped one of her arms into her coat, Lewis approached her. When he tried to calm her down again, she pulled away from him, the safety she had felt with Lewis now gone. He could see how shocked she had now become.

'Please, Sarah; just think for a minute. You were in no harm. I simply showed you what the box held within it.'

She stood in front of him, running her hand through her hair as if thinking.

'Lewis, I'm grateful for your help earlier. Truly, I really am, but conjuring up your dead wife wasn't quite what I was expecting!' She thought about what he had just said and added, 'What did you mean by – what the box held within it? And how did you open it?'

She stood there in her coat, her hat in her hand. Her rucksack was still on the sofa where she had left it. She breathed out deeply, and strangely felt that she was no longer in a rush for the door as curiosity swept over her. Lewis, thankful she was calming down, tried to ease the situation by moving away from her. When he spoke, his voice was calm and measured.

'The box gives the viewer a chance to see what they want to see. It allows us to see time.'

'What does that mean?'

'Like I said, it allows the viewer to see and relive a moment in time. I chose a Christmas here with Evelyn.'

Sarah stood aghast. 'Are you being serious? How the hell can you pick and choose what you want to see?'

Lewis simply replied, 'Did you not see for yourself?'

Sarah didn't respond. She turned away from him while she considered what he had told her.

'Sarah, I'm sorry if I have upset you. I should have been clearer with you.' She could see the look of disappointment on his face as she looked back at him, and felt a pang of guilt. Shaking her head, she said, 'No, I'm sorry. I'm just confused and unsure of what has happened.'

The distance between them remained for a while, with Lewis regretting that he hadn't explained more clearly what would happen. He thought she would still leave, but as he watched her, he could sense her mind race as she tried to make sense of the events.

When she sat back down with the box in front of her, she nervously tucked her hands underneath her legs and gently rocked herself. Lewis joined her on the opposite sofa.

'So, tell me again,' she said. 'Are you telling me that you can pick and choose the moment you want to view?'

'Yes, I am.'

'I take it you have used this before?' she questioned. The wry smile appearing on her face seemed to help break the tension between them. Lewis didn't reply. The look on his face answered her question.

Sarah leant forward; her hand hovered over the box. Lewis looked on as she lowered her hand onto the box and tried to remove the lid. It remained closed. She tried again to loosen the lid, each time she increased her grip and tried, but failed.

'I don't understand. How did you open it?'

'Do you remember earlier how I told you that I found how to open it?'

'Yes, but…'

Lewis interrupted her and added,

'Love opens the box, Sarah.'

She turned her head to him, her mouth slightly open. She expelled some air and shook her head again. 'Love? How can love open a box? That's ridiculous!'

'Is it? Have you not listened to all I've said? Did you not see what happened here tonight?'

'But Lewis, you realise how mad that sounds?'

'Yes,' he added. 'I also thought that at the time.'

He moved next to her and could see that she was struggling to make sense of it all.

'I'm talking about real love, Sarah. Not the romantic stuff of hearts and roses and all the imagery of it all. But deep love. Love that lies deep in your soul. That part of you that never dies; it's the love that bonds and unites us. Over time people have gone to extraordinary lengths for the sake of love. Have you not felt that, Sarah? Have you not longed for that? For the comfort and reassurance that it would provide? Would that not be the perfect gift?'

He could see the emotion rising in her and hoped that she had understood his meaning. As Lewis had spoken, Sarah's mind had wandered to the events of the last few years. She felt tears welling up inside her as he continued.

'That's what opened it. That and the image in time I thought of. I thought of a time one Christmas and the box took me there. As it could you…'

A single tear rolled down her cheek as she heard his words. Through a mouth that felt full of feathers, she managed to say, 'You mean, I could use it to see a moment I want to see?'

He simply replied, 'Yes.' She brought her hands to her face and used the back of her hand to dry her eyes. Lewis saw the hurt and aching in her as she looked at the box and thought of what he had said. For a while she sat still, then slowly extended her arm towards the box. He could see her fingers trembling slightly as she lowered her hand and touched the box. She screwed up her eyes and almost shook herself. As she lifted her hand, the box lid slowly came away.

As before, nothing happened initially. Lewis saw the wonder on her face as she realised the lid had come off. She still sat with it in her hand. Then, from the darkness, light soared from out of the box. The light was the same intensity as Sarah had seen before, though no coldness enveloped her this time. The pressure in the room fell so greatly she could hardly breathe; almost unable to move, she sat there as the room span around her.

Lewis remained by her side as the light brightened further so that neither of them could see. The pressure on her body had now slackened; though still blinded, she was unaware whether or not the room continued to spin. When the light suddenly faded, Sarah found herself standing in another room.

This room was a lot brighter than Lewis's, and she found herself looking down at a grey carpet. To her side was a small nest of tables. She looked up, but not to familiarize herself with the room, for she knew it well. Lewis was unaware of his surroundings. The vivid colours which were so familiar to him were not present, but he found the clarity in the room was incredible, particularly as it was late evening.

A small Christmas tree stood at the far end of the room. Decorations twinkled and sparkled as light was reflected in them from a white candle burning on a fireplace, beside which stood a man and a woman. To Lewis they were unknown, but as he looked at Sarah, he began to realise exactly where they were.

They appeared older than Sarah could remember. The man looked to have lost weight while the woman's hair was shorter than the last time they had met. Sarah stood transfixed as the man moved closer to the woman and embraced her. It seemed as though the strength had gone from the woman; tears fell from her sad eyes.

Six years ago Sarah had stormed out of this very room. The shouts still echoed around her head to this day. As the couple held each other, Sarah's eyes were drawn to something the woman held. When she finally managed to move toward the couple, she saw that it was a silver photograph frame.

The picture contained a scene taken at a fairground. It showed the man and the woman standing behind a young girl in a red cap, who was laughing so much she looked as if she was doubling up. Sarah felt tears well in her eyes as she remembered so vividly the day the picture had been taken. They had called at the fair by chance on their way home from a trip to the coast. Sarah had effused about the simple fairground attractions, insisting on going on every ride, later winning several times on the stalls. The vivid memory of that day seemed to have lasted with the couple, as if it held all the emotion they now felt. Sarah looked on as the woman placed it on the fireplace alongside others of herself.

Tears rained down Sarah's face as she stood alongside the couple, who simply had no idea she was there. Lewis looked on unable to speak or move. He now knew where he was and who these people were, even before Sarah spoke. Sarah held her head in her hands, her long hair spilling over her face. She lowered them and, holding one out, Lewis could see it was shaking as she spoke. 'I've missed you so much…'

She lifted her arm and placed it on the woman's shoulder. The couple slightly moved as if sensing something. As they did, a great surge of energy engulfed Sarah, the force of which held her hand in place. A rush enveloped her whole body. Her hand seemed to vibrate then resonate with light that sparkled like diamonds on snow as it crept up her arm. As it reached her chest, she jerked as images flashed before her.

Many of them were of childhood; some she couldn't place. Birthday parties where her puffed-out cheeks blew out endless candles. She looked and saw herself laughing, dressed in a white dress set against a blue sky, holding onto a garden swing as she soared high above. As it descended, her eye fell over a sun-drenched beach. She saw herself running along the edge of the shore, her small legs splashing in the water's edge. A red bucket full of shells swung from her hand. Then she found herself lost among a crowd on a seaside pier, her head spinning frantically in search of her parents. Within seconds she was running again as she saw them in the distance. The safety and sanctuary she felt as she fell into those open arms, flooded through her. There were other darker images, some again unclear to her, though one of a hospital bed stood out. In it, she lay motionless while medical equipment flashed and beeped around her.

Her father held her hand while her mother gently, slowly stroked her hair. She had years ago back-stepped out into traffic on a side street and been hit by a passing car. Apart from being knocked unconscious, her only other injuries had been a dislocated shoulder and broken arm. She turned away as a small brown rabbit, long forgotten, brushed her leg. Old toys passed her, and a doll whose name she couldn't remember smiled up at her, an arm outstretched. There were so many images, she could hardly keep track of them.

In the centre of all this she still held onto her mother's arm; the tears continued to fall, as did her mother's, but Sarah felt an invisible hand brush her face. It touched her so gently, so softly, that the tears faded away. An aching and numbness she had felt deep within her suddenly seemed to lessen, as invisible arms held and comforted her. She felt herself lifted as she was taken from her nightmares and held safely until morning, not just the feeling of one person, but of two. Such was the unity of the tenderness that swept through her.

Initially, what she felt most could only be described as hope – a feeling she thought had abandoned her. She felt so light on her feet that she believed she was almost hovering above the floor. The feeling swept deep within her, no part of her body was untouched. She could only stand and look as the light travelled around her, shooting out of her fingertips, tingling through her hair, caressing her skin so sensitively that it then dawned on her what she was feeling and, to some point, seeing.

On her train journey home, she had continually asked herself one question. She was unsure if an answer could be given, but here in her parents' house – her true home – as the endless scenes danced around her, she realised that what she could see and feel was the one thing that she had yearned so much for these past six years. It was the feeling of being loved. Whether she still was had been her question.

Sarah closed her eyes to the images and she felt her hand break away from her mother's shoulder. The scenes began to fade. As they did, the swirling light that had surrounded her travelled back down to her hand, along her fingers, before pulsing and disappearing. For how long these events took place, Sarah had no idea. Her parents were still holding each other as if the scene had been mere seconds. The events she had witnessed had gone unnoticed to them, as she was herself. When her father released her mother, a soft smile crossed her mother's face. She saw her father stroke her mother's face; he held it in his hands and gently kissed her forehead.

Then, embracing again, they looked again at the photographs on the fireplace.

Sarah slumped to her knees and wept. For a long time, the tears cascaded down her face. The aching and hurt inside her had subsided, but she felt so emotionally drained.

At her knees was the box, with the lid lying alongside. Still light came from the box, though its brightness was much weaker and darkened as the fading images returned within. She was aware now of Lewis looking down at her as he had done earlier on the rain-soaked road. Then she was scared and in pain, now she felt somehow serene. He offered her a hand, which she gratefully took. Picking up the box and lid, she smiled at him and, without saying anything, as no words seemed appropriate, put the lid back on the box. Sarah took one look back at her parents and noticed that even though the sadness was still so strong in the room, she felt as if somehow some had lifted.

The room darkened as before and Sarah and Lewis found themselves back in Lewis's house. For a while Sarah stayed on the floor beside the box, as if lost not only in her thoughts, but in time. Eventually she rose and sat back on the sofa, having returned the box back to the table. Lewis sat close beside her, but neither of them spoke. For a while, only their loneliness was shared.

Sarah rested her head on Lewis's shoulder; the tears had slowed but still fell. Lewis held her, stroking her hair. So intense had been her weeping he felt it would not stop.

Slowly though, as she lay beside him, they did subside and she broke away from his shoulder and lay her head down against the sofa's arm. How long she stayed there she was unsure, but she seemed to have fallen asleep as she woke to find a blanket over her. The box was now back on the table, to the side; a table lamp cast a faint light around the room. Sarah returned into a dreamless sleep.

Christmas morning dawned and Lewis, as ever, rose early. When he came downstairs and entered the lounge, he expected to find Sarah still sleeping. Instead he was surprised to find her with her coat on, sitting on the edge of the sofa. Her eyes looked wide and fresh, a broad smile graced her face. 'Merry Christmas to you, Lewis,' she said.

Early morning light streamed into the room from the window, though the sunlight was quite weak. Sarah had brushed her hair and wore no make-up except for a small amount of lipstick she had managed to find in her bag. This had managed to partly conceal the cut on her lip. Her cheeks showed more colour and a greater look of peace had been cast upon her face. Her best wishes had surprised him, for so long had he come down to an empty house. Company had not been a guest on Christmas morning for many years.

'And to you, Sarah. Merry Christmas.' On the table he found that Sarah had made some tea and, as he sat down, she poured two cups. 'You look better this morning. Good to see.'

'I am, thank you. Much better.'

Sarah had sat for an hour before Lewis joined her, thinking about the events of the previous night. So used to sleeping rough, she had put her coat back on, feeling a sense of protection from it. At no point did she think that she had imagined anything that she had witnessed the night before. The feeling in her was so intense. She recalled the wonder of how the room had been transformed, marvelling at what she had seen. The clarity of her vision had stunned her. Then the horror (or was it shock?) as Evelyn had returned.

The contrast of her journey home when the box was reopened had had the greatest effect on her. She knew this morning she would make her journey complete. Had this been a glimpse of reality, or had she seen or felt what she wanted to?

The fear that had accompanied her on the train ride back home had been replaced with a greater sense of peace. Now the sunlight from the window had faded and shadows darkened the room. They sat in silence as they finished their drinks, before Sarah rose and said, 'I should head off.'

Lewis asked her no questions about the previous night. Let her feel her hope, he thought. Picking up her rucksack, she walked into the hallway. Guilt at leaving Lewis alone concerned her. But when he joined her in the hallway, he said, 'Now don't be worrying about me alone here, I'll be fine. You have somewhere you really should be.' Stepping out into the morning, she noticed and felt the day was much colder. A biting wind touched her face as she turned back to face Lewis. In the wind, snowflakes danced around the street.

'Thank you for everything, Lewis,' she said. She leant forward and kissed his cheek.

He held her close for a while. Her body had no signs of the shakes that had accompanied her crying the previous night. 'You take care now,' he told her, 'and good luck.'

Down the steps she went and waved as she walked down the pavement.

Lewis waved and watched her go until out of sight, and then he turned and slowly closed the door behind him.

An hour later a young girl stood at the gate of a house; a house which stood back off the road; a house unseen for so long. She walked through the gateway, down the driveway, past the immaculate lawns. Light snow swirled around her as she neared the house. No lights had been visible from the road but, as she approached the property, she noticed a small table lamp on in a downstairs window. When she reached the doorstep, snowflakes gently fell on a wreath fixed to the wooden door. There she paused, breathing out deeply as she slowly raised her arm and pressed the doorbell.

The cat kept mainly to the shadows, which were much greater now as darkness fell.

Light snow continued to fall. As the cat reached the main road, it turned away from the noise and traffic and soon reached a row of houses. These attracted the creature as here there would be shelter and, hopefully, the chance of finding some scraps of food.

There was no movement from any of the houses, and no signs of any food.

The cat soon reached the end house where it sheltered under the bushes that stood next to the property. To the side lay an area of open wasteland where a cold wind blew across, making the cat appreciate the cover from the weather and the slight warmth the shelter provided. A noise from the house drew the cat's attention. It jumped up onto the windowsill and peered up to the window. Though the house was in darkness, the curtains in the window drawn, a small crack of light shone from the edge of the curtain.

Here the multi-coloured light glowed, swirled and pulsed as it reflected in the cat's eyes.

Sevarine

Only the fire lit the room. Away from the yellow and orange flames, the night was inky black. Other than the crackle and hiss of the wood slowly burning, no other sound could be heard. The figure that sat in the chair stirred slightly; its aged body ached, the fire's warmth its only comfort. Slowly the figure rubbed its hands together in a weak attempt to gain some more warmth, but the rough, cracked skin caught in places, the sensation unwelcome. Even the long yellow nails were cracked, some split on the top, while a couple were so long they turned over at the tip where dirt was trapped underneath. Raising its head slowly, the figure's eyes remained tightly shut, the wrinkled skin hanging in loose bags all around them. Breathing out, its mouth opened, gradually exposing pink gums which bled slightly around the jagged, uneven teeth. The blood gave off a distinctive coppery taste, which felt warm along the long tongue that now ran over the bottom lip. The breath was fetid as it breathed. The pain the figure felt was so uncomfortable, though it had long known what the aching meant, and in a perverse way, it welcomed the pain because the pleasure was sure to follow. For now though, the figure waited. Dawn was not far off, and then it would make its move.

It would soon be time to feed.

The man held his breath, knowing that the slightest movement could be crucial. Knowing that he would most likely only get one shot, the only part of his body he risked moving was his right-hand index finger. Having held his position now for several minutes, he could feel the muscles in his arms beginning to ache. For nearly a mile he had patiently tracked the deer, always keeping to the front of the main herd, and the stag which appeared to be leading the others had soon become his target.

When it paused briefly to drink from a stream, he had moved further ahead and entered a clearing in the forest, where he had settled himself behind the remains of a fallen tree. With superb luck, the stag now walked into the clearing and he had quickly lined up his shot.

This is where he lay now with the movement of his body frozen, as he strained his eye to peer through the eyepiece of the small sight. Any second now he would release his finger and he could then relax. His luck was definitely in today, as the deer had walked to within only thirty feet of him. He needed the animal to just raise its head a fraction and he could get the perfect shot. Almost as if on cue, the stag raised its head and slowly breathed out.

The muscles in its neck stood out strong, the antlers catching the sun perfectly as he pressed his finger down. The Nikon D700 camera clicked as the image was captured before him. He smiled to himself: perfect!

The deer stayed there for several minutes allowing Daniel to take another dozen photographs, content now and no longer worried about any sound his movement made. When he rolled onto his back, his rucksack offered him good support as he pressed the memory button on his camera and viewed the shots he had taken. His first picture was good, but he actually preferred a couple of the later ones. The one in which the stag had arised its head just before turning away, had perfectly captured the strength and beauty of the animal. The ones he had taken earlier of the rest of the group hadn't really pleased him; they were all too similar, the backgrounds too bland. These shots had more than made up for them.

Slipping his rucksack off his back, Daniel reached into one of the side pockets for his water bottle. The cool water felt good as it hit his dry mouth and throat, and he looked up at the blue sky while swallowing, before breaking off a couple of pieces of chocolate from the bar he had been cooling under his bottle.

It was a perfect June day. Though only just after 9am, the day was already warm. With the forecast set good for the next week, he intended to make the most of the long daylight hours. Daniel replaced his water bottle in its pocket and lifted the rucksack onto his back. It was pretty heavy, though he was used to carrying the weight. Aside from all his usual walking gear, his bag carried two cameras, an amount of food and a small lightweight tent, in case he decided to camp overnight.

So far he had stuck to his route after his girlfriend, Becky, had dropped him off at 7am on the edge of the forested area. He was lucky to have her get up so early to drive him out here, and made a mental note to get her something as a thank you.

Today, though, was all about his walk. Leaving the deer to resume their grazing, he made his way down through a patch of long grass until he reached the forest path once more.

Daniel's plan, or the route as he preferred to call it, was to walk from one side of the forest to the other. The previous night he had spread his maps across the kitchen table and, with the aid of a green highlighter, marked off his route. Becky had packed the food he now carried for his trip and had returned to the film she was watching. He had seen it before, and although Michelle Pfeiffer tried on more than one occasion to catch his eye, each time he turned away. Over a second cup of coffee, he studied his route.

His westward journey would mainly skirt the top of the forest before heading south to pick up the forestry road. Here the ground rose to the highest part of the route, with views over to the Cheviot range. A large section of the forest was natural woodland, while the rest was made up of conifer plantations. Thankfully the regimented shapes of these areas had been cut back over recent years, and the more natural look of the forest area was slowly returning. Then his route would take him back, eastwards, through the denser part of the forest. This section would need care as the terrain there was more challenging. The whole walk would be just over 16 miles. While he had a rough idea how long it would take him, Daniel had a tendency to stray from his plans at times, usually to enable him to take in some extra scenery.

Andy Collins pulled on the handle of the Nissan and lowered the tailgate of the pick-up truck. Once down, he began lifting the old fence posts into the back of the vehicle. The day was warm now and his brow beaded with sweat, making him use the back of his gloved hand to wipe it away. Despite the heat, Andy could still smell the damp that the rotted sections of the post still held. When the last of the posts were loaded, he removed his work gloves, leant into the truck's cab and picked up a couple of water bottles. It was stifling inside the cab, and he wound down the windows to allow the heat to escape. Walking over to his workmate, he looked across the landscape where they were working.

They had started early today, doing various jobs along the way, until they had reached the area where the bulk of their work was centred. Here were two large sections of fencing which needed to be repaired to prevent the deer herd from straying too far. The work was estimated to take them several days to complete. The fence they were currently working on was deep in the centre of forest and only the 4x4 could have got them up the steep forest road to where they were. He handed one of the water bottles to James Lloyd, who nodded him a silent thank you. James was well over fifty years of age, more than double that of Andy, who was constantly surprised at how fit his workmate was for his age. They both drank simultaneously from their bottles before sitting back on the grass to enjoy their break in the sunshine.

James had worked for the Forestry Commission for nearly twenty years and loved the variety of work the forest provided. Andy was only working over the summer; he was starting a new job with a bank in September. James's previous assistant had left suddenly, without so much as a word, and Andy had joined the team a week later when he responded to an advert in the local paper. A little unsure of the remoteness of the work at times, he had soon been put at ease by James's friendly manner and started to enjoy the older man's company. He found he had quite a knack for the work, and the two of them worked well as a team. James had told him that it was difficult to attract younger people to the job; most preferred 'the bright lights of the cities', as he put it. Though born in a city himself, Andy found that he felt comfortable being out in the forest and thought he'd remember days like this one when he was stuck in a stuffy office all day. For now, he would enjoy the sunshine and the peace and quiet.

But there were times, especially late in the day when the sun lowered and the shadows began to stretch, that the forest seemed darker and more sinister. Nothing he could put his finger on, nor could describe if asked, but sometimes he had the strange feeling he was being watched.

'We've got some company,' he heard James say, distracting him, and looked across to the forest road to see a lone walker nearing them. Daniel had, unknown to them, already used the figures of them both to add a sense of scale to one of his photographs. The spot where they were sitting was close to the side of the faint road which curved gradually into the distance. The dark forest to the side of them had been bordered with an expanse of early summer flowers in the foreground.

'Hello there!' Andy said loudly as Daniel approached, returning the greeting and adding the same to James.

'Going far?' James asked, passing a coil of wire to Andy as he spoke. He took his glove off and pulled a handkerchief out of his pocket, using it to mop his brow. 'Not seen many people out today,'

'Quite far actually, I've skirted the forest from the west. From the crossroads in a couple of miles, I'll be heading south and following the forestry road.'

James looked impressed and nodded his head in approval. Daniel noticed they both had the forestry logo badges on their shirts; the same logo was emblazoned on their jackets laid to the side.

'That's a good choice you've made,' James continued. 'Done it myself a few times. One for the summer, when you have the daylight. Funny how everyone calls it the crossroads as it's more of a T-junction really; the path to the east fades away after a bit.'

'I noticed that on the map,' Daniel remarked. 'Still, I'll be heading south, once I'm there. It's been nice talking to you.'

'And you,' James replied. He took another mouthful of water before adding, 'Enjoy your day.'

Andy nodded a farewell before returning his attention to his work in hand with James, and Daniel headed back on his way.

When Daniel reached the crossroads, he decided to have his lunch. While he ate, he watched a pair of red kites circle high above. They were too far away to warrant a picture, but that didn't detract from the enjoyment in watching them. He had read recently how successful the recent breeding programmes had gone, to the point that they had now become a regular sight in the area. He sat to the side of the crossroads, which did look more like a T-junction as the forestry worker had remarked. The bracken had almost enclosed the path opposite.

From his rucksack he brought out his map and found the area where he was. The map showed the overgrown path continuing east for about half a mile then, after some woodland, the area opened up into open country. Tracing his finger across, he saw nothing of interest standing out from the map, but began to think that there may be some good opportunities for photographs possibly looking across to the Cheviots. He had eaten enough and, after another drink, collected his gear and walked down to the crossroads.

Standing in the centre, he looked at the panoramic view around him. It really was a beautiful spot. His intended route was to the side of him, but he had an interest to see the view from the end of the smaller track. It would only take half an hour at most; he still had plenty of time left in the day.

As he began walking through the bracken, it soon became quite thick and on a couple of occasions he lost his footing. Just as he was beginning to consider giving up and re-tracing his steps, the path reappeared and the bracken thinned out, eventually joining up with a larger forest path. Here the path ran in a curve, the view ahead blocked by the trees. Daniel took the pathway and, after about a mile, found that the path split again, so he followed the faint path to the right, attracted by two large oak trees that came into view. He stopped and took a couple of photos. The trees were old; the bark had split, the branches thick and gnarled in places. He tried to guess what age they both were. Running his hand across the bark of the tree, he considered taking a photograph but, keen to re-join the pathway, decided against it before returning to the path.

The woodland was quite varied now and Daniel saw other oaks, though much smaller, interlaced between ash and elm trees. When the path finally straightened, the trees thinned to his right and he stepped off the path and headed toward a clearing in the distance.

Pine needles cushioned his footsteps as he weaved in between the conifers he now passed. Aside from an occasional twig snapping, his soft footsteps were the only noise he could hear. Daniel was aware of how silent the woodland had become. He was a good distance away from any stream, brook or anything else that could cause a sound; yet the forest had become as still as night. No birdsong could be heard as he stepped into the glade. Here the trees thinned considerably, although he did pass some small silver birch, which looked to be struggling to take hold, alongside some older tree stumps. Remnants of when the forest had been much denser remained in places, and foxgloves grew around many of the old tree stumps, but no bees or insects hovered around them. Only the sound of his own breathing could be heard.

He was reaching for his map in one of the rucksack side pockets to check his position, when he heard singing. It was faint at first and for a moment he felt he had misheard, but when he listened again, the sound came again to his ears.

The singing sounded like a children's nursery rhyme. It was sooth-ing and almost hypnotic in the warmth of the sun. The singing seemed to be coming from an area over to his right. Here the land dipped away, close to where a few elder trees stood, and when he looked down he noticed the shoots of young trees poking through the long grass.

Taking care to step over the tender saplings, Daniel scrambled up an incline to reach a small ledge, which enabled him to look down below into what opened up into a large hollow in the ground.

The woman was kneeling towards him with her head bowed, her red cloak standing out sharply against the green all around her. Her features were obscured by the long black hair which hung down onto her cloak; he saw that she was picking small yellow flowers which she placed in a wicker basket beside her. As if sensing his presence, she slowly raised her head and smiled at him.

Daniel was taken aback by her features. Her deep brown eyes almost looked a little too large for her head. High cheekbones led down to full generous lips, which parted as she smiled, her teeth shining bright white in the sunlight. As she stood, he could see she was quite tall, almost six feet. Her cloak fell open and Daniel noticed that it had a large hood which lay flatly across her shoulders. Through the gap in her cloak, he could see she wore a cream coloured dress underneath, which seemed to fit closely to her slender figure. On the ground beside her he could see other baskets which, aside from holding other varieties of flowers, contained pieces of wood, bark, and mosses.

'Hello there,' said Daniel. 'You made me jump. I heard your singing, it was nice.'

Still smiling, the woman lowered her head slightly. She looked slightly embarrassed by his compliment, but before he could apologize she spoke.

'Thank you, that's very kind of you.'

She placed the wicker basket down and, as he neared her, her cloak fell away from her arm as she offered him her hand.

As he shook it, he said, 'I'm Daniel.'

Her skin felt soft and delicate even though her handshake was strong. As he released it, she said, 'My name is Sevarine. I don't see many people out this far into the forest.'

'That's some name,' he replied. 'Is it foreign?'

Her expression changed as she thought about what he had said. Shrugging her shoulders, she said, 'I'm afraid I'm not sure.'

She turned and began bunching the baskets together. There were six in total, too many for her to carry on her own and he wondered how she had got out here. He noticed under her cloak that she wore soft canvas shoes which appeared to be handmade. They had no soles or heels and were held in place by long laces that wrapped around her slim ankles.

Her clothing was a stark contrast to what he wore. Though early summer, he was dressed for the remoteness of the place, and had all the necessary gear with him in case the weather turned or he got into difficulty. For him, boots were a necessity; the woman looked like she would be more at home in a garden in the middle of town.

'What are you doing out here?' he asked her curiously.

'I live here,' she replied, her eyes still holding her smile.

Daniel was surprised by her answer. The road Becky had dropped him at was at least seven miles away. Only the forestry vehicles could get out to such a remote place.

His Ordnance Survey map had shown no properties in this area and he could only think that there was easier access elsewhere.

'You live out here?' He looked around him, puzzled by her answer. 'Where?' he asked.

'I live in the next clearing. I have a little cottage there.' She smiled again as if to reassure him, her deep eyes entrancing.

'Come,' she continued. 'I'll show you. I'm going there now. Would you help me with my baskets?'

Daniel felt a shiver run through his body, as if a trace of unease was trying to surface despite the warmth of the day. A chill caught his skin and he momentarily shivered, but then looked across to the woman's baskets and the moment passed. They took three each and set off across the glade. As the trees thickened again, Daniel began to doubt that there was such a cottage, as the tree canopy thickened above them and the light became poor. In places the ground became uneven, fallen branches trying in vain to stop their progress, but still Sevarine sang her song gently and carefully led them through the trees. High above, a tawny owl looked down. It felt relatively safe at its height but kept perfectly still, all the time sensing their movement below. Away from this area of forest, birds kept their distance, all wildlife kept to their nests, rabbits were hushed deep in their warrens. A pair of foxes, usually brash and aggressive to all they met in the forest, cowered nervously in their den, with the male's paws trembling before him. Stags and deer lay silently in front of their young, all bravery held back as they sensed the air. Aside from the couple who walked below the owl, all were still. Such was the fear throughout this part of the forest; it felt as though the forest itself was holding its breath.

As promised, Daniel could see the cottage as they left the gloom and stepped once more into the warm sunshine. His heart lifted at the sight of it; its location was beautiful. The dark forest edged the rear of the property, but there were few trees nearer to it. A small, but neatly trimmed lawn stood in front of the cottage, which was surrounded by a small dry-stone wall. A white gate led towards the front door, around which hung several baskets all full of colour. Petunias of pink and red hung down, intertwined with purple freesias. The cottage was painted white, with a red tiled roof. Two windows, one each side of the front door, had further flower baskets on their sills. Again, each of these was bursting with life and colour. Closer up Daniel could see the cottage appeared to be L-shaped. The section to the rear he presumed was the kitchen or maybe a further bedroom.

A small but tall chimney sat on the far side of the roof and, even though the day was very warm, smoke gently rose from a fire within. Against the wall foxgloves gathered, their soft purple flowers attracting all sorts of insects. Bees droned around the garden and plants, along with several multi-coloured butterflies that danced and spiralled entrancingly in the sunshine, landing occasionally on the white petals of tall daises. The whole scene was charming.

As they approached the cottage, Daniel noticed that a road led from the cottage on the far side. It looked as if it hadn't seen any traffic in a long time.

Sevarine spoke again as they reached the gate.

'You see, what I told you,' she smiled and opened the small gate. Passing through she added, 'It's warm today, I'll get something cold to drink. Would you like something?'

'Please,' he replied. 'That would be nice, thank you.'

They placed the baskets beside the door and Daniel saw there was a small bench below one of the windows, so he slipped his rucksack off his back, welcoming the loss of its weight as he sat down. Oddly, he was pretty tired now and the rest felt good. Sevarine had disappeared into the cottage and he noticed several sculptures and works of art standing against the garden wall. These had not been visible as they approached. As he walked over to them, she reappeared carrying a tray, with a filled jug along with two tall glasses.

The sculptures were strange. They were of human figures and appeared to be made of wood and different forms of metal. Lengths of dry, shaped timber made up the limbs, while the head, arms and feet were made of parts of old machinery. They were, on closer inspection, very effective. Skill and thought had gone into their design. The paintings, however, were completely different. These were of forest scenes. The colour was strikingly vivid, dramatic skies were mirrored with dark woodland images. The base of each picture showed flowers and plants in fine detail, a sharp contrast to the skylines. Each picture was on canvas, on wooden frames; the colour had been applied generously but with great care. When she spoke he almost felt as if he had awoken from a trance.

'Do you like my work?'

'I do actually,' he replied. 'It's very dramatic. The colours are sensational. Are they oils?'

'Kind of. I make my own materials from things I find in the forest. I use some oil, but mainly it's extracted from plants, berries, and fruit and…' her words trailed off, as though she was lost for a moment. When she continued, she looked at him as if studying him.

'You would be surprised what you can find out here that you can use.'

'I take it you are an artist?'

'I am,' she replied. 'I work from here mainly. I sell to a select few. To some people my work is in great demand.'

47

They sat outside on the bench where Sevarine poured them each a drink. It was lemonade with ice and cut lemon in it. On the top, amidst the lemon and ice, floated cranberries. It felt sweet and wonderfully cooling when Daniel tasted it. It was after midday now, and the sky remained a clear unspoilt blue with the temperature hovering in the mid-seventies. The scent and smell of the garden was overwhelming and Daniel felt completely relaxed.

'Come inside,' she said. 'I have other work in there you might like.'

They took their drinks inside the cottage and Daniel felt the welcome coolness. The inside was charming as well. A settee and two chairs sat around the fireplace, and he could now see the fire from which the smoke had risen. It added slight warmth to the coolness the stone walls cast. To the rear he could see the kitchen, which was mainly pine, but it was to his left that something caught his eye. Here she had her studio. A much larger window was to the side and this provided most of the light inside the cottage. A large easel dominated the scene, though no work or canvas stood on it. Palettes, pots, other easels and various paints in jars or hand-made tubes lay around; brushes of various sizes gathered in small bowls. Against one wall stood more frames, awaiting canvases. On the other side of the studio, several completed works lay next to various sketchbooks which lay open; sketches of figures and wildlife filled the pages. Sevarine watched him as he looked around her work. He knelt and picked up a striking picture of what appeared to be a huge wolf, though the scale and size were out of proportion.

'This cottage was once owned by the Forestry Commission,' she told him, 'but it fell into disrepair some years back and I managed to buy it.'

He had replaced the painting as she crossed over to him; her arms remained folded as she continued.

'When I saw it, I thought it was perfect for my work.'

'Don't you get lonely out here?' he asked.

Daniel looked on as Sevarine walked over to the large window, where she stood for a while gazing out. She looked as if she had almost forgotten he was there, and when she turned to him she had a concerned look on her face. The look vanished as she spoke again.

'Sometimes, when it's dark, I do. Then at times I fear it, but I have my girls for company.'

Daniel was surprised by her statement, he had thought from the way she spoke that she lived alone. Now she walked into the kitchen and stopped by what he imagined was the back door. She removed her red cape and laid it on the kitchen worktop, her black hair again spilling onto her shoulders. She must have been warm wearing it, yet she still looked cool and calm as she opened the back door.

'Meet my girls,' she said.

When she stood back, Daniel was surprised to see what appeared to be two large wolves slowly walk into the cottage. He took a few steps back, securing himself behind the settee. His breath caught and he found his nerves straining.

'Jesus! They're wolves!' he said.

Sevarine laughed and threw her head back. She was still smiling as the two animals sat silently beside her.

'They're not wolves, silly! They are Laikas or, if you prefer, Russian hunting dogs.'

She knelt beside them and gently stroked each of their heads. The two dogs looked content now, nuzzling up to her but although they looked calm, Daniel remained behind the settee.

'The name comes from the word "Layat", which means to bark. To me they are simply my girls.'

When she stood and walked over to him, the dogs remained seated. Her long black hair stood out against the paleness of her dress. The cut in her dress front allowed him to see her slender legs as she walked. She looked stunning, but Daniel suddenly felt somewhat uncomfortable, not just in the dogs' company.

'I like them, because they are quite primitive,' she said softly as she passed him. 'Please relax, Daniel, they won't hurt you. They do exactly as I tell them.'

From a silver dish placed on one of the kitchen worktops, Sevarine took out two large bones and tossed them in front of the dogs. They still sat motionless, their eyes fixed on her, ignoring the offerings. Sevarine looked casually at Daniel then raised her hands, clapped them together once and said 'Eat!' At her command the two dogs pounced on the bones, their powerful jaws crushing them as they sought the marrow within. Soon there was little trace of the food and Daniel stood amazed at the hunger the dogs seemed to have. Sevarine then told them to leave and, again at her command, they walked out of the cottage leaving her and Daniel alone.

Now more confident with them gone, Daniel walked over and shut the door himself. He could feel his heart racing and breathed out deeply, hoping it would soon relax him.

'Please come and sit,' she asked him, tapping the back of the sofa. 'Would you like some wine?'

Daniel moved his rucksack beside the arm of the sofa and, as asked, sat down. The three-seater sofa was covered in a decorative floral pattern, which more than matched the room. Though not new, he found it very comfortable as he stretched out his legs. Sevarine returned with a bowl of grapes and two glasses. She placed the bowl on one of the side chairs and handed him a glass of wine. Sitting beside him, she asked, 'So, Daniel. What do you do in the world?'

'You mean for work?' he enquired, somewhat unsure of her choice of words. 'I work for a building firm, mainly costing new developments. Mostly I work indoors, so I like to get out walking as much as I can.'

Sevarine watched him as he spoke; his strong jaw line caught her attention. He was well-built, she presumed in his mid-thirties and obviously kept himself fit. She could tell he was attracted to her; when she crossed her legs she felt his eyes linger on her slim legs. As she drank from her wine, she smiled at him, comfortable in his company. The sun streamed in on her studio behind him, making the canvasless frames stand out as the warm rays caught them. The water in pots sparkled and shone and the palette knives glinted in the sunlight, reflecting on the ceiling above him. Oh, how she welcomed his company.

'Well, out here is perfect then for you,' she replied. 'As I said to you when we met, I don't see many people out here. Mostly people stay to the paths, so I feel quite honoured to have a guest.'

Daniel sipped his wine slowly. Although he was happier that the dogs were outside, he didn't feel completely relaxed. The woman sitting before him was very attractive, yet he had a small feeling of unease in the bottom of his gut that seemed keen to surface. She continued to talk, mainly about her art, and he listened attentively. The wine was pleasant but very sweet. He leant forward and took a few grapes from the fruit bowl, hoping their taste would help lighten the wine. As he relaxed back into the sofa, he noticed his hearing had weakened and, although he could see Sevarine's mouth move as she spoke, her words were distant and slow. He took more wine and tried to swallow deeply, hoping this would clear it, but now his vision began to blur and the room swayed slowly around him. Daniel tried to stand up, but his limbs felt weighed down, his whole body seeming immobile. Sevarine moved closer to him and, through his blurred vision, he saw her face move right next to his own. Again she seemed to be talking, though he now heard nothing.

Her eyes seemed so dark and alluring, her jet black hair blurred into the background as her mouth moved, almost as if she was repeating the words of a rhyme, only stopping as she leant in to kiss him. He felt a weak sensation on his lips before his vision failed and he blacked out.

He seemed to dream. He was falling rapidly, yet no wind rushed past him. Light shone above him, but when he tried to look up, he found this quickly faded as he continued to fall. Strangely, when he suddenly stopped, he found himself standing upright. There had been no impact on landing and he found difficulty in understanding where he now was. In the darkness, unseen, he began to feel the company of others around him.

A weak light began to shine in the distance, through which he began to get his bearings. There were walls around him that appeared to be partly covered in panelled wood. The space seemed about ten feet wide, how deep he could only guess. When he reached out to feel the uncovered walls, they felt damp. When he moved his feet he realised that he was standing on wet earth. He now heard movement to his side and turned quickly to see what had caused the sound. Out of the darkness, figures began to approach. Far too many figures for the confined surroundings. They appeared to be dressed in rags, their features pale and watery somehow. On several of the approaching faces, he saw deep wounds which showed signs of decomposition, and he felt bile rising in his throat as the smell of their foul breath reached him. As they closed in around him, their hands reached out for him, each one speaking the same words over and over again, 'Help us, help us...'

The light began to fade as the figures engulfed him. He could no longer move as he tried in vain to escape. Unheard and into the blackness, Daniel screamed.

Daniel awoke with a jolt. A scream lodged deep in his throat. He found he was still sitting on the sofa where he must have fallen asleep, but he noticed that the room in the cottage seemed different. The fire had died, and long shadows now stretched across the room, yet it seemed to him that only minutes had passed. By the light in the room, Daniel realised the sun was now setting. He found that his watch was missing, yet he still clutched at where it had been. By the light he guessed it was now late evening, meaning he must have been asleep for over six hours.

Daniel slowly stood, but his legs felt weak and unsteady, while his head pounded with pain. He felt his bottom lip and found it swollen; a cut ran from it onto his chin. When he took his hand away he noticed a small amount of blood, and there was dirt underneath the nails and between the fingers. His shirt was open and now he noticed scratch marks across his chest. Blood marks stained his trousers and, when he looked down at his boots, he saw thick clumps of wet earth on them. His mouth quivered as he recoiled in horror. Fear raked his mind and body. What the hell had happened? When he tried to move, his steps were unsteady and he fought hard to keep dizziness at bay.

Sevarine was nowhere to be found. He looked around the cottage and saw that the flowers in the vases had withered, the dank water within carried mould on its surface. The grapes in the bowl had rotted away and he found the whole room in general had a scent of decay about it. The only part that still seemed warm and inviting was the studio. Here the other easels had now been erected and various empty canvases awaited an unseen artist.

His rucksack and fleece were missing and as he looked around the room for them, he thought he heard soft laughter. Keeping perfectly still he strained his ears and listened again. This time it was clearer, the sound almost a chuckle. He looked across to where a door stood shut, presumably leading to a bedroom. The sound could only have come from there. Slowly he approached the door, his ear still listening intently for any sound or movement. He felt compelled to open the door and find the source of the laughter, even though a cold sheen of sweat covered his fear-filled body.

It must be Sevarine, the woman who had seemed so serene and calm when he had met her, yet he remembered the unease he had felt. With his size and weight he thought he could easily overcome her if she attempted to threaten him in any way, yet now his unease did little to settle his nerves. His hand was shaking as he reached for the door handle.

He laid the map out on the bonnet of the pick-up truck and, after finding himself looking at the wrong side, James Lloyd turned over the double-sided map. Andy had gone back to his lunch and James soon found his bearings. Beside him stood Jean and Martin Page.

The couple had come across the two forestry workers as they reached a junction in the network of forest roads. Having moved onto their next section of fencing, the men were erecting a new signpost beside it. Bright blue and yellow markers stood out strongly on the new sign, and showed the varying routes that could be taken.

James and Andy had stopped for their lunch and were sitting on a grass bank enjoying the sunshine as the couple approached. Now, over the unfolded map, James explained the different options the Pages had for the rest of the day. The couple were in their early sixties and looked on as James used his index finger to mark the route back to their car. Martin afforded himself a wry smile as the route he had suggested to Jean had been confirmed as right. James and Martin spoke for a short while longer, while Jean took the opportunity to take a drink.

The afternoon was very warm and Jean was pleased they had decided to come for a walk instead of doing the household shopping. Groceries can wait, she thought, the day was too good to waste. As her husband finished his conversation with the forestry workers, he headed back over to her. They shouted their goodbyes to the men as they passed, continuing with their walk, following what would soon be shown on the new sign as the yellow route. Their voices faded into the distance as James and Andy resumed their work.

Daniel had to allow time for his eyes to adjust to the light in the room. As they did, he could see that a large bed with an ornate brass frame dominated the room. On the bed were dark irregular shapes, which were still unclear to his eyes. There appeared to be no window to this room, though there could have been a curtain in place. Around the room were several lit candles, some of which were placed on large plates beside the bed, while others stood on tall pillars. These were thicker than the others and now appeared to provide most of the room's light.

'Sevarine, are you there?' he asked, his voice sounding nervous even to himself. When no response came, he moved toward the bed. On closer inspection he saw what the dark bundles on the bed were. Mostly they were piles of clothes, all neatly stacked. Underneath some of the piles were various bags. The largest one he recognized as his own rucksack, his coat folded in a neat square on top. Alongside his own, was a pile of green clothing, upon which was a small badge showing two trees against a hillside background. Daniel had seen this logo earlier in the day when he had spoken to the forestry workers. Each bundle was wrapped in a cloth bow.

He heard movement to his side and he held his breath as Sevarine stepped out of the gloom. She wore her cloak again, though it hung off one shoulder. Her dress was open to the waist and one of the shoulders was tucked back under her cloak revealing one of her collar bones, the shading along the bone standing out strongly in the subdued lighting. He noticed that her hair had changed. Now it hung in long curls, masking her face as she walked towards him. Daniel felt more than unease within him now, to the point where she greatly disturbed him. As she neared him he noticed a tall dressing mirror to the other side of the bed where, as his vision had become more accustomed to the light, he began to see her reflection.

She stood and leant her head against his shoulder. Her skin smelt of scent and her hair held a sheen which was accentuated by the candlelight. She didn't speak and Daniel again looked into the mirror. Sevarine then turned her back to him and stood just in front of him, looking toward the mirror. Her hair felt silky and clean as it brushed his face and, when he lowered his head, he inhaled the freshness of her hair. However, when he looked again in the mirror, he suddenly jolted when he saw the image it now cast.

While she still stood just in front of him, she now appeared much smaller. Across her shoulders, the hood of her cloak seemed to have been raised as if her back had become humped. The cloak and dress were still off one of her shoulders, but here the skin was aged and cracked in parts. Her hair was still curled but it was etched with grey, with the clean smell gone, being replaced by a foul odour that rose from her. As she raised her head, allowing her hair to fall away from her face, Daniel saw that her deep eyes remained but the rest of the face was almost disfigured. Aged skin stretched across her face. A soft hissing noise came from her mouth, which opened slightly to reveal jagged yellow teeth. Saliva ran from the sides of her mouth, the hissing noise now replaced by a deep rasping noise that came from deep within the figure that appeared to have once been Sevarine.

Daniel backed away from her, his hand blindly scrambling behind him for the door handle. The air smelt fetid and corrupt, the cottage which had felt so welcoming earlier now held an atmosphere that was as though all goodness had been removed, and only evil resided there. He felt bile rising in his throat again as the stench of the place seemed to increase, his breath coming in short gasps. He pulled the door open and backed out of the room then scrambled across the lounge, his shin smacking against a small coffee table, sending a table lamp on it flying. The lamp holder shattered as it hit the ground. The pain from the blow to his shin was intense, his eyes winced as the pain increased, yet the deep fear in him seemed to sanitize it as he tried to find his way to the front door. Daniel sensed that the figure had followed him into the lounge, yet he couldn't bear to look back and see it again. He paid scant regard to his belongings as he burst through the front door and out into the garden.

The heat of the day hit with full force, even though his face was coated with cold sweat. By the doorway the hanging baskets hung life-less, the bright colours of earlier now lost.

He turned and backed away from the cottage until his legs banged against the gate. No figure emerged from the cottage; whatever lay within had not yet reached the doorway. Daniel quickly looked around him to see which way to go. The roadway nearby seemed the best option, though little traffic had ventured down it in recent times; the grass stood long aside the tyre tracks. He would also be running blind into unknown territory.

He jumped the gate, his shin feeling on fire as he landed. His head-ache felt just as bad.

Now he did look back, just as a figure started to emerge from the doorway. Daniel could only imagine what the place now held within it and fled with fear and dread.

Away from this nightmarish scene he raced, heading the same way that Sevarine had brought them earlier. When he reached the clearing he prayed he would find the crossroads again and could pick up the forestry road and hopefully get help. His mind swirled. Help? But from what? He would worry about his rucksack, gear and coat later. Now all he wanted was to be away from this nightmare.

Soon he entered the trees, where the bright sunlight again faded underneath the thick canopy. Several times he stumbled and almost lost his footing, but he continued on and soon ran into the glade where they had met earlier. Seeing the ledge he had stood on in the distance, he raced towards it, trampling the saplings he had carefully avoided before. As he reached the top of the ledge he saw that birds were taking flight from the trees around him. Dozens took to the skies; owls, hawks, blackbirds and thrushes were amongst those whose shapes filled the air above him. Their cries rang out over the trees, though the noise that followed chilled the blood within him. Two separate howls rang out, their sound long and distinctive. At what distance they were, Daniel could not tell as they began to echo around the confines of the trees.

Sevarine must have let them loose. God only knew what commands she had given them. He remembered her calling them hunting dogs, the thought doing nothing to make him feel safer. They may just as well have been wolves, though in reality he knew wolves kept to their own territory and would normally have kept clear of him. These, though, were something completely different, but it didn't seem to matter what breed they were. What did matter was they were after him. Daniel had no time to wait, he had to reach the forestry road and pray someone would be there.

From the side of the cottage, the two Laikas were released. They set out with their noses alive to his scent; their powerful senses would soon stalk their prey as they bounded away from the cottage.

Daniel feared looking back to see if he could catch sight of them. Terror drove him on. As he continued, he started to recall his way and a small amount of hope crept into him as he began to feel as though he might make it. Several times he had to duck under low tree branches and, when he looked up above, he could see the number of birds leaving the forest had lessened. At a junction in the forest path, he stopped. He seemed to have run much further than he remembered walking. Here the bracken was thicker than he remembered and he realised that he had to veer right. The forest road should only be about half a mile away.

Surely he could not outrun the advancing dogs. He only hoped they had got lost in the woodland somehow. There was simply no way he could avoid making a noise as he tried to put distance between himself and the dogs. Maybe someone else would hear him coming and could help somehow. His heart beat strongly against his ribcage, almost threatening to burst through. He could feel his body coated in sweat and he knew the cuts on his chest were bleeding slightly as the strain on them was increased by his running. More than once he rubbed his eyes to clear his vision. They stung with sweat and tears. Despite the pain from his legs, he ran on.

His mind remembered how the path bent round to the right, the way forward lost for a short while. Here the branches of the tall conifers hung over the path in places. As he looked ahead of him, he caught sight of one of the dogs. It was about four hundred yards ahead of him, moving at great speed. Through the trees and foliage he only caught glimpses of it, but it appeared even from this distance to be much larger than he recalled. Its back was raised higher and the head and jawline seemed more elongated.

To his rear, a distance away, the other one stood on a rocky ledge. Around it the fading sunlight struggled to penetrate. The shafts that did were coloured blue and green; they shone down illuminating the edges of the Laika. It raised its nose, sensing the air. Stretching its head high, it gave out a long howl.

Daniel stuttered to a halt. He now seemed surrounded and his mind raced as he considered his options. The one behind still sounded a distance away but, as he stood there catching his breath, he imagined it racing towards him at speed. The other, he presumed, had gone on to cut him off and would be waiting on the path up ahead. He seemed to have no option.

To his left he saw small breaks in the trees and presumed that a small clearing lay beyond. He set off running again, hoping there might be some cover there, or a way of shaking off his pursuers.

This section of the woodland appeared to be much older than the one he had come from.

A few tall trees stood, but most had withered and died. The lowering of the sun caused shadows to lengthen, making the centres of several hollow trees look dark, the scene foreboding.

Stumps stood all around, what shoots and branches they once held were gnarled and rotten. A scent of decay hung over the area; the occasional bird still fled the sky, though most were high up as if this was the limit of their safety. Now when he walked, no dogs followed, and he soon found himself in the centre of the clearing.

This area seemed so remote even though the rest of the forest and woodland surrounded it. Just what had caused such devastation to the area he couldn't imagine. No flowers or plants grew here, whatever grass remained was tinged with yellow and brown stains. Where moisture lay, mould had found a refuge.

Daniel looked around him. No sound came, but as he turned back in the direction he had come from, he saw Sevarine standing against a broken tree stump. His breath caught, as he had not heard her approach. She wore her red cloak which hung over her now smooth shoulders. Her hair was black and straight again, the skin young and unspoilt once more. In her left hand she held a shaped shaft of wood, which looked like a shepherd's crook. Although she was smiling again at him, his fear still remained. He felt he was being toyed with and at any moment all hell would be released upon him, so he was surprised when she spoke.

'You shouldn't have come here, Daniel. You have no right to be here. The forest is mine, it is part of me, as I am part of her,' she told him. 'The child I am, of its very own earth.'

Daniel could make no sense of her words. Her voice was tinged with anger and he began to slowly back away as she continued, 'People have no right to come out here. They abuse the place and they leave their mark and scars here.'

'So, what about here then?' he replied. 'I can only guess that you did all this.' He waved an arm around at the dead woodland as he spoke.

'It was mine to take!' she screamed at him, furiously stamping her stick on the ground. 'People should keep away or else I'll make them pay!'

As she glared at him, her cape fell open. To the top of her body, her pale dress stood out clearly, but below, within the cloak, was only blackness; blackness so intense it seemed light could not penetrate it. She held the crook against her. Her other arm was at her side, but now she trembled as her anger seemed to grow.

He continued to back away from her, his breathing becoming tight as his heart raced.

'What the hell are you?' he asked, his mouth trembling as he spoke. Now she laughed a laugh that warmth could never touch. It mimicked him, taunted him and when she looked again at him, her eyes were filled with hate.

'You could never imagine...'

Daniel looked on as she stretched out her arms and began to slowly rotate them. Into the air she rose with her cape flowing around her. The darkness still clung within her cloak, which opened more and more as she spun in the air. She stretched her hands out and moved them around in circles, the stick floating wildly around her. She laid her head back and to one side and began to sing the song he had heard before. There was grace only in her movements as she spun in the air, her speed never increasing. He stood transfixed by the sight before him, and when he looked at the ground beneath her, he saw that the darkness had extended down to the ground. Out of it stepped the two Laikas. Their bodies had now become disfigured, the backs hunched, the shoulders more prominent. Their fur was mottled in places, with dirt and leaves clinging to the lower parts, presumably picked up from the chase. The paws of the dogs were now the size of his hands, but it was their heads and jaws which stood out most. Almost twice the size of before, the teeth were exposed as they sneered and growled at him, saliva dripping from the sharp points. Daniel looked up again, and saw that Sevarine was changing once again; her hair was greying, her arms and face seemed to age as he looked on. Still she spun in the air, but her singing had been replaced by cruel laughter.

He could bear no more, he realised that the dogs had led him to this place; the distance he had run, they could easily have caught him. Despite this knowledge, with the mad and ever-changing Sevarine still spinning against a perfect blue sky, he fled once more.

It was after seven o'clock by the time James and Andy finished their work for the day. They had erected a further two signs after completing the section of fence they had been working on, then headed north to renew netting to a fence which deer had already trampled down. Both were tired now, though each felt the satisfaction of a good day's work. The extra hours would ease the workload later in the week. The sun was beginning to lower as James swung the 4x4 onto the forest road and they headed south once more.

When Daniel reached the pathway again he felt close to collapsing. The path still veered to the right and his heart, if not his body, lifted as he saw the entrance in the bracken where the path led back to the forestry road ahead. From behind he thought he could hear movement, and guessed the pursuing dogs were again close, but his breathing was so heavy he could barely hear. With the crossroads about a quarter of a mile ahead, he looked to his side and thought he saw a glimpse of red between the trees. When he looked again it was gone. Now he did hear the dogs; they were far out to his right when he glanced across, almost as though they were herding him onto the road. In the distance he could see a vehicle coming into view. The dark colour made him think it must be a forestry workers' pick-up truck, maybe the two he had seen earlier. Once more his hopes rose, if only slightly. His whole body ached and his heart pounded as he neared the road. He was only three hundred yards from it when he saw a flash of red to his side again. Thicker trees edged the road ahead where the path met the roadway, and he lost sight of the colour again. He glanced over to his right as he ran harder than ever with the dogs approaching fast.

The vehicle was nearing, though still some distance off. He raced off the path through the bracken, hoping the dogs would misread his movements. As he tumbled onto the small pathway he had taken a lifetime ago, he caught a glimpse of red at the corner of his eye. He heard the dogs approach, then saw a figure step into his vision.

In a brief second he saw her cape flow to the side. From a clear blue sky came a glimpse of her crook as it descended. There was a moment's intense pain as it struck him, and then only blackness as his neck snapped like a twig.

Jean and Martin banged their boots again on the ground, the last of the soil and grass falling away. With the rear door of their estate car open, they sat and finished their drinks and looked back across to the forest. They had enjoyed the day immensely, the scenery had been excellent, and the walk had left them both tired but exhilarated. As Martin collected the last of their gear, Jean stood and stretched, already looking forward to a long hot bath when they got back.

Each of them looked forward to returning again soon. Once they were both in the car, Martin started the engine and, after leaning across to kiss each other's cheeks, they headed for the main road again and their journey home.

The Laikas carried his body back to the cottage with Sevarine walking alongside, stopping every so often to pick flowers which she spotted. After collecting them into a bunch she then used several long pieces of grass to tie them tightly together. By the time they reached the clearing where the cottage stood, dusk was upon them.

She had gutted the body by the time darkness had fallen. Separate bowls lay out around the kitchen, filled with different organs. The rest was greatly enjoyed by her girls, who feasted out of huge silver bowls that clattered noisily on the tiled floor.

Sevarine herself ate, though her choices were more particular. She sat hunched over the table as she fed. Soon her youthful looks would be established again and the aching in her body would begin to ease. It would be months now before she needed to hunt again. The bones were collected together. These would later be crushed and ground, mixed with the remaining bloods and certain other items, and her stock of paint and materials would soon be replenished. The skin hung from the ceiling in large strips. This would be stretched over the waiting canvases and her work would begin again. Outside in the darkness, the forest came to life once more, a sense of normality returning again. The foxes hunted with ease and confidence, the deer were more settled, and stags now slept easier.

Smoke rose from the chimney of the cottage and, in the moonlight, an owl flew by, its wings flapping silently in the still of the night.

'Ye have not chosen me,
but I have chosen you…'
John 15:16

The owl landed silently on the fence post. Around it, the shadows lengthened as the remains of the day's sunlight faded away. The mist that hung over the surrounding fields began to thicken as the bird took flight again. It headed towards some nearby woodland, which slowly became illuminated as a vehicle passed by on the country road. As it passed, the headlights briefly caught the edge of a house which stood in the distance beside an isolated wood. With the brief intrusion of light now gone, the house returned to darkness.

Within the woods small creatures stirred as the approach of darkness brought the woodland slowly to life. Some would soon become prey for the hungry owl. Inside the house all was still. The rooms remained unoccupied, doors remained firmly shut and locked.

As the owl started its search for food, the house waited patiently as it had done for many years. Along a silent corridor, small footsteps were joined by another set, as darkness fell with the oncoming of night.

The dog searched in vain for the ball. It pushed its nose through the long grass as it sought its scent again. In the distance it could hear its owner's voice calling but, desperate to return with the ball, the dog searched on.

Where the hell was that dog? Reaching into his jacket pocket, Donald Hughes brought out a packet of cigarettes and stopped to light one. He had been smoking for forty years and, now in his seventy-seventh year, he considered if they hadn't hurt him yet, when would they? He walked once more when he heard the dog barking.

Though he considered himself still fit, he felt tired this morning. A recent cold had knocked him back, and he hadn't been able to walk his dog as much as he would have liked. Today was the longest walk the two of them had taken for a couple of weeks, and his legs felt tired. He ducked below a tree branch, upon which the first buds of early spring were beginning to open. As he skirted the edge of the woodland he caught sight of the dog away to his right. It stood barking towards the house that came into view as he approached.

'Alright, Jessie, where's that ball?'

Donald smiled to himself at how often Jessie lost balls; as a retriever, she more than often failed in that role. The dog turned to look at him as he approached, before continuing with her barking.

From his pocket he pulled out a set of keys. Jessie resumed her hunt for the ball, while Donald looked up at the property before him.

The house looked sadder than ever, the sunshine on its stonework failing to add any warmth. In the ten years it had been empty, he had once a week or so come down to check on the house as asked. The latest agents to have the property on their books were only a couple of miles away but, being the nearest resident, Donald had long ago agreed to help keep an eye on the place. Occasionally he missed a week, but no-one checked up on him and when he phoned the agents, usually every other month, there was a general lack of interest on their part about his list of minor repairs the place needed. It seemed to Donald that the house had become forgotten, and now no-one really cared about it.

So he kept up the usual routine. He checked for any sign of break-ins or damage, and made a few additions to the increasing list of repairs the house needed as neglect began to take hold. As he sought the main door key, he remembered the time when the house was much happier; now only sadness seemed to be in residence.

The small gate creaked as he pushed it open. Over the years lengths of ivy had become entangled in the rusted hinges. Walking down the path, he found the door key as Jessie came bounding across to join him. He ruffled the dog's fur as he bent down to welcome her, noticing that there was still no trace of the ball.

She soon returned to the side of the gate, with her tail tucked between her rear legs. She lay close to the ground, as though her nervousness toward the property still lingered.

To the side of the doorway, dead leaves had collected in an over-grown bush which had grown across a small sign showing the house name. Donald reached across and brushed them away to reveal the word, *Greystoke*. Away from his view, the forgotten ball lay in the grass alongside the metal railings that surrounded the house, a small hand reaching out for it as Donald entered the building.

All the magazines carried the same stories. They were all filled with self-indulgent celebrities, craving publicity in any form. Surely people didn't really care about these people's sad lives, though judging by the number of articles each magazine carried, some obviously did. Wondering who was the saddest, Amy Latimer thumbed through another magazine looking for something to read while she waited for her hair appointment.

Amy had booked for 10am and it was now 10.25. She thought that if the two stylists cut more and talked less, they could keep to their scheduled appointments better.

Amy returned her attention to the magazine she held and took a sip of the coffee she had been given. As she turned the page, she suddenly stopped. She felt her breath catch in her throat and her heart rate increased rapidly as she looked at the page before her. The whole of her body suddenly felt numb; she couldn't believe what she had just seen. Her haircut now seemed unimportant and she tried to shake the numbness off, her body jolting as she rose from her chair. Her leg caught on the side of a low table, causing the other magazines to spill onto the floor. The stylist nearest to her stopped, her arms frozen in the air like a statue, as she looked open-mouthed at Amy's sudden movement. Amidst the commotion, she saw Amy grab her coat and, still holding the magazine, race out of the shop pulling on her coat as she left.

Donald always found the entrance hall welcoming. This was where most of the light entered the building. The windows on the lower floor had shutters drawn across them, and when Donald checked these rooms he usually used a torch as the electricity had long since been turned off. He could easily have opened a few shutters, and occasionally he did, but mostly they remained closed almost as if the house itself had its eyes closed.

Above the front door was an arch-shaped fanlight window; across the top, decorative glass showed various shades of colour. On brighter days these glowed across the floor when Donald entered the house late in the afternoon. Above this was a large round window. He looked across to the grand staircase which rose up before him. Halfway up, under a large window, it separated left and right. Light from the window streamed down into the hallway, adding a warmth that failed to shift the dampness which had marked and stained the once elegant wallpaper. The wooden balustrade on the stairs no longer held shine, nor did anywhere else, as dust and grime gathered. Either side of the stairs stood a door. Each door was closed, as were the ones either side of him as he stood in the middle of the hallway. He removed his hat, rolled it up and put it in his jacket pocket. He raised his head and felt the warmth the late spring sunshine offered through the glass.

Closing his eyes, he recalled days long gone when warmth and laughter had filled the many rooms of *Greystoke*. He had only occasionally come inside the property back then but now, as the only visitor, silence held court, broken only by his visits.

He followed his usual routine, checking all the downstairs rooms which were mostly empty. Others had odd pieces of furniture shrouded in pale white sheets which glowed weakly as he shone the torch over them. The glass of a tall bookcase reflected the light back at him in one room, allowing him to briefly glimpse his reflection. Closing each door behind him, he left every room as he found it. It was as he closed the kitchen door that he heard the noise of soft footsteps on the floor above him.

Blake Henning turned off the car engine and reached into the back seat for his jacket, then looked up at Amy's small terraced house and wondered what all the excitement could be about.

Amy had telephoned him a couple of hours ago asking him to come over as soon as possible. It had meant cancelling his planned trip to see friends over the weekend, as Amy had said she needed to see him. She had told him she would explain all when he arrived, but he could tell from the enthusiasm in her voice that it was good news.

They had been friends for nearly two years now and, while they had dated a few times early on and almost got intimate, Amy preferred him simply as a friend. Blake, on the other hand, while accepting her wishes, had fallen for her the moment he had seen her.

Of all places, they had met in a bank. Amy had been having a heated exchange with a charmless cashier, and had turned abruptly to leave. In doing so, she had walked straight into him, knocking him to the ground. She tried clumsily to apologise to him while he still sat on the floor but, instead of annoying him, she had seemed almost angelic to him. Despite her mood, the sunlight that had shone through one of the bank's windows had lit up the curls of her blonde hair. Her apologies had continued over a cup of coffee in a nearby café, where Blake had been able to soothe her temper and completely charm her. They found they both shared the same sharp sense of humour and had spent three hours talking over several more coffees, soon becoming firm friends.

Breaking his mind away from his memories, Blake pulled on his jacket and, after locking his car, had to wait for a car to pass before crossing over the road to Amy's. After letting himself in with the key Amy had given him, he heard her shout 'hello' from upstairs.

'I'm up here. The kettle should have boiled by now. Bring up some coffee and prepare to be stunned!' she called.

Amy always kept her place neat and tidy, with the exception of the kitchen. Here chaos reigned, and Blake struggled to find two mugs for their drinks. He couldn't understand how anyone who lived on their own could have so much washing up. He managed to spill some coffee on his hand as he climbed the stairs, cursing quietly under his breath.

When he entered the bedroom, only her blonde curls were visible above the piles of books, folders and papers on her bed. Amy was kneeling on the far side and appeared to be reaching for something underneath the bed.

He placed the cups on two coasters on top of a cupboard, as Amy surfaced from under the bed, clutching a book, with a huge grin upon her face.

She bounded over the bed towards him, sending other books and papers spilling to the floor in the process.

'What's got into you?' he asked her, smiling himself now.

Amy held the book beside her and, leaning forward, said, 'I've found it.'

'Found what?' he asked, enjoying her excitement. When she held the book out to him, he guessed what had got into her, in the moment before she added, 'I've found my house!'

Donald wasn't surprised by the sound, having heard it many times over the years. As he turned at the bottom of the staircase, he held his hand on the banister and strained his ear for sounds of movement. The sound came again, though much stronger now. The footsteps had been joined by others; it was these ones that were more familiar to him.

He heard Jessie bark outside as he started to climb the stairs. There was no way the dog would enter the house now, the unease the animal felt about the place often caused her to keep her distance and more than often bark in protest. By the time he had reached the divide in the staircase, he heard the soft laughter.

Originally the rooms to the left of the house had been used by the owners as their private rooms. There were five bedrooms, two bathrooms, and a room that had been mainly used for storage. At the end of the corridor, there was a small nursery.

Donald checked each room to the left, in his usual manner. Free from shutters, the upstairs windows allowed the sunlight to fill the rooms and gave each one much needed warmth. The two bathrooms were cooler though; here the small frosted windows gave little illumination. He saw that the old baths in each room were becoming discoloured over time, along with the sinks. There had been a time that he had seen all this gleaming and polished. The bedrooms all still contained beds, which were also covered in white sheets. The last room he checked was the nursery. Outside of it he paused, his hand on the door handle. He put his ear to the wood and listened. He heard movement and a brief snigger which seemed to echo within the confines of the room. He turned the handle and opened the door.

The room was empty; it usually was, though he recalled a day when it had appeared quite different. It had been a summer's day, two maybe three years ago when he had called on the house. The visit had been in addition to his usual checks. He had felt the compulsion to visit, almost as if the house itself was calling to him.

He had been in the left of the house, as he was now, when he heard a noise coming from the nursery. The place had been quiet on his previous visits, so the noise had surprised him.

He had left one of the bedrooms and, as he approached the nursery, the door had opened by itself. The weather had been warm for several weeks and as he entered, the sunlight streamed across the room. In the middle of the room, there stood two young girls. He knew their ages and who they were, but still the surprise made his breath catch. Both had smiled at him and then, turning to each other, started to dance.

Their movements had been soft and mostly silent. The small footsteps seemed to bounce off the floor. Each of the girls held a garland of flowers and, as he watched, he noticed flowers in each girl's hair. As they danced, their footsteps caused the dust on the floor to shift and move. The dust motes danced in unison around them, caught in the sunlight that shone brightly in from the three large windows, the grime Donald was used to seeing on the glass now gone. The only place the sunlight had seemed to weaken was as it hit the forms of the young girls, who sang a soft lullaby as they continued to dance around the room. Donald had looked on, enchanted by the scene, their movement seeming to have a hypnotic effect on him. Outside cloud must have moved across the sky, as the sunlight began to fade. As it did, so did the image of the girls. He had blinked his eyes and the immobility he felt gently lifted. When he looked again, the images had faded, the room was again empty, the house silent once more.

Donald continued now with his room checking. The right hand side of the house mirrored the other side, apart from the nursery, and he checked these rooms quicker due mainly to his urge for a cigarette. Though empty he still never smoked inside the house, as much out of respect as from a safety point. No further sounds came as he left.

Outside once more, he checked the front door was locked and found Jessie chasing a rabbit through the long grass opposite. He was tired now and thought a long hot bath would ease his weary joints. He lit his cigarette and enjoyed his smoke as he and Jessie made their way back home.

From an upstairs window, two figures watched them leave.

Blake held her book as she told him of the events in the hairdressers.

'So you're going to get yourself arrested for magazine pinching are you?' he teased her. She laughed as he flicked through her small book.

Inside were several copies of her original photo, alongside maps, drawings and sketches of what she thought the house looked like inside.

Amy had spent years trying to find the house; endless hours in estate agents, hour upon hour in libraries poring over books, even putting the photo on the internet on various websites – all to no avail. Now, in a small hair salon less than a mile from her rented home, she had found it.

It amused Blake that Amy rented her house; she was more than capable of buying it and most of the other properties in the road. On the eve of her twelfth birthday, Amy had lost both of her parents in a traffic accident. She had noticed the police car pull up outside her school one day, and had wondered who they had come to see. Moments later, when they entered her classroom, she had felt a strange unease in her body which only increased as her teacher and the two policemen turned to look at her.

Her only uncle on her father's side had become her legal guardian, as the world she then knew seemed to suddenly end and everything changed without warning. Unknown to her at the time, she had been left

74

a large estate by her parents. Amy learned the scale of her new wealth on her twenty-first birthday, when her uncle had handed her a letter from her parents' solicitors. She had known her parents had owned a large number of properties and land, but the sheer scale of the amount had stunned her. Most had been sold following her parents' death, and the money raised had become her inheritance. The following day she had left the solicitors' office in a complete daze.

She had continued in her job, working for a publishing company in the city. It was the life that she knew and understood, so she saw no reason to change it. With such an amount involved, she took onboard all the advice about investing her inheritance wisely. Once invested, she had left the money alone, as she simply didn't have a plan of what to do with it. One spring afternoon eleven years later, browsing around a book fair, she had found it.

'Well, now you have found it, what next?' Blake asked.

'I'm going to phone the number on the bottom of the page and ask to view it.'

'Thought you would have done that straight away.'

'You, of all people, know how much this means to me. So I thought I would tell you the news first and phone while you're here,' she told him.

Blake was touched by her words and sat down on the bed, steadying the pile of books and papers, while she dialled.

He listened while she spoke. As she did, she ran her hand through her hair. This was always a sign that she was getting excited over something. Quite what she wanted to do next he was unsure; he was still thinking when she hung up. Amy dropped the phone on the bed and punched the air. She hugged Blake, as the excitement flooded through her.

'Take it the phone call was a success?'

She released him and picked up the house photo from the bed.

'I'm going to view it tomorrow. The house is called *Greystoke*, and it's up in Cheshire. Apparently there is someone who lives nearby who used to work at the house as a gardener; he has the keys, and can show me around. I have to phone him and arrange a time to view.

'So, I've done it then!' she told him, with her face like a child's on Christmas morning. 'I have finally found my house.'

Blake saw a distant look in her eyes as her mind drifted elsewhere. He didn't ask if she wanted him to go with her. He knew the answer to that. This was her own dream, and suddenly he felt she was more distant to him than ever before.

'Have they had much interest in it?' he asked, focusing his mind on the here and now again.

'No,' she replied. 'The magazine is a year old. I am the only person who has enquired.'

Looking at the number on the paper in her hand, she picked up the phone again and dialled.

She was younger than he had expected. Her voice on the phone had seemed wiser than her years now as he looked at her. She was, he guessed, in her mid-thirties, dressed in a brown waistcoat over a loose white blouse. Her jeans were tucked in small ankle boots. She removed her sunglasses as a warm smile spread across her face.

'You must be Mr Hughes,' she ran her hand through her hair and held out her other hand, which he shook. 'I'm Amy.'

'Hello and welcome, but please call me Donald.'

He stepped aside and gestured for her to enter. As she passed him, he caught a scent of jasmine on her. Jessie gave a soft bark and wagged her tail furiously as Amy knelt beside her, rubbing her back.

'Oh, this is Jessie. Don't be taken in by those sad eyes, she'll have you rubbing and throwing things all day. Please take a seat.'

She sat on a large sofa which faced a small fireplace. Between them, a long coffee table was covered in various books. It looked as though Donald had been reading when she had arrived, as a pair of glasses lay on top of an overturned book. The small cottage was well cared for and had a warm cosy feel to it. The kitchen was just off the lounge and Donald made them some tea as she told him about her journey. She had meant to be here much earlier, but had got caught in traffic on the M6. He was pleased to hear that his directions, once in the countryside, had been accurate.

She stood and walked over to a window which gave the room the most light. A vase of spring flowers stood in the middle, their scent strong but subtle.

'The scenery is gorgeous out here, so green.'

'I take it you are pretty much a city girl?' he said as he returned with their drinks.

'Mostly, though I grew up on a farm in Lincolnshire. I lost my parents when I was young and I went to live with my uncle in London. At the time it was a great change, though I'm used to it now.'

'I'm sorry to hear that,' Donald added compassionately. 'That must have been tough for you.'

Amy looked out of the window as she replied, 'At the time, yes.'

Turning back, she hoped that she had held her emotions hidden as she asked,

'Do you have family?'

'No, not myself,' Donald replied. 'Just me and Jessie here.' Moving some books to the side, he placed their drinks on the small table in front of the settee on which Amy again sat. She leant forward, saying thank you as she took a sip. Her mouth was dry and she felt herself relaxed now from her journey, as Donald sat alongside her.

'On the phone you said something I found curious; you said you wanted to buy the house.'

Amy laughed, surprising Donald. Even though her response had been unexpected, it was not mocking in any way.

'I'm sorry if that sounded odd,' she replied, knowing she needed to reassure him. 'I meant I would like to buy it. Some years ago I was at a book fair and I was looking through a box of paperbacks, when I noticed a box of old photographs. There were various scenes of the countryside along with some coastal scenes. In there though, I found this.'

She handed him a small envelope, out of which he took a photograph. It was a black and white print of *Greystoke*. The picture had been taken from the end of the lane which leads to the main road, with the wood just visible on the far left. Donald tried to work out when it had been taken, but was unable to do so.

'How strange,' he replied.

'For some reason I was fascinated by it. I looked through the rest of the photos, but that was the only one in there. As you can see, there is no name or details on the back. The woman on the stall didn't know where the place was.'

Her face had a warm glow to it as she spoke; she had real passion in her voice.

'I tried for ages to find out where the house was. I looked through countless books on houses trying to find it. Blake, my friend, thinks it has become my obsession. I've lost count of the number of dreams I've had about the house. Then last week, I was in a hairdressers flicking through a magazine, when I saw the article also in the envelope.'

Donald took out a sheet of paper, folded in four. The article showed empty houses in England. The house at the bottom of the page was *Greystoke*. Beside it was a small article which mentioned that the house had been empty for several years and was currently on the market. Anyone interested should telephone the agent listed below. The woman who sat alongside him had done just that.

They took their drinks into the small garden, where they sat on a couple of chairs to the side of a small table. The spot was nicely sheltered and Amy enjoyed the day's warmth. It felt good to be away from the noise and pollution of a city, and she caught the scent of several flowers that bloomed around them, bees droning peacefully on some. Jessie followed them outside, carrying a soft toy in her mouth, which she dropped beside Amy.

'Who were the former owners?' Amy asked as they sat.

Donald cradled his drink in his hands as he answered her.

'The house was the home of the Morrell family. Thomas Morrell was the owner until about ten years ago. He lived at the house with his wife, Jean, and their two children, Isobel and Emily'.

Donald shifted in his seat. As he did so, Jessie pawed Amy to pay attention to the toy. She settled for a stroke.

'Thomas was an exporter of furniture. Made a good living, though his work kept him away from home a lot, which his wife found hard. She felt happier when the girls came along. The children were born in the house and they all lived there quite happily until the accident. Sadly, Mr Morrell was away at the time.'

Amy saw the compassion in the old man's grey eyes as his memories were brought to the surface.

'What sort of accident?' Amy asked.

'I was working in the rear garden when it happened, tending the rose bushes. I heard a scream from the house and rushed in to find out what was wrong. When I came into the hallway, I found Mrs Morrell quite hysterical. The children lay beside each other at the bottom of the stairs. Turned out, they had been playing with a skipping rope and somehow they must have got themselves all tangled up in it. Mrs Morrell saw them fall on the staircase. They landed at the bottom of the steps; the fall broke both their necks.'

Jessie had had enough of Amy's attention and now wandered off, but Amy failed to notice and stayed quiet, leaning forward with her elbows on her knees as Donald continued.

'We called a doctor, but it was no use, the poor mites were gone. Mr Morrell was working in South Africa at the time and it took some time for folks to track him down. Friends came to stay and comfort Jean, Mrs Morrell, but she was too remorseful to help. She kept blaming herself for the accident. A few days later she disappeared. Half of the nearby village searched for her…'

He rubbed his eyes as the memories flooded back. Amy wanted to ask if he was okay, but felt he was best left as he was.

'At the far end of the grounds, there is a small lake. It is a cold bleak spot, has an isolated feeling about it, if you know what I mean. I found her there, floating on the surface. Everyone presumed she had taken her own life, as much out of her own guilt as anything. By the time Mr Morrell got back to the house, he was too late for everyone.'

'Gosh, that's terrible! So sad,' Amy said.

Her voice seemed to break Donald from his memories and a warm smile fell across his face.

He rose from his chair and took his cigarettes out of his pocket.

'Do you mind if I smoke?' he asked.

Amy shook her head and watched as he headed back inside. In the kitchen she saw him take a box down off a shelf. He returned outside, the smoke circled around his head as he sat back down.

'I have some old photos you might like to see. There is one of all the family, a couple of the children and some of the house in happier days.'

Over the table they looked at the forgotten images of the house and family. One showed the family grouped on the rear lawn. Mrs Morrell wore a large sun hat, which shaded her features; the children sat at the front smiling, with their blonde hair catching the sun. They all looked so happy. How sad, Amy thought, that such a tragedy could happen to them. Another showed the two girls running down a corridor, which Amy presumed was inside the house. On the family photo, she thought Thomas Morrell cut a dashing figure above them all, making Amy wonder what state his mind had been in afterwards.

'What happened to Mr Morrell?'

'He left almost at once. Of course, he stayed for the funeral. It was such a sad day seeing those small coffins, let alone Mrs Morrell's. The rain fell so heavily that day, the wind battered the churchyard, and the service seemed endless. It took place at the nearby village, Toolston. After the funeral, Mr Morrell wouldn't set foot in the house. He told his solicitors to sell all the furniture and to, as he put it, close the house. He couldn't bear to stay here any more. He left the next day for South Africa; I never saw him again.'

Amy looked at the other photos of the house as he spoke; the gardens, though not large, were beautiful. Though she knew the house would be different now, she couldn't wait to see it. A breeze blew into the small garden, blowing Amy's hair across her face, and, as she stroked it back, Donald noticed how striking her blonde curls were and how familiar. Still cradling his cup, he carried on talking.

'About eight years ago, I received a letter out of the blue. The postmark and stamp said it was from South Africa. When I read it, it informed me that Mr Morrell had died suddenly while out at work. Even though I didn't hear from him much then, the news still came as such a shock. I still tended the garden, even though no-one now saw it, but *Greystoke* stayed locked and empty. I was also informed that the house was now on the market and found I had been made the sort-of caretaker to show potential buyers around.'

'Have many people come to see the house?'

'A few people have visited; though not many. A couple came over from Ireland, but the woman hated the atmosphere of the place. One chap, an actor I think, viewed the place. I think out of interest mainly. You are the first for about five or six years. I don't remember time as well these days.'

Amy had been completely enchanted by the old man's tale. Looking again at the two girls smiling in the photo, she compared them to herself at that age. Emily's hair was curled, just like her own. Donald collected the empty cups and rinsed them in the sink. Amy joined him, bringing the photos he had left on the table.

Jessie was now outside at the front, barking at another invading rabbit and Donald smiled, shaking his head at the dog's exploits.

'Well, if I haven't frightened you off, young lady, would you like to look at the house?'

He knew he didn't have to wait for a reply; her smile said everything.

A small lane led from the cottage to where it joined the road. Amy left her car there as Donald suggested she might like to walk to the house.

It turned out that Donald had been left the cottage in Thomas Morrell's will, which he had been stunned to hear. At the time, it had come with the gardener's job and he had thought that it would be sold along with the rest of the property. The early afternoon was warm now; the sunshine flickered through the canopy of the trees as they walked past the edge of the woodland that led to the house. There was a deep kindness and peace to Donald that Amy was taken to. They seemed to stroll along like two old friends, each enjoying the other's company. He was keen to know more of her interest in the house, but for now he kept his thoughts to himself.

Along a corridor, small feet ran. Stopping by a window, her breath hushed, she waited. She had been looking for her sister, when her attention was drawn to something. The curls of her hair swayed gently as the girl looked out of the window.

She raised a hand to the glass, stopping an inch from the pane. Someone they knew was coming, but this time he was not alone.

The trees hung over the pathway as they neared the house. Amy lifted the smaller branches so that Donald could pass, then she ducked under and, as she stood, the house came into view. It took her breath away as it had done the first time she had seen the photograph years back.

The door stood central, a decorative arch curved over it. Smaller copies were over the six windows either side. A border of carved stone separated the upper floor from the lower. Here the windows were taller; again, the same decoration topped them. Three tall chimney stacks gave the property even more height. The stonework looked weathered and, as her eyes scanned the roof, she saw some loose roof tiles.

Several crows flew out of a nearby tree, their loud caws causing her to look away from the house. When she looked back down, she saw Donald watching her.

'Well? First impression?' he asked.

'It's beautiful. I knew it would be.'

She smiled a smile that left Donald breathless. There was a beauty about this young woman that reached deep below her striking features.

Her walk was graceful and unhurried, as if she made the pace of the day her own. He watched her walk towards the property. She seemed to be taking in every minute detail, as if she had waited so long for this moment that she wanted to savour every second, like a child looking at a Christmas present before tearing the paper off to see the gift within. The gate creaked as she opened it; she waited on the steps for Donald to join her. As he did, he took the house keys out of his pocket. He selected and handed her the long silver front door key.

'Would you like the honour?' he asked.

Amy hugged herself and, reaching for the key, smiled and said, 'Thank you.'

A curious thing happened to her as she walked into the hallway. She stopped in front of the staircase, raising her head and turning round to look up at the ceiling. She had expected to be overcome by the size and grandeur of the house, but the actual feeling she felt was so different. It was a feeling that at first surprised her, then completely overwhelmed her. It felt like she had come home. Donald watched as she held her arms out and span round, her hair flowing as gracefully as her movements, as she shouted out,

'I'm here, I'm here!'

When she finally stopped spinning, Donald asked her,

'Would you like the tour?'

He thought she looked like someone about to start an epic journey, her eyes full of excitement.

'I would like that very much.'

He led her through the downstairs rooms. Between them they opened some of the shutters, the rooms seeming grateful for the light that had been offered. They left doors open behind them as they went. The kitchen was much smaller than she had imagined, but the number of rooms left her bewildered. He told her small details about each room, and how they had been used in the Morrells' time. By the time he led her up the staircase, he could tell that she already loved the house. He showed her the rooms to the right of the staircase first, explaining that they were the rooms the family had used for guests. In one a tall wardrobe caught her eye, as its door was slightly ajar. Amy closed it and turned the small key in the lock, thinking that with the door closed it made the room seem in order. When they moved to the other bedrooms in what Donald told her was the west of the house, she looked out of one of the windows.

Below she could see the overgrown garden. A metal fence separated this from the rest of the grounds; weeds and small bushes entangled themselves around the railings. Beyond the fence, a path could be seen leading into the distance. This, she presumed, led to the small lake.

In several of the rooms there were small fireplaces, but she discovered these were all dwarfed by the fireplace in the master bedroom. It stood at nearly six feet and dominated the room, even though the room was twice the size of the other bedrooms.

When Amy sat on the bed, dust motes from the sheets floated in the air around and caught in the sunlight. She had noticed how the many windows offered the house so much light, and wondered how it would alter as the day passed and the sun set behind the woodland. She loved the master bedroom instantly and decided that this was to be her room. It was a room she felt she could be at peace in. A closed sanctuary away from the rest of the world.

The nursery was the last room they visited. Not that Donald had planned it that way; he had let her lead her own path. By chance or coincidence she had followed the route he took on his inspections. He pointed out faults and small repairs that needed doing. A couple of rooms suffered from leaking roofs, and she remembered the dislodged tiles she had seen from outside. The remaining carpets were worn and faded badly by sunlight.

In the nursery no-one greeted them. No-one danced, ran or giggled. The room was as silent and still as the others. For a moment he thought he saw her pause as if listening, but the moment quickly passed and they continued. They spent all of three hours in the house. Donald sat and rested on the stairs as Amy went round the house over and over again. When she joined him in the hallway, he saw the look of wonder hadn't faded in her eyes. As he stood once more she looked up the staircase and said gently, 'They're still here, aren't they?'

Donald looked as curious as he could, and asked her what she meant.

'The children. They are still here.'

She saw great honesty in his eyes as he replied, 'Yes, they still are.'

He had thought of mentioning it on their way over to the house, but he hadn't wanted to dampen her excitement. Now, standing for the first time in the house of her dreams, she had sensed their presence. Maybe she had been influenced by his story; maybe she just felt it, like she felt the love for the house which only a short while ago remained unknown.

On their way back Donald told her of his various sightings of the girls over the years. Most were brief glimpses yet others, like the day in the nursery, were much clearer.

Some days he would find doors open, which he knew he had locked on his previous visit. He told her how people from the nearby village had also reported seeing strange lights shining in and around the house.

Once the police had been called when two youths had broken into the house, only to return to the village screaming about figures they had seen there. Not much damage had been done; if there had, there was no-one other than the estate agents and himself to report it to. Mostly people kept away, occasionally Donald saw people looking at the house while out walking their dogs. In the main, the house stayed isolated and alone.

Amy shook Donald's hand and thanked him for his help, then got back into her car and made her way down the lane. At the road junction she gave a wave out of the window; Donald waved back and watch her go. He stayed for a while thinking about Amy. Jessie came out to join him and he knelt down besides her, stroking her head.

'Well, girl, I think we may be getting a new neighbour.'

The village of Toolston was quiet as Amy found a place to park. The place had a peaceful charm about it which she found relaxing. A large green dominated the middle, around which a row of shops curved. She parked near to the post office where she saw the Estate Agents' sign, three doors down. As she looked over to the edge of the village, she noticed a small church nestled between rows of beech trees. She wondered whether this had been the resting place of the Morrells, which Donald had mentioned. When she looked back, two elderly women passed her and said hello.

A small bell rang above the door of Erskine & Chambers as she entered. She introduced herself to the manager, Mr George Rayman. When they had spoken on the phone, he had sounded rather dour. On meeting him, she thought his manner and voice were well matched. He was a tall thin man, with even thinner lips. His handshake was as luke-warm as his demeanour as he gave her details about *Greystoke*.

He offered her a seat, and took out a file from a tall cabinet.

'I am surprised that you are interested in the place,' he told her as she looked through the paperwork.

I bet you are, she thought to herself. She wondered if he was married; if so, she pitied the poor woman. His voice droned on though Amy gave only a slight ear to it. To Mr Rayman, it was just another property; another item to be listed, unlisted and eventually filed away in his soulless little office. To Amy though, *Greystoke* was everything. When she had read through everything, she asked, 'If the house is sold, where would the proceeds go?'

Mr Rayman seemed taken aback at her direct question. He settled himself in the chair across the desk from Amy before he answered.

'You know, I've never been asked that question.'

For the first time a touch of warmth entered the world of Mr Rayman, as if the question had sparked some life into him.

'Thomas Morrell, as you may know – I presume Mr Hughes will have informed you – died shortly after the events at the house. However, he had updated his will before he passed away. His will stipulates that in the event of his death, with him being the only surviving relative, the proceeds of the house would be donated to various children's charities.'

In some way his answer was the one that Amy had almost expected; the piece of information she needed, which made her long quest for answers complete. She made an offer close to the asking price there and then. Amy informed him that she would get the necessary surveys and checks done as soon as possible. The look on the face of Mr George Rayman as she left brought a content smile to her own face which matched the warmth she felt inside her.

The warm sunshine bathed her as she walked back to her car. As she slid behind the wheel, moisture formed in her eyes, and a single tear ran down her cheek. Her feelings were a mixture of hope and expectation. The strange thing she then realised was that, apart from Blake, she had no-one to tell her news to. Aside from a couple of friends at work, she led a near solitary life. Now she was close to obtaining a property with nearly thirty rooms, along with the grounds the house included. The excitement of her venture now took hold and her mind focused on the here and now as she started her car. She drove the short distance to the small churchyard and parked close to the small lych-gate, where the scent of freshly cut grass came in the breeze that blew across the churchyard. A small gravelled path led to the stone church; to the side she saw a man with a shock of red hair, wearing blue overalls, raking grass into a pile.

She asked him if he knew where the Morrell family plot was. Leaning on his rake, he smiled slightly and directed her to the far side of the grounds. The plot, when she found it, was dominated by a tall marble plinth on which were the family names. A brief bible reading crossed the bottom, barely visible through the long grass around it.

Amy wondered whether this was to be tended to later by the groundsman. But she suspected that it would be left and forgotten like their home. A blackbird made an appearance in front of her, before flying up into a nearby tree, around which the scent of jasmine hung strongly in the air. She stayed a few minutes longer, before she walked back to her car and drove out of Toolston.

Time went by slowly for the next couple of weeks as she waited to hear about her offer. Several times she thought of contacting the estate agents, even getting halfway through the telephone number once before changing her mind and hoping that her patience would hold. One evening she went to the theatre with Blake, but the play failed to catch her attention. Her mind was elsewhere, as it had been since her one and only visit to *Greystoke*. When she managed to get some sleep, the rooms and corridors of her special house filled her dreams and she woke feeling as though she had actually been there, the feelings so strong within her.

She got the phone call she wanted a week later.

Trees obscured the view of the lake as they approached. Again the sun shone brightly and, with little breeze, the coolness the water offered them was welcoming. The size of the lake surprised Amy. She had expected it to be much smaller and at that moment, as she and Donald sat beside it, it was far from bleak. She had phoned Donald to tell him that her price had been accepted. He was delighted for her and pleased to hear she was travelling north again to view the property once more. This time she spent more time outside of the rooms of *Greystoke*. She took countless photographs both inside and out, yet for some reason she decided not to take one of the lake. In her mind this was still a private place, a place which still held onto sadness. Why here, more than the house? She couldn't say. Over a shared lunch, Donald felt at complete ease with her as she spoke about *Greystoke* and the plans that she had.

'I've got a surveyor coming to take a look, as well as a couple of builders. If I give you the times and dates, could you show them round?'

'Of course I will.' He looked across as a bird took flight from the water, its movement disturbing the calm surface. She saw great warmth in his eyes when he spoke to her.

'Be happy there, Amy, and bring some love back to the house.'

The surveyor found countless faults with *Greystoke*, and the building companies did the same. Both advised against purchasing the property due to the expense of the repairs. The surveyor, who had less charm than Mr George Rayman, suggested other properties he knew which were on the market. It seemed everyone she brought to the property advised her to look elsewhere.

She moved in within a month. There was no electricity, no heating and no running water. Thankfully by that time it was mid-summer and the daylight hours were long. Donald suggested she moved in with him as he had the space, but he knew that while his offer was appreciated, Amy had her heart set on moving into *Greystoke*. Blake hired a small truck and, between the three of them, they unloaded her few belongings. He presumed she had more to follow but for now she had enough to get by with. Not surprisingly, she chose the master bedroom as her own and used the bedroom alongside as her lounge. Donald was unsure of Blake at first, mainly of his feelings for Amy. It was obvious that he adored her, and her wealth would attract many, but when he saw them together and heard the banter and felt the warmth between them, he was reassured.

He backed her passion for *Greystoke* but knew and respected that this was an adventure she wanted to savour alone. When Blake left, she set about exploring the house. Donald left her to it, telling her to call by if she needed anything. Jessie lingered for a while at the gate before joining him as they headed back.

The house remained silent. The newcomer had the entire house to herself. At times she felt a slight presence, a chill in her bones which she simply put down to a draught. Amy rose early each day and, by the end of the first week, the layout of the house had become familiar to her. She cooked on a camping stove, drank bottled water and slept in a sleeping bag on top of her bed. An onlooker would think her mad, but Amy was completely happy. Donald called to see her most days. Each time he would find her, dressed in overalls and a baseball cap, her hair tied up and hanging out of the back of the hat. She would usually be covered in dirt and dust, as she cleared out and cleaned the rooms. The downstairs shutters had been opened, and light filled the entire house once more. Amy informed him that the electricity was to be restored soon, but a local electrician had to do extensive alterations first. A roofing firm was due to call to start the repairs as well, as she wanted to ensure the roof was watertight before the winter came. For now, though, the warm settled weather remained.

Donald had thought that she might have looked like an intruder in the house. Over recent years he had spent so much time alone here that occasionally he had felt the house had become his own. But now, as he walked around the house with her, she looked completely at home. Not in a way with which Donald felt uncomfortable; it was almost as if she belonged there. Donald informed her that she had become the talk of the nearby village. People were surprised that she was living there alone. The older generation remembered the tragic events around the house and most preferred to keep their distance. Throughout the house, Donald felt and saw nothing of the girls. Amy herself didn't mention any sightings or anything untoward. It felt as though they had left.

A few weeks later Amy was fitting two light fittings in the hallway. Early that day the water supply had been restored, though the colour of the water was not yet clear. It was late afternoon and a warm wind blew into the hallway from the open door, ruffling her hair as she unpacked the small glass shades for the fittings. There were eight shades in total on each of the fittings, and she found she could only hold two each time she climbed the metal steps. The shades looked wonderful, even from close up, and soon she was fitting the last two. She knew she really should have moved the steps, but felt she could reach the last one. Maybe it was her eagerness to see the lights complete but as she leant across, her blouse caught on one of the closest shades, causing it to slip off its holder. So as not to break the one disturbed, she leant over further still. Now she had suddenly become overbalanced, and the shade slipped from her hand while her other arm caught on the top of the steps. Her body twisted round suddenly and the next thing she knew she was looking up at the ceiling, before the room spun as the steps went from under her and she fell. Amy hit the ground hard just seconds after the light shade she had carefully held shattered on the floor beside her.

Donald had just finished his dinner when Jessie suddenly rose and started barking.

'Hey, Jessie, quiet there!' he called to her. Jessie, though, continued to bark, the hair on her back had risen sharply. Now she bounded out of the front door of the cottage and onto the pathway outside. Donald looked up and half-expected it to be Amy calling round, though Jessie never barked when she did. It could have been another visitor, but when Donald joined Jessie outside, no-one was there.

Whatever had spooked Jessie refused to let go, and now Donald began to grow concerned. In the back of his mind something was beginning to form. A feeling of unease that something was not quite right. He checked around the garden but all seemed fine. Jessie had set off in the direction of *Greystoke*, the sound of her barks growing less as she ran off. He shut the cottage door securely and headed after her.

Her entire body ached. She found that she had become immobilised. Her head hurt most of all and she blinked hard to try and clear her vision, soon finding that she was looking toward the staircase. To her side she could see the broken glass of the shade, and felt grateful she had managed not to land on it. As she looked back to the staircase, in the sunlight that streamed over her, she thought she could make out the outline of two small figures at the top of the stairs. She closed her eyes, but this only caused her head to hurt more as stars danced behind her eyelids. When she opened them, she expected the image to have gone, but instead the image was taking greater form. Slowly they began to descend the steps, their blonde hair glowing almost like gold. The image of the girls was so clear now that Amy could see that the hair of one of the girls was brushed straight, while the other was curled like her own.

Another strange thing appeared to be happening. The carpet they walked on began to grow in colour. She looked to her side and found the same was happening to the walls and ceiling. The flocked paper, which had been faded and marked with age on her arrival, was now rich in colour. The small light fitting she had earlier fitted to the side of the staircase had been replaced by a thin chandelier, which sparkled like diamonds in the late afternoon sunshine. Now the two girls neared the bottom of the steps and Amy noticed a look of concern etched on their faces. She tried to speak, but she found her words were lodged deep in her throat. It was then that she felt her body being lifted.

As she began to turn, the image of a woman came into view. Amy felt the arm that had been trapped under her straighten, as she came to rest on her back. She knew the face of the woman, but the pain she felt was blinding her memory. She felt her head rise slightly, though no further pain came. When it fell back it landed on something soft which, though the pain continued, felt comforting. The two girls now ran silently to the woman who embraced them. Amy could see tears falling from her sad eyes and, through her fading vision, she thought she saw the woman mouth the words, 'thank you' before darkness overcame her and she blacked out.

She appeared to be dreaming. Images flashed before her, some faded like old sepia tone photographs. In others the colours were so vivid. The darkness suddenly returned and she became nervous and unsure. She heard laughter in the darkness, though not menacing, and reached out her hands towards the sound. Her hand hit something solid. The surface seemed flat; she moved her hand around and found something cold and hard. By its shape she could tell it was a handle. In the dark she realised she was standing at a door. Turning the handle, the door opened inwards and light filled her eyes. The laughter came again as her eyes adjusted to the light.

She found herself in a room full of colour and light, a room known to her, as was the girl standing beckoning her. As the girl's hand moved, her straight blonde hair swayed gently. Entering the room, she walked towards the girl and, as they neared one another, the other girl embraced her. The impact caused her head to spin, the light became dazzling and she found herself falling. Her arms flayed all around her as she fell, no sound could be heard as the darkness enveloped her again.

Around the time of her fall, the weather broke. The weeks of sunshine had been replaced by grey leaden clouds and a strong south westerly wind which brought heavy rain. Deep puddles gathered in the rutted lane beside the cottage, as the hard ground held back the water. Wind and rain drove across the front windows of *Greystoke*, their noise the only sound heard within. The house had become silent once more.

Donald was uncomfortable in hospitals. Maybe it was the smell, maybe it was the fact that if you were in one you were not in good shape, or that someone you cared about was ill. Whichever the feeling, he didn't like it. The doctor had been in with Amy for a while, no doubt explaining the nature of her injuries now that she had awakened. The staff at the hospital had told him that Amy had been very lucky, although Donald didn't think so as he looked at her in the bed. Her right eye looked badly bruised and swollen as did her hand, which stuck out of the cast on her arm. Propped up on her pillows, her hair hung lifeless to one side. Following her arrival at the hospital, she had drifted in and out of consciousness for two days. She had a fractured skull, a broken arm and three cracked ribs. How long she was to remain in hospital, he was unsure. No doubt he would find out when the medical folks came back out.

Donald sat on a small sofa in the waiting room, while he waited for Blake to return with drinks for them. He had come straight up from London on hearing the news. He had stayed day and night near to Amy. Donald had offered him the spare room at the cottage, but he said he wanted to be at the hospital when she awoke. He looked tired when he returned, dark rings circling his eyes, his smile weak as he passed Donald his drink. The sweetness of the drink was comforting to them both.

'Thank you, Blake,' he said. 'You come sit down and stop worrying, she'll be fine. Be up and dancing before you know it.'

Amy smiled as she saw them both enter. Blake leant in and kissed her cheek gently. She relayed to them what the doctor had told her. Blake's face was etched with worry, which didn't go unnoticed by Amy. She did her best to reassure him, but he expressed his concern at her being in the house by herself. There was also the fact that he felt she was working too hard and that her accident was in a way no surprise. Amy had taken objection to that comment and Donald felt a bit awkward, like an intruder in a private matter. Donald told them he would give them some privacy and went to stretch his legs in the corridor outside. By the time he returned, Amy was alone. He sat in the chair beside the bed and held her hand to check she was okay. She gently squeezed it. Her smile was warm, but he thought he saw moisture in her eyes.

'You should get some rest,' he suggested.

'I know,' she replied. 'Thank you for being here with Blake. I know he means well, but sometimes I feel swamped by him.'

'He's a decent man, though Amy. Those are hard to find sometimes.'

It turned out Blake had gone to the toilet and Amy was grateful for the chance to talk to Donald alone. 'I saw them, while I lay on the floor. I saw them.'

'You mean the girls, Isobel and Emily?' he asked.

'No, not just the girls, but them and Mrs Morrell.'

She went on to tell him what she had seen. As Amy recalled the details of her accident, her face looked strained but he listened and thought how detailed her description was. An outsider might have thought her imagination was running riot following her head injury. But Donald knew better, by the countless events he had been witness to which were unknown to anyone else. Blake returned and Amy soon changed the subject, listening quietly to them both as they talked about her rehabilitation. Donald looked at Blake as Amy spoke with him, and thought he saw a crack in Blake's way with her. Only a slight crack, but a crack that ran deep. One which the recent events could widen over time.

On the drive back to Donald's home, Blake was silent for most of the journey. The rain had cleared by the time they reached the cottage. As he opened the door, he thanked Blake for the lift home. The younger man told him he would see him soon, then turned the car around on the narrow lane. Through the open window, Donald heard him say,

'That house. It's her life now.'

It was a curious statement, one which Donald had no answer to. He waved and watched the car journey down the lane and turn into the road.

When she was released from hospital, Amy stayed at the cottage with Donald. He was pleased she had taken up his offer and, although he worried that Blake might object and suggest that she convalesced nearer him, they both understood her need to be near *Greystoke*. Amy was greatly frustrated that her injuries prevented her from continuing her work. She agreed over a late supper with Donald one night that she had spent years looking for the house, so a few weeks away weren't going to matter. Her heart ached to be back there, more then her injuries did at times. She longed to walk the rooms and corridors and feel the grace and beauty of the place. Amy had a stubbornness which he hadn't noticed before, one which reminded him of himself when he was younger. Donald had never married and never had to care for a sick child or any person other than himself, so the feeling was unusual for him. He saw great similarities between them both in the time they shared each other's company. Each had no family, no dependants. He had lived near to *Greystoke* long before he had become the gardener there. His love for the house had grown from his first day working in the garden. After the tragic events the house had witnessed, it had kept the feeling of a home even when solitude and darkness were in residence. Now years on a woman, who carried that deep sense of love for the house even long before she had stepped foot in it, had arrived to keep alight whatever flame burned within the heart of the house.

Over the same supper, Donald told her something he had kept back from her during her time in hospital. When he had found her that day after her accident, he told her he found her laid on her back. One of the white sheets, used to cover the old furniture, had been rolled up in a bundle and placed under her head, supporting her body.

At the time, the paramedics thought that Donald himself had done this on finding her.

The place she had fallen was the same place Emily had fallen all those years before.

Each of them wondered whether this had been an accident or that the events had been destined to happen to release the family from the house. They began to believe this more when Amy returned home to *Greystoke*.

Her strapped-up arm restricted her activities, so Donald and Blake were pleased when she gave into their requests and got workmen in to continue making the house habitable. As the work continued inside, Amy and Donald turned their attention to the garden. Donald had done some drawings of what the layout of the garden had once been like. When she informed him she wanted to return the garden to its former glory, he was overcome with emotion. For his seventy-ninth birthday, Amy restored him as head gardener. She asked him to recreate the garden as it had been in the time of the Morrels He was paid a fine salary and even had staff under him – a couple of local gardeners that Amy brought in to help.

By the following spring, the west side of the house had been redecorated and, although some rooms were quite sparse of furniture, the house began to take shape. The heating had cleared the cold and dampness from the place, lights glowed and sparkled from the renewed ceilings, and the now watertight roof had given the house great shelter throughout the winter. The house had once more become a home.

The following summer Donald took a walk late one evening with Jessie. Though the sun was quite low now, the day's warmth remained. The warm breeze carried the scent of nearby honeysuckle, and by the side of the roadway butterflies danced around several poppies that swayed gently, their shadows now lengthening. Jessie walked alongside him carrying a stick she had found. They both walked down to an old tree stump, and Donald sat down. He lit a cigarette and looked over at *Greystoke* in the distance. In the space of a year the house had been transformed. Though plenty of work still needed to be done, the sombre look the house once held had been lifted. Somewhere within, Amy would be working away on yet another project. Now fully recovered, the energy she possessed seemed endless. She had managed to inject the same elegance and grace she had herself into the house. Blake seldom visited now, which Donald found sad. He had hoped Amy would soften in her feelings for him but he knew, as Blake did, that Amy's heart belonged elsewhere. The house itself seemed to have become her lover.

The gardens were beginning to take shape as well. The renewed rose garden had taken well, though he doubted he would ever see it as mature as it had once been. He blew out smoke and watched it drift away on the breeze, as Jessie chased a butterfly across the long grass. The sun had now dropped behind the woodland, long shadows etched across the front of the house. In an upstairs window, lights glinted softly through the glass.

Donald wondered how many more summers he would sit up here, how many more rose bushes his ageing bones could tend. And whether, after he was long gone, his own spirit would return to walk the rooms and corridors of *Greystoke*.

As others had done before and maybe, at times, still do.

Crenin Point

Cornwall, England. July, 1979

The clouds had been gathering for some time now, though the boy paid them no regard. All that currently mattered was that he held the handle tightly as he ran. The wind continued to blow his hair across his face, and he found he was forced to run with his head to the side to enable him to still see the kite up above. The orange tail continued to swirl and loop in the strong wind. Behind him he could hear Rebecca's laughter, even though most of the sound was lost as the wind buffeted him. Running close to the water's edge, his bare feet sank slightly into the wet sand which the waves had just brushed smooth. When another wave crashed onto the beach, he found the spray cooled his body in sharp contrast to the hot sunshine that bathed the coastline. Rebecca was running alongside him now and her brown curled hair blew wildly as she reached out for the handle. Still moving fast, they carefully exchanged it.

When she grasped it, the force of the wind pulled on her young arm, but she managed to keep a grip even though the wind carried the kite even higher. Still watching Rebecca, he turned towards the water once more and watched his feet splashing among the returning waves. Jumping into the air, he punched at the sky as the adrenalin flowed through him, and he pounded his small feet harder into the water, laughing as the surf splashed all around him. When he looked across towards his friend, he saw that she was a good distance ahead of him; the enticing water that had occupied him now let go as he resumed his chase. In the distance he could see she had reached the ridge of rocks that split the bay in half.

Running on towards her, he could see that she had stopped on the edge of a section of rocks. His heart lifted when he saw that her hand was still holding the kite. The boy lowered his head as he ran harder to see why she had stopped, but by the time he reached the rocks he could no longer see her. He stopped and raised his hand to shelter his eyes from the sun as he searched for her, his breathing coming hard now.

Rebecca was nowhere to be seen. He retraced his footprints and found another set which he presumed was hers. Both sets stopped at the rocks. Climbing over the short ridge, he felt the wind increase further as the sunlight began to fade. The direction of the wind was also changing, so that now it came straight off the sea.

As he reached the other side of the rocks, he saw that the sand below was covered in strange markings; patterns he could not figure out. Beside the markings, it looked as though something had been dragged across the sand.

Turning his attention back to the beach, he found he could not make out Rebecca's footprints, though other prints were visible below him which were uneven in size and shape.

The sun had now slipped behind a large bank of cloud that had drifted in. Without the sunlight, and now standing alone, he began to feel cold and unsure of his surroundings. Out to sea he could see that the size of the waves was increasing rapidly. He watched as one crashed onto the edge of the ridge, forcing him to retreat to keep dry. The waves brought an even stronger scent of salt and brine to his nose, as the mass of water spread out across the beach as the wave collapsed. The force of water took with it all trace of the markings he had seen, leaving behind just smooth sand. He suddenly remembered his kite and looked up into the now blackening sky for a trace of it. Spots of rain began to fall; a few landed on his face as he looked skywards, sheltering his eyes with his hand, trying to spot the kite.

At first there was no trace but, when he looked out to sea, he saw the small outline high up above the water. The tail was now lost and neither the handle nor line could be seen.

He shivered, alone now on the ridge, clutching his arms around him. There was no sign of Rebecca as he looked either way across the beach. Unease was quickly turning to panic and the need to be away from this place was overcoming him; he desperately needed to get back to his family. Looking back inland, he set off running again. The rain fell heavier now, soaking him to the skin as he searched for the pathway off the beach. Behind him the waves sounded larger than he could imagine, as the noise of them breaking on the shore pounded in his ears. His hair was plastered across his face and the tears that fell from his eyes mixed with the salt of the sea spray. Fear was his only companion.

Present Day

The traffic steadily increased as they approached Manchester Airport. When the car in front of him turned suddenly without indication, he was forced to brake sharply to avoid colliding with it. Shaking his head, David Lonsdale looked over at the vehicle as it drove away.

'Hope that's not your pilot!' he said amusingly.

Beside him, Rachael Shannon was grateful for the touch of humour on David's part. For most of the journey there had been a tense silence between them and her previous attempts to lighten the air had fallen flat. David saw the sign for the terminal which Rachael required, and pulled his car over into the inner lane.

'You sure you have everything?' he asked her.

Rachael again checked through the documents in her bag and lightly tapped him on the side of the head with her passport. She saw a smile cross his face which calmed her somewhat. When they reached the front of the terminal, a line of black taxis occupied most of the dropping-off area, but luckily one pulled out and David was able to park the car in the space left. While Rachael reached into the back for her coat, he took her cases out of the boot.

Rachael had almost pulled out of her trip when things had escalated between them recently, but David had convinced her to stick to her plans. Besides, her business trip gave her the opportunity to visit her father while she was in Boston. It had been three years since they had last seen each other, so it was too good an opportunity to miss. Her work often took her away for long periods and, as things had been strained between them recently, she thought the space between herself and David might heal their differences.

'Remember, David, get some rest while I'm away. If not for yourself, do it for me, please.'

'Okay, okay. I'll be fine,' he told her, holding her shoulder as he tried to reassure her.

'David, are we okay?' she asked, as he lifted her cases onto the luggage trolley.

A month ago she had dragged him to the doctor's when his headaches had got worse; she was unconvinced that all was well, even when the relevant tests showed no cause or problem. Neither could they explain the dreams he suffered nightly. He looked tired and withdrawn as she looked at him, the lack of sleep becoming more evident on his face. His smile seemed genuine to her, though his eyes held the worry he obviously had.

'We're fine, stop worrying. Listen, you have fun and give my love to your dad.'

'I will, though ten hour days with corporate lawyers is never my kind of fun.'

Another group of passengers climbed out of a taxi beside them, their laughter catching Rachael's attention. When she looked back she saw that David was smiling at her and she lost a little of the anxiety she felt about leaving him. She linked his arm as he pushed the trolley into the airport foyer.

Once she had checked in and her cases had been cleared, she held him tightly, leaning on his shoulder as he ran his hand over her hair. When she eventually released him, he kissed her forehead softly and noticed moisture in her eyes as they said their goodbyes. She gave him a final wave as he turned and headed back to the car. Rain was beginning to fall as he reached his car, making the people arriving at the airport in search of warmer destinations hurry that little bit more. As he slipped behind the wheel, David caught sight of his reflection in the rear view mirror. The area around his eyes showed just how tired he had been for the past few weeks. He needed a shave and, most of all, some sleep. Tilting the mirror away from him, he pulled out into the flow of traffic as the rain began to fall heavier.

By the time he arrived home, the rain fell steadier and was now accompanied by rumbles of thunder. The previous days of continuous rainfall had saturated the ground outside the small block of flats where he lived, and David was forced to jump onto the third step to escape the water gathered at the entrance. Inside the foyer, he swept his hand through his hair to clear the rainwater. He was halfway up the stairway when he heard the phone ringing from his flat.

At first he didn't recognize the voice; it had been quite a while since they had spoken.

'David? It's Billy Denton. How are you?'

'Hey, long time no speak. I'm good thanks,' he lied. David hated lying but, sometimes when it came to his personal life, it was easier to say everything was okay. Besides, most people do it anyway, he thought, as he slipped his jacket off, allowing it to fall on the floor.

'Have you got the television on?' Billy asked.

'No, I've only just come in. Why?'

'Well, stick Channel Five news on. Should bring back some old memories.'

He looked around the room for the remote, spotting it on the window-sill, then put down the phone as he reached for it. Sitting down on the sofa, he pressed the channel button and watched as the picture appeared. Reaching for the phone, he said, 'Right, got it on. What have we got?'

He was going to ask his old friend more, but the image immediately caught his attention.

The waves looked enormous. The grey coloured container ship rose as a wave crashed against its huge body, the spray of the wave lost in the storm that spiralled around the ship. Turning up the volume, David listened as a news reporter was talking about how the ship had fallen foul of the storm raging off the south west coast, a stretch of coast he recognized from long ago. The headland stood out strong on the screen and, when the picture changed to an aerial view, his eyes widened further as he saw the full shape of the bay. He almost jumped when Billy spoke again,

'Recognize it?'

He didn't need to answer. The memories were still strong. As he watched, another huge wave broke against the side of the ship. In the background, Crenin Point held its breath.

For the next two days David did as he had promised Rachael, and got some rest. He had hoped to catch up on some reading and had put several books by his bedside but, when he tried to concentrate, his mind continued to drift. Thankfully he managed to sleep reasonably well, but his dreams continued to disturb him at times. Each morning, he found as usual he couldn't remember any details or any events. All he was left with was a headache, which refused to leave. He continued to watch the news coverage of the stricken ship on the television, and left it switched on while he went and bought several newspapers to see the photographs they held.

Although helicopters continued to hover over the ship, the outlook was becoming more hopeful. Thankfully the storm abated over the next few hours, three tug boats managed to move close by and the bay escaped as the ship was finally pulled to safety. Once safe, the various news channels dropped the story and Crenin Point no longer made the news. When David finally switched the television off, the place stuck in his mind as it always had done since that summer's day. Having made himself a cup of coffee, he went into his bedroom and stood on the bottom of the bed, reaching for a box on the top of his wardrobe.

At one time the box had contained a coffee machine he had received as a gift some years back; now it contained old photograph albums. Placing the box on the bed, he sat beside it and searched for the album he wanted. The blue album had a label on its side saying Cornwall, and

David saw the dust motes float in the air as he pulled the book out and opened it. Had it really been so long?

It was as if someone had opened a hidden file in a dark corner of his memory, as he looked at the images of his childhood. Images long forgotten all fought for his attention. He smiled as he looked at a family photo, his parents standing beside him at Lands End. They were standing in front of a white sign which showed the number of miles to destinations around the world, including their home town. Deep within him an ache he had learnt to live with began to surface, as he remembered his departed parents. He turned the page and sought other memories, till eventually he came across the picture he was looking for.

His legs looked incredibly thin in the photo and again he smiled to himself as he remembered the yellow shirt he was wearing. He had worn it for most of that holiday, insisting on it being washed several times over the two weeks. His hair was blown to the side by an unseen wind, but not as much as the hair of the girl beside him. She stood several inches taller than him, slightly leaning into the photo. And, although her brown curls obscured half of her face, David was still able to remember her clearly.

In another photograph, one of Billy and him, the girl could be seen in the background. Again her hair covered most of her face, something that seemed unusual. It had been several years since he had last looked at the photos of that holiday, and he didn't recall noticing that there wasn't a clear picture of her. Picking up the original photo he had held, he turned it over and read the words written on the back.

'Me and Rebecca at Crenin Point, 1979.'

He flicked through the rest of the album, which concentrated mainly on family, and he separated out all of the ones which showed the beach and the Point. When he tasted his coffee again, he found it had gone cold and he winced at the bitterness the coldness brought. Walking into the kitchen, he carried the photo of him and Rebecca and studied it while he waited for the kettle to boil.

David and Billy had originally lived next door to each other and hadn't especially got on to begin with. It was only when Billy's family had moved a few miles away that their friendship had begun to grow. Looking back now, he thought that they had always had plenty to catch up on when they met, but before they had constantly fallen out because they were living on top of each other all the time. Both sets of parents had always been close, and it had been in 1975 that the idea of going on holiday together was first suggested. Once agreed on, the holiday had been such a success that two other holidays had followed. They always travelled down to Cornwall and always stayed in the same rented cottages. While they travelled around the area during the two weeks, one place in particular had become a favourite of David's; a place where the beach seemed to stretch endlessly and the emerald green sea brought in huge waves that sounded like thunder as they crashed onto the shoreline.

In the humdrum days of school, David's mind would drift away from the lesson he was supposed to be paying attention to. He would close his eyes and dream of the waves breaking on the beach at Crenin Point.

The third and last holiday the two families had, was the one when he had met Rebecca. They had been having a picnic at Crenin Point on a sun-drenched day, a day when David seemed to be constantly in trouble. He and Billy had fallen out over something long forgotten and he had decided to take himself down to the beach. It was only a short distance away and enabled him to keep in sight of his parents. As he had trudged onto the beach with his hands deep in the pockets of his shorts, he had come across a young girl drawing pictures in the sand. Most were of giant fish, sharks, octopus and, as he looked across, a huge whale. He saw that water had been drawn blowing out of the top of the whale's head. David was amazed at the detail that had gone into each of the drawings, and watched as the girl drew another smaller fish with the long stick she held in her hand. As he approached, she stopped and, looking at him, smiled.

She had the greenest eyes he had ever seen. They looked like the colour of the sea at the spot where he and Billy had thrown stones in the water some days ago. Her pretty face was surrounded by brown curly hair which seemed to have no style or control. After saying hello, she told him her name was Rebecca; her simple words lifted both his mood and the whole day. From that moment on, they became instant friends.

Of course he was more than impressed to show off his new friend to Billy, who also thankfully made friends with her, though not as close as with David, who basked in the glory of having a friend who was all of eleven – a world away from his nine years.

For the next few days they had become inseparable, spending most of their time on the beach, where they made huge drawings of every sea creature they could think of.

At the start of the second week the weather broke, grey clouds moved in from the Atlantic bringing with them persistent rainfall. On one of the days when the rain fell lighter, both families travelled down to the small coastal town of Mevagissey. Rebecca was asked to come with them, once it had been approved by her parents. David remembered standing in front of her father, who towered over him, as he asked if Rebecca could spend the day with them. As they all clambered into the car, everyone had laughed when David told them that Rebecca's dad had smelt like old fish. David and Rebecca had sat together holding hands as they sang songs on their journey. When they arrived in Mevagissey, they found the place was busy as plenty other tourists seemed to have the same idea for a day out. When they had eventually parked, David had been enchanted by the place and had loved the sounds and the smells of the small harbour. In the rain, which had now turned to showers, they had wandered around looking at all the different boats, imagining great adventures on wild seas. They had both ducked when a gull flew low over them, its loud screech mixing with their laughter as they fell to the ground to avoid it. While the two of them had enjoyed an ice cream, David's eye had been drawn to a small gift shop across the street. They had walked over to look into the window where, among the usual seaside gifts, a display of tall lighthouses drew his atten-tion, beside which stood a large blue kite. As he gazed through the window, David had thought the kite looked just about as big as he was. This was to be the gift that gave the two of them so much pleasure, but one that was to change the holiday for ever and, with it, their lives.

Later that day, David's father had patiently showed them how to launch the kite into the eager wind. Although a few crashes had followed, they soon picked up how to get it flying and, by the end of the day, the kite flew strongly at what seemed to them to be unbelievable heights. For the next few days the kite filled their days. It would look down on the two small figures, who by now had learned to run while still flying it. Up above that late afternoon as the tide roared in, clouds had begun to gather and the sunlight to weaken as David and Rebecca ran below.

David rubbed his eyes and felt some of the tiredness begin to lift. Having driven for over three hours, he really should have pulled over for a rest much earlier. From the flask on the passenger seat, he poured himself a cup of coffee and opened the car door. Sedgemoor service station was busy, even for a weekday, and he was pleased that he had decided to park away from the main area. Several coaches were parked up to the side of the lorry park, and he watched as several elderly people made their way towards the service station's main building, adding to the congestion within. He was pleased that the coffee still tasted hot as he leant back against his car and drank. Another two hours and the coast of his childhood memories would be in view. Refreshed and rested, he rejoined the motorway and thought back to that day on the beach.

He remembered he could barely see by the time his parents found him. The tears had been flowing down his face as his father held him by his arms. He had felt swamped by everyone's attention; his voice so hidden within him he had found he could barely speak. Breaking away from his father's grasp, he had managed to point towards the beach, eventually mumbling Rebecca's name.

He had watched as his father, along with Billy's dad, ran off through the driving rain in the direction they had been shown. David still recalled

110

the feeling of the blanket his mother had wrapped around him as his tears continued to fall.

For the next two days the search had continued for Rebecca. David had watched as the helicopter flew low overhead, the bright yellow of its body standing out strongly against the still black sky. He had sat with his parents as the two police officers had asked him endless questions. There didn't seem to him much to say, other than that she had disappeared somewhere near the ridge of rocks. One of them had asked whether either of them had been in the water, to which he had answered no; his last sighting of her had been well clear of the incoming waves. Everyone from the nearby villages seemed to have gathered by the harbour as the police and coastguard had continued the search.

When David and his father had walked down from the road toward the harbour, he had been amazed to see the sea so far onto the beach. The water in the harbour had been so high that the steps, which he had seen people use to go down to their boats, had just been visible above the water's surface. Several people had smiled at him reassuringly as they neared the crowd; one or two ruffling his hair as he passed by them. Suddenly there had been movement ahead of him as a police Range Rover eased its way through the crowd. Above the noise of the people, David could hear the police radio crackle as one of the officers stepped out of the car. Someone was talking excitedly, although he had been unable to make out the words. He became aware of an increased tension around him, along with the strain of a headache which was now appearing. He had pulled his father's coat, and he turned to look at him as David's vision began to distort, his headache increasing to a point where he started to sway on his feet. As the background noise faded, David began to hear a voice calling his name, yet it sounded like it was coming from within him. He found his breathing had become difficult as he tried to make sense of what was happening. The voice became clearer as he reached out for his father.

'They've found her,' he said pulling on his father's coat. 'She's in the water!'

With that, his legs had finally given way and he blacked out.

The clouds began to lift and break as David approached the coast. White waves could be seen breaking on the blue green water as he looked over towards Crenin Point. He slowed the car to a safe speed as he took in the scenery he hadn't seen in years. At a T-junction he turned left, following the sign for Crenin. He knew from memory that the road ended in the village at the harbour, where a small car park stood beside a row of cottages. As he approached the village, he could see that the tide was out and the broad expanse of sand on the other side of the harbour shone like gold in the sun that broke through the clouds. The rocks where Rebecca had disappeared could now be seen through the trees, which partially obscured his vision as he drove down the hill towards Crenin. His directions for the bed and breakfast he had booked into, showed it to be just on the left as the road levelled out. As it turned out, The Rock Guest House was the first building he came to.

Three large flower tubs stood outside the place, giving a warm touch of colour for the time of year. There were, he had been informed, only four guest rooms; he presumed that in a past era the house had been a large family home. A small wooden sign, showing the house name, hung from the white painted building. The weather had begun to take hold on the sign, and the paintwork on a few of the letters was beginning to peel away. Pulling the car into the driveway, he noticed there were several buds beginning to show on the trees that overhung the driveway beside the property. Unsure of where to park, David tried to get as close to the far wall as he could, while still being able to get out.

The sea air, carried on a slight breeze, smelt even better than he remembered as he stepped out of the car. From the boot he took out a couple of small bags, just as a woman appeared in the doorway. He guessed she was the owner, Mrs Hobson.

'You must be Mr Lonsdale?' she asked in a friendly voice.

He didn't detect a local accent as she spoke, and presumed she had moved to the area.

They said their hellos and, after signing in, she showed him to his room. She reminded David of an aunt he had years back, with her jolly face which carried a smile well. While rather a large woman, she moved quite gracefully as she led him to a room at the front of the property, which was light and airy and overlooked the village in the distance. Fresh flowers stood in a vase on a small table, while a set of clean towels had been placed on the bed. It looked as though Mrs Hobson took a great deal of care with her guests' rooms. A small boat bobbed up and down to the side of the harbour as he looked across.

'You booked for three nights. Is that still the same?'

'Yes, thank you,' he replied and told her a few brief details of his past holidays here.

'Well, my husband and I are quite new here. We only moved down last year, so we are still getting to know everyone,' she told him. 'We're still quiet this time of year, so if you want to stay longer, you're more than welcome.'

With that she left him to unpack and made her way downstairs.

David opened a window slightly to allow in more air; again the sea air seemed to calm him and, as he lay back on the bed, he already felt refreshed. There was no sign of a headache at all and, as he closed his eyes, his mind was clear for the first time in quite a while. The watching figure had seen the window open earlier and, fearing being noticed, had stepped back behind the wall beside where David had parked. There it remained for a few minutes until all was still; only then did the figure turn and head back down towards the village.

David awoke to sunlight streaming in the window onto his face. He enjoyed the warmth it offered him before he opened his eyes. Checking the clock on the wall, he saw that he had only slept for about twenty minutes, yet his body felt as though he had rested for hours. He unpacked a few of his clothes, putting a couple of shirts on hangers in the wardrobe, then placed underwear and socks, along with a few T-shirts, in the drawers provided.

When he came downstairs again, he was greeted by Mrs Hobson's husband, Brian, who was laying fresh tablecloths out in the small dining room. His handshake was strong and powerful and his apparent fitness belied his age. Obviously he had been used to physical work over the years. David presumed the bed and breakfast they now ran must be less strenuous, though still hard work. As he was the only person staying there, Brian had chatted with him for a while about their move down to Cornwall and how spending more time together had brought them closer. David briefly wondered if the same could happen to him and Rachael. He forced himself to clear his mind as Brian continued with the tables. 'So, what are your plans for today then?' the older man asked.

'Well, I'm trying to find a family that used to live here years ago,' David replied. 'I thought that you might be able to help but, as you are relatively new here, I guess not.'

As he spoke, Mrs Hobson joined them, carrying a tray of drinks.

'Thought you might like a drink,' she told him.

Over their drinks, she gave him the name of a woman she knew in the village.

'She's been here all her life, I was recently told, so she should know.' She wrote the name and address on a piece of paper and handed it him. 'Her name is Mrs Wenderby.'

The gull flew low over the surface of the water. Through the breaking cloud, shafts of sunlight lit the water, the warmth spreading across the bird's body. In the subtle heat of the sunshine the bird rose swiftly, its wings outstretched; while its wings remained still, its head kept moving side to side as it continued to scan the area.

Earlier in the day, the bird had – among others – followed some fishing boats far out to sea, where it had fed several times, diving deep into the water to catch the plentiful fish below. Now though, there seemed to be a change in the water. Rain began to fall as the birds picked off the scraps discarded from the boats, and the gull had broken away from the others, heading inland. The shoreline was in sight now, where the sunshine remained constant. Suddenly the bird flew higher, more concerned now for its own safety. Below it could make out shapes under the surface, far too big for fish, moving at great speed. It was enough to make the bird uneasy and it called out loudly before it banked to the right and returned to safer waters.

The row of small cottages stood back from the main village road. David noticed that several roof tiles had been replaced on the end two cottages. No doubt they took the force of the wind during the harsh days of winter. Most of the five properties had window boxes on the front of them which, like the ones at the guest house, were full of early spring colour. Mrs Wenderby's was the end cottage nearest the harbour, he had been told. And as he got out of his car, he saw a woman sitting on a wooden chair close to the doorway. He smiled to reassure the woman as he walked over.

'Hello, I'm looking for a Mrs Wenderby.'

'That's me,' she replied. 'How can I help you?'

He guessed she was in her late sixties; her hair had a touch of grey, but her clothes suggested she was younger. She wore a jade coloured blouse, which hung loosely over her trousers. Her features stood out most and, while the skin was lined around her eyes, they still held great beauty. As she spoke, she stood and scattered pieces of bread onto the lawn at the side of the cottage. In nearby trees, birds gathered eagerly.

'My name is David Lonsdale. I'm spending a few days down here and I was wondering if you could help me locate someone in the village.'

He went on to inform her that he had been given her name by the owner of the guest house. On his way over, he had thought that an unannounced visit might have appeared rude, but her response soon put him at ease. The warmth he had detected in her eyes was only enhanced as she smiled at him. She brushed her hands as she removed the last of the breadcrumbs, then extended one hand to him. He shook it as she answered.

'Yes, I'm Mrs Wenderby, but please call me Dianne.'

She gestured for him to come inside and he followed her into the cottage.

As they sat, she asked, 'How can I help you?'

'I'm trying to find someone who used to live near here. I used to holiday with my parents and friends here when I was younger. We used to rent a couple of cottages near to Portreath. On one holiday, the last we had here, I made friends with the girl of a family who lived here. I was wondering if they still did.'

Dianne had listened with great interest to him as he spoke. She looked pleased at how warmly he had spoken of the place.

'What was the name?'

'McFarlane.'

It was strange how just the saying of a single word could change the atmosphere. Not that she made it evident. It was just a flicker in her eye that caused him concern, as if an old memory had been pulled to the surface; one which she wished had been left undisturbed.

'The girl's name was Rebecca.'

The concern appeared to strengthen in her eyes, and David felt uncomfortable at the change in her. However, she soon composed herself well, although she didn't initially respond. Not wanting to cause offence, he broke the silence between them.

'Have I said something untoward? I hope I haven't said the wrong thing.'

When she smiled, David felt some of his unease shift.

'No, my dear, not at all,' she said reassuringly. 'Yes, I know of the McFarlanes, and especially Rebecca.'

Dianne rose and headed towards the kitchen. By the doorway, she looked back.

'I'll get us both a drink and then I'll tell you about the McFarlanes.'

As he leant back on the small sofa, he looked around the room. The cottage was tastefully decorated and a collection of watercolours on the far wall added great charm to the room. Beside him there were several silver-framed pictures on the mantlepiece. A young man featured in many of them; one he could see had been taken close to the harbour in Crenin. As Dianne returned with their drinks, his attention was drawn away from the pictures and turned to a black and white cat which appeared and jumped onto his lap. Thanking her for the drink, he stroked the cat's back.

'Say hello to Thomas. He's my neighbour's actually, though he seems to spend most of his time here.' Placing his drink down onto a coaster, she sat in a seat beside a small table.

'How old were you when you used to holiday down here, David?' she asked, sipping her drink.

He thought for a moment, then recalled, 'I guess I would have been about eight or nine at the time. I met them in I think 1977, or it could have been '78.'

David had relaxed now, although he was intrigued to hear what she had to say about them. He told her how they had met, and was just about to mention the day of the storm when she asked him,

'You're the boy, aren't you?' She put down her teacup. 'The one who was with her when she disappeared?'

He was surprised by her comment and felt no need to say otherwise.

'Yes, I am. Do you still remember it?'

'Oh goodness, yes. The storm was a particularly bad one. A lot of damage was done to the village, and besides, someone going missing at the same time was quite an event here. What brings you back now though?'

He told her about watching the stricken tanker on various news reports, though failed to mention anything about his headaches and dreams. That seemed too personal for him to disclose, and he didn't think it was connected then.

'So, as I have some time off work,' he continued, 'I thought I would come down here and see the place again. It's as beautiful as I remember.' Then he added, 'I just wondered if the McFarlanes were still here.'

He saw shadows cross her face as she looked down before she spoke.

'There have been McFarlanes in the village for as long as I've been here. I went to school with a cousin of Rebecca's, who I used to be quite close to. I must tell you that they weren't the most popular of families though. Rebecca's parents, whom you met, bought up a lot of land over the years; land which they didn't use. They liked to keep themselves private, which is fine, I do myself, but the land they misused was good land which could have been made better use of. The village has always been short of housing. You need that to keep the young folk here, the same as you need to do all that you can to keep local people in the village. Nowadays it seems everyone just wants the bright lights of the city, and all it offers. Me, I like the quiet. Anyway, the McFarlanes let the land go to waste, and that is what irked most people here.'

David listened intently to the woman speaking, so much so that when he took a mouthful of his drink, he noticed it had gone quite cool.

'The family, over the generations, were always regarded as somewhat strange.'

'In what way?'

'Oh, nothing dangerous or anything like that. Maybe it's because they liked their privacy so much. In a small place like this, most people have to get on with each other.'

He sensed there was more to her tale than she was letting him know, but he didn't push her to explain further.

'Are they still here?' he asked. 'I remember their place stood near to the headland.'

'Yes, you remember well. But they are no longer there. In the late eighties, a high tide brought with it a storm similar to the one you recall. Rebecca's parents were out with some friends on a fishing trip. They were making their way back, when one of the large waves hit them and overturned their boat. The boat was lost and, even though there was an extensive search, they were never found.'

'Oh, I'm sorry to hear that.' David was surprised at this news.

Dianne saw the hurt on his face. He wouldn't have known unless he had seen it on the television or heard it on the radio. She liked David, even though they had just met; there seemed a great deal of compassion in him.

'I'm sorry to be the one to break the news to you.'

118

He smiled weakly at her. 'That's okay. I'm pleased you told me. Rebecca and I used to write to each other like pen friends for a while; the letters became fewer over the years. The last I heard she had gone to art college in London, I received one from her there, but after that didn't hear from her again.'

Dianne could see the memories were still with him as he spoke.

'I guess Rebecca moved on afterwards?'

Now the flicker in her eye returned, and David thought it was more evident this time.

'No, actually. She's an artist now; I guess college worked well for her. When she lost her parents, she came back and still lives here. She lives alone now at her parents' place, though whenever I see her she is normally down at her workplace on the opposite side of the harbour. She has a studio in the old lifeboat station.'

David was more than a little surprised to hear that she was still here. The loss of her parents must have been hard on her. As an only child himself, he could relate to her loss and the feeling of isolation; something he had never got used to. The temptation to move away and rebuild her life must have crossed her mind, yet she had chosen to remain here. Even in the short time he had been back in Crenin, the beauty of the place had moved him as it had done as a child. Maybe that was what held her here. His thoughts were broken as Dianne spoke.

'David, it's been a long time. You will both have changed from when you were children.'

It was said almost as if she was trying to warn him, yet in the comfort of her warm home it seemed sympathetic. Almost as if she didn't want him to get hurt.

'Oh, I appreciate that,' he told her. 'But for some reason, that day has never left me. Maybe I just want to settle old ghosts.'

His own smile brought warmth to his comment, yet Dianne thought he was trying to reassure himself.

'I get the impression you have your own thoughts about not just the McFarlanes, but Rebecca herself,' he added.

Dianne collected the teacups and took them back to the kitchen. When she returned, she was wiping her hands on a teatowel.

'My business with Rebecca was long ago, and it's gone now. You shouldn't concern yourself, though you should take care around Rebecca. She seems nice, but first impressions aren't everything.'

Not wanting to pry, he asked her sensitively what her dispute over Rebecca had been.

'I have a nephew called Ben,' she replied, passing him one of the photo frames he had seen earlier. In the picture a young man was kneeling on a walkway in front of a large yacht. As David held the photograph, she continued, 'Ben was quite a sportsman years back; he won a lot of trophies for sailing. The boat in the photo you have there was called Cassandra, which was always his favourite.'

David wondered what all this had to do with Rebecca and placed the photo back down.

'One summer on a sailing trip around the south coast, Ben came to stay with me for a few weeks. We had always been close when he was younger, and it was nice to spend time with him again. During that summer Ben met and fell in love with Rebecca. As the weeks went by, he extended his stay, spending more and more time with her.'

'I take it you didn't approve?' David asked.

'Actually I did. They were good together, I thought. But, as the summer passed, I noticed a change in Ben. He saw less of her and began to sail less as well. He would spend hours just sitting looking at the sea. When he first arrived, he had rarely been away from it.

'I guess it sounds daft, but he seemed unsure of the water somehow. I remember asking him if there was anything I could do to help. It was then that Ben told me more about Rebecca.'

David listened intently as Dianne spoke; he noticed that he was beginning to feel nervous. He couldn't think why. He was merely listening to someone's story, yet he felt as though he was connected to it somehow.

'He told me how she seemed to change with him sometimes, how dark her moods could become. She would disappear for days without saying where she was going. Whenever he asked her about it, she would have a faraway look in her eyes and not respond to him. By the time he left, I do believe that Ben was scared of her.'

Outside, a couple of birds fought in a small tree, distracting them both. The noise faded as the birds flew off. When David looked back, he saw that Dianne was smiling as though she had lifted herself from her memories.

'So, what do you think scared him?' he asked her

'I'm not sure. For a while after Ben left, Rebecca kept away from me. When I saw her in the village I sensed she was avoiding me. Then one day she turned up here, with some flowers and a couple of books which belonged to Ben. She said he had left them at her studio. She asked how he was, yet didn't say why she had avoided me for weeks.'

'At least she came to see you.'

'True, though I really think she was prying for something else.'

David stood and picked up the frame he had looked at earlier.

'Has Ben seen her since?' he asked.

'I don't think so,' she replied. 'He often writes and sends pictures to me, but he never mentions Rebecca and hasn't been back here since.'

They spoke for a while longer, mainly about Crenin, before he thanked her for her time and help. He told her if he had the time he would call back and see her before he left. As they stood at the doorway, they noticed that the two fighting birds had returned and chased each other across the small lawn.

'Give my regards to Rebecca, if you get to see her,' Dianne added.

'I will, and thanks again for your help.'

In spite of the sunshine, David felt a chill in his body as he climbed into his car. He was surprised he had learnt so much from his short visit, and more surprised by the woman's revelation about her nephew and the news that Rebecca was still here. When he looked at his watch he saw it was after five o'clock but, despite his strong feelings to return to Crenin, he felt that he would wait till the following day to explore. He decided while there was still daylight he would drive out to the cottages his parents had rented for their holidays and see if they were still as he remembered. Starting up the engine, he turned the CD player on, hoping the music would calm him as he drove away from the village.

Back in the cottage, Dianne watched his car wind its way up to the main road. She brought her hand up to her mouth and rested her fingers on her lips. For several minutes she stood there, her eyes closed then, shaking her head, she walked into the kitchen. On her way, despite the time of day, she drew the front curtains in the lounge and slid the bolts across her front door.

When David eventually found the temporary home of his childhood escapes, he discovered that the two cottages were no longer used as holiday homes. The one that Billy's family had used had been extended at the rear, while the one he had stayed in remained as he recalled. He spoke briefly to the new owner, a man in his early fifties, who was tending to the front garden. The man informed him that he had lived there for over seven years now and had no idea when the other cottage had become privately owned. Thanking him for his time, David left him to his garden.

On his way back to Crenin, he spotted a country pub which was serving food. By the time he had ordered, he realised that he hadn't eaten since early morning and was now quite hungry. The pub was cosy and only occupied by a couple of locals who were sitting at the bar. He took his drink and sat by the window. After his meal, which turned out to be worth the wait, he sat and finished his drink. From his jacket pocket he took out an envelope, from which he removed the photograph of himself and Rebecca as children. Running his finger over her obscured features, he wondered if she would even remember him. Only one way to know, he thought. Thanking the landlord, he left his glass on the bar and left.

It was almost dark by the time he parked by the harbour. On the drive back, he had felt he couldn't wait until tomorrow; his impatience was growing all the time. As he locked his car, he saw a man out walking his dog. They spoke briefly before he pointed David in the direction of Rebecca's studio. There were no lights to be seen, so he cupped his hand against the glass and tried to peer through. When he saw nothing, he walked back to his car, and took a small notepad from the side pocket of the door.

David wrote her a short note, telling her that he hoped she didn't mind him calling in to see her after all these years, and hoped she was well. At the bottom he wrote the name of the guest house where he was staying. When he pushed it through the letterbox, the flap banged loudly as he let the note go, the sound echoing across the quiet harbour; yet nothing around him stirred.

Even though he felt extremely tired, David showered before he went to bed; the warm water soothed his mind and body. How long he stayed there under the spray, he was unsure. Later he lay in bed with the curtains open, allowing the moonlight to coat the room with a pale light; he was asleep in minutes.

For another night he slept right through. When he awoke, he felt completely refreshed; no dreams had troubled him. For a while he lay still in his bed, slowly letting the sleep escape him. The undisturbed nights had been wonderful, and even though he knew he would again carry his painkillers with him constantly, his headaches remained at bay. The sound of birdsong came gently through the window, adding to his relaxation. After cleaning his teeth, he drank a couple of glasses of water. He had become used to drinking water simply to help swallow tablets; now, on its own, the water tasted refreshing. He ran some water through his hair, pulled on a pair of black jeans and, from the wardrobe, he chose a grey shirt along with a pair of trainers. When he looked in the bathroom mirror, he thought he could manage another day without a shave. As he rubbed his chin, he noticed his eyes looked refreshed;

the dark lines that had etched themselves around his eyes seemed to have faded. Later when he came down into the hallway, he picked up a newspaper off the table alongside the stairs and caught up on the news. As he did, Mrs Hobson came out of the kitchen.

'Good morning, I was hoping to catch you,' she told him. 'This was left for you this morning.'

David was surprised to see that she was holding a folded piece of paper. When she handed it to him, he could see his name was written on the front.

Thanking her, he again picked up the newspaper, pretending to be more interested in the news as he waited for her to return to the kitchen again.

The note was a sheet of paper, folded in half; his name had been written just above a wax seal. Indented on the wax was the outline of a small fish. The seal cracked as David opened the paper, and several pieces fell to the floor. Ignoring these, he opened the sheet and read:

> *Dear David,*
>
> *How lovely to hear from you, what a wonderful surprise.*
>
> *I'm sorry I wasn't in when you called. I had to go to Helston for some supplies.*
>
> *It would be good to see you while you are here, please come for lunch at the studio today. I'll be down on the beach from late morning collecting driftwood.*
>
> *I'll leave a drawing so you know I'm there!*
>
> *With love,*
>
> *Rebecca*

After breakfast, he read the short note again several times, trying to picture her in his mind as he read. In his hand, he felt the strange texture of the paper. There was a slight odour when he smelt it - not unpleasant, but one which he couldn't place. The edge of the sheet was serrated, which made it look like old parchment. The fish symbol he had seen on the wax seal stood at the top above her words; this time it had been wrapped around a small rock. He folded the note again and made his way back to his room.

The day had dawned brightly, though the air was noticeably cooler. Thin clouds streaked across the largely blue sky, their tails curling up at the edges high above. The wind had taken the edge off the temperature and David lifted up his coat collar as he walked down to the village. It felt good to leave the car behind and stretch his legs; the walk would only take him about fifteen minutes. Daffodils swayed in the breeze along the roadside, and he could hear gulls calling overhead as he approached the harbour. He thought how peaceful these small villages along the coast must be before the hordes of summer visitors arrived. Though it was late morning, there were still few people about. A young couple walked hand-in-hand along the harbour wall as he neared Rebecca's studio, while an old man walked by with a black Labrador. The dog came over and gave David a sniff and a wag of its tail; leaning down, he stroked the dog before it caught up with its owner.

From the end of the harbour he could see that the tide was now fully out, a line of discarded seaweed running along the top of the beach. He descended a set of steps not far from where an old tree stood. Many of the branches had been bent and twisted over the years by winter storms. The sand felt soft as David stepped onto the beach, so much so that in places his feet sank in which made walking difficult. He soon found his balance as he had done as a child on this very beach, and made his way across to the figure in the distance.

He could now see other people walking by the water's edge several hundred yards away, their voices carried softly on the breeze. There was no mistaking that the figure he was heading for was Rebecca. He had already seen her bend down a couple of times and pick up objects from the sand. Even from this distance he could see the long curled hair that again obscured her face as the wind caught it.

She must have seen him approaching as she waved over to him, pushing her hair back as she did. David quickened his step and waved back, though he was now close enough to hear her voice.

'Hello stranger, fancy seeing you here,' she said warmly.

Her eyes appeared as enchanting as they were when he was young; even the slight lines etched from the corner of them did little to age her and only seemed to complement her features. The mouth was slightly wider than he recalled and, as she smiled, it lifted her cheekbones slightly, giving her face great beauty.

'Hello, Rebecca,' was all he could say.

The black coat she wore brushed the sand as she bent to pick up the basket she had been carrying. Various pieces of dried wood lay among strips of seaweed and shells.

'Hope that's not lunch,' he added, nodding toward the basket.

She laughed, shaking her head. Leaning over to him, she kissed him on the cheek.

'Hello, David, how are you? It's been a long time.'

'Good, thank you,' he replied.

'Fine wind for flying a kite, don't you think?' She winked slightly as she looked out towards the sea. 'Come, I've got something to show you,' she added, before walking off. When he caught up with her, he noticed she was standing in the middle of an ornate drawing in the sand.

She had drawn a series of waves on which figures of a boy and a girl surfed, while over their heads she had drawn several kites. Each had a long tail that swirled around the picture, adding a sense of depth to the image. Though simply drawn, Rebecca had managed to capture a thousand memories. Now it was his time to laugh, and they began to walk across the sand. There was plenty of driftwood entangled in the line of seaweed. Further back, pieces could be seen among the rocks which separated the beach from the land beyond. David could also see a couple of plastic bottles along with other litter; she caught him looking at these.

'The winter seas bring in so many interesting items, sadly too much rubbish as well.

The pollution we make disgusts me, there has to be a limit to what the ocean can take.'

'I saw the container ship on the news. You must have been glad when that was moved away,' he answered.

'Oh, very much so. We all were.'

There was a relaxed atmosphere as they walked, chatting occasionally. Each step seemed to close each year apart and by the time they turned back, all of David's nerves about them meeting up again seemed to have vanished.

'I was sorry to hear about your parents. I didn't know. I spoke to Mrs Wenderby in the village. She told me about them and where I could find you.'

'Thank you,' she said tenderly. 'There's not much goes on around here that she misses,' she added, though from her expression he thought she had held back on her comment.

She asked about his family and was sorry to hear of their passing. She then asked whether he still saw Billy.

'Not as much as I should do. I guess we all move on.'

Their pace was easy now and Rebecca kicked out her legs as she walked, flicking the surface of the sand.

'So, are you married now?' she asked.

'No, I'm not. Never met anyone daft enough to have me.'

Again she laughed warmly. 'I sense there is someone though,' she said.

As they walked, he told her about Rachael, about her being abroad and even mentioned the problems they had been experiencing recently.

'Oh, I'm sure you'll be fine. The break might help you,' she told him.

'Maybe. So, how about you; you ever get married?' He thankfully diverted the attention away from himself.

'No, my love has always been the ocean.'

Now they had reached the harbour and he took her basket as she climbed the steps. There were no other people around by the time they reached her studio. She unlocked the door and led him inside.

'Welcome to my world. My little place of sanctuary.'

The inside of her studio was larger than it appeared from the outside. He could see various displays of work set back against the walls. The centre of the room was dominated by an ornate carving made, he presumed, from driftwood. The wood had been skilfully carved into the shape of a large fish surrounded by what appeared to be a large rock. He remembered the design from the heading on her note. On the body of the fish, instead of scales, were several ocean scenes of mermaids, giant sea creatures and other strange shapes. The carving was a stunning piece of work, but then his eyes strayed to some of the other items. Most were made of different kinds of pottery; some were polished, shaped glass that reflected various shades of colour, while the remainder of the display were wood carvings.

'You make all this?' he asked as she watched him.

'It's all my own work. The ocean helps me to see things so much better. Do you like my work?'

'Rebecca, it's beautiful.' She could see a look of wonder on his face as he looked around her studio. 'You have a real talent.'

Again she thanked him, then invited him over to a wooden staircase that stood at the rear of the room. As he climbed the steps, he passed a couple of small benches containing various tools and partly completed work.

If the downstairs had impressed him, the room upstairs blew him away. A large lounge stretched out across the building as he reached the top of the staircase. To the side was a small kitchen, where he could see she had been busy earlier. Walking into the room he could now see the doorway to another room, where a double bed stood beside two book-cases. Three huge beams spanned the building, supporting the angled roof, and giving an open plan look to the lounge and kitchen. At the front of the building a large half-moon window looked over the harbour and out to sea, casting most of the light which crossed the room.

The stone walls were covered with other pieces of work – mainly small ones – beside large cloth murals, some of which were as high as the room. The murals showed ocean scenes similar to those he had seen on the wooden carving as he had entered the building. Around the room were four table lamps, two of which were lit despite the daylight, their soft light reflecting off the glasswork alongside them. From the beams hung small mobiles of dolphins and fish which swirled gently in the warmth of the room. Two armchairs sat next to a low fireplace, in front of which several books lay on top of an old wooden table.

Rebecca removed her coat and David could see she wore a green dress underneath with a black pattern wrapped around it. A line of buttons sparkled on the front; the top few were undone to reveal her slender neck. Her hair hung onto her shoulders and looked darker now than it had outside.

'Your place is lovely. I hope your talent extends to the kitchen,' he said, averting his eyes.

'I wasn't sure what to do,' she now moved behind the counter which separated the small kitchen from the rest of the room. 'So I have made some fish and a salad. Will that be okay?'

Walking over to her, he removed his own coat and placed it on the back of one of the chairs. 'Sure, that sounds good. Is there anything I can do to help?'

'Thanks, you could cut some bread for me, if you like?' she replied and showed him a couple of French sticks. The bread smelt fresh and felt slightly warm.

Rebecca talked about her artwork as she grilled some pieces of plaice.

'Do you live here or at your parents' old place?' he asked her.

'Both. I tend to mainly work through the winter. The storms bring an abundance of materials as I mentioned earlier. My parents' place is a little big for just me; I prefer it here closer to my work.'

'I guess you mainly open over the summer?'

'Mainly, but as you saw from my sign, people are welcome to ring my bell any time.'

While she talked she passed him a wooden bowl, into which he placed the cut bread.

'I had a couple come in before Christmas, who spent over an hour in the studio and didn't buy anything. Nor did they say thank you for opening up for them. Then the next day I had an elderly woman in for ten minutes who bought over two hundred pound's worth of stuff.'

She asked him to pick a bottle of wine from her display in the lounge area and, while the fish cooked, she prepared a salad. As she did, David poured them each a glass of wine. She put on some background music while they ate, which only added to the warm atmosphere over the table. On top of the fish, Rebecca had toasted some almonds which added a surprise taste. The meal went well, as they caught up on each other's lives. He asked about the paper that she had written her note on, and was surprised to find it was made of stretched seaweed. Rebecca showed him some other sheets, as well as several pieces of jewellery she had made. She handed him a necklace made of three interwoven chains; small shells linking the chains together. A selection of carved moons added more decoration to the piece.

'Please take that for Rachael.'

'Are you sure? It's lovely.'

She nodded gently. 'I hope she likes it.'

'I'm sure she will.'

They left the table and took their drinks and sat down by the fireplace. Rebecca moved the chairs together so that they were closer and tucked her legs under her as she sat. She noticed that David had become quieter now and saw him frown as though he was deep in thought. He suddenly broke the silence.

'I still remember that holiday so clearly,' his face looked haunted as he looked at her. 'I remember looking for you in the storm. The sea looked terrifying; I couldn't find you, so I just ran. I was so scared, scared that you might have thought I had just left you, and you had fallen into the water.'

'But I was safe in the end,' she replied.

'You were, but how, how did...?'

As his words trailed off, Rebecca drank from her glass and looked at him reassuringly.

'How did you find me? I guess you just called to me.'

'I called to you? What do you mean?' he queried.

'I found myself in the water and I could hear you calling me. When I surfaced, I could see people running into the water towards me. I don't know how, but you found me.'

David shook his head as if trying to make sense of her words.

'But that was over two days later; you must have been somewhere else other than in the sea.'

'I guess so, but it was years ago. Remember we were only children. I really don't know, David.'

He saw a look of peace on her face, as though she simply accepted the events of those days. As if it was just a distant memory, only brought to the surface by his visit.

'But why has part of me always stayed there?' he asked, before telling her about his headaches and bad dreams. Dreams which woke him suddenly, ones which he could not remember when he awoke.

'The funny thing is, they have stopped since I came down here.'

'Maybe it's the sea air; you might just have needed a break.'

She saw his frown lessen and, when he looked up, he seemed brighter. She got up and went into the kitchen and brought back a bowl of grapes.

Placing them on the table, she poured them both some more wine. He took a handful of grapes and sipped from his refilled glass.

She found it nice to talk to someone; too often her days were spent in solitude at her work. His company was relaxing and she didn't feel as if she had to please or impress him, though she felt the need to change the topic of conversation.

'Tell you what, David,' she ran her hand through her hair, 'if you're free tomorrow, we can go over to the Point and lose some old ghosts.'

David thought for a moment, and at first she thought he was going to decline her offer, but the brighter look he had shown earlier gradually returned.

'I'd like that, thank you.'

Cloud increased while they talked and by late afternoon rain could be heard falling across the half-moon window. As he listened to it, he heard the bell for the studio ring downstairs. Rebecca asked him to excuse her and made her way down the stairs; he could hear her talking to some people below.

He looked over the edge of the stairway and could see a middle-aged couple enquiring about some glassware in the window. Returning to the lounge, his eye was drawn again to the mobiles hanging from the beams. The majority of them were of moons in different stages but, from the angle he had approached, he saw several different ones towards the far wall.

A full moon stood at the top of these while below what looked like small strips of wood hung down. Each display had about seven or eight of them, and when he looked closer he saw markings etched onto each one. For some reason they were familiar to him, maybe he had seen them on something down in the studio. He reached up and felt the carving with his fingers. He felt the outline of the design with his index finger and tried to recall where he had seen them before.

'Do you like them?' Rebecca's voice startled him as he hadn't heard her approach. The mobile gave off a slight ringing tone as he let go of it suddenly. She had come right over to him now, the light from one of the table lamps reflecting strongly in her green eyes and David found her entrancing.

'The mobiles. Do you like them?' she asked again.

He broke away from her gaze and moved over towards the sofa. He found his heart was beating fast now as he sat down. Rebecca held her hand out, steadying the mobile, and the strange moment appeared to pass as she sat down beside him once more.

'Sorry, I was miles away there. They are beautiful, all your work is,' he finally managed to say.

'Thank you, it takes some hours to produce it all.'

'You manage to sell anything down there?' he asked, referring to the recent visitors.

'No, just looking,' she replied, before taking another sip of wine.

The daylight had almost faded by the time he left. The more persistent rain had thankfully cleared, though a few drops still fell occasionally. Having arranged a time to meet in the morning, he thanked her for the meal and the welcome. His head felt quite light from the wine as he walked back up the hill out of the village.

Looking back, the last remnants of the setting sun broke through the clouds, casting a red glow over the outline of the village. He breathed in the sea air deeply and watched as the sun disappeared behind the cloud once more and darkness began to fall.

Rebecca waited patiently for the clouds to break. For nearly an hour now, she had sat by the half-moon window and looked out into the darkness. She held a drink of coffee in her hands and sipped from the cup as she waited. Finally the first breaks in the clouds began to appear and the moonlight once more bathed the ocean. She loved the water at night, from the tranquillity that now showed to the full force of the waves in winter storms. All the ocean's moods captivated her. Leaning forward, she unlocked the small hinge on the bottom of the window and opened it slightly. The coolness of the night crept in and caused her to shudder gently in her nightdress. The steam from her coffee blew towards her as the soft breeze entered the room, causing the mobiles hanging from the beams to spin and turn. Rebecca lifted her ear nearer to the window and listened. On the wind, moving swiftly across the surface of the water, travelled voices; ones that if the room had been full of people, only she could have heard. They rose over the harbour and into the studio. Some called her name, while others were singing. She watched as the mobiles began to spin faster as the voices caressed them. All the time the excitement within her grew. She looked up at the almost full moon; soon it would be time for her voice to join the others. As the sound faded, the clouds drifted back in and the moonlight once more began to fade. She returned to her bed, the window still open, and dreamed of the ocean.

David got no reply when he knocked on the studio door the following morning. Cupping one of his hands, he attempted to peer through the window but saw no light on inside or any sign of Rebecca. He checked his watch and saw it was just after ten o'clock. Just as he was wondering where she was, he heard her calling his name. Looking away from the window, he saw her standing over at the harbour wall with a group of people. He waved and made his way across to her.

Rebecca was dressed in a grey woollen jumper, along with blue jeans and trainers. Her hands were now deep in the pockets of a black jacket; her hair tied back this time. This only seemed to emphasize her cheekbones more and David was struck with how beautiful Rebecca had grown over the years. She smiled as he approached and finished talking to the people, who then moved off.

'Good morning,' she said. 'How are you today?'

'I'm good, thanks,' he told her. 'I slept really well.'

They began to walk back towards the studio, and David asked her who the people were.

'Oh, they live nearby. They bought some of my work as gifts for their relatives. They were telling me how much they had liked the presents.'

'Guess that must give you quite a buzz, all that praise?'

She laughed, though not modestly. Rebecca had a great deal of confidence in herself, which David found was rubbing off on him. He had reservations about going to Crenin Point, as it was his first visit since that day they had become separated. He had come to try and silence the ghosts of his childhood and was grateful that of all people, Rebecca would be with him. She unlocked the studio door and picked a rucksack up off the floor.

'I made us some lunch,' she said, holding up the rucksack. 'Just a few old fish heads and whelks. Hope you're hungry!'

'Sounds perfect. I can hardly wait.'

Before she locked the door, Rebecca placed a note in the window which he read as they walked off. It read:

'Gone to enjoy the day, love Rebecca'

Crenin Point could only be reached from the path which led from the harbour. The western side of the headland had cliffs which, while not high, had taken the impact of countless waves. This, in turn, had made the ground unsteady. The headland, or the Point as it was known locally, stretched out for over half a mile, rising to just over two hundred feet at its summit before dropping away to the sea. Here at low tide a small sandy cove was sometimes exposed, though it was rarely used due to the varying tides. The cool breeze stiffened as they made their way along the path. As they began to climb, David was forced to walk behind Rebecca where the path narrowed. Looking back, the view over the village became more and more impressive and the colours of the sea began to change. Now he could see differing shades of green and turquoise which merged into a light blue as the water neared the shore.

Within half an hour they were standing on the highest part of the Point, where David remembered the day when he had first climbed it with his father.

The view from the summit showed how much the headland sheltered the village; below he could see a small boat making its way towards the harbour. The grass on the summit was quite sparse where, over the years, endless feet had slowly worn the ground away. He imagined that in the summer the spot would be popular with picnickers but today, with the cool breeze off the water, they were the only people there. As they descended towards the cove, the wind decreased and the sunshine felt noticeably warmer.

'I had forgotten how beautiful this place is,' David said.

It was the first time either of them had spoken since they first set off. Both of them had been lost in their own thoughts, although it had been a comfortable silence.

The water level was still deep enough to cover the small cove, so it wasn't possible to descend to the shore. As they stood looking out to sea, Rebecca suggested that they sat a while.

'Tell me about Rachael,' she said.

Her comment surprised him. Drawing his legs up and resting his hands on his knees, he asked her why she wanted to know.

'I'm curious, that's all. What's she like?'

'She's fun to be with, she's got a good sense of humour. She always seems to have time for people, oh, and she always seems to be working. She works for a legal company based in the States, which is why she's over there at the moment.'

'You miss her?' she asked.

'I guess so, though I admit the distance between us might help.'

'In what way?' she asked. 'Would you not be better off together, talking about how you feel?'

David laughed at her comment and looked away from her.

'She says I'm too distant at times, that I don't open up enough to her and keep my feelings to myself too much. Guess she's right. I don't talk honestly about how I feel.'

When he turned back to her, he saw compassion in her expression. In her eyes there was a level of understanding.

'You're doing it now though, David,' she added.

He realised that he was, and that he had a level of understanding with Rebecca that he found difficult to understand.

'But you're easy to talk to.'

'And she isn't?' enquired Rebecca.

'It's just different, I guess. I feel like I've always known you.'

He half-expected her to react to his comment, but instead she let him continue. 'I knew I had to come back here, maybe even before I saw the television coverage last week.'

He stood and moved toward the water's edge, where he leant down to pick up a stone. Holding it in his hand, he seemed to find comfort in it somehow and tossed it in his hand a few times before throwing it out to sea. As it disappeared into the water, he turned to face her.

'It's funny, but the nearer I got to here, the more I thought about you.'

Rebecca stood and folded her arms as she walked over to him. She kept her head down as if she was watching her own steps, but didn't reply to his comment. David failed to notice that she had moved closer to him as they walked slowly on.

They followed another path then which took them over to the cliff side, where the air became cooler as they became exposed to the wind again. In the distance Rebecca pointed out her parents' place at the bottom of the headland; the roof just about visible. He was surprised by its location; as a child he had thought it had been further away. Walking back along the cliff tops, David listened intently as she talked about the birdlife along the coast. She pointed out various types to him while they sat down on the grass. They watched a pair of cormorants on rocks close to the swell of the water. While one picked at the white plumage on its chest, the other stretched out its wings, a sign – Rebecca told him – that the bird had recently dived for fish and was now drying its wings. She pointed out sandpipers and oystercatchers feeding down on the water's edge, though from the distance they were, he admitted they all looked the same to him.

'When you're closer, you can tell the difference,' she told him. 'The oystercatcher has a white underbelly and pink legs. Also, the sandpiper rocks its tail while it looks for food.'

She caught him smiling at her, and asked what he was thinking.

'I can see you really love this place, and how it must inspire your art,' he replied.

'It does, though it's the whole thing really; a mixture of the land and the sea.'

The keen wind was still noticeably cool as they descended back down to the tip of the headland, where they ate the lunch Rebecca had prepared for them.

'I have to say I was looking forward to the fish heads,' he joked as she passed him a sandwich. She laughed and tapped the rucksack beside her.

'Maybe later,' she mused.

'I really should have taken you out to dinner; you'll have nothing in your fridge soon.'

'That's okay, I prefer it here,' she replied. 'Restaurants are some-what stuffy, I feel.'

Now sheltered again from the wind, the sunlight felt warmer as they finished their ham salad sandwiches. She had also packed them some fruit and coffee, which David enjoyed. The sea air seemed to have given him an extra appetite.

'I'm pleased it was fine today,' David told her. 'The forecast said it should be nice for a few days.'

Finishing her coffee, she looked at him and shook her head.

'I'm afraid they're wrong,' she poured them another drink then added, 'the coming high tide will bring in a storm. A bad one.'

'What, are you telling me the forecasters are wrong, and you aren't?' David was surprised by her comment.

'Yes.'

'But how? What makes you say that?'

'Because I know. I can feel it. The tide will be at its highest soon and the wind and rain will join it. You watch.'

They spent the rest of the afternoon on The Point, enjoying the weather and each other's company. Down on the bay, Rebecca took her shoes off and walked barefoot on the sand, though keeping clear of the water's edge. David found a few flat stones which he skimmed across the surface of the water. When he returned to her, he saw the wind blowing her hair across her face, reminding him of the photo of them when they were young. She tucked her hair behind her ear and leant towards him.

'Thank you for coming, David,' she said, kissing him gently on the cheek.

David was surprised by her affection and it must have shown on his face, as she apologised. He said she didn't need to, and the awkward moment passed as they walked on.

'I need to go to my parents' place,' she told him as they reached level ground. 'Would you mind coming?'

'Sure,' he replied. 'Lead on.'

Despite the late afternoon sunshine, Dianne Wenderby added another log to the fire. It hissed and crackled as the flames began to spread along the dry wood. She pulled her cardigan tightly around herself, as much for reassurance as for warmth. From the front room window she could see that the wind was strengthening. She looked up and saw that cloud was beginning to edge in. It was only high up at the moment but, when she looked across to the skyline, the first signs of an approaching storm could be seen on the horizon. Walking back into the room she took one of the silver framed photographs off the mantlepiece, and sat down clutching it to her breast. Closing her eyes, the tears soon followed.

To the rear of Rebecca's studio, a small lane led to her parents' house. Occasionally vehicles made deliveries to a small storage unit halfway down the lane, but otherwise the road was rarely used. In parts the trees and bushes overhung the road and David and Rebecca were forced to duck underneath the branches as they made their way to the house. A set of ornate gates dominated the entrance, the paint flaked and pitted with rust in places. Tied around the gates was a thick chain, on which a large padlock hung. As Rebecca unlocked the gates, David noticed a small path leading to the side of the house. From its direction he guessed it led over onto the headland, and was wondering why they hadn't used it to reach the house. Just as he was about to ask, he heard the gates screech and protest as Rebecca pushed them open. They sounded as if they hadn't been opened in quite a while and, as she led him down the pathway to the house, he saw that weeds had taken hold of most of the path.

'Guess you've not been here for a while?' he asked her.

'It's been a while,' she replied. 'As I said, I prefer the studio.'

The house was L-shaped, with two floors made mostly of stone. Most of the windows had the curtains drawn; the glass itself grimy, as was the front door when Rebecca opened it.

'I won't be long,' she told him, before disappearing into the house. He found it strange that she didn't invite him in as openly as she had done at her studio, but guessed she preferred some privacy with the memories the place obviously held. Within a few minutes she had returned and locked the door, pushing her hand against it to check it was secure before they left.

David noticed that she had brought nothing out of the house and appeared preoccupied with her thoughts as they closed the gates again.

'Everything okay?' he asked as she snapped the lock shut again.

'Yeah, fine.' Her warmth of earlier seemed to have vanished and she kept her hands deep in her pockets and her head down as they walked back down the lane.

By the time they had reached the studio, her mood had lifted and she seemed to have lost whatever had concerned her.

They stood by the door to the studio as Rebecca felt for her keys in her coat.

'Thank you for that. I really enjoyed seeing it again,' he told her.

'My pleasure,' she smiled as she let them in. She took off her coat as they entered, and added, 'I'll make us both a drink.'

He looked at her work again as she made their drinks. Again the beauty of the work struck him as he removed his own coat. He was afraid to touch some of the pieces due to their delicate texture, but did run his hand over the smooth glasswork. As he did, Rebecca reappeared and handed him his drink. As they sat, he saw the concerned look on her face as she let down her hair. She ran her hands through the curls as she sipped her drink.

'I have to go away tomorrow. So today will be the last time I can see you,' she told him.

'Has this got anything to do with calling at your parents' house?' he asked. 'You've seemed preoccupied since you were there.'

When she looked up, she could see from his face that his comment had been well meant. There was no intrusion in his manner and his company had made her feel good. She knew herself that there was a bond between them which the years had failed to diminish. Leaning forward in her seat, she clasped her hands together as she looked at him.

'David, I have something I need to tell you, though I'm not sure how.'

He could tell she was struggling to find the words she wanted, but was at a loss to know what was on her mind. Finally she began to find the words which she had struggled to bring to the surface.

'The day you found me in the water; you knew where I was because I called you.'

'What do you mean?'

She could tell her comment had unnerved him. Fighting hard to find the right words to say, she continued, 'The day I first met you on the beach, I knew you were there. I heard you calling. You were angry and annoyed when you walked onto the beach. I felt that, and found you.'

He looked at her as though her words had made no sense, yet still she continued.

'I've been calling you for weeks now, David, but you haven't heard me.'

'What the hell are you talking about?' His emotions were rising.

'The headaches you've been having; that was me calling, and they were caused by my inner voice. Not understanding that, you simply shut me out. You felt the need to come here, didn't you David?'

'Yes but…' his words trailed off as he tried to make sense of what she was saying.

'They have stopped now, I guess, because you're no longer afraid.'

'Afraid of what?' he asked.

'Afraid of this place; afraid of what happened to me. You said yourself that the place had affected you.'

'And you're trying to tell me that you are the reason for this?'

'No, David, please listen to me,' she held his hands now. When she looked into his eyes, he saw a look of pleading.

'In the water, I was never in danger.'

The words were softly spoken, yet somehow they sounded different. They had a clarity to them that shook him; there was no background noise, no distance between them both as she spoke. He would have thought he'd imagined them, had they not be so clear. The thing that shocked him most and caused him so much doubt was that the words had appeared in the middle of his head. Her lips had never moved.

He backed away from her now, unsure of what had just happened. To reassure him Rebecca moved towards him, but he held out his hands to stop her.

'What was that?' he asked. 'I heard you speak, but your lips didn't move.'

'I simply opened your mind – a form of telepathy. You and I are able to do this as our minds are quite alike.'

'What do you mean?' he was confused.

'It's how my people communicate at certain times.'

She could see that David was still not making sense of her words. He stood up and walked to the half-moon window before turning back to look at her. He ran a hand through his hair while he thought about what she had said. For a moment she thought he would leave, but he seemed to settle down and walked back over to her.

'Rebecca, I want to understand you, but you're not making any sense.'

'I knew this would happen. I shouldn't have said anything.'

He could see how vulnerable she looked now and asked her to explain again what she meant by 'her people'.

'I didn't just disappear that day on the beach. Someone came for me.'

'Who?' he asked.

'That doesn't matter. What does is *why* they came. When I was a young child, about five I think, I was on a boat trip with my parents and fell overboard. I was in the water for a long time before someone was able to pull me out. While I was in the water, I found that after a short while I was able to breathe.'

David looked at her as if she was losing her mind, but let her continue.

'I felt okay when I was back in the boat, but everyone else seemed to be in a panic. Later, when we were back at home, I asked my parents what had happened to me.

'They told me a story about people who could live both on land and in the sea. Several places around the country you will find similar stories. Most of the people go unseen, rarely venturing onto land, but others are the opposite and live just like normal people. My parents explained to me how, at certain times, they would hear the calling – usually around the highest tide – and return to the sea.'

'What, like mermaids?' his tone was almost mocking.

'Kind of, but they had another name then. I can no longer remember.'

'But what has this to do with that day years ago?' he asked, shaking his head.

'It was when I first knew that I was like those people.'

'You're kidding me, right?'

'No, it has happened many times since then. You weren't here to know about them.'

'And what has this madness to do with now?'

'Every time there is a really high tide, we all communicate like I showed you earlier.

'We all call out to each other. You heard me calling you, though you would not have understood what was happening to you. When you saw the news report, it just triggered off an old memory, but also the fear in you.'

She saw him shake his head again slowly and could see that he did not believe anything she was saying. Again he stood. He held his head in his hands as he spoke.

'This is nonsense, all of this. Do you really expect me to believe any of it?'

Rebecca stayed seated as he paced the room. She could feel his agitation rising; he looked up at the mobiles hanging around him. It could have been a slight breeze or even his movement but, as he looked, they all began to slowly turn; the wooden symbols giving off a strange ringing tone as they touched each other.

'Sometimes, you simply have to believe,' she said softly.

David picked his jacket up off the back of the sofa and slipped his arm into the sleeve, struggling to find the other opening in his agitation. He flapped the jacket as she moved toward him; she held his arms and looked pleadingly into his eyes. When they met, he could see the green of her eyes strongly. She moved her face close to his as she tried to calm him. Her lips brushed his cheek and she felt his tension lower; raising a hand out she stroked his face. All he could now see was madness in her; he pulled away. As he did, he saw her eyes fill with moisture and her bottom lip tremble slightly. He felt he could have none of this madness and headed for the stairway. He heard her call out his name, could hear the pleading in her voice, but still he kept moving. His fingers were trembling as he unlocked the door; he gulped air into his lungs as he stumbled away from her place.

The sleep that had initially found him now drifted away. He wished that he had closed the curtains earlier, as now the moonlight illuminated the room. Try as he might, he fought to keep the words Rebecca had spoken earlier out of his mind.

Thankfully no-one had been about at the guest house when he returned; he had been shaking by the time he got to his room. Now he brought an arm across his face to shield his eyes, hoping the darkness would bring him nearer to the depth of sleep he had experienced the last two nights. No noise came but he became aware of a presence in the room. Unease crept through his body as he slowly lowered his arm. When he looked across the room, a figure stood close to the door. He reached for the bedside light, but in his haste caught it with the tip of his fingers and the light fell to the floor. By the time he looked up, the figure had moved next to the bed. Before he could move, a hand rested on his chest and he caught the scent of her perfume before she spoke.

'It's okay, David, it's me,' spoke Rebecca softly.

He wondered how she had managed to get into his room, let alone the guest house. As he tried to speak, she placed a finger across his lips.

As his mind raced, he became aware of another scent. The strong scent of the sea hung heavily in the air.

He tried to speak but found his voice lodged in his throat. Rebecca leant over him, her hair brushing his chest as she kissed his ear. As she faced him, he thought he saw the moonlight glint of her eyes. The pupils appeared to expand until the whole of her eyes blackened.

Her mouth moved opposite his, and she placed her hand underneath his neck, lifting him slightly. As she leaned in to kiss him, her mouth opened and water poured from it as she pressed their lips together.

Somehow, he again heard her words in his head, as the salt water filled his mouth.

'Just breathe, David. Just breathe.'

David tried to push her off, but found weakness enveloping his body. The water continued to fill his mouth and throat. He could feel his eyes bulging in their sockets as he fought against the water; his chest ached as his body tried in vain to resist. The hand at the back of his neck pulled him closer and, in his panic, he feared he was going to black out. He could feel his lungs filling and no longer felt the air in his nostrils. His eyes started to close; the lids heavy as he gulped in the mass of water.

His struggling became weaker as he felt himself sinking backwards. Surely he was drowning; his body could simply not take such a volume of water. He no longer felt her hand on his neck, nor could he feel her mouth on his. When he opened his eyes again he saw that she had moved away from him. His eyes must have been playing tricks, for as he looked at her, her hair seemed to bounce and flow gently around her face. David was still aware that he was falling backwards, away from Rebecca, and he waved his arms frantically to stop his fall. This seemed to slow him down, and he flapped his arms even more as his strength appeared to return. As he rose, she moved nearer to him so that their faces almost touched. Again he could hear her voice, though her lips didn't move. As he flapped his arms, he was aware that his own hair was flowing just like Rebecca's.

'You see, you just need to believe and then breathe.'

She reached for him now and placed an arm around his waist. He followed her gaze as she looked down and he saw nothing but darkness below him.

'Look above,' he heard her say softly in his mind.

He cautiously looked upwards as moonlight broke through the surface of the water above them. He pushed her away as his mind took in the sight above him. As he tried to comprehend what was happening, she reached for him again. When he looked, he saw that her fingers were webbed, the nails on her long fingers almost to a point. Taking his hand in hers, she pulled him along. They moved at speed and he found his fear reducing as she moved her body next to his. As she embraced him, a great warmth began to flow through his body. Now, all the fear and doubt he had felt earlier seemed to leave him. There was no pain now in his chest, only a feeling of complete peace. The speed they had moved at had been exhilarating, to the extent that he felt light-headed.

When Rebecca released his hand, he found himself falling again and quickly realised that he had to move his arms to keep himself stable. He felt his chest rising as he tried to control his breathing again, yet still he failed to see how he was managing it. Rebecca's hair brushed his face as she passed by him once more; she stopped in front of him, her arms moving as gracefully as her hair as it flowed around her face. The white blouse she wore hung loosely around her breasts and his eyes were drawn to where it opened by her waistline. The moonlight that shone from above illuminated her skin and as his eyes ran down her body, he saw her hips move gently. As she rose, he noticed how her legs seemed to merge together. From her waistline a pattern emerged, emphasized by the increased light; each scale fitted perfectly into the next. As he looked down her body, he saw the scales gradually became smaller, and at the tip of her feet he saw the outline of a fin emerge. It felt as though his heart had leapt into his mouth, as his mind tried to take in what he was seeing. He shook his head and tried to move back from her as he saw the smile on her face wane.

Up above he saw the light was fading as his panic increased. When he looked he could no longer see Rebecca; weakness again overcame him and he felt himself falling.

He tried to shout out for her, but now the darkness began to envelop him, the images swirling around him as he continued to sink. When David suddenly found himself sitting bolt upright in bed, he struggled to catch his breath. It felt like he had swallowed his tongue and he began to panic as he coughed and tried to gulp in air. Slowly he began to steady his breathing then felt his heart rate slow as the panic subsided. He managed to step out of bed and, although his legs felt weak, he was able to reach the doorway and find the light switch to the side. To the side of the bed he could see the lamp he had knocked over; thankfully he had missed the glass of water at his bedside. As he picked the lamp up, he noticed his hands were shaking badly. His breathing continued to slow and he ran his hand through his hair as he tried to calm himself. His hair was soaking wet, as were the shirt and shorts that he wore. Water ran down his hand as he held it out in front of him. As he looked down, the bed sheets were all tangled and soaking wet. When he lifted his fingers to his mouth, he could taste salt water on them.

As his breathing settled, he lay back on the bed, his mind still racing as he reached for his glass of water. The coolness and purity of the water freshened his mouth, but he thought he felt a bitter taste on his lips as he drifted into a deep sleep.

The storm swept in from the south west, much further north than forecast. By morning the village was being lashed by driving rain and gale-force winds. Few people ventured out, the warmth and safety of their homes holding them still. From her cottage Dianne Wenderby watched as the wind carried small branches in the air from the nearby trees. She pulled the small blanket she wore around herself, as if feeling the chill of the wind. Her breakfast remained untouched, as did the drink she had made. While she watched, she had continued to stir the drink even though it was now cold, as she tried to focus her mind. Now mid-morning, she listened in as the local radio station continued to report on the damage being caused by the weather.

By lunchtime, concern was rising over the height of the evening tide.

David failed to understand why his eyes felt so heavy as he tried to open them. When he finally did, he became aware that pain had settled on them and his headache had returned. He lay on his side, staring across the room, too tired to move. His jacket hung over the chair where he had left it the night before. Something about it was different, though; something at first he couldn't place. Turning onto his back, his whole body seemed to protest painfully. Looking back to his jacket, he realised what had caught his eye. It was the light. The shadows that lay across the far side of the room were the shadows he noticed toward the end of the day. He could hear rain being driven against the window pane by a strong wind. When he looked over to the clock on the wall, he saw that it was after six in the evening. It couldn't possibly be so late, he thought, yet the light told him otherwise. He crawled out of bed and picked up his jeans, the watch in his pocket confirming the time.

What the hell had happened to him? Running his tongue over his lips, they felt swollen and cracked. He reached for the glass by the bed. There was no water left, yet he noticed a small amount of sediment lying in the bottom of the glass. When he smelt it, he failed to detect an odour.

In the bathroom he ran water from the tap, using his cupped hand to drink until he felt his mouth clear. His reflection did little to ease his mind as he looked in the mirror, his stubble now showing clearly. Around his eyes and other parts of his face looked swollen. The memories of the night before came to him. He doubted whether it had even happened; surely it had all been a dream. Yet when he stepped beneath the shower to help not only waken him but to clear his head, the images sharpened in his mind. David looked at the water running over his hand and remembered the webbing he had felt on Rebecca's hands, how her hair had flowed all around her face and the pattern of scales as he had looked down her body. He thrust out a hand to block the water and the jet sprayed across the bathroom as he closed his eyes and shook his head.

Picking up the first clothes he could put his hands on, he dressed as quickly as his body would let him. He found he had to sit on a chair to pull his trainers on; his head ached too much when he leaned over. As he left the guest house, Mrs Hobson tried to catch his attention. He paid little regard to her as he passed her, pulling on his jacket, and hurriedly made his way out onto the road. He was in no fit state to drive; just running seemed to take all his concentration. The rain had soaked him by the time he reached the harbour, the wind so strong now that at times he struggled to stand.

Somehow he knew that Rebecca would not be found at her studio. As he passed it, he saw curtains had been pulled across the windows hiding the display he remembered. Again, as in his childhood, he was drawn to the pathway which led to Crenin Point, and it was this path he chose to take. He thought she would be at her parents' house and remembered the pathway he had seen near to the house entrance. Hopefully he would be able to find this in the fading light of the storm.

As he ran, he wondered why he was chasing after her. There had been madness in her words and yet he found no reason to dismiss them so easily. If she was leaving, wouldn't he be safer away from her? What would he do if he managed to find her? If she had spoken the truth, would he be able to stop her? Was it the connection she had said existed between them, or something much deeper that he felt for her?

The gale-force wind now made it hard to run, so he headed down towards the beach, hoping to pick up the path further down.

He ran along the sands of his childhood. Then the sun had coated the coastline, now – in fading light – the wind and rain combined to try to halt his progress.

Before he had run towards the threatening storm, now it engulfed him. The rain drenched his clothes further; his trousers clung to his legs, making them clumsy and heavy as he continued to run into the wind. He tried to clear his vision with his hand, and his mind raced back to the time before. His heart beat as fast as it had as a child, though the fear he had then failed to materialise. Now something else, something he couldn't understand, drove him on.

In some ways it seemed as though he was on a different stretch of sand. He remembered the wide expanse of beach then, now the tide was so high that by the time the ridge of rocks came into view the waves forced him to find higher ground.

As he clambered over the rocks his pace slowed considerably; nearing the grassed path he slipped on the edge of a rock, losing his balance. He managed to put out a hand to cushion his fall, but his shin caught the edge of a rock, the pain causing him to cry out. His hand stung from the impact and, when he regained his balance, he felt his shin. David cursed loudly and, despite the pain in his leg, ran on. The wind increased even further by the time he reached the gates of the house, the gusts still causing him to stumble a few times. The chain and padlock were back on the gate, yet he still pulled on the gates hoping they would open. The fencing either side of the entrance was far too high for him to scale, so the only option was the gates themselves. He found he could get some good footholds as he started to climb. The pain from his leg seemed to increase as he pulled himself up. At the top he nearly fell as he swung his leg over the top, only his jacket catching on one of the spikes prevented him from falling. He heard the material rip as his weight carried him down the other side, the impact on his injured leg causing his legs to buckle under him as he hit the ground. Lying on his back he let the pain subside and caught his breath. Overhead the dark storm clouds continued to swirl and the rain fell heavier as he made his way to the house.

There appeared to be lights on inside as he reached the doorway. He pounded on the door with his fist, repeatedly calling out Rebecca's name. There was no answer, nor did he expect one. Moving to the side of the door, he tried to peer through a window but found, like other ones he went to, the curtains remained drawn tightly across. Back at the front door, he began to kick at the lock, hoping the wooden door would give way. For several minutes, despite the pain he felt, he continued kicking until at last he felt something give way. He forced his shoulder against the door and burst through into the hallway. Amid the crash of the door, the howling wind and rain entered the building. He could see a large room ahead of him, in which the furniture had been shrouded in white sheets. In the hallway beside where he stood, he could see several boxes stacked up against the walls. David shouted out her name and began to search the rooms for her. Some of the downstairs rooms were locked and he cursed out loud each time one blocked his path. There was no sign of Rebecca as he searched the rooms on the upper floor either; only when he descended the steps did he hear movement. When he turned at the bottom of the steps, he became aware of a strong scent of sea and brine. And when he saw Rebecca, he found she was not alone.

Had it not been for Rebecca being there he would have fled the building immediately. She moved towards him as if she sensed his fear. Reaching for his hand, she stopped when he backed against the wall.

'David, what are you doing here?' Her eyes still held their beauty but he saw the concern on her face. 'You should have stayed away.'

'Rebecca, what's going on? I had a strange dream about you last night...' he said, still trying to pull away from her. 'Who the hell are they?' He looked over her shoulder. For a moment he felt as though he was still dreaming, as that would have put his mind at ease about what he saw.

There were eight figures in the room, all varying in size and in appearance. Two stood at nearly seven feet tall, their heads almost touching the ceiling. The shoulders were hunched over, and on the edge of the figures' necks, a form of ribbing clearly stood out. This pattern tapered down their arms to hands which seemed exaggerated, even for the height of the figures. On a couple he could see webbing between the long fingers, on which black curved nails also showed. Four of the other figures appeared to be female and resembled Rebecca's appearance. What he thought had been a dream was now turning into a living nightmare. He watched as two others moved next to where Rebecca stood; these were older than the rest and somehow his mind recognized them. The faces were familiar to him, even though the ears were swept back and skin hung down beneath their chins to where it joined their chests. What appeared to be the females held a strange sort of elegance to their features; each seemed to have their own beauty and grace. The males were more menacing to him, and he could see their chests rising. Occasionally he heard them exhale; the sound itself seemed threatening. The more he took in the sight, the more he noticed that each of them – except Rebecca – was soaking wet, the smell of the sea strong on their bodies.

He looked back as the one he thought he recognized moved even closer. As he spoke, his features began to change. His ears moved back to their normal position while the skin around his bare shoulders and face moved at great speed, smoothing out the features, the skin drying in an instant.

'Rebecca, we really have to go,' the figure told her.

The voice was as clear to David as it was that day he had first met him, towering over the youngster as he asked if Rebecca could come to Mevagissey all those years before.

'You told me your parents were dead,' he scorned.

'No, David, I never said that. I agreed with you that they had gone. Now they have come for me.'

She held him by the face now and he saw the Rebecca he knew as a child, her eyes bigger and her face more youthful, yet her voice stayed the same as she spoke.

'When I told you that we all call to each other at the highest tide, you were not only hearing my voice, but every one of us. It's how we know to gather.'

'But how can I hear it?' he managed to ask.

'Because you have the ability to hear as you have the ability to change, like me.'

He tried to push her away as he attempted to dismiss what she had just told him. Although her face still appeared as a child, her grip was strong as she held him still. In his mind he heard her voice again, so clear that every other sound was lost around him.

'Remember that day on the rocks, remember what you saw…'

He watched as her features changed back to the present. Yet when she let go of him he found himself standing on the rocks by Crenin Point. Up above he heard the sound of his kite's tail flapping in an unheard wind. When he looked over to the sea, he saw huge waves approaching; above him a storm neared. Yet the only sound he could hear was the kite's tail. Then he heard Rebecca call to him and saw her pointing across the shoreline. He slowly turned to see what she was pointing at. The area of sand on the far side of the ridge was covered in markings, the ones he had seen all those years ago.

In his mind he could see the mobiles in her studio slowly spinning and remembered reaching out to touch the same markings. The flapping of the kite faded and was replaced by the sound of the wind, though not as loud as the oncoming storm suggested. Rebecca's voice came to him again, deep within his mind.

'The markings are the signs I had to look for. They told me I had to leave. Each one gives its own message. So, as I told you… I was never in danger.'

The light began to fade and he saw her turn and head back along the ridge, then step between the rocks and out of sight. The next thing he knew he was back in her home, Rebecca holding him once more. He could also see now that they were alone. He feared he was losing his mind; it seemed too much to take in. Before he could speak, Rebecca moved swiftly to the side of him. She turned her head as if she had heard something. As she did so, she reached down for his hand then led him down a set of steps into the bottom floor of the house. Into darkness they went and David became aware of a change in temperature. His face caught a slight breeze which brought with it the renewed smell of the sea. She led him through the darkness until his feet felt the ground dip away as they began to descend steps. Reaching out, his hand felt the coldness of rock, and in places water ran over his fingers. David began to fear that he would overbalance and gripped Rebecca's hand tighter. Finally the ground levelled out and the darkness was penetrated by the flames of a torch of wood, fixed to the wall. As his eyes readjusted to the light, he saw that the pathway that followed was lit by further torches which burnt much brighter, reflecting their light around the passageway. Rebecca quickened her pace and, still unsure of his footing, David struggled to keep up with her. Now a stronger breeze blew down the passageway, on which the scent of the sea carried. In the distance he could hear water, the sound increasing as the passageway began to open out into a large cavern.

Here the torches that had lit the passageway stopped, their light no longer required. As David caught up with Rebecca, he saw that the new light source had outlined the edge of her hair, illuminating her curls. The sight before him did more than take his breath away. It was enough to make him stagger for support on the ledge where he stood with Rebecca.

Turning to face him, the light only emphasized her beauty, her cheeks looked as pure and clean as fresh snow. The dampness of the air had caused her curls to spiral closer together; the tips of her hair lay flat against her clothing. As she smiled, her eyes seemed to sparkle so much that the green of them looked like emeralds. His ears began to pick up a sound that at first seemed like a buzzing noise, as though his ears were ringing. As it increased he heard the sounds separate and become more individual. He followed her gaze as she raised her arm out toward the noise.

'They are singing.'

Now he knew where the other figures he had seen had gone. They stood beside the water which flowed into the cavern; the light that emanated from them reflected off the surface of the water.

'Why are they singing?' he managed to ask her finally.

'It's how we gather everyone in, how we join,' she explained softly. 'The tide will soon be at its highest and you will have to leave, David. This cavern will soon flood.'

As he reached for her hand, she felt his grip, though hard, held tenderness.

'Please leave now, David. I need to know you will be safe. You might not have time to make it back to the house. There are other passages where the water can cut off your route. The quickest way is to follow the path onwards and you will soon come to an opening – the opening I used when I was young. Once you climb out, head back on yourself. You will see the village in the distance.'

She then leant against him, kissing him gently. With that she released him and stepped down the uneven rocks and into the water. As he watched, he looked for any change in her and failed to see anything different, but as the water reached her waist, she leant back her head and he saw her body shudder. She held out her arms and leant back into the water. As she did, the others joined her. Two of the other females swam towards her as Rebecca slipped beneath the surface. David stayed rooted to the spot, unsure whether she had gone or not. Below the surface he could make out a faint light, which grew in strength as Rebecca emerged once more. She had lost the white blouse she had worn and her hair lay flat, curling only around her shoulders. For what could only have been seconds, they looked at each other. No thoughts or words were exchanged between them, just a warmth and understanding in each of their smiles.

With a last wave, she swam away with the others, their tails breaking the surface as they moved. All the light they had given the water now faded; the torches along the passageway were burning lower now and the shadows merged with the darkness around him. The swell of the water lashed the rocks by his feet and he knew he had to leave at once. Along the passageway, away from the house, he left. Up ahead he could hear the wind roaring and guessed it came from the opening she had told him about. When he reached it, what little daylight remained penetrated enough for him to be able to make his way to the surface of the rocks.

The full force of the wind hit him as he left the shelter of the passageway. The wind instantly chilled his body, his clothing which had dried slightly soon soaked by the driving rain. He turned his face away from the wind and tried to see the lights of the village, but a strong gust knocked him forward, causing him to fall to the ground. Pain from the impact crept into his arm and he clutched it tightly. As he attempted to stand, he caught his shin on the edge of a jagged rock as the wind continued to drive into him. He could see his leg was cut and he winced as he touched it through the material of his trousers. Bringing his hand up, he saw blood mixed with the rain water that ran down his fingers. It was impossible to tell how far away the village lights were and how far across the rocks he had travelled through the passageway. Along with the rain, he felt spray across his face when he looked back. He tried to keep moving, unsure of the tide behind him. The uneven ground was making it impossible for him to make headway, the pain from his arm and leg increasing all the time. Hoping for more shelter, he began to make his way to the side of the ridge. While the rain continued to fall, his descent had at least given him more shelter and he was able to increase his pace.

Behind him the tide had now reached the place where he had emerged from the passageway. Here the two bodies of water converged, causing a huge swell in the flow of water and, joined by the endless waves, it raced along the ridge. In the distance David could now make out the familiar shape of the lights beside the harbour, though the distance still seemed too great for his liking.

He released his injured arm as he looked back to see what had caused the increase in noise behind him. For a brief moment he glimpsed the image of Rebecca's face. Scenes of the last few days flickered before his eyes; scenes he would have scarcely believed days ago. The roar became almost deafening as the huge mass of water hit him, sweeping him away.

Far out to sea they swam, most were in groups while others swam alone. Above the water the rain had begun to clear and the moonlight across the waves drew them nearer to the surface. Its light was now strong enough to break beneath the surface in parts, where it illuminated their bodies. The colours reflected back across them as they swirled around each other at great speed. Between them they continued to sing, the sound lost within the confines of the water. Though whenever one broke through the surface, their song could be heard above the roar and crashing of the waves.

Earlier on, one of them had looked back to the shoreline where the lights could still be seen. As she had emerged through the water, her matted hair clung to her neck and shoulders. She cried out inland, hoping someone would be listening and hear her voice.

The swell of the waves raised her body high and the moonlight caught the green of her eyes, as she disappeared once more beneath the waves.

Early morning was always quiet, a time where the stillness of the night lingered, mixed with the hope and belief of a new day. It was close to her finishing time, but Molly Shawcross wanted to change the flowers in the corridors, even if that took her past her shift finishing time.

Unlike many of the staff, she liked the night work. True, there wasn't as much to do as during the day, but she somehow felt her time was of more use. She greatly believed that the unseen care was the most precious. By eight o'clock the Woodlands Care Home would be busy with the start of a new day, so she decided to get on with the flowers. Taking a bunch of withered flowers out of a vase, she opened the small window to freshen the air. The disturbed water smelt stale and the cool breeze that flowed through the window helped to freshen the air. As she looked outside she could see the leaves of the copper beeches were falling steadily now; autumn had reached its peak and the long days of summer seemed far away. She took another vase with her into the washroom and, after washing them, filled each one with fresh water. Before long the fresh flowers filled the two windowsills with colour once more. Returning to the washroom, she lifted the vase she had prepared earlier, walked down the corridor to the end room and quietly entered. The young woman beside the bed looked up from her magazine and smiled at Molly as she entered with the flowers. Each time Molly saw Rachael Shannon, it made her heart break.

She visited most weekends, spending all her time in the room talking away or reading from books and magazines. Just opposite the room, a guest room had become her own over the past few months. Sometimes when Molly saw her, she was quiet, other times when she looked in all she could hear was her sobbing. Molly placed the flowers beside the bed on the side table and stroked the side of Rachael's head. She whispered a good morning to her, though she could have shouted it, as nothing disturbed the man who lay silently in the bed.

The staff had openly encouraged Rachael to talk as normal. Research had showed in many cases that it was possible that David Lonsdale, although in a coma, could hear her every word.

'I see you have some more cards, David,' Molly said, handing them to Rachael.

Molly saw Rachael look up at the other cards above the bed, putting her magazine down to read through the pile of cards. In the five months he had been in the home, she could by now recognize most of the handwriting. It was the smallest of the envelopes that she opened.

Inside, along with a colourful card, was a short letter which Rachael would read to him later. Taking a pin out of the notice board, she added the card to the others after reading it. Rachael liked Dianne Wenderby's handwriting. It reminded her of her mother's; she wrote in the same graceful way. On the card she had simply written, 'Thinking of you'.

Over the course of time since the storm, the two women had become good friends. Without the details Dianne had told her, Rachael would have struggled to find out what had happened.

It had been two days after she had returned from Boston that Dianne had contacted her. Some of the jetlag had seemed to accompany her on the drive down to Crenin; only a numbness keeping her mind focused. Dianne had been the one who had found David unconscious on the shoreline, and for that Rachael would always be grateful. So much damage had been done to the village by the storm that the emergency services had already been nearby to help. David had been taken, along with three other residents, to Truro Hospital, from where Dianne had contacted her. Rachael kept David's wallet with her all the time, and thought the girl who looked back from the photo inside, looked much younger than the one who stared back at her in the mirror these days. Rachael had made the decision to move David closer to home when the hospital staff could do no more for him. His initial injuries had healed; the evidence of them now gone, he lay in his bed as though he was sleeping. A sleep, though, which seemed neverending. Throughout the long talks, she had learned that David had met up with his old childhood friend, other than that she knew little about the woman called Rebecca.

The storm had taken the lives of two elderly people, struck by a fallen tree, and that had been the main focus of attention. Each person in the village had their own story to tell and their own cares to attend to, instead of worrying about a woman who often left the area for short periods of time. No sign of her had been seen since then. Dianne told her that the woman's studio and home remained unlived in. Dianne had often checked, but both places remained silent.

Crenin slowly returned to normal and the endless tide continued to ebb and flow as time moved on.

Molly left Rachael alone with David, telling her she hoped to see her on her next visit. When Molly had collected her coat and bag, she passed the doorway and could hear the woman reading the new letters to the man in the bed. Had she looked in, she would have seen the single tear that ran down Rachael's cheek as she spoke.

Granton House

Part One – The Visits

The early morning frost lingered in the parts of the garden that still held onto the shade. On the recently mowed lawn, the curled edges of the fallen leaves sparkled as the approaching sunlight fell across them.

Several crows had gathered across the grassed area which lay either side of the long driveway; all enjoying the early morning sunshine. Soon it would spread across the rest of the garden as well as the woodland, which ran the length of the grounds up to the entrance gates. Despite the pleasure the late autumn warmth gave them, two of the crows suddenly became agitated with each other, spreading out their wings and cawing loudly. Another one, slightly bigger than the other two, decided to leave them to their fighting and flew away towards the house which stood at the top of the driveway.

The sand-coloured brickwork of the house had yet to catch any of the sunlight, the small windows held no reflections, there was total blackness within. Each window had a decorative border of red bricks around it, as did the entrance. This was set to the right of the building next to a larger section, which led to an angled roof where a short chimney stack stood. It was here that the crow landed. With its wings now tucked in along its black body, the crow cocked its head slightly as it surveyed the garden below. Across the grey slated roof, other crows gathered on the main chimneys of the house. These chimneys were much larger; the red vents on their tops matched the colour of the windows' red borders. No smoke came from the chimneys, as it had been several years since they had been used; the approaching sunlight would soon be the only warmth they would now feel.

Inside the house, each room was empty of furniture. No curtains hung at any of the windows, the carpets had largely been removed and the wooden floorboards now supported only memories and dust. Each room was locked, yet the key remained in each door. The silence of each room was only broken now by the noise of the crows outside deciding *en masse* to take flight. They settled in the tall trees of the woodland, though the noise remained, only slightly muffled by the few remaining leaves. The sunlight had now reached the front of the house, casting a golden glow across the brickwork. It shone through the upper windows, casting light into even the darkest corners of each room. This was repeated a short while later on the lower floor, and in the archway which housed the oak front door, through which visitors would soon enter.

The country lanes were mainly in shade, the trees and undergrowth yet to see any sunlight. The car that travelled along the lanes held the roadway well as it made its way around the tight bends. Jody Sedgwick gripped the steering wheel tightly, enjoying the feel of the road and the fact that she appeared to be the only person up so early. She kept mostly to the speed limit, but on the straighter parts Jody put her foot down, enjoying the sensation the speed gave her. She sang along with the music playing in her new Mini Cooper as she drove through the crisp morning air.

Jody had the volume on low, so she could hear the instructions from the SatNav. Her father had bought her the device after he became increasingly concerned about her getting lost in the country on her appointments. On her recent twenty-fifth birthday, he had met Jody outside Langdale Estate Agents, where she worked, and surprised her with the present.

Jody had worked at Langdale's for over a year, mainly in the office, taking phone calls and dealing with customers walking in off the street. Recently though, she had started doing viewings for potential buyers. Mary Hamilton, the co-owner, had accompanied her on the first few appointments, guiding her along with the viewers. She had been pleased with Jody's manner and humour with customers and thought she would soon gain much more experience by doing some of the viewings by herself. The company had even supplied her with a mobile phone, so that they could contact her, as well as for her personal safety. On the passenger seat beside her, a black folder lay with her phone alongside. Her folder contained the necessary papers for the call she was heading to. At the next junction she slowed down, before turning left. From the screen of the SatNav, she could see that her destination was now less than a mile away.

The gates that led to Granton House eventually came into view and Jody pulled her car over to the side of the lane just before them. When she looked across, pockets of the overnight frost still held at the base of the hedgerow beside the gates. She didn't expect much traffic using the road, but had still run two of her wheels onto the grass verge to allow any cars to pass. Turning her music off, she wound down the window beside her, looking now toward the gates.

The stone pillars, which held the driveway gates, stood at well over ten feet. The gates themselves were closed, a thick chain holding them together, on which a large brass padlock hung. Though it was partially obscured by the still low sun, she could see the house at the end of the driveway. Opposite the gates, open country led to higher ground which captured the morning sunshine beautifully. The nearby trees that lined most of the surrounding fields had become topped with ochre coloured leaves.

Jody felt in her pocket for the house keys. While she looked through them for the padlock key, a large crow landed on top of one of the gate pillars. It looked down at her as she found the key she sought and undid the lock, freeing the gates from the chain. Above her, the crow called out loudly, catching Jody's attention. Pushing open one of the gates, the hinges protested loudly and several flakes of rust fell, caused by the unexpected movement. Some of the flakes landed gently on her hands. The noise caused the crow to take flight and head back toward the nearby woodland.

By the time she had fully opened both gates, the bird could no longer be seen. In the long grass either side of the drive, she noticed two large stones, which she used to hold the gates back. Through the open window, she could hear the gravel crunch beneath the weight of the car as she approached the house. When she stopped, she reached for her folder and took out a paper containing a couple of photographs. Granton House appeared much larger than the image she now held. The picture had obviously been taken some time back, as it showed the surrounding trees fully out, and the lawns more unkempt. Jody thought the place looked much better in reality, as gardeners had recently been at work tending to the grass and bordering hedges, all making the surroundings look more presentable.

Before opening the car door, Jody looked at her hair in the rear view mirror. The previous weekend she had had her long hair cut to almost shoulder length. She had worn her hair long since she was a child, so her new look still surprised her whenever she caught sight of it. Running a hand through her hair, she felt the sharp edge of the tips, pleased with her new look as much as with the green two-piece suit she wore today. Underneath, the cotton of her white blouse felt cool against her skin as she finally stepped out of her car, noticing that her breath was caught by the still cool air.

The sun had risen higher now, bathing the garden completely in sunshine. Jody somehow thought that Granton House would look quite different on a grey winter's day – much less welcoming – so she was grateful the recent fine weather was holding.

Turning her attention to the house itself, she noticed that the windows failed to reflect any sunlight. Many months had passed since they had all been washed; around the window frames the paint was cracked and peeling and she could see some of the brickwork was also in need of repair. Several of the brick faces had been lost on some of the lower parts of the building, where damp had allowed frost to penetrate.

Jody enjoyed showing people around properties, though none so far had been on as grand a scale as Granton House. On her drive over, she had wondered how the house name had originated. There was no place nearby with a similar name, and she had wondered whether it had been an old family name or something. Either way, her first appointment would be here soon, as it was almost ten o'clock. She had originally planned to be here much earlier so she could look around the property first and get her bearings before the first of the viewers came. But numerous phone calls had delayed her.

When she had pulled up outside the house, she had left her car beside an overgrown, oval-shaped flower bed which, at one time, had no doubt dominated the top of the driveway. Now only weeds and grass filled it. Across the thicker weeds, several spiders' webs could be seen. Straightening her suit, Jody walked purposefully towards the house, again hearing the gravel beneath her shoes. Via a single step, she made her way into the archway that housed the front door. From her coat pocket she again took out the house keys and unlocked the door. At first the lock resisted and it took a couple of attempts before it finally turned. The old door hinges protested as loudly as the gates had done, as she swung open the door. The noise of the hinges broke the silence the house held within. The undisturbed air smelt stale in the hallway and Jody yearned to greet her viewers with the smell of fresh coffee and flowers which the glossy property magazines always recommended.

To familiarise herself with the property, Jody looked quickly through the relevant paperwork before the first viewer arrived. There were to be four viewings today, each an hour-and-a-half apart. Off the top sheet of her file, she read the viewers' names:

Hartwell & Longton Ltd.

Mrs and Mrs Farnham

Mr and Mrs Lyall

Mr A. Burscough

Thankfully she had brought some lunch with her, as she expected to be here for most of the day. On the cover of each set of paperwork, there was a smaller version of the house photograph she had looked at earlier. Inside, there was a floor plan of each level, along with the measurements for every room. Details about the outbuildings and the extent of the land which accompanied the property, were also included. Other than a brief paragraph at the end of the brochure, there were few other details regarding the history of the house or who the current owners were. Oddly, the itinerary also recommended that the upstairs rooms should be viewed first. Jody imagined that this was so that the grounds of the house could be viewed better. Reading through the paperwork again, it seemed to show the house in an order of rooms. The final paragraph stated that any future enquiries should be made through Langdale Estates; the address followed, along with a curious final line:

"Please leave the house as you find it, with nothing displaced."

Jody could make no sense of this line, and paid it no concern as she then decided to quickly go through the rooms and familiarize herself with the layout of the house. In the hallway, a door stood either side of her. Another one slightly to the right of the staircase led, she presumed, to the kitchen. The door was shut with the key in the lock, like all the others she would soon come to. The wide wooden stairway stood ahead of her, rising for several steps before turning towards the left of the property, then back on itself and out of sight.

Despite the time of year, the house wasn't cold inside. There was dampness in the air in parts, and the stale air she smelt on entering still lingered, but that could only be expected given that the house appeared to have been unoccupied for a long period. The windows of the house had seemed small from outside, and she doubted that they would cast much more light into any of the other rooms. Jody was thankful the electricity was still connected and she could at least add additional light if required. She began to climb the stairs, running her hand up the banister. At the top of the stairs, she arrived at a passageway which ran the length of the house. The brochure had informed her that there were five bedrooms and two bathrooms on the upper floor. Downstairs, there was a main lounge, a dining room, a kitchen with a morning room off it, a library without books, as well as a study.

Jody approached the first door and noticed the key in the lock. When she looked down the passageway, she saw other keys hanging down from the relevant doors. Every door upstairs had a decorative plate around its lock; each contained a different ornate pattern, the colour of which matched the fob on the keys. In contrast to the front door, she found each door opened easily.

She opened all the bedroom doors, along with the two bathroom doors. The rooms were completely bare. Only the bathrooms held furniture and these were only two tall cabinets which were fixed to the wall. Each bedroom had its own fireplace, the grates of which were empty. On some Jody noticed coloured tiles decorating the large frames. These gave the rooms a much needed touch of colour. All of the bedrooms looked out over the front or side gardens, while the passage windows – though small – gave fine views across the rear of the property. In the largest of the bathrooms, Jody noticed a round-shaped mirror above the discoloured sink, and checked her appearance in it.

As usual Jody wore little make-up; only her deep red lipstick added extra colour to her face, as her skin still held its colour from the warm summer and her holiday to Cornwall with her father. While she was in-between viewings, she reminded herself, she must phone him and see how his trip was going. During the periods he worked away, she missed his humour and company. In the eight years since her mother had walked out of their family home, she and her father had become closer than they had ever been when she was younger. Jody and her mother had barely spoken since.

She left the bathroom and noticed, when she walked back into the passage, that all the doors she had opened were now shut. She tried the handle of the one nearest to her and opened it slowly. There was no draught anywhere in the house and she watched the door to see if it swung back on itself, but it remained as she had left it.

Jody reopened the other doors and stood at the end of the passage waiting to see if any closed by themselves. None did. She was confused by what had happened and felt a little uneasy for some reason. Checking her watch, she saw it was 10.15am now, so she made her way back downstairs and looked through the other rooms.

The main lounge was the largest room in the house. It boasted a huge marble fireplace, as well as two large mirrors hung at each end of the room. To the side of the fireplace, two alcoves added welcome depth to the room; it was the only one in the house which was carpeted. The lounge led to the library, which was shelved up to the ceiling along three of the walls. The small study could be reached from the library, as well as from the kitchen, something she later discovered when she retraced her steps to the hallway. The kitchen was in dire need of modernisation, but was given great charm by the morning room which it led onto. Here French-style doors opened onto a small terraced area. Jody saw that weeds had taken a firm hold among the stone tubs and vases outside, the grass standing tall between the grey flagstones.

Back in the kitchen, she found another door which led to the study and then realised that you could walk all around the house by the connecting doors. As she had upstairs, she opened each one with its own individual key, leaving the doors open behind her. None had closed when she returned to the lounge, and she put the odd event upstairs down to the way the house had settled over the years. Leaving the room behind her, she stepped into the hallway as the sound of an approaching vehicle could be heard on the driveway. It was 10.30am exactly; her first viewer was on time.

James Hartwell and Darren Longton had barely spoken to each other on their journey. They had driven past the main gates and been forced to make a tight three-point turn by a field entrance much further down the lane. James knew that if he had made a comment that Darren's excessive speed had been the reason for him missing the driveway, it would only have added to the tension between them. Both had a feeling of relief when they finally pulled up outside the property. Darren stepped immediately out of the Audi A4, and spotted Jody coming out of the front door. James watched as he shook the woman's hand with great enthusiasm, before readjusting his suit jacket. The woman's smile seemed warm, and she looked genuinely pleased to meet him. Most people were. James could think of a thousand places he would sooner be than with Darren today. Although they had been business partners for five years, the friendship that had forged them together rarely surfaced these days. Through the windscreen he saw Darren beckoning for him to join him and the woman from the estate agents. Reluctantly he opened the door. The air at least refreshed him; the sun felt warm, yet the air held a coolness to it which helped lighten his mood slightly.

Jody introduced herself to him; her smile was even warmer close up, he thought. She asked them if they had had any difficulty finding the house, before leading them inside. While James continued to talk, Jody handed them each the paperwork for the property. She suggested they start the viewing upstairs, to which James and Darren both agreed.

At the top of the stairs Jody noticed the doors were open as she had left them and she began leading the two of them through the bedrooms. She pointed out features in each room, referring often to the brochure. The ceilings were of great interest to James. The time and skill that had been put into the house became more obvious to him as they toured the house. Darren, however, seemed less interested, Jody detected, and she noticed how he kept interrupting her as she talked about the house. It was true that Jody knew little about this particular house, so she worked on the same routine she used at other properties. However by the time they came back downstairs, Darren Longton was really beginning to annoy her. He had now made his own way through the lower floor rooms. James had sensed Jody's annoyance and had seen the tension showing on her face. As Darren walked off into the kitchen, James caught her attention.

'I'm sorry my business partner's manners aren't too good these days,' he told her.

'Did he ever have any?' she asked.

'Once, but I think he sold them on eBay.'

Jody laughed at his comment and felt herself relax a little. Darren was out of earshot now and Jody asked James about their interest in the house.

'We run a development business, mainly in new property. Darren, my charming partner, thought that this place had potential for redeveloping. Or, put another way, it's mainly the land he is interested in.'

Jody was surprised by his revelation, but appreciated his honesty. She admitted to him that it was the first time she herself had been to the property.

'It's actually a beautiful place. It would make a fine family home,' he told her.

'It would. Listen, I'm going to leave you guys to look around by yourselves. I'll be in my car if you need me; I have a few phone calls to make. After, if you like, I can show you around the grounds and the few outbuildings that there are.'

James thanked her and went in search of Darren. He realised that he hadn't yet seen the downstairs rooms and found himself quite taken with the dining room.

The ceiling was on a much grander scale than the bedrooms. Ornate friezes lined the edge of the room, while two round ceiling roses had at one time been home to chandeliers. Now just a long flex hung from each of them, with a light bulb on the end. He walked over to the brass light switch and flicked it on. A weak light was cast across the room by the light bulbs which, far from giving the room any warmth, only seemed to add to the already gloomy feel of the house. He switched the light off and unlocked the connecting door into the kitchen; from here he headed for the library. The paperwork stated that over two thousand books could be housed within the room. It now held little cheer; only two small windows offered light and the corners of the room were deep in shadows. Closing yet another door behind him, he returned to the kitchen which he thought offered greater potential. True, it needed modernising, but the space was good and the connecting room added much more daylight than the previous rooms. Sounds of movement came from above him and he guessed Darren had returned upstairs. He called out to him as he took the steps two at a time, but heard no reply. When he looked down the passage for his partner, he noticed that all of the doors to the rooms were closed.

Waiting outside the first door, he called out Darren's name again. No reply came again as he tried the door. Strangely, he found it was locked.

Turning the key, he looked inside. He remembered the details Jody had told him about this particular room. It boasted a fine view down the driveway and, when he looked through the window, he saw Jody standing beside her car talking on her phone. Turning his attention back to the room, he noticed a tall dressing mirror standing in the corner. James couldn't recall seeing it when they had entered the room before. Walking over to it, he saw the frame was made of oak or something similar. It stood at over six feet, and the tapered oval shape held strength as well as beauty. James caught sight of his reflection in the mirror. He thought he looked tired in the image before him. He wondered why he had put on a suit and tie today, when he had no business meetings. Maybe it was force of habit. He decided to lose the tie and was unbuttoning the top button of his shirt just as he heard Darren calling him.

'In here!' he called, still looking in the mirror. From where he stood, James could see the doorway through which the edge of one of the passageway windows could be seen. The voice startled him, making him turn around quickly.

'There you are, I've been looking for you,' Darren's voice still seemed loud as James hadn't seen him enter the room. He walked over to the window and looked back out.

'So what do you think?' James asked as he turned around.

'It's not suitable really. The land is great, but it's miles from anywhere. There are better sites in town. Besides the place is a dump.' Then he added with a smile, 'Still the skirt was worth coming to see, eh?'

How blind had Darren become, James thought? Was work all that really mattered now? He remembered a time early on in their partnership when they had had not only targets, but dreams. They had both wanted to improve their standard of living, but Darren had become so ruthless, caring little for anyone else along the way. Just as long as they made a profit. He could hear Darren talking now, but paid him little attention. He walked over to the mirror and looked at himself again. Was he turning into Darren himself?

Early on he knew he would not have lasted five minutes in the business. Darren had taught him so much, but now his own knowledge was enough for him to stand alone. James smiled to himself in the mirror and wished Darren would just shut up and get out of his life for good. Looking in the mirror to where his business partner stood, he found he couldn't see his reflection. Turning, he found Darren had walked back by the doorway, yet when he looked back in the mirror he couldn't see him, just the empty doorway with the passage beyond. Now his partner walked over and placed his hand on his shoulder.

'Let's go find the skirt and get out of here.'

James still stood alone; no figure was beside him in the mirror. He glanced across, saw and felt the hand squeeze his shoulder. He heard the footsteps walk across the floor, yet no figure showed in the mirror. Doubting his own eyes, he touched the glass as if it had just been a vision. The glass felt hard and cold to his touch. James felt lightheaded as he left the room, and the extra light at the top of the stairs strained his eyes. He heard Darren down in the hallway talking to Jody; looking back down the passageway, he saw that all the doors were open again. When he looked back in the room he could see no trace of the mirror.

'James! You there?' he heard from below again, and backed out of the room. His mind was reeling as he hurried down the steps. As he joined them outside, the sunshine failed to warm him in any way. He felt his hands and face, noticing how cold they were.

He rubbed them together vigorously in an attempt to warm himself. Jody noticed how pale James looked as he joined them. She was about to ask him if he was alright, when Darren stepped in front of her.

'Come on, we're going to have a look around the back of the property.'

'I thought you weren't interested?' James asked him. Noticing his partner's eyes following the woman around the building, he knew the answer to that question.

They stayed for about another ten minutes, walking along the terrace at the back of the property. Jody again referred to the brochure, but sensed that she was failing to catch their attention. She noticed how quiet and nervous James had become, and how he constantly kept looking back up at the building, especially at one of the rooms on the upper floor. She tried to include him in the conversation, and for a while his mood lightened, but the distant look soon returned. Soon though, even Darren's interest faded, and they both paid their compliments to Jody for letting them view the house, and thanked her for her time. As Darren stood by their car, Jody asked him to contact the office if they should require a further visit or any additional information regarding the property. Jody noticed how his eyes travelled down her body, making her feel uncomfortable. She folded her arms to shield herself from Darren, which seemed to work as he turned to open the car door, his interest lost. James was already sitting in the car; the nervousness about him hadn't faded. Jody gave a final wave as they headed down the drive, grateful that the first viewing was over.

Alone now by the house, she watched as their car turned onto the lane. The silence soon became noticeable. Looking across the drive and gardens, she wondered what was unusual all of a sudden. At first she couldn't put her finger on it, and then it dawned on her. It was completely quiet now, no breeze, no birdsong or any movement in or around the house. The garden was as quiet as a tomb.

Jody shuddered as she began to put fear in her mind. She couldn't shake the image of James's face and how quickly his warmth and humour had evaporated.

Now in the archway, she felt unease about entering the house. When she stepped into the hallway, she thought it felt noticeably cooler than before. Deciding she was simply spooking herself, Jody shook her head and attempted a weak smile. Pulling the door firmly shut behind her, she decided to sit in her car. Her mood lifted when she remembered she had a flask of coffee by the passenger seat. She sat behind the wheel sipping the coffee and found herself relaxing again. She scolded herself for being so jumpy and chose a CD to listen to, while she ran through the paperwork again. She was also annoyed with herself for being so unprepared for the first viewers. Although the singer Sarah Mclachlan sang about heartache and loss of love, the music soon began to soothe her. She hummed away as she enjoyed her coffee. Unseen to her, the upstairs doors slowly closed one by one.

If the first viewers had dampened her spirits, Jody didn't let it show. She felt more confident having fully read through the inventory, and she greeted the next viewers with a renewed passion. The sun still shone and she noticed birdsong again as she stepped back out of her car, the silence seeming to have lifted. Jody was soon put at ease by Grace and Stephen Farnham. They were accompanied by their young son, William. When introduced by his parents, he told Jody that he preferred to be called Billy.

The Farnhams were both in their early forties, well-spoken and very well-dressed. Their appearance matched the immaculate Mercedes they had arrived in.

Jody immediately liked Grace, and the two of them were soon complimenting each other on their suits. In contrast to the green of Jody's, Grace's was ivory coloured, with a fine grey stripe on the jacket. Worn over a black blouse, the cut of the suit looked expensive. Stephen and Billy exchanged glances and both raised their eyebrows as the two women continued to talk about clothes. Stephen though soon had them heading towards the house and before long they all stood in the hallway.

'I have a guide with details about the property,' she told them as she took copies off the stairs, before passing them each one. She got an awkward smile from Billy as she passed him one, but this soon widened when he realised that he was being included. 'As you will be aware, the property is unoccupied and the place is unfurnished. I'll show you briefly round, than let you explore yourselves. That okay?'

'Thank you,' said Stephen, as everyone nodded. 'Please lead on.'

As before, she started upstairs. As they reached the top of the stairs, she explained that the upstairs passageway ran the length of the house, and mentioned which were bedrooms and the bathrooms.

'I notice each door has its own key,' Grace said, as they entered one of the bedrooms.

'That's right, even downstairs,' Jody replied. 'You'll see that each one is colour-coded as well,' she smiled, 'but please don't ask me why. I presumed they were left by the previous occupiers for ease of access. I have the main door keys and the relevant ones for the outside buildings.'

Grace went on to ask about the previous occupiers, looking a little disappointed when Jody was unable to answer her questions.

'The place has been empty for several years now; very few people have viewed it, I'm informed. Today we have four viewings, the first since Langdale Estates took the house onto its books.'

As they went from room to room, Grace and Stephen exchanged comments about the property between themselves. Jody noticed how the couple held hands as much as possible as they walked. The long black coat which Stephen wore looked as relaxed on him as his manner. They both liked one particular bedroom. It was the largest one and the fact that it was next to one of the bathrooms only added to their interest. Jody looked over to Billy as his parents talked about knocking through walls and any alterations they thought would improve the place. Billy looked a little uncomfortable under her scrutiny, though seemed to brighten up slightly when Jody asked him what he thought of the house.

'It's certainly big,' he told her. 'I'm not sure why you would need so much space.'

'Well, there's plenty more downstairs. Do you like to read, Billy?'

'Sure,' he said. 'Why?'

'Wait till you see the library downstairs. You could have thousands of books in there.'

Billy smiled; his parents could see that he was beginning to enjoy himself. On the journey to Granton House, he had seemed withdrawn and had barely spoken. Grace was grateful it was the half-term holidays from school. She always liked the fact that they spent the week or so together as a family. Most years they had a week abroad, usually in France, but this year they had planned mostly days out. Stephen had been talking about moving to a bigger house recently and, although she had been against it at first, she was beginning to warm to the idea. Besides, she felt the area they lived in had declined over the years. During dinner one night, they had talked about moving to the country and getting away from the noise and pollution of town. She had found the advertisement for Granton House in a property magazine and they had all agreed to go and take a look. William had been the least enthusiastic of the three of them.

Since moving to senior school in September, he had struggled to settle in his new surroundings. The day he came home, when the school had broken up for holiday, was the happiest she had seen him in weeks. Grace had tried to ask how he was getting on at school and if he was having problems with anything. William's work was good and she was more than happy with his latest grades, but he was becoming more and more withdrawn over something. Grace was concerned that he was being bullied at his new school.

The downstairs of the house impressed the Farnhams. They both liked the ceilings and the fireplaces. Stephen warmed immediately to the small study, which Grace gave up to him jokingly as she claimed rights to the large kitchen. Again they talked about changes they would make to the property, should they decide on it, and how much they liked the place. Jody continued to chat warmly with them and loved the look on Billy's face when he saw the library. She showed him a fold-up set of steps, which could be used to reach the higher shelves. On the base were two small wheels, which enabled it to be moved easily and safely. Billy soon appeared on top of the steps, showing how high he could reach, and insisted on shouting from his now high vantage point. Grace was appreciative of the way Jody included him in the conversations and how she seemed to have cheered him up. After they had completed the viewing of the main house, Jody led them outside to show them the outbuildings and gardens.

To the side of the house, set back, was a double garage which was badly in need of repairs. Part of the roof had collapsed and the doors looked ready to fall off at any minute.

Alongside the garage were a couple of large outhouses, which Stephen and Billy soon explored.

The late autumn sunshine was quite warm now as Grace and Jody walked across the rear lawn. This, like the ones either side of the drive-way, had been mown recently though the general condition was poorer. Weeds had laid siege over most of the far end. A high patch of nettles stood against a pile of grass cuttings, no doubt from the recent mowing. From the nearby woodland the sound of crows, restless in their nests, could be heard. As Jody and Grace reached the end of the garden, they saw how impressive the view of the house was from here. The gardens themselves were finished off by another smaller terrace, on which a row of stone flower tubs stood, these sadly overgrown. For a moment they sat on a stone seat beside the flower tubs, and Grace took her shoe off, removing a small stone that had found its way in. When they stood again, the uneven flags they walked on wobbled slightly. Grace and Jody spoke about the house most of the time; occasionally they heard Stephen and Billy talking. At one point some joke was shared between father and son, which ended with a playful chase down the lawn. Halfway down Stephen called over to them.

'We're going to have another look inside. Do you want to come?'

'Sure, we'll catch you up,' Grace replied.

'Billy's a nice lad,' Jody told her as they made their way back towards the house.

'Thank you,' Grace smiled at Jody, 'although he's not been himself recently.'

Jody listened as she continued. 'He changed schools recently, and doesn't seem to have settled.'

'Which school does he go to?' Jody asked.

'He's at Westmoore.'

'That's close to where I live,' she told her. 'It's a good school, I hear.' Her words seemed to do little to convince Grace. 'Maybe the break will do him good,' Jody suggested.

'I hope so,' she replied, her voice sounding less confident than her words.

From high in the trees the crows took flight, circling high up above as they approached the house. Stephen had wanted to take another look at the study. There were times he needed to spend time working at home for the promotions company he owned and ran, so a study or somewhere for an office was essential. The outbuildings had potential, but he felt that somewhere he could more or less start work from was more suitable. So while Stephen assessed the room, Billy announced that he was going to have another look around.

'Okay, mate, you watch how you go,' Stephen told him.

Billy closed the study door behind him; the key fob swung slowly as he walked across the lounge. The rooms seemed enormous to him. Maybe it was because the rooms were empty, or maybe it was the height of the rooms. He knew he was small for his age; no matter how many times he had told people he had no say in the matter, they never seemed to listen. Things seemed so different recently. His only refuge seemed to come at home with his loving parents. He had shared in their obvious pleasure when he had started at Westmoore School. He knew the sacrifices they had made to send their only child to a private school, but now wished that they hadn't. All his friends from his previous school had gone elsewhere, and he seemed to be the only child who had known no-one on his first day.

Craig Doyle and Matthew Cartwright must have spotted him straight away. From that moment on, Billy hated the place. First it was his height they taunted him about, then the fact that his parents didn't have "real money", as they called it. They seemed to know all his personal details; how, he had no idea. There was nothing about him they seemed to like or that was out of bounds with their taunts. Over the next two weeks, they increased the threats to him. One lunchtime they had dragged him into the sports hall and begun to land punches on him, Billy had never figured out why. His eyes had filled with tears as he had tried to make sense of what was happening. The blows had been painful, but when they had stopped, the sounds of their laughter hurt just as badly as they both walked off. After a couple of similar incidents, he decided not to take it again and began to keep a permanent eye out for them. In the lessons he shared with them, he caught them glaring at him; even their looks caused him unease and nervousness. Most lunchtimes he would have to hide away from them, and the chases that usually ensued when school was let out terrified him. On the day they broke up for half term, they had followed him over to where his parents were waiting. Billy looked on in disbelief as Craig and Matthew introduced themselves to Billy's parents.

The false charm and politeness seemed to impress his parents somehow, and Billy's heart had sunk when his mother had invited them both for tea.

'You must both come to tea after the holiday,' she had told them. 'Wouldn't that be nice, William?'

How they had smiled, almost laughed, when his mother had called him William. They had stood and watched as he was driven away from the school. On the way home he had struggled to hold back the tears inside him. His only sanctuary seemed to come at home, where he would watch his parents openly express their love for each other. That he was loved himself, he never doubted. His parents were his rock; he felt though that he could break so easily against everybody else.

Across the hallway from the main lounge there was another door, which Billy didn't remember seeing before. He was kind of sure that the woman from the estate agents had taken them in there, but he couldn't remember. He walked curiously over to the door, and saw that the key held a sky blue key fob. The decorative plate around the lock on the door, again matched. The number of keys seemed a puzzle to his young mind. He was about three feet from the door when the key suddenly turned. He jumped and felt his breath jump in his mouth. The key fob now swung gently, disturbed by the turning. He half-expected the door to open and one of his parents to appear. Instead though, he heard his father moving about across the lounge, so it must be his mother or the other woman, Jody. Not wanting fear to overcome him, he called out his to his mother. No voice came. Slowly he reached for the handle and turned it. The door had been unlocked and it only dawned on him as he opened it, that it must have been opened from the inside. Yet the key remained in the front. Billy tried to clear his mind as he entered. The room was about twice the size of the study. Again there was no furniture. The floorboards were in poorer condition in this room, and in several places, gaps could be seen between the boards. Even the paper on the walls seemed aged, in parts it was split, allowing the plaster beneath to show through.

A much larger window than he had seen in the rest of the house gave the room much more light; the bright sunshine shone a shaft of light into the centre of the room, in which a small boy stood.

Billy wondered where he had come from. He wasn't aware that anyone else was in the house, certainly not anyone of his own age. The boy wore a grey shirt with black trousers, his hair was long and unruly. Billy also noticed that the other boy wore no shoes. Only when the boy smiled did Billy become more relaxed. He wasn't aware that the door had closed behind him by itself. All he noticed was the warmth of the sunlight through the window as he approached the boy.

'Hello, Billy, how you doing?' the boy asked him.

Billy answered okay, before he noticed that the boy had used his name.

'What are you doing here?' Billy asked him. 'How did you get in here?'

The boy seemed unfazed by his questions, and slowly shook his head.

'That don't matter, what does is how you are?' The boy spoke with a strange accent which Billy couldn't quite place. He seemed to leave words out of his sentences when he spoke and seemed greatly concerned with how Billy was.

'I'm okay,' Billy repeated.

'Do you like house?'

'Yes, though it's a bit big.' Billy noticed the boy beckoning him nearer, and his nerves started to rise. 'What do you want?'

The boy laughed, his head rocking back as he let the humour out. His eyes focused on Billy as he now stood by him. He put his arm around Billy's shoulder and moved his head closer to his ear. 'Billy, I've come to help you,' he whispered.

Just before entering the house again, Jody received a phone call. She asked Grace to excuse her, and assured her that she would catch her up. By the time she returned, she found Grace in the hallway just as Stephen came down the staircase. As they met at the bottom, Stephen kissed his wife's cheek softly. Grace reached for and squeezed his hand as he kissed her. Jody thought their open touches of affection were nice; there was no falseness in the couple at all, and she had enjoyed spending time with them both. When Stephen reached the bottom of the stairs, he asked them if they had seen Billy. Stephen called out the boy's name as Grace explained that they had only just come back in. Jody told them she had taken her phone call outside but hadn't seen the boy there. Again Stephen called out to Billy, but again there was no answer.

In the short time the boy had been speaking, Billy had noticed that the sun had moved around enough so that the two of them stood in the shade, the sunlight now further across the wall. Out of the sun, Billy noticed the room felt much cooler.

'So you want it to stop, right?' the boy said, as he moved away from him.

'Of course,' Billy told him. 'I wish for that more than anything.'

185

He then heard his name being called; the voice muffled at first, as if his hearing was weak. Now the voice sounded much louder, and Billy turned his head quickly to the door. He was about to call out, when he decided to tell the boy he had to go. However, when he looked back across the room, the boy was nowhere to be seen. Billy called out weakly, but got no reply. He had gone but where to Billy had no idea. As his father called again, he moved over to the door. As he opened it, he realised it was the only door the room had.

It was Jody whom he came across first when he entered the kitchen. The woman smiled at Billy and told him his parents had been looking for him. By the time they reached the hallway, Stephen and Grace were now both coming down the stairs.

'There you are. We've been looking for you.'

'Sorry, I got kind of lost. The place is so big,' he told his father.

'Well, as long as you are okay,' Stephen ruffled his son's hair.

They looked around the upstairs again – the four of them together – before Stephen said they had seen enough. He and Grace spoke for a while, while Jody watched Billy. The boy seemed more relaxed than when he had arrived, and she sensed his parents – especially Grace – felt that the trip had been good for him, if nothing else.

As they descended the stairs, Stephen told Jody that he would get back to her about the property. They both liked the place, and could see a lot of potential in Granton House. The location was a bit remote from what they were used to, but they felt that could be overcome in time.

As they approached the front door, Billy was looking at the room opposite the lounge, where he had seen the boy. He caught Jody's attention and asked,

'This room, what is it for?'

'This? Oh, it's just for storage. A kind of cloakroom.' She moved past him and turned the key in the lock. Pushing the door back, Billy looked into a room no more than three feet square. Along each side of the windowless room, black coat hooks hung on the wall. Underneath were a couple of buckets, and a small handbrush leant against the wall. Billy was completely stunned. He looked around the hallway for another door, almost as if he had chosen the wrong one. But as Jody shut the door, he saw the sky blue finger plate as well as the matching key fob when Jody released the key.

They thanked Jody for her time and promised to be in touch soon.

Billy seemed preoccupied as she said goodbye to him. He gave her a brief if awkward wave as he got into the car. Stephen beeped his horn as they circled the oval flowerbed and moved off down the driveway. Jody could see Billy leant over the back seat, looking back up at the house as they drove off.

She phoned Mary from her car as she ate her lunch. Now gone twelve, her next caller was due at one o'clock. She told her boss about the two viewings and how different they had both been.

'So, you'll want to stay office-bound if everyone was like the first two then?' Mary joked with her.

'Oh, one was okay, though he seemed to get spooked by the house,' she told her.

'You okay with the place yourself?' Mary asked.

Jody thought about the incident with the doors and the quietness that had descended outside the house. For a moment, she thought about telling Mary about them. Deciding she would sound silly, she replied instead that she was fine. It was just an old house that hadn't been lived in for a long time. Then she remembered a saying her grandmother had said to her as a child, 'most ghosts we carry in ourselves'. The women spoke for a while longer, before hanging up. Jody finished off her sandwich, and took a bite from one of the two apples she had brought with her. Her coffee still held its heat as she poured herself another cup.

As she sipped her drink, a large crow landed on the bonnet of her car. It folded its wings back and hopped close up to the windscreen, watching her curiously. Jody could see its black eyes seemed to shine as the sun caught them. Two other crows landed beside the car; they looked up at her through the side window, but remained still. The one on the bonnet appeared much larger than the other two and Jody began to consider it could possibly be a raven. It still studied her, but where its head had cocked from side to side before, the bird now stood motionless.

Unease began to creep into Jody, when several others landed on the front lawn. Thin cloud had drifted across the sky, temporarily blocking the sunshine. The gardens fell into shade and the warmth of the sun through the glass was now lost. The crow or raven – she was still unsure – moved its beak right up to the windscreen. Jody moved back in her seat slightly, still feeling uneasy. She wound down her window and shooed the two beside her away. She threw her part-eaten apple out of the car, hoping they would follow it. Both ignored the discarded apple but took flight, calling out loudly in protest. Others called out from the lawn, which now began to fill with sunshine as the cloud thinned. On the car bonnet the larger bird continued to stare at her, not at all fazed by her actions. She noticed its beak slowly open, but no sound came from the inquisitive bird. Jody pressed the horn, certain now that the bird would fly away. Instead it remained still. The bird's stare was now becoming almost hypnotic. Then, without reason it seemed, the crow turned its head towards the house, the sound of its wings flapping almost silently as it took flight. Once more, sunshine bathed Jody's Mini and she kept the window down as much for air as for the warmth. When the crows moved further down the lawn, she felt their interest declining in her and she began to relax a little more.

There was no sign of the larger one which had studied her so closely. Jody slowly opened the car door, expecting movement from the birds again. When none came, she stepped out of her car; as she stood, she noticed her legs were shaking slightly.

The country air smelt wonderful. Even though she was occasionally forced to wind the window up when the others complained about the draught, she still felt invigorated by it. Georgina Lyall glanced into the rear view mirror, but saw only the road disappearing behind her. On the rear seat, out of sight, her daughter Lily lay sleeping. In the passenger seat, her sister Jane continued to struggle with the road map she held.

'Well, we can't be far off now,' Georgina suggested to her.

'Guess so. This must be the right road. If it would only straighten out, we might be able to see something,' her sister advised.

On the back seat Lily awoke and shuffled herself upright, pulling on the seat belt to make herself more comfortable. While she had slept, her brown hair had fallen across her face. Pushing it away, she asked how much further they had to go. As she spoke, Jane called out, 'There it is, up ahead on the left.'

Thankfully the road had now straightened, and Georgina let the Volkswagen Golf slow down as she looked over to where Jane had pointed. Through the near leafless trees, the outline of a house came into view.

'Think we're here, Lily,' Georgina said, looking in the mirror again. This time her eight-year-old daughter could be seen smiling back at her.

'It's a shame Daddy couldn't be with us,' Lily said softly.

'Daddy has to work, honey, but if the place is nice we can come again and let him see it. Just think of it as our treat first,' she told her.

Nathan was always bloody working, she thought to herself. Earlier in the day, she had been so annoyed when he had phoned her to say he was caught up at work and would they mind going without him. Of course she said she would go, but this was supposed to be their big project. The big dream. For months now they had looked for somewhere to renovate, somewhere in the country; the place where they could find some peace away from the chaos of living in the city. Georgina already had part of the finance required, due to selling her share in the interior design business she and Jane had set up together. She didn't need to tell Jane that Nathan wasn't coming. When she had called around to see them off, she could read it on her sister's face. That's why Jane dropped everything she was doing to accompany her sister. The solicitors which he worked for gave Georgina and Nathan so much, especially since his new promotion, and they both had much more than Jane could ever dream of, but the hours he spent away from his family weren't doing any good. Especially with the way Lily was now.

As they approached the driveway, each of them felt their anticipation increase. Any other thoughts disappeared as they turned into the drive. They slowed to a halt so they could take in the view. The sandstone coloured driveway led straight to the house before it circled around what appeared, from where they were, to be a large flowerbed. A red Mini, which Georgina thought must belong to the estate agent, was parked to the side of this. The house was much further back from the road than she imagined; the property bigger and instantly appealing to her. Jane was first to get out of the car when they parked, lifting her sunglasses onto her long brown hair as she looked up at the house. A young woman appeared through the archway which housed the front door. Jane thought how well the colour of her suit looked on her. She looked young and fresh to Jane; a look she remembered occasionally. Now almost forty, she was two years older than Georgina and hoped she looked as good as her sister did. Recently though, the tiredness around Georgina's eyes seemed to be showing more. Although her smile and graceful ways managed to distract most people, they didn't fool her own sister.

'Hello, I'm Jody,' the young woman said, holding out a hand for her to shake. 'You must be Mrs Lyall.'

Jane shook her head as she took the young woman's hand. 'No, I'm Jane, Georgina's sister.'

Behind her, Jody could see the other woman helping a small girl out of the car. As the girl stood up, her lilac coloured dress fell down below her knee. The frame of a leg brace could be seen; Jody tried to avert her eyes from it as she smiled at the girl. When the young girl returned the smile, Jody felt more comfortable and walked over to them both.

'Welcome, I'm Jody, as I'm sure you heard. And you are?' She looked directly at the girl, who replied, 'I'm Lily. Pleased to meet you.'

Everyone seem to laugh gently, as Lily pointed out how formal they had all been with their introductions.

'Please call me Georgina,' the girl's mother told Jody. 'I'm afraid my husband can't make it today, so it's just us.'

'Oh, that's fine.' Jody smiled at Lily. 'It's all girls together then.'

Jody showed them all inside and went through the same routine she had followed with the two previous viewings. Again she handed them a brochure for the house, though this time she took them through the downstairs first. She had left the lounge door open and explained about the keys in each door. Lily thought the keys were cool; Georgina was more interested in the rooms themselves. As they walked from room to room, she loved the high ceilings and the extra air the height seemed to give each room. Though the décor was aged and worn, there seemed little dampness. In the kitchen she asked Jane what she thought of the place.

'Georgie, it's lovely.' She had always called her sister Georgie, even against Nathan's wishes. Recently she had made a point of saying it whenever she was at their house. He never said anything, but Jane knew it riled him.

'This could be wonderful,' Georgina said about the kitchen. 'You could do so much with it.' In her current house Georgina had completely refitted the kitchen at great expense, even though the room was pretty small. The size of this room, however, gave her a greater scope of ideas. Elsewhere in the house, Lily loved the library, insisting on shouting out 'hello' as she stood in the middle of the room. Despite the noise her clumsy leg made, she laughed at the slight echo the room gave off. Jody told Lily about the boy who had been at the house on the previous visit, but declined to mention the ladder she had shown him earlier. It dawned on Jody suddenly, as they re-entered the hallway, that the stairway to the upper floor could be awkward. Before she could express her concern, Jane swung an arm under Lily's arm, lifting the girl quickly up to rest her on her hip, then started to climb the steps.

'Let's go see upstairs, Princess.'

Jody could see the warmth in Georgina's face as she watched her sister with Lily. The look she gave Jody seemed to express much more than words could ever say. They joined them at the top of the stairs, where Jane told Lily she was getting too heavy for an elderly lady. Lily laughed and told her aunt she wasn't old, to which she replied, 'Well I feel it, carrying you around these days.'

Jody enjoyed the humour between them, as if it was their way of dealing with problems. Looking down the passage, she saw that each door was closed. No key fobs swung, and nothing was untoward as the early afternoon sunshine continued to warm the house.

Jody led them into each room, talking about the various features. They flicked through the brochure occasionally, both preferring to listen to Jody. Lily couldn't decide on which bedroom she liked the most, eventually picking what appeared to be the smallest, though it was much bigger than her current one at home. Her mother picked the one next to the bathroom, to Jody's amusement. She had bet herself that would happen. Jody joined them all in the largest of the bathrooms, where Lily tried one of the taps in the discoloured bath. Nothing came out as Jody explained that the water had been turned off to stop the pipes from freezing in the coming winter.

Water or no water, Lily made sure the tap was off before they left the room. At the top of the stairs, Jody rubbed her hands together and said, 'I'm going to leave you to look around for yourselves, I'll go and open up the back door and show you around outside when you're ready.'

Turning in the passageway, Jody added, 'Most things are mentioned in the brochure but please feel free to give me a shout if you need anything.'

With that, she descended the steps as they returned to the bedrooms, winking at Lily as she left them. Jane and Lily began looking at one of the bedrooms, while Georgina went into the larger of the two bathrooms. The bath seemed far too small to her; the depth was normal but the length seemed much smaller. As she ran her finger through the film of dust that lay on the edge beside the taps, she heard the sound of music. It was faint at first, and then started to get progressively louder. At first, she thought it was a mobile phone going off, but she knew only she had one with her. The music was clearer now. It was the sound of a piano being played.

She began to recognize the tune, one she had not heard for many years. She smiled and sat gently on the edge of the bath as she recalled the words from her childhood… 'Half a pound of tuppenny rice, half a pound of treacle, that's the way the money goes…' Her thoughts were broken when she heard a noise from outside the door.

'That you, Jane?' she called out. No reply came. Walking over to the door, she half-expected Jane or Lily to appear. Neither did. When she looked down the passageway, she found it was empty. Then she looked down and saw a small blue ball rolling towards her across the floorboards.

'Very funny, guys,' she said, laughing. She was puzzled by the silence that greeted her comment. She was wondering where the two of them had got to by the time the ball stopped rolling just in front of her feet. She leant down to pick it up, her hair falling across her face as she did. Pushing her hair back, she picked up the ball. At the same time the door at her side slowly opened.

Georgina grinned to herself as she realised that they were simply trying to make her jump. She pictured them both hiding behind the door, giggling. Any laughter in Lily she didn't want to miss, so she decided to play along with them both.

Walking into the room on her tiptoes, she pushed the door back, shouting 'Boo!' There was no-one there, the room was empty. This was the room that Lily had eventually said she liked the most, having changed her mind several times. The window looked out over the front of the house – as did all of the bedrooms – but also gave a good view over to the nearby woodland. When she looked out, Georgina could see some of the crows gathering in the highest branches. Looking down across the garden, she could just see the two cars parked by the side of the oval flowerbed. Jody stood talking, though her voice could not be heard. Georgina thought she must be on her phone, but when she stepped back Jane and Lily came into view.

The sight of them almost made her jump; she had been convinced that they were still upstairs with her. She ran her hand over the pane of glass to clear the view. The dust and grime held firm on it at first, and she found she had to rub her hand hard to shift the dirt. As she rubbed, she began to hear the soft music again. She sensed movement behind her and turned swiftly, looking towards the door. Out of the corner of her eye she thought she saw a figure pass the doorway. Only a glimpse, but a definite figure. Now unsure of herself, she looked back outside and could no longer see anyone down below. Still the music played. Though it was the same nursery rhyme, the tune was much slower; each note seeming to hang in the air. It reminded Georgina of how a child would play when learning the piano, with a single finger.

Georgina walked slowly to the door, now convinced she had seen something or someone go into the bathroom where she had been a few minutes earlier. The music continued as she looked left out of the doorway and saw that the bathroom door at the end of the passageway was closed. The fob on the key in the door swayed slightly, as if the movement of the door closing had disturbed it. As she approached, she found that she was gripping the ball quite firmly now. Her knuckles appeared white as she looked at the back of her hand. The music began to speed up now, erratic at first, like it was going out of tune. Then it sounded as though someone was banging their hands hard on the keys as the tune increased. Georgina had tired of this game now and wanted the music to stop; the beginnings of a headache were starting to form as she reached for the bathroom door handle. As she turned it, she found it unlocked. The music suddenly stopped. With the door now fully open, only an empty room greeted her. Georgina could feel her heart beating fast against her ribs now, her mouth had become dry and a cold sheen of sweat seemed to wrap itself around her. When she heard the voice behind her, she did jump this time.

'Georgie, are you okay?'

Georgina span around, a scream lodged in her throat. This was soon replaced by a huge feeling of relief as she saw her sister coming down the passageway.

When she glanced in her hand, she noticed there was no trace of the small ball. 'Where have you been? We've been looking all over for you.' Jane could see that her sister looked uneasy; she thought she even saw concern in her eyes. Only when she saw her smile did she relax. Georgie had looked genuinely scared as she had turned around. She never looked like that. Even through the bad days with Lily, she always managed to hold her composure. Jane had never seen her look as unsure as she had then.

'Sorry, I was miles away,' she told Jane, as she closed the bathroom door behind her.

'You sure?' Jane persisted. Her sister did her best to put her mind at ease as the two of them made their way downstairs. Lily was waiting for her in the hallway and insisted on looking in the library again. The child's attention seemed to relax Georgina, yet she was still unsure what had happened upstairs. When they revisited the study, she asked Jane if she had heard any music. Jane seemed confused by her comment, telling her she had heard nothing. For the next half hour they looked round the outbuildings and the gardens. Jody was very helpful and quite charming; at no time did she ask about Lily's condition. Georgina felt the need to tell her though and chose a moment between them while they were alone on the rear terrace.

'Lily loves the place,' she told Jody as they watched her with Jane. 'Do you have any children?'

'No, but one like Lily would be nice,' Jody replied.

'How do you mean?'

'She's fun and seems very bright.'

'Most of the time she is, but her condition troubles her. Lily has a degenerative illness which affects her spine. Without the brace, her leg would not hold her weight.'

The day felt suddenly cooler as Jody listened to Georgina talk about her daughter. She presumed it was only her reaction to what Georgina had told her. Looking across, they both saw Jane lift Lily up, holding her on her hip again as she walked over to them. Jody wondered whether the young girl was tired, or whether she just liked being held close by her aunt. Jody felt very lonely as she watched the two women with the child, which was odd for her; even odder, she felt keen to get back inside the house now.

Back inside, Jane took some measurements in the kitchen, and made sketches and a few notes for her sister, while the rest of them gathered in the hallway. Georgina thanked Jody for allowing them time to have a good look around.

'That's what I'm here for. I have a final viewing that should be here soon, and then I just have to lock everywhere up.'

Lily reached for her mother, who lifted her, allowing the child's head to rest on her shoulder.

'I like the house, Mummy.' Her simple comment seemed to sum up all their feelings. In a quiet moment between them, Jane insisted that she should seriously consider the place. It had everything that the two of them were looking for. Georgina tried to quell her enthusiasm by telling her that Nathan would have to come and take a look. She still felt troubled by the events upstairs, and had revisited the rooms with Jane to see if anything happened. Of course nothing untoward happened; the rooms remained quiet and still. It was almost as if she had imagined it.

Lily still lay across her chest; the walk around the place had taken its toll on her. A good sleep was what she needed on the way home. It seemed too much for someone so young to cope with at times. She could feel Lily's light breathing against her neck. At these sorts of moments, Lily seemed so fragile. Georgina just wished she could take away all her pain and worry. She stroked the girl's hair as Jane rejoined them in the hall. When she had finished stroking her daughter's hair, she held her tightly, kissing the top of Lily's head. She saw that flecks of dirt lying across her hair and Georgina looked at the palm of her hand. She had forgotten all about wiping the bedroom window; some of the dirt still clung to her hand as she began brushing it off Lily's hair.

'Sorry, baby, I didn't realise my hand was dirty. It's okay now.'

Lily seemed unconcerned by her mother rubbing her hair and giggled as Jane messed it up with her hand, before pretending to run away slowly. Georgina followed her outside, lowering Lily carefully down on the driveway beside the cars.

Jane thought that Georgina would have been overjoyed with Granton House, yet she seemed almost preoccupied. She did, however, perk up as she thanked Jody for showing them around.

'My pleasure, I hope it was of interest to you. If you want to arrange another visit just give me a ring. You know the number.'

Jody knelt down in front of Lily and gave her a small hug. Georgina saw Lily's smile beaming as she returned it. They both helped the little girl into the car and soon they were all boarded. Jane asked her sister if she was okay as she pulled on her seat belt.

'Yeah, I'm fine. Just got a headache coming on.'

They stopped at the top of the drive and gave the house a final look. By the arched doorway, they saw Jody waving farewell. They all waved back as Georgina steered the car out of the driveway and down the lane.

Again Jody was alone. Only one more viewing and she would be done. Now gone two-thirty, her final viewer was running slightly late. She tried to phone her father, but only got his answering machine. The sound of his voice as the recorded voice told her to leave a message, gave her a small amount of comfort. She left no message, planning to try again later.

The sun was beginning to lower slightly now, although the sunlight would be sufficient until past five. Her experience with the crows had spooked her while she ate her lunch and she wanted no repeat of it. She wound down both of the car's windows and turned her CD player on.

She chose an upbeat CD and turned up the volume. Not too loud, but loud enough to keep the birds away, she hoped. She could see a few of them high up in the trees; none seemed to be close to the house. Another thing she decided to do was to stop the house itself from making her feel uneasy. She left the front door open and walked into the hallway.

From there she went straight to the kitchen and opened the back door. With not even a slight breeze, there was no risk of wind blowing through the house. She left the remaining brochure on the bottom stairs as she climbed them once again. She opened all the upper doors and laid the keys on the floor beside each one. In each of the two bathrooms she managed, with a struggle, to open a window to let some air in. The music from her car drifted in through the window of the one she stood in and she checked her hair in the mirror above the sink, before returning downstairs. Her confidence increasing, she sang along to the music as she walked downstairs. She decided to leave the keys in the doors downstairs, so that the next viewer would be able to use them if they wished. In the library she placed the fold-up ladder against one of the bookcases, and managed to open a window to freshen the room a little. Of all of the rooms, this one felt the stalest; Jody thought that a library was the last place you wanted to be damp. From the library, she walked through the study and entered the kitchen.

Along the floorboards of the upper passageway, the dust began to move slowly. There was no breeze or anything obvious to disturb the dust, but it began to swirl and spiral. The same was happening across the landing and down the stairs. The sunlight was stronger here and highlighted the dust motes in its rays, as they spiralled higher almost touching the ceiling. As quickly as it had started, the movement began to slow down, until no trace of any disturbance could be seen.

Jody turned her head slightly, straining her ears and noticed she could no longer hear the music playing. It wasn't as though it was between tracks, as the gap was too long. Besides, she knew the running order of the songs. She had been returning to the library when she noticed it was still not playing. She stood with one foot slightly lifted so hat her toe remained on the floor, as if she had stopped mid-step. Still no music came from her car as she resumed her walk towards the lounge.

As she stepped into the library, a loud crash came from the hallway, shattering the silence around her. Her hands flew to her mouth as she stifled a scream. She rushed into the hallway to see what had happened, each step increasing her apprehension. Jody felt her legs weaken and found she was forced to lean against the wall in the hallway, as she saw what had made the loud crash. The seven keys she had removed from each of the upper doors lay in a pile on the floor in the middle of the hall. They had landed there with such force that Jody could see the disturbed dust floating above the keys, as it shone in the sunlight. Her breathing was becoming much shorter now and she desperately needed to get out of the house. Still looking at the keys on the floor, she backed quickly towards the front door. Sensing movement behind her, she turned and screamed as a figure appeared in front of her.

Jody's scream seemed louder than ever within the confines of the archway of the door. She felt trapped in between whatever was happening behind her in the hallway and the figure in front of her. A combination of the shadow at the doorway and the sunlight behind, caused the figure to appear in silhouette. Her scream had taken her voice away and her mouth felt dry and swollen as panic overcame her.

There was no way she was going to look behind her, and was bracing herself for the impact of the new arrival, when the figure moved back through the archway. The sunshine immediately lit the figure, and she almost screamed again when it spoke.

'Hello, I'm sorry if I startled you.'

Jody didn't know whether to laugh or cry. Instead she leant back against the door frame and ran her hands through her hair. She closed her eyes and tried to control her breathing. When she looked again, she saw the man was still standing there, an awkward look on his face.

'Hello, I'm Adam Burscough. I have an appointment for 2.30.'

Jody attempted to compose herself, and stepped outside beside him. She continued to breathe in deeply. The air outside felt so clean and so pure after the events in the hallway. She nodded and raised her hand to him as if to say, 'give me a minute.'

Her last viewer was, she guessed, in his mid-to-late thirties. He was dressed casually in black jeans, with a jade coloured shirt, over which he wore a brown jacket. His appearance matched his calm face. Jody thought his short black hair had recently been cut, and a scar on his right cheekbone stood out in the partial shade in which he now stood.

'I'm sorry,' Jody said smiling. 'You gave me quite a fright there. I never heard you come.'

'Seems we're both sorry now then,' he replied. He offered her a hand which she shook.

'You must be from Langdale Estates?'

'That's right, please call me Jody.'

Adam waited by the doorway as the young woman brought back a bottle of water from her car. As she took a mouthful, she seemed to have settled from her fright. He noticed how she composed herself well, before slipping back into work mode. Her eyes, though, still held concern. Jody handed him the brochure on the house from the stairs, as they stepped into the hallway. She explained, as she had to the others, that the brochure should contain all he needed to know. While he flicked through it, Jody looked over to where the keys had appeared. They still lay in a pile, undisturbed. Unsure as to whether she should touch them, it was Adam who then mentioned them. Jody made an excuse about dropping them as she had been startled by him. He seemed to accept this as she leant down and began picking up the keys. When she had reached for the first one, she almost expected something to happen when she touched it. Nothing did. In a few moments she had collected the keys in her hands and tried to smile as she faced Adam.

'This says,' he waved the brochure, 'that we should begin upstairs.'

'That's right. I did with a couple earlier, although you are free to do as you wish.'

'No, that's fine, we do as the brochure suggests. If that's okay?'

She nodded and they made their way to the stairs. That was fine with her, the sooner she was out of the place the better. She could make no sense of what was going on in the house. The doors that closed and opened by themselves, the keys appearing in the hallway, even the birds outside continued to scare her.

As they turned on the stairway, Adam asked her about the house. There was, as she had told the others, little she could tell him about it other than what the brochure held. Due to the remoteness of the property, Langdales had decided to make any appointments for the same day.

'This is the first time I have done the viewings here,' she told him. 'Of the others who have been today, I'm not sure how interested any of them have been.'

Now at the top of the stairs, she saw all the doors were again closed and began to show him the upper rooms. She found every door locked and selected the appropriate key for each door, before returning each to its proper place.

'I was coming up here to put the key in each door,' she lied. 'For some reason each door has a separate key, as you will see. Each is colour-coded.'

'Seems a strange idea.'

'Seems a strange house,' she replied, smiling as she spoke. In the bedroom they entered, Adam looked through the window and commented on the fine view.

'It is in each bedroom, though one looks mainly over to the side of the property,' Jody replied.

When they reached the last room – the end bathroom – she had replaced every key in its original lock. She half-expected the doors to slam or swing madly, but nothing happened. Adam continued polite conversation and looked around each room with interest, before they headed downstairs. As he was to be the last visitor, she closed the upper windows she had opened and locked each door behind her. She explained that he was free to look around the house again at his leisure, if he so wished. Through the downstairs rooms they went, till they stood in the library. Adam's face seemed to light up as she saw him raise his head and fully take in the room.

'This room is beautiful. I can picture it with reading lights all around it. It would be stunning.'

It was strange how each viewer had picked out an individual room as their favourite. Adam's choice was the library. With just one viewer, Granton appeared much bigger to Jody. The two of them seemed small, almost insignificant. At times the rooms of Granton House could seem almost overpowering.

'Do you have family?' she asked. 'It would make a fine family home.'

When he didn't answer her, she felt she had said the wrong thing. He looked straight ahead of him at an empty bookcase for a few seconds, then seemed to focus again. He continued to look around the room as he finally answered her.

'I don't, actually. I lost my wife a few years ago and have been busy with work ever since.'

'I'm sorry,' Jody told him. 'I didn't mean to intrude.'

'Oh, don't worry.' He raised his hand as if to reassure her.

'What work are you in?' she asked, changing the subject

'I'm a musician; I play piano and cello. I used to do the usual orchestra thing, but now compose my own work. I was looking for some place I could play undisturbed.'

'Well, the neighbours wouldn't complain about the noise here,' she reassured him.

They both laughed and continued on the viewing. He asked her while they were looking around the kitchen if she liked to cook. Jody appreciated his interest and admitted she could more than hold her own when it came to cooking. Food was a real passion of hers, though she confessed she should be more adventurous at times with it.

The study, as she had guessed, was of interest to him, though he preferred the morning room off the kitchen due to its size.

By the time they walked out onto the rear terrace, Jody felt much calmer. The sun was lowering slowly now and shadows were beginning to fall across the rear garden. The sunlight still held warmth though, and the full scent of autumn was now in the air.

At the far end of the grounds, they were looking back at the house when Jody noticed Adam take a compact camera out of his jacket pocket.

'Would it be okay if I took some photos?' he asked her.

'Sure, I don't see why not.'

Adam took several photos of the back of the house, as well as the outbuildings. He seemed to take his time with each photograph, as if composing each shot. Inside he took fewer, concentrating mainly around the hallway.

She accompanied him into a couple of the rooms downstairs, though she preferred not to join him upstairs. The upper floor seemed to cause her the most concern. Adam spoke seldom, and when he did his voice was measured and thoughtful. He was obviously quite interested in the house which, to Jody, seemed far too big for one person. Maybe he was looking long term and had other plans. As he returned to the lounge, she left him alone and walked outside.

Jody wondered whether she should mention what had happened with the keys she had moved upstairs. She felt guilty about taking them out of the doors. It was almost as if she had offended the house somehow; as if she had shown a lack of respect towards the property. What nonsense, she told herself. She didn't believe in ghosts or anything like that, but something or someone had moved the keys. Maybe the same someone had been opening and closing the doors. Yet she remained convinced that the house was empty. She noticed Adam's car parked a little away from her own. The paintwork reflected the roof of the house as Jody passed by. Standing by the edge of the lawn she watched the crows, who had gathered at the far end of the lawn. They took little interest now in her as she walked slowly across the garden. The more she thought about the day's events, the more she remembered the first viewing. At the time she wondered what had changed in the mood of one of the two businessmen. The one called James had seemed completely on edge as they left. Now Jody wondered what had happened to him while he was alone in the house. Even Grace had seemed more distant by the time she left. Had each of them had similar experiences? Or was she just letting her imagination run riot? Jody pulled her arms around her as she looked towards the house. In the stillness of the late afternoon, the house looked serene. Yet she felt each window seemed to follow her as she walked towards them, almost as if the house itself was watching her.

It was the smell that Adam noticed first. At first it was barely noticeable and he thought he had been mistaken, but when he stood still it gradually became stronger. He had been taking some photos in the lounge when he first noticed it. It was the smell of a distant memory; one which unlocked a feeling held deep within him. It was the smell of almonds. Again he thought he had been mistaken, and opened the door into the study.

Yet this only seemed to increase the smell, to the point where it was almost overpowering. It became clear that the smell was coming from the kitchen.

It wasn't the smell of almonds being used in baking; the scent was more subtle than that. He had to blink his eyes repeatedly when he entered the kitchen, as he thought his eyes were deceiving him. The floor of the kitchen was covered in pale pink flower petals. In places there were so many of them that his feet dragged them along as he walked through. As his feet disturbed them, the petals rose into the air, floating and spiralling around his legs like feathers. Still the smell of almonds filled the air and he bent down to take a closer look at the petals. They felt like velvet to his touch as he rubbed one between his fingers. He had known what they were the moment he had seen them; they were from the flowers of dozens of almond trees.

They had come across them by chance one day as they drove across southern Spain.

Anna had asked him to pull over to the side of the road so that they could take a closer look. Now, as he stood again in the kitchen, Adam

204

could recall the welcome relief from the sun's heat that the shade of the trees had offered them. He knew at that moment that his love for Anna had reached the point where he needed to tell her of his feelings. Ever since he had lost his wife, Eve, he had shared his grief with the one person who knew how he felt, for she felt the loss in equal measure. Her sister had been the only family she had and the emptiness that they both felt had brought them ever closer.

Now, two years on as they had sat under the falling blossom of almond trees, the tears of joy and regret had flowed down Anna's face as he had spoken to her. From that moment Adam had believed that they could never be separated. How wrong he had been. The lowering sun outside the house was beginning to make the inside of the kitchen gloomier. He walked across the room with the petals still sticking to his feet. The doors leading to the rear terrace offered more light to the morning room. The petals were fewer in here; the smell of almonds was beginning to fade. Adam felt a need to keep the smell within him and turned back toward the kitchen. Here, too, the petals were beginning to fade. He began to try and pick some up, as if to preserve the memory, but each one faded as he touched the petals. He fell to his knees as he thought of Anna. She was on his mind daily, yet he had not seen her for three long years. How he wished he could hold her again, reassure her doubts and fears. He knew the guilt she felt toward her sister had made her leave; nothing he could do at the time could have altered her plans to leave. He could feel tension across his face and he clenched his fists, his eyes tightly closed. When he opened them, there was no trace of the scent he had noticed; the petals had all gone. He was alone again.

It took a while for Jody to close the house up. Having already closed the bathroom windows, she struggled to close one of the other ones she had opened but thankfully Adam stayed and helped her pull the frame shut. She was also grateful that he offered to help her lock up the house. She had been nervous about closing the place up by herself. Jody had come across Adam on the rear terrace. He had told her he had finished taking photos and the two of them had returned inside. She didn't notice anything different about him, his quiet manner remained, and he spoke mainly about the property as they moved about the house. Of all the viewings, Jody thought this one had gone the best. Maybe that was because it had been the final one and soon she would be away from the place. Having already locked the rear door when they had come back in, between them they closed each of the lower doors, locking each as they left. Soon they were back in the hallway, and Jody felt tired and drained. The day itself seemed to have tired her, let alone the strange events that had happened. With relief she closed the front door. Turning the key, she breathed out as she backed away from the property. She found that Adam was waiting for her by his car.

'All locked up?' he asked, as she put the keys in her pocket.

'Sure is,' she said as she nodded. 'Thanks for staying on.'

He said he would be in touch regarding the property and thanked her again for her help. She watched as, like the others, he drove away from the house. The sun had sunk behind the woodland now, long shadows stretching across the lawn as she drove down the driveway. Jody left her engine running as she pulled up on the other side of the gates. She moved the stones away from each of the gates and pulled them together. They both protested at being disturbed, though not as loudly as before. Once she had wound the chain around the two gates, she stood looking down the driveway. Granton House seemed dark and unwelcoming in the fading daylight. The small windows held a deep blackness which caused her to momentarily shiver. Two of the crows she had seen earlier flew across and landed on the lawn in front of her. They remained silent and watched as she slid the gate padlock through two of the chain's links. Then the two birds flew back to the woodland, joining the others who called out from their high nests.

Jody noticed the first strands of mist forming in the fields opposite; she felt cold and vulnerable as she climbed into her car. Turning up the heat inside, she welcomed the flow of warm air over her. No traffic came down the lane as she left, thankful to be away from Granton House. The garden and woodlands held a stillness now, as did the house, as daylight faded. Across the gardens, the largest of the crows flew, its long legs hanging down from its body. The wings of the bird widened out as it slowed, before landing on the top of one of the gate pillars. The mist off the nearby field encroached on the gardens as the remnants of the sunlight faded. The crow remained on the pillar, thoughtful and watching. Behind it, within the rooms of Granton House, only silence now remained. The doors stayed shut and locked.

Part Two - The Wishes

The wet weather failed to dampen Darren Longton's mood as he stood looking out from the fourth floor window of Rennington House, the view below looking out over the city's railway station. Below him he watched a train as it passed by, its long body slowly snaking its way towards the shelter of Piccadilly Station. Rain had been falling for most of the morning and the heavy grey clouds threatened more. Darren managed to hide his smile, and quickly shifted to his serious business expression as he turned away from the view of the Manchester skyline.

'So, are we done then?' he asked the two men who had been sitting beside the oval table. Both had now stood up.

'We are, thank you,' replied Mark Rennington. His brother, Edward, seemed less than convinced to Darren. The paperwork they had all been debating on for the last hour was now neatly piled in the centre of the table. Darren shook both of the brothers' hands, all the while keeping his composure and his smile well hidden.

The Renningtons had called the meeting when the extra costs that the project they were currently working on had soared. Darren had listened tentatively as both of them droned on about the individual cost of each item of material. All the time they spoke, Darren had clicked the pen he held in his right hand. He was aware how irritating the noise became after a short while, but found that people kept their talks brief whenever he did it. Rennington Limited were constructing the small office block beside which Darren had earlier left his Audi A4. Several people seemed busy at work as he had looked across the site; one or two of the workers paid him a casual glance as he took his suit jacket off the hook in the back of his car. Despite the rain, he had walked the few hundred yards to Rennington House. The meeting had started amicably, but had soon become heated as the two brothers had wanted Darren to agree to an extra twenty per cent on costs. In the end he had got them to agree to fifteen and they had both signed the relevant paperwork and committed themselves to the new figure. Darren could have gone as high as thirty per cent, as the office block was already sold for a price far greater than he and James had expected. The saving he was making by screwing Rennington Limited only made him feel even more content.

Darren left the two brothers alone in the office as he made his way down the stairs. He thanked the young woman on reception for her help, as well as the coffee she had provided during the meeting. She felt uncomfortable as she noticed his eyes upon her legs, and swung her swivel chair around so that they were covered by her desk. Still smiling at her, he turned and left the building. The rain still fell as he made his way back to his car. Unseen by him, the receptionist raised the middle finger of her right hand and stuck it in the air as Darren Longton walked away, before returning to her work – a smile falling across her own face.

Darren pressed the key fob of the Audi A4. As it unlocked, the lights flashed briefly, their orange colour reflecting in the puddles that lay around the vehicle. He placed his briefcase on the car roof as he opened the door, then dropped it on the rear seat along with his jacket. The noise of a lorry reversing beside the office block caught his attention as he was about to step into his car.

Across the road from him, a row of small trees lined the side of the road. On them, a large number of crows landed silently. Several called out, though Darren paid them no attention and looked away. He could still hear the birds within the confines of the car, but they were soon drowned out by the loud music that starting playing from the stereo as he started the engine. Pumping the accelerator of the powerful vehicle, he took a final glance over to Rennington House, before he drove away from the site.

On the other side of the city, James Hartwell had just left his optician's when his mobile phone started ringing. He sheltered from the rain under the shop's canopy as he reached into his coat pocket for his phone. In the window beside him, an advertisement for sunglasses seemed inappropriate, given the weather. The heat in the optician's had been stifling while he had his eye test, so the cool air outside was a welcome relief. He put his new prescription in the inner pocket of his coat, as he answered the call.

'James, it's me.'

He had seen it was his partner calling on the display screen, and for a moment considered not answering. Darren no doubt had got what he wanted from his meeting, or otherwise he wouldn't be calling. As he heard the details, James imagined the smirk on Darren's face.

'Look, I hope you're not driving,' he interrupted. 'You can always tell me later.'

'It's okay, I'm done now. Remember, it's all money, buddy.'

With that, Darren hung up.

It was all money, James agreed. That's all it had become. Now, though, he felt he had had enough. Over the last few days he had been to see his accountant to see how he stood financially, and how he could get out of his partnership with Darren. At a pelican crossing, he stepped onto the road, allowing an elderly couple to cross first before he ran the last few paces. He noticed that there was a small coffee shop ahead of him, and he decided to have a drink before heading back.

The traffic steadily increased as Darren crossed the city. As the main road joined the city centre dual carriageway, he put his foot down, passing the row of vehicles he had been behind with ease. The music continued to blare out and he felt more than content with his day so far. Now mid-morning, he had a couple more meetings to attend, as well as an auction for some flats which James had been interested in. Darren was getting increasingly frustrated with James, who hated risk or being ruthless. That part was always left to him. Not that he minded. He loved the adrenalin rush he got from the power his position gave him over people.

The dual carriageway tapered back into a single lane as the road left the city, and the land alongside the road began to open out. He pulled his car in swiftly, causing the lorry he passed to flash at him. Despite the loud music, Darren heard him sound his horn. Darren raised two fingers up at the driver as he sped away. The wipers of the Audi were now on full speed to cope with the spray that swirled across the road. The rain and recent poor weather seemed relentless. Maybe he should think about getting some sun over the winter? Give himself a well earned rest. He reached for his phone on the passenger seat as it beeped, telling him he had a text message. He thought about ignoring it, and then reached across, the car swerving slightly as he looked at the screen.

It turned out to be unimportant and, after shaking his head, he put the mobile back down and focused on the next lorry on which he was closing. As his speed was now greatly reduced, Darren banged his hand against the steering wheel and cursed the driver. A couple of times he drifted out to the side of the vehicle to see if he could pass, but he was too close for a decent view and had to swerve back each time as cars approached him. Finally the road straightened out once more and Darren floored the accelerator of the Audi.

The response from the two litre engine was instant. As he passed the lorry, spray from the heavy vehicle flooded his screen, and for a moment his vision was lost. As it cleared, he saw a small van in front of the lorry had been the real reason for the slow progress. Ahead, he could see another vehicle approaching, the oncoming headlights appearing weak through the rain and spray. With the car's power he had more than enough room to pull in, but the car that overtook the approaching vehicle completely surprised him, so much so that it was now completely blocking his view.

He was forced to lose speed as now two cars approached. At the same time the lorry and small van reclaimed some of the lost ground on him. The approaching car slowed rapidly as the driver became aware of the threat of an oncoming collision. As it pulled back in, Darren had no alternative but to head for the narrowing gap. Squeezing through the reducing gap, he felt the rear of his car clip the front of the van. He could see headlights being flashed as the traffic passed him on the other side. Behind him the lights of the van and lorry dazzled him. Now through the gap, he laughed, though more through relief than anything else. The spray from the oncoming traffic now flooded his screen and when it did clear, the Audi still held its speed but it was far too great for the approaching bend. The Audi was still swaying slightly from the collision and Darren was forced to pull hard on the steering wheel to enable the car to take the bend. His mobile began to ring as the horns of the vehicles around him blasted. The noise caused him to be distracted and he felt his grip slacken, as he started to lose control. The rear wheel now connected with the kerb of the roadway, the impact jolting his body. As the rear of the car mounted the kerb, he could feel the back end scraping along the crash barrier which protected the corner. This soon dipped away as the road straightened, but the Audi didn't. As the front of the Audi swung round into the path of the van and lorry he had passed, he was momentarily blinded by the headlights. If the impact of the van wasn't enough, the impact of the lorry certainly was. It drove the Audi off the edge of the road, the wheels spinning wildly in the air. Darren, for some reason, glanced into the rear view mirror. Oddly, his seat appeared unoccupied in the reflection he saw. The music that had been playing had now stopped, as had the ringing mobile, and for a few seconds Darren could only hear the silence around him. The impact of the trees his car ploughed into soon put an end to it.

The heavy rain continued to fall across the roadway, on which the badly damaged van and lorry had finally managed to stop. In the ditch that ran beside the road, the ruptured fuel tank of the Audi now ignited. The bright flare illuminated the group of trees, from the top of which a group of crows took flight.

Craig Doyle was pleased to be back at school. He had become bored and restless over the half term holiday and needed to be away from home. His annoying parents had dragged him around endless relatives, and the evenings out at his father's golf club had driven him almost crazy. How he hated golf. His father was constantly on at him to start having lessons, yet he had no interest in the stupid game.

Craig had arrived early at Westmoore School, so that he could meet up with Matthew Cartwright. With his parents filling each day of his holiday for him, Craig had not had time to see his friend. There was also the fact that his parents didn't care for Matthew; they seemed to believe the two of them wasted too much time when they were together.

As he reached the school gates, he saw Matthew running over to meet him. For the next twenty minutes the two of them caught up, occasionally breaking into a mock fight which left them both struggling to stop their laughter. Now nearing eight o'clock, cars were beginning to pull up in the road beside them.

Matthew had thought little about Billy Farnham while they had been off, but soon learned of the plans Craig had for their schoolmate. He wanted to take up Billy's parents' offer of coming for tea, wanting to get the youngster in the safety of his own home. Between the two of them, they decided that they wanted Billy to know that nowhere was safe for him. He looked along the line of vehicles for the Farnhams' car. The early morning sunshine was shining straight at him as he looked down the road, and he was forced to shelter his eyes behind his raised hand. Matthew had drifted away to talk to a group of other pupils and Craig was forced to interrupt Matthew's conversation as he saw the car he had been waiting for approach.

Two vehicles pulled away from beside him, the parents or family within waving hard as they departed. The Farnhams' black Mercedes stopped and for a while no-one appeared. No doubt 'William', as his parents called him, would appear flanked like bodyguards by at least one bloody parent. Sometimes Craig knew that the gutless Billy would fool him by sneaking in one of the side entrances and going straight to whatever lesson he had. Today, though, would be different.

Craig saw the rear door of the Mercedes open and Billy stepped out. To his amazement, the car moved away, leaving Billy alone. There must have been a wave sent over to Billy, but he didn't return it; he simply raised his head slightly as if in recognition, before walking toward the school. His walk was upright and confident, a world away from what he had been when school had broken up.

Craig pulled on the sleeve of Matthew's blazer as he tried to get his attention. Matthew, however, was already watching with slight concern showing on his face. He too had not expected Farnham to turn up alone.

'Hi, guys!' Billy called as he passed them.

The two of them glared back

'What's with you, Farnham? Or should we say, William?' Craig laughed.

'Just saying hello, that's all,' Billy returned, before walking on into the school.

Grace Farnham felt relaxed as she drove away from the school. She had been dreading Billy's return to school, yet he seemed unconcerned by the start of the new term. The homework he had been set had long been done, and the previous evening he had spoken openly about the coming week at school. Grace had asked Stephen if he had seen any difference in him; anything that she should be aware of. As ever, her husband had done his best to reassure her, telling her that Billy was just fine. It seemed her fears had been unfounded as she headed home.

There was only one lesson which Craig and Matthew shared with Billy, the one just before the lunch break. The lesson would soon be over, even though he thought the clock on the far wall of the classroom was actually slowing down as it seemed so long. Craig needed to get some fresh air. The heat of the classroom was stifling, making his mood worse; he longed to open the window he sat beside.

No matter how many times he glared at Billy, his classmate continued to ignore him. As the teacher droned on and on, Craig glanced at his watch. Only five more minutes and they would be out of the lesson. He caught Matthew's eye and he nodded back, smiling as Craig stifled a pretend yawn. The teacher began to wind down the lesson and, across the room, pupils began gathering their books.

Billy's eyes were drawn to the small trees that flanked the grassed area outside the window. On the branches of the trees, several crows had landed. One cried out, yet the sound was lost to him as the noise of chairs being pushed back across the floor filled the room. As the room emptied, more crows began to gather.

Billy's confidence was waning fast now as he headed for lunch. He had tried hard to ignore the attention of Doyle and Cartwright, and hoped as the day went on they would keep out of his way. He had planned to confront the pair first thing, but had changed his mind when he saw them by the gates. As he turned into the corridor which led to the dining hall, a couple of other boys rushed past him, causing him to stumble. He composed himself again as they moved off, but seconds later he felt another, much harder push in the back. At the same time that he was pushed, he felt another arm twisting him around. His back connected hard with the door to one of the toilet blocks.

By the time Billy steadied himself, he found he was up against a row of sinks with Craig Doyle and Matthew Cartwright facing him.

'Farnham, you are so irritating me today,' sneered Craig.

Matthew swung round the bag he was carrying, Craig laughing loudly as it hit Billy on the side of the head. Although it hurt like hell, Billy refused to rub it or to show any emotion to the pair.

'Just leave me alone,' Billy told them, and tried to push past. Craig stuck out a leg, catching him painfully on the shin. The kick sent Billy falling to the ground, the impact of his fall taken up mostly by the bag which he had over his shoulder.

Craig was standing over him now, the laughing Matthew egging him on.

'You're going to get such a kicking now, you little shit…'

There must have been more, Billy thought, something else which should have been on the end of Craig's sentence, but he never waited for it. He got quickly to his feet before Craig noticed it; Billy's fall had caused great humour between him and Matthew. Craig felt the wind leave his body as Billy grabbed him by his shirt and tie, pushing him back fast.

Despite Craig's height and weight advantage, the unexpected move had caught him off guard. He found himself being driven quickly back, his arms flaying at his sides as he was forced to use them to keep his balance rather than to grab hold of Billy. It was the smaller boy's face that caused Craig such concern. Billy's face was contorted in anger, his mouth slightly open and his teeth clenched together. But it was the look of sheer hate which Craig saw in Billy's eyes that held his attention. On the wall behind him ran a row of coat hooks, which enabled pupils to hang up their belongings while they used the toilet block. A long, angled hook stood at the top of each coat peg, while a smaller thicker one was situated below. It was this smaller one with which Craig's head connected. The momentum that Billy had going by the time they reached the wall, jolted even him, but the impact on Craig was far more severe. The hook crashed into the back of his head, shattering his skull, the upper coat hook driving even deeper. Billy heard Matthew scream as blood and fluids from Craig's formerly arrogant head began to cover the wall. When Billy released him, his lifeless body hung from the hook like a bizarre puppet whose strings had been cut.

Matthew needed to be as far away from here as possible. He began to feel moisture forming in his eyes; he could feel bile rising from his stomach, and he backed toward the door. Over the weekend before school had started again, Billy had helped his father to clear out the garden shed. On a shelf they had cleared some lengths of wood which his father had told him were solid oak. The wood was very hard, he heard his father saying in his ear; the other voice was telling Billy that he soon needed to put an end to his fears. The boy in the large house had told him what he needed to do, how to make a stand for himself. He had to turn the fear around and make both of them pay. From the bag on his shoulder, Billy took out one of the pieces of oak. Matthew was too busy scrambling for the door to see the blow coming. Billy brought the length of wood down hard on his back, as the now screaming Matthew turned around to face him. The next blow from the wood connected hard with the boy's collar-bone, shattering it instantly. His screams soon faded as further blows rained down, mainly on his head. By the time the blows stopped, Billy doubted that even Matthew's parents would be able to recognize his face.

Outside the room, Billy could hear raised voices heading toward the toilets. He walked out onto the corridor still holding the bloodied length of wood. Other pupils called out to each other as they saw him leave the room. Now everyone backed away from Billy; no-one came to threaten or confront him.

As the pupils moved back, Billy caught sight of a shoeless young boy who walked away through the crowd. When the boy looked back, Billy could see a broad smile on his face. Now people began to raise their voices and occasionally he heard his name mentioned, but he was too busy trying to spot the other boy. From a nearby classroom, several people spilled out into the corridor and Billy lost sight of him. A female member of staff walking by, dropped the files she was carrying and screamed as she saw the blood splattered over Billy's uniform and face. Several of the papers left the files, spiralling around in the air, before they were trampled on by the commotion that erupted in the corridor.

It was after one o'clock by the time Jody left work at Langdale Estates. During the morning a severe headache had begun to set in, making her concentration stray. Mary had said that she would do the only afternoon viewing they had, and let Jody take half a day off because it was quiet. The time spent at Granton House, although five days before, had left her mentally drained. She was struggling to get a decent night's sleep, and recently just getting herself to work each day had seemed an enormous effort. She drove with no music on for a change on her way home, all the time trying to relax now that she was out of work. Being the early afternoon, the traffic across town was light and she would soon be home. The sound of sirens could be heard, and in her rear view mirror she could see flashing blue lights approaching. She slowed her speed, along with the other cars around her, as the two police cars raced by. Half a mile further on, she saw the police cars had been joined by three other vehicles, including an ambulance. They had all stopped outside Westmoore School.

Maybe it was curiosity, morbid fascination, or the feeling Jody had within her that made her turn around, but she pulled over to the side of the road and let the traffic pass before turning her car fully around. She headed toward the school.

As she approached, she pictured Grace and Stephen Farnham in her mind for some reason, and Jody sensed that something was wrong. At the end of the road leading to the school, a line of yellow traffic cones had been placed across the junction. Two police officers, both wearing high visibility jackets, had begun running a blue-and-white tape across the road to seal off the area. Another officer was diverting the traffic away from the scene. Further up the road, a group of people stood watching. Jody managed to pull her car over as another left, leaving a gap. When she stepped out of her car, she could hear a couple of women talking. One of them looked at her as she approached.

'Can I ask what has happened?' Jody asked. She could see the woman had recently been crying, her eyes were still puffy, and her face pale. It seemed to take all her strength for her to speak.

'Oh, it's terrible! Someone has apparently killed two of the pupils.' Then, looking further down the road, she added, 'The lady down there has also heard that one of the pupils did it.'

The woman began to cry again and Jody rested a hand on her shoulder as if to support her. Jody felt her headache increase as she left the women talking. Her stomach was beginning to knot and she began to feel nausea sweeping over her. With relief she sat back in her car, and found that she had to wait a few moments while she settled. She hoped nothing had happened to Billy. Her mind again pictured Grace and Stephen Farnham, this time racing towards the school. Jody rubbed the bridge of her nose, her headache now strong. She wound down her window to let in some much-needed air, before driving off. She turned the car around again and glanced down the closed-off road as she passed. By the side of a large van, she saw three figures enter the school gates, their blue overalls pulled closely around them. In the upper branches of the trees that lined the school fence, Jody saw several crows looking down as the figures passed below them.

Jody stayed in the shower for over twenty minutes. Within the confines of the hot water, she started to calm down. She had turned the television on as soon as she had arrived home. *Sky News* were already reporting on the story.

The reporter and several others were standing close to the school, but in a different part to the one Jody had seen. They were giving out little information; only that two twelve-year-old pupils had reportedly been killed and that the area had been sealed off. Police investigations were continuing, and the school – understandably – would be closed until further notice.

Her father, Barry, had taken the remote control off her and turned the sound down on the television.

'Maybe you're wrong,' he told her. 'It might have nothing to do with the boy you met.'

She had told her father everything about her visit to Granton House; all the strange happenings and the people who had viewed the house. She was pleased he was now home again. Her father had listened with his usual calm and understanding manner, which always gave Jody great strength. He could see the look of concern in her eyes and the effect it was having on her.

'I know something is wrong,' she had replied. 'Don't ask me why, I just do.'

With the sound muted, Jody continued to watch the pictures, even though the screen now showed the normal presenters and had moved on to another story.

'Listen, love, you go and dry your hair and get changed'.

Knowing he was right, she stood and hugged her father. They smiled at each other, before he kissed her on her forehead.

'I'll make us a drink if you like,' he called to her as he headed to the kitchen. When he turned, she was already heading up the stairs.

For the third consecutive night Jody struggled to sleep. She kept waking with her duvet tangled all around her. Despite the coolness of the night air, her body was coated in perspiration when she awoke. In the times that she did manage to drift off to sleep, she dreamt.

In her dreams she found herself on a gravel path. She was dressed in a white nightdress, the sleeves of which were ripped. On her arms she could see scratches across her skin. Although it was night in her dream, the area she walked in was bathed in moonlight. When she looked down, she saw she was barefoot; her feet showed dirt across them. As she walked, the path felt cold beneath her feet.

She had no idea where the path was or where it led. Around her a grey fog descended that she could not see through. She walked on, only silence accompanying her, before a house came into view.

Moonlight lit the front of Granton House; the windows had been removed and the house now looked like an empty shell to her. The roof had collapsed in towards the centre, so much so that only a couple of chimney stacks remained. From above, she heard a sound coming to her ears; it was the sound of hundreds of wings being flapped. When she looked up, she saw the dark outlines of birds circling above her.

There was movement on the path behind her now, and she saw that the fog was thinning. The path she was on had widened out and she could see a grass area either side. Out of the thinning mist came thousands of crows which landed all around her, the fluttering of their wings rippling through the night air. When they were eventually still, Jody saw that the full moon coated them all in a pale light.

Before dawn, Billy Farnham had awoken to the sound of buzzing coming from the overhead light. It cast a weak light around the room in which he had spent the night. The sheet that had been over him when he had drifted off to sleep had fallen to the floor during the night and he reached down to wrap it around himself. It seemed strange to wake up alone. Up until he had been allowed to sleep, everyone wanted to talk with him. He had spent several hours at the police station after being picked up from school, Billy's constant requests to be allowed to go home with his parents being refused.

A large crowd had gathered outside his school as he had been led to the police car. The female police officer to whom he had been handcuffed remained silent, even as she sat in the car beside him. To Billy there seemed to have been blue lights flashing everywhere. The other pupils had seemed fascinated by the events unfolding around them. He had heard shouts and jeers being directed at him but, when he had looked at people, they had tended to back away from him, fear in their faces.

The calmness he felt at being free of his tormenters had lessened as he had stood in the police station. He had been asked by a tall thin-faced policeman to empty his pockets, who had then taken his fingerprints. Billy had started to feel scared. He wanted his parents now and nobody else. They would surely be able to understand what had happened. They knew his fears and doubts. Hadn't he told them? He was sure he had, but his mind was beginning to spin wildly, confusion clouding his thoughts.

Two other men then questioned him briefly, but he couldn't find the answers that they wanted. Later he had been able to see his parents for a couple of minutes, but he barely recognized the two distraught people who had entered the room. His mother's face had been racked in pain and she had been unable to even stand properly without the support of his father. The eyes of his father had been tear-stained, his shoulders notice-ably slumped. In that one glimpse of time, he knew he had lost them both.

Before he had been allowed anything to eat or drink, a woman had come to speak to him from Social Services. She had explained to him that

220

he would have many more interviews as well as psychiatric evaluations. What they were, he could not imagine.

Feeling warm now, Billy discarded the sheet once more and perched himself on the edge of the bed – the same position he had been in when they had left him alone. He was still clothed, his hair ruffled. Above, the light continued to buzz. He looked down at his feet; his shoes had been removed for his own safety the night before, as had his belt. His feet were now bare.

Georgina Lyall was awake long before the alarm went off. She lay looking at the ceiling of her room, listening to the rain falling steadily against the window. While she glanced at the bedside clock, she stretched out her arm across the empty space beside her. Whenever Nathan worked away, she found it hard to sleep by herself. She liked to wake early, as she had done this morning, and watch him sleep. Sometimes she would see his eyelids flutter as if he was dreaming, occasionally a smile would fall across his face as he slept. Georgina would find herself gaining strength from the moments before he woke, enabling her to cope with whatever the day threw at her. The clock showed 6.25; in five more minutes the alarm would shatter the quietness around her. Today Lily had her latest appointment with her doctor. Although Lily had become used to these now, Georgina still found them depressing.

Georgina could always tell from her daughter's expressions, rather than what she said, how she felt about being prodded and probed. When her sister, Jane, had once said that to Lily, she had laughed at the comment – to Georgina's amazement. They would take her brace off and run a course of tests on her as normal, and all the time Georgina would be crying inside at her daughter's plight. This would be the second successive appointment she would attend without Nathan. It annoyed her that he had to work, instead of being the real support Lily needed. The company themselves, she felt, should allow him the time he needed with his family; he was, after all, making enough money for them to be able to afford it.

The clock began buzzing and Georgina leant across to switch it off. From downstairs she thought that she heard movement. She lay back across the bed as she listened again.

Lily's bedroom was downstairs. Three years ago they had converted the garage and utility room into a lounge-cum-bedroom for her when her condition worsened. It was hard to imagine that the room had once been home to tins of paint, dozens of boxes and general rubbish. From the moment Lily had seen the converted room with her own personal decoration, she had absolutely loved it. The noise came again, closer this time; Georgina blinked her eyes hard in an effort to fully wake up. Now she heard the noise again. Had she not known that Nathan was away, she would have thought that he had got up to get a drink of water from the bathroom. The sound she heard was the loose floorboard on the landing which creaked whenever anyone walked on it. Someone just had, and Georgina could feel her pulse racing. Dear God, what if someone was in the house? She had to get to Lily and make sure she was safe. When she stepped out of bed, she looked across to the bedroom doorway just as a figure appeared.

In her left hand, Lily dragged along the golden figure of Winnie the Pooh; her hair was as unruly as her pyjamas. She kept her bare feet close together as she stood upright without her brace. Georgina felt her breath lock in her throat as her daughter spoke.

'Mummy… something's different.'

The rain continued to fall heavily as she waited for the traffic to start moving again. Georgina ran a hand through her hair as she tried to compose herself, breathing out deeply. Watching the raindrops running down the side window, she thought of Lily.

She failed to understand everything that had happened to her during the morning. An hour before her appointment she had burst into the doctor's surgery carrying Lily, frightened to let her stand by herself in case the new-found strength was lost. For nearly half an hour her daughter had walked around the house with Georgina, showing how much better her leg and back felt. The tears that had fallen down Georgina's face had been a mixture of shock and emotion.

As the traffic began to slowly move, she reached again for her mobile phone. She flicked down to Nathan's number and pressed dial. When the automated voice told her that the phone was currently switched off, Georgina had banged the steering wheel in frustration.

'Turn the bloody thing on!' she had shouted within the confines of her car. Again the lights of the roadworks turned to red, and she found herself stationary once more.

The doctor had been as stunned as she had when he had examined Lily. His initial examination could find nothing untoward. Lily appeared as healthy and normal as any other eight-year-old girl, yet she wasn't, Georgina thought. For almost three years, Lily's condition had continued to worsen.

Now, for some reason, she seemed fine. Following a few phone calls, they had taken her straight to hospital. Georgina had phoned Jane to ask her to meet them there, telling her she would explain everything later. While they were waiting to be seen, Jane had seemed to cry even more tears than Georgina as she found out what had happened. Using a pay phone in a corridor, Georgina had tried Nathan's mobile several times. Each time the phone was still switched off, and again her anger began to rise. When she phoned Drayton Solicitors where he worked, her heart had warmed as they informed her that the final meeting Nathan had been attending would now have finished. His train should be getting in just after one o'clock.

He must be taking an earlier train, she thought; he wasn't expected back from London till late that evening. When she had returned to Jane and Lily and told them about him coming back earlier, Jane had suggested that she go and meet him at the station.

Now approaching one o'clock, she hoped she would make it on time. The roadworks now behind her, she found she was less than a mile from the station. The rainfall increased and Georgina was forced to put the wipers on to high speed in an attempt to clear her vision.

What if Lily was, by some miracle, well again? She knew that was impossible. You couldn't just heal as quickly as that, especially with her condition. Yet she had seen it for herself, as had Jane and Lily's doctor. She needed Nathan with her, though. She needed his strength and understanding to support her through whatever the future would bring.

As she found a parking spot outside the station, she thought how much she had to tell him. From the news of Lily, to the house they had recently viewed. She thought there was no need to get her brolly off the back seat, as she would be able to run over to the cover which the station entrance gave. People were already exiting the station; when she looked at her watch, she found she was exactly on time to meet his train. The rain felt cold against her face as she stepped out of the car. She was forced to stop her run for cover when a group of birds flew across in front of her.

A couple of the crows landed in front of her as she stopped, while the others flew on to the entrance canopy. Over the sound of the rain, she could hear the birds crying out as she approached the entrance. She could see Nathan through the gap in the doorway and began to wave over to him, but he had failed to see her through the crowds of people around him. Beside him, Georgina could see a woman move closer to Nathan. Georgina stopped in her tracks as she saw them link hands. The two of them moved to the side to let the mass of people pass. Georgina stayed where she had stopped, the rain now beginning to flatten her hair. Her hand was still raised in readiness for another wave; yet unmoving, she looked like a statue as the crowd moved around her. Finally she took small steps towards the entrance and could see her husband clearly. She saw him raise his hand and link the fingers of the woman; Georgina could see she was quite beautiful, a few years younger than herself. The colour of her red coat stood out sharply against Nathan's long black coat. As the woman played with his tie, Nathan raised his other hand, placing it behind the woman's neck before he angled her head and leant in to kiss her passionately on the mouth. It was what Georgina had called "their kiss". Their own personal intimate thing. The kiss he always gave her; the one he had used when he had proposed to her in a restaurant in Rome; the one he had given her the day they had exchanged vows on a spring day – her memories still held the smell of the flowers that had filled the church; the same kiss that told her everything would always be okay.

Georgina found she couldn't move. Her hair was now plastered across her face, her clothes completely soaked by the falling rain. A coldness, not only caused by the weather, wrapped itself around her. She felt rainwater dripping off her bottom lip as her mouth remained open. Behind her, a taxi moved closer to the entrance in an attempt to pick up the waiting passengers outside the station. The driver sounded his horn, but Georgina seemed oblivious to the noise. When the taxi driver gave a long blast, she jumped and turned toward the noise. She heard the driver shout something at her through the partially opened window as she stepped aside. Looking back, she saw that the people at the front of the station had looked across to see what the commotion was all about, including Nathan.

She saw him release the woman and even step aside of her, as if nothing had happened. The other woman now looked worried, as if she had realised who Georgina was. Nathan had a picture of her and Lily in his wallet, and Georgina wondered whether this woman had seen this picture. In her mind she imagined the open wallet on a bedside table, while the two of them shared a bed together.

Tears now began to mix with the rain running down her face as she held her trembling fingers in front of herself. Nathan moved towards her, making her step back. An elderly lady with a small dog stepped in front of Nathan as he tried to move forward, forcing him to check his step. Through the driving rain Georgina fled, reaching in her trouser pocket for her car keys as she ran. Her hand shook so badly as she tried to open the door that she thought he would catch up with her, and spin her around by her car. When she finally slipped behind the wheel and looked back, she saw he was still a distance off, other passengers still holding him up. She fired the engine and pulled her car out without looking; her lips continued to tremble as the tears still fell, an increasing ache creeping through her body.

Georgina scraped the edge of the vehicle in front of her as she pulled out, causing her car to jolt. Ignoring this, she turned the car around as she saw Nathan running towards her.

She put her foot down, needing to put distance between what she had just seen. To the side of where she had turned, a road joined the approach to the station. The road was mainly used by delivery drivers making drops at the industrial estate nearby. Out of this road, a 7.5 tonne Royal Mail parcel lorry moved. The driver looked away from the road for the briefest of moments, checking his paperwork as he moved down the road. When the Volkswagen Golf pulled across him, he had just looked up again. He was forced to brake hard to avoid colliding with it; the papers he had been checking spilled to the floor of the cab. As the other car raced off, the lorry driver swung the vehicle out into the road. No other traffic came, yet he still had one eye on the disappearing Golf. The rain continued falling across his windscreen, and he failed to see the figure in the long black coat which ran out in front of him. The impact of the collision was felt by the driver who stalled the vehicle, his chest hitting the steering wheel, causing the horn to sound. Shocked by the impact, he could hear screaming coming from outside. He opened the door and stepped down from the cab, as people began to gather around the front of his vehicle. A woman in a red suit stood screaming, her hands holding the sides of her face. Others were turning their heads away as they looked at the sight before him.

The man lay on his side, his body hideously twisted. His eyes were oddly open, though no expression or life was reflected in them. Blood ran heavily from the body, merging with the broken glass and plastic of the vehicle's lights. The images of the onlookers reflected in the water that lay on the ground around him. A mother turned her daughter's face away from the scene, the movement causing the girl to drop the small blue ball she had been holding. Falling to the ground, it eventually came to rest against the briefcase Nathan had been holding. The traffic was now stopped on the road leading to the station, with people's attention being drawn to the crowd that gathered further up the road. No-one took any notice of the large group of crows which took flight from the station roof.

Mary had listened intently as Jody told her about what she had seen the previous day at Westmoore School. She had seen the pictures herself on the television last night, but hadn't watched as long as Jody had. Across from her, she noticed that Jody was now looking through the newspaper which covered the story over two pages; the names of the two children who had died had been released, but little else.

Jody told her about her feeling that the Farnhams were somehow involved.

'Jody, there are hundreds of kids at that school. The odds on it being the Farnham boy are massive,' Mary tried to tell her. 'Besides, you said that Billy was a bit quiet.'

'He was, yet something's nagging at me.'

She reached across her desk and picked up her diary. Mary knew what she was doing before she dialled the number she had found. The phone was ringing as she leaned back in her seat. She closed her eyes in partial relief when the call was answered.

'Hello, is that Grace? It's Jody Sedgwick from Langdale Estates.'

The voice that answered was weak and barely audible.

'No, I'm a friend of hers. Grace isn't here, I'm afraid.'

'Oh, I'm sorry,' Jody told the woman. 'I was wondering if she had any feedback on the viewing she made recently at Granton House.'

She thought for a moment that the line had been disconnected as she could hear no sound. When the woman spoke, Jody almost jumped.

'Now is not a good time, I'm sorry…'

The line did go dead this time and Jody sat looking ahead of her, unable to think. Mary had seen her reaction to the phone call; the noise of the phone being placed back in its cradle broke the silence between them.

'Well?' Mary asked.

'She wasn't there; it was someone else who answered. She sounded awful.' Jody looked across at Mary. 'There's something wrong, I know it!'

The quietness of the area she lived in made Jody feel more relaxed by the time she arrived home. There was nobody about in the quiet tree-lined road where Jody lived with her father. She parked her car against the garage, and then let herself into the house. From the floor she picked up a couple of letters that had come in the morning post. As she placed them on the stairs, she spotted a yellow post-it note which had been stuck on the small table where the house phone sat. She smiled as she read it. Her father liked to leave her notes; it always amused her. The note told her he would be home in nearly an hour, having gone out to see a friend. As she made a drink of tea, she read another yellow note stuck on top of a casserole dish. It read, "put me in the oven for thirty minutes". Jody gave a mock salute to the request and, after turning on the oven, placed the dish inside. She put the yellow note with others on the notice board in the kitchen. A picture of her and her father, taken on the Cornish coast, looked back at her, making her smile as she walked into the living room.

She kicked off her shoes before sitting down on the settee. On the table beside her, a newspaper had been left, her father's reading glasses beside it. The picture in the corner of the paper caused her to catch her breath, the hot liquid scalding her hand as she let go of the mug.

Her father found her running her hand under the cold water tap. Jody had cleaned up the spilt tea and had been reading the newspaper for a while before her hand started to sting. The water eased it a little but, when her father looked at her hand, he went and got some cream from a first aid kit he kept in the bathroom.

'So, how did you do this?' he asked her, rubbing the cream onto her hand. She broke away from him and went to pick up the newspaper. Turning it to face him, she pointed at the picture which had caused her to drop her drink.

'That's Darren Longton. He was the arrogant property developer I told you about who viewed Granton House.'

Barry asked Jody to pass him his glasses before he went on to read the article. As he did, Jody rubbed some more of the cream onto her hand. When he had finished he lowered his glasses, before rubbing the bridge of his nose.

'Such a waste of a young life,' he said looking at her. He saw that his daughter had been troubled by the article. Her mood didn't improve as they set the table for dinner, and she was quieter still while they ate. The casserole was wonderful, but Jody found she had little appetite. Her father was wise to her ways and asked what was on her mind.

'I'm afraid the incident at the school and that article in the paper are related,' she told him.

'How could they be?' he asked.

'I don't know, but one of the people who viewed Granton House is dead and I think that something has happened to one of the other viewers.'

'You don't know that, Jo. Anything could have happened.'

Her father always called her Jo when he was trying to help her; he had done since she was young. She had only been seventeen when her mother had left them. Neither of them had seen it coming. Barry often spent time away from home on business for the sales company he worked for. Jody had never had an inclination that her mother wasn't happy with her life; her parents rarely argued, held grudges or had issues with each other. Yet one day as Jody returned home, she found her mother putting suitcases into her car. The fact that she never kissed Jody as she left or even gave her an explanation, cut deep into her; from that day on, she realised that her father was all she now had. The rebellious teenager was forced into an adult in the space of a single day. Her father had told her later that night that her mother simply wanted a fresh start, adding that there was no other person involved. Barry was unsure about that, Jody just didn't care.

Standing now, Jody came round the table and put her arms around his shoulders.

'I know, Dad,' she said, as she kissed the top of his head, 'but I know something is wrong.'

For the next few days Barry worried about his daughter. She came in completely shattered from work, something she rarely did. It was over a week now since she had gone for a run. Normally she went twice a week, really pushing herself over her ten mile route. He usually found her pacing up and down the house as she wound down. Now as he watched her, she lay on the settee completely worn out. She was also eating very little. When he asked her about dinner, she said that she had already eaten. She was being polite, but he still worried. The one thing that did focus her mind was Granton House. More than focusing her mind, it was beginning to dominate it. Most of the time it was all she would talk about. Their usual range of conversation had fallen into the background as the house took over her life.

Jody must have sensed him watching her and looked across. She smiled warmly at him and asked if he wanted a drink. Rather than say that he would make it, he said yes and felt pleased as she headed for the kitchen. The day before she had told him that she had spoken to James Hartwell on the phone. She had passed on her condolences and, although she hadn't liked Darren Longton, had felt sadness at the news of his death. Jody had told her father that James had admitted to a sense of freedom since the accident, explaining how he had wanted to go his own way and get out of the partnership with Darren for quite a while.

While they were finishing their drinks, the telephone rang. When Barry answered he was pleased to hear Melanie Duggan's voice. Melanie had been friends with Jody since they went to the same Junior School. Although they were later to go to different senior schools, their friendship had remained and strengthened. Barry spoke with her for a while before he handed the phone to Jody.

'It's Melanie, maybe you two should have a night out?'

Smiling weakly, Jody said hello and Barry left her to talk with her friend. He cleared away the dinner plates and, after washing all the remaining pots, cleaned down the kitchen work surfaces. When he returned to the dining room, the phone was back in the cradle. From upstairs he could hear the sound of Jody running a bath.

Jody spent the following morning at work alone. Mary was out on a few calls, and the part-time staff they used were not due in till the following day. That suited her fine as she wasn't in the best of moods, and didn't feel much like talking. Just after eleven o'clock, the post arrived. For some reason the usual postman always made a point of calling in and handing Jody the post himself. He would often try to make conversation with her or compliment her. This amused Mary no end as Jody was bliss-fully unaware of his interest in her. Most of the post was for Mary, others were advertising leaflets, as well as a couple of thank you cards from recent buyers. The other item of post was a letter addressed to herself.

If her father had received the letter, it would have had less of an impact. He was of the age when people often received news by letter, but Jody had grown up in the era of twenty-four hour communication, used to hearing news via mobile phone, e-mail, or instant messaging. She did, however, hold onto something from the past when she opened the envelope with a letter knife. This was something her grandmother had shown her as a child and something she still used at work.

Unfolding the paper, she began to read. The woman's handwriting was neat and, by the time Jody finished reading, tears were running down her face.

Despite its location next to a busy road junction, the churchyard of St Gabriel's Parish Church offered a welcoming peace. A row of yew trees blocked out most of the traffic noise, allowing people to spend time quietly with lost loved ones. The grounds looked well tended and fresh flowers had recently been laid on several of the graves. An anniversary card had been placed under a small bouquet of roses, which Jody stopped to look at as she made her way over to the church. When she read the card, she saw that the couple had been parted over ten years now, yet the bond and deep love still remained.

The cars bringing the family and relatives of Nathan Lyall had already arrived; by the time she joined the rest of the mourners, the service was about to begin. Jody sat on one of the pews at the back, surrounded by strangers, her view of Georgina obscured by close family who sat supporting her.

In the week since she had heard of Nathan's death, she had continued to dream of Granton House. Her dreams were becoming progressively darker. The house continued to deteriorate as she watched it, the number of crows increasing all the time. Yet it was her appearance in the dreams that caused her the most concern. She still walked up the driveway in her white nightdress but now, as she approached the house, a figure slowly emerged from the doorway. Jody began to follow the figure in each dream, but when they reached the rear garden she always woke up. The clarity of the dreams remained with her all day, clouding her thoughts. She had so little energy that she phoned in sick the day before Nathan's funeral. The previous evening she had gone to bed early. Though tired, she had lain awake for over an hour before she drifted off to sleep.

Now in her dream she appeared closer to the house. Where before she had walked down a much longer driveway, she now stood next to the oval flowerbed. Up above her, the moon cast its light across the house and garden and illuminated the figure which emerged from the doorway. Jody could tell from the walk that the figure was a woman. Dressed totally in black, she moved silently around the side of the house. Jody followed. She noticed that the white nightdress she wore in her dreams was ripped as normal on the sleeves, the scratches on her skin beneath seemed deeper, yet none bled. As she reached the rear terrace, the woman in black stopped and looked up to the sky. With her back to Jody, she was still unseen. As crows began to appear, the woman started to move again, quicker now, forcing Jody to struggle to keep up. Across the lawn she walked; all the time the number of crows increased. As she approached the smaller terrace at the bottom of the garden, Jody saw a large rock sticking out of the ground on the edge of the lawn. There had been no sign of this when she had viewed the house, but now it was quite prominent. The woman began to climb the rock and, by the time Jody approached, the woman was kneeling on it, her head and shoulders bowed. The dream held as Jody stepped nervously towards the woman. The crows around them still held flight. As they looked down from above, they saw the woman beginning to extend her arms. She had been wearing a black shawl, which now fell from her shoulders, yet she kept hold of the flowing shawl with her clenched hands. Underneath the woman was still dressed in black; her long skirt lay across the rock; on her upper body she wore what looked like a tightly-drawn bodice, its ornate stitching highlighted by the moonlight. The skin of her arms and waist, which was visible below the bodice, looked like porcelain as the woman fully extended her arms. Jody now walked over so that she stood about ten feet in front of the woman. A gentle breeze began to blow around her. On her back the nightdress was blown again her skin, cooling her. On the woman the breeze blew, swirling her long hair around her, occasionally showing the straps of her top. The mass of crows circled above her in the moonlight. Occasionally a few would swoop down and land on the woman's arms. Still she held them out; her hands gently waving as if caught by the very breeze itself. Where the crows landed, Jody could see small cuts on the woman's arms where their sharp claws had caught the skin. Jody noticed how several began to bleed, as did the ones now on her own arms when she looked down. All she had seen faded into insignificance when Jody became aware of the woman's face. When the breeze had begun to blow, the long black hair had covered most of the features. Now the head was further back, the chin raised, the long hair flowing around, seeming to merge with the black shawl that somehow floated around her shoulders. Jody knew the face so well, yet refused to believe it was true. She knew every inch of it as she had seen it reflected back at her all her life in every mirror or object that caught her very own features.

She wanted to wake from the dream, but seemed unable to. Instead Jody began to run away from the image before her and away from Granton House. The grounds beyond the terrace were overgrown with bushes and small trees. Despite these, she ran on, eventually becoming entangled in branches around her. She thrashed out at the branches which gradually became softer, light starting to fill her vision, only her duvet restricting her movement now. She was awake once more.

Around her now, the mourners' heads were bowed in a final prayer for the now departed Nathan. The service came to a close. From the coffin-less room, the family led the mourners as they all filled out. When Jody looked across, she saw Lily through a gap in the people. Her eyes were red and puffy as she looked up at her mother, before she lowered her head slightly. She kept hold of her mother's hand as she left the church. Outside Georgina spoke to a few people, mainly family, before climb-ing into the back of the funeral car. Jody watched as Lily stepped in beside her. There was no sign of the brace, the only restriction in the girl's body was caused by the grief the child felt and carried. Through the people around her, she caught sight of a woman moving towards her, and realised it was Georgina's sister, Jane. Her kind smile masked the sadness within her as she shook Jody's hand.

'Thank you for coming,' she said as she kissed her gently on her cheek. 'I'm sorry I didn't see you earlier.'

'I felt I had to come. I was shocked to hear about Nathan in your letter. Please give my love to everyone,' Jody told her.

'I will, thank you. There is a reception nearby if you would like to come?' Jane told her.

'That's kind,' Jody replied, 'but I feel that should be for close family.'

'Either way, you'd be most welcome.'

Jody again declined. As Jane turned to leave, she asked her about Lily and saw moisture reform in Jane's eyes as she spoke.

'You know, she's fine. Somehow she seems well again. All her doctors and such can't find anything wrong with her. It's unbelievable that Georgie gets what she wished for at the same time as losing her husband, don't you think?'

The words hit Jody like a punch to the stomach. It felt as if the very air inside her had been suddenly sucked out. She had no words to answer. Jody watched Jane leave with the others, before the rest of the crowd filtered away. Soon she found she was the only person standing beside the church. From the stone of the side of the building, the weak sunshine gave off a slight warmth yet it failed to warm Jody, as she stood thinking about Georgina and Lily. In the space of two weeks since the visits to Granton House, two of the three viewers had suffered a devastating bereavement. Darren Longton and Nathan Lyall were both dead, the events around the Farnham family unknown. Jody still held hopes that young Billy was not involved. Each time she thought of him, her emotions ran riot. The only person so far untouched by anything was Adam Burscough. She knew she had to find him as soon as possible. The noise of the traffic was a welcome distraction as she reached the road and headed back to her car.

It took Jody over half an hour to find somewhere to park. All of the short stay parking spaces at Manchester Airport seemed to have been taken. Whatever time of the year she came here, it always seemed so busy. Once or twice she considered just parking and risking a ticket, but eventually she found a space at one of the hotels nearby. Not that she had to rush; Adam Burscough's flight wasn't due in for another hour.

She had finally got hold of him on his mobile phone after days of trying, even calling at his home several times only to find his house in darkness.

Luckily, on her latest visit, as she had walked away from the house, a neighbour had called over. The woman, in her mid-fifties, had asked if she could help. Jody had told her she was a cousin of Adam's, hoping to pay him a surprise visit. If there was one thing Jody detested, it was lying but she kept telling herself she was just telling white lies to try and help people. For a while it seemed to work, later though she felt even guiltier. Adam's neighbour had told her that he had been away in Europe on business and was due back on Saturday at lunchtime. Having even got the flight time off her, Jody had thanked the woman by going and buying her some flowers from a nearby shop. The woman had seemed confused by the sudden act of kindness; Jody's guilt seemed lighter to carry around as she left.

Now, two days later, she walked hurriedly into the airport foyer. More than once she was forced to step to the side as crowds swarmed around her. She saw his flight was on time, and decided to go and get a coffee while she waited. Jody found a seat tucked away in a corner and hoped Adam would understand why she was meeting him at the airport. The coffee tasted bitter; another spoon of sugar helped slightly.

Adam had certainly been surprised when she had managed to finally get hold of him. She had left six messages on his answering machine, asking him to phone her with regard to Granton House. Originally she had been going to tell him everything that had happened to the other viewers, but the more she ran the words through her mind, the crazier it all sounded. When the moment to talk to him had finally come, she had lied – again – that the price of the property had been drastically reduced for a quick sale. Adam had been initially interested at the news, and told her he would contact her over the weekend, but Jody wasn't going to wait for that phone call. She needed to find him and warn him. That was the reason she now sat waiting for his flight to land, drinking an awful cup of coffee.

Now that she could get a clear view, the woman standing close to a car hire advertising board was convinced it was him. She had first spotted him as she waited for her own suitcase. His hair was shorter than she remembered, his dress sense still as sharp though. Now, seeing him more clearly, she thought Adam Burscough looked as though he had put a little weight on. Not that it looked bad on him, as his height held it well. This was the first time Anna Muscroft had seen him in almost three years, but the moment she had seemed to instantly bridge the gap in time. Having now collected her own case, she held back while Adam continued to watch cases go by, trying to spot his own. She wondered why she was waiting. Anna had completely uprooted her life to keep away from Adam, so that she could keep her sister's memory as she wanted it. Now she stood looking across at him, wondering what on earth she was doing.

Leaning forward, Adam spotted his case and eagerly grasped the handle, thankful that his wait was over. Following the people ahead of him, he continued on his way; behind him, Anna moved closer, deciding that at least she would say hello to him. As Adam emerged into the airport concourse, Anna watched a young woman approaching him. She was in her mid-twenties and smartly dressed. Her looks were quite striking, her black hair shining as it was caught in the brightness of the overhead lighting.

Anna looked on as Adam approached the woman, and could see a warm smile fall across her face. The young woman was obviously so relieved to see him that it made Anna keep on walking, hiding her face slightly with her hand as she passed and scorning herself for opening up her feelings once again.

Increasing her pace, she walked towards the exit, keen to regain the distance between her and Adam. As she emerged from the exit, her eyes were caught by a group of crows sitting on some discarded luggage trolleys. They seemed completely unfazed by the number of people moving around the airport exit. Despite what had just happened, Anna managed to smile at the crows. It was almost, she thought, as if they were themselves waiting for someone.

Adam was surprised to see Jody Sedgwick coming toward him. At first he couldn't place her, given the different surroundings. When he looked at her and they made eye contact, her face seemed to show relief. When she stopped, Jody stumbled her way through a confusing explanation about why she was meeting him. Apart from a few moments on his trip, he had thought little of Granton House. A couple of nights he had dreamt of Anna, but had put it down to his memories being disturbed by the house. He listened as Jody told him about a new price on the property. As she spoke, he began to move toward the airport's exit. She continued to talk as his eye sought an available taxi. As the final one pulled away, he turned to her and spoke.

'Miss Sedgwick…'

'Please call me Jody,' she said, interrupting him.

Adam stood still now; he felt his shoulders slump a little as he looked at her. A cool wind blew across the exit of the airport and in the distance he saw a group of birds quickly take flight.

'Jody, I appreciate you coming to meet me with the news regarding the house, but I really need to get home. I'm tired from my trip and, to be honest, have no real interest in the house at this moment.' He saw her enthusiasm didn't diminish in any way as he continued, 'I promise I'll get back to you if I change my mind. Now, if you'll excuse me.'

A black taxi pulled in beside him, and he moved across and opened the side door. The driver emerged around the side and started to load his case into the boot. Adam could see Jody still looking concerned. He considered that his words might have sounded harsh when he had spoken to her.

'Jody, are you alright?' he asked. Adam could see that her face appeared a little paler than when he had first spotted her.

'I'm not sure,' she answered. 'I guess I just wanted you to have the news.'

With that he thanked her again, before stepping into the taxi. The exiting passengers continued to swarm around her as she stood motionless for quite a while. She felt she had failed in her attempt to alter his plans. Eventually she pulled herself away from the airport, feeling a coldness within herself. Her earlier renewed energy had gone. The roaring sound of an aircraft taking off filled the air around her as she walked slowly back to her car.

Anna looked at the empty seat beside her in the back of the taxi, and slowly stroked it. She had hoped that she could have at least had the chance to stop and say hello to Adam, but the intervention of the young woman had soon put a stop to that. The taxi driver was chatting away to her, but she paid him little attention. Instead she watched the rain-filled streets pass by out of the window beside her. How she wished they could have met again and talked. Maybe even shared the taxi together.

The temporary traffic lights the taxi had just pulled through meant that joining traffic from the two side roads had to filter into the line of traffic whichever way it was flowing. The young driver of the Ford Focus had been busy lighting his cigarette and failed to realise the direction in which the traffic was heading by the time he reached the junction. His speed was such that he had little time to brake and was forced to pull out blindly to prevent his car from skidding. The passing taxi took the full impact of the collision.

Anna screamed as the side of the taxi imploded. She felt the taxi being pushed sideways, as the side of the vehicle was crushed inwards. Putting her arms up to shield her face from the glass, she pushed herself against the door beside her to avoid being caught up in the wreckage. Through the now shattered window, she could see the crumpled bonnet of the car which had hit them. A figure was slumped over the steering wheel. The grinding of metal seemed to merge with the shouts of the taxi driver, who had managed to bring his own vehicle to a halt. Anna, for the briefest of moments, thought of Adam. Someone had opened the door beside her, and was trying to unbuckle her seatbelt. She let out a sigh of relief as she was helped out of the wrecked taxi, so thankful that Adam hadn't joined her. The space where he would have been sitting was now completely taken up by the damage to the vehicle.

A small crowd had gathered alongside the accident and several upturned traffic cones lay on the pavement beside her. Anna felt a strange feeling of relief rather than shock come over her as she stood. Her legs began to feel weak and she feared she was going to collapse. Whoever had come to her assistance now helped her to sit. The wet ground soon soaked her clothing, the falling rain flattening her hair. In the distance, she could hear the approaching sound of sirens.

When Adam finally arrived home, he left his suitcase in the hallway of his house, his coat discarded on top of it. While he made himself a drink, he stood rubbing the back of his neck. He could feel tension in his muscles as he worked his hand along his neck and shoulders. During the ride home in the back of the taxi, he must have fallen asleep. He had felt his body jerk when he suddenly woke. His body seemed to ache down his right hand side, especially along his arm, shoulder and neck. Later, as the aching eased, Adam put it down to the angle he must have been sitting at while he dozed. It was almost as if he had felt the impact of something against him. He sat in the kitchen with his drink as he stretched and flexed his right hand. The aching seemed to be fading, and his body soon only felt the strains of tiredness as he headed upstairs.

Once he had showered and got into bed, sleep soon found him.

Given that it was a Saturday, Jody was lucky to find them both a table in Starbucks. As usual, most of the seats were taken up by groups of people – or lovey-dovey couples, as she called them – but dotted about were a few people on their own reading or working on laptops. What on earth, she thought, made people want to go on a computer in the middle of a coffee shop?

Jody shook her head gently and waved across to Melanie, who stood by the till collecting her change. More than once she struggled to keep the tray holding their drinks level, as she weaved through the other customers. Her friend blew her cheeks out as she sat down, passing Jody her vanilla latte.

'We should have gone to a quieter and cheaper place,' Melanie said, as she ran her fingers through the edge of her red hair.

'You asked me!' Jody replied. 'Besides, we can chat here for ages.'

It was good to see Melanie again. They often spent weeks without seeing each other, then followed those up by seeing each other daily. Jody sipped her drink, enjoying the privacy that the corner seat gave them even though it was by a window.

'Your new hair colour suits you,' Jody told her. It was the first time that she could clearly see it close up. Over the years Melanie's hair had been several colours and whichever colour she chose, it was always accompanied by dramatic make-up. Today her eyeshadow was rust coloured, running to a green edge, which matched her eyes.

'Yeah, well. I'll still attract weirdos and sex maniacs.'

Jody laughed, enjoying the feeling Melanie's company gave her. She watched as her friend's face contorted as she tried to tear open a sugar sachet.

'Bet it's the weirdos you hate most though.'

Pointing at her, Melanie answered, 'You got it, kid.'

Over their drinks, they chatted and generally caught up on each other's lives. Jody failed to tell her the details about Granton House, although as Melanie talked, Jody felt as though she could be someone who would understand, given their friendship. She now saw that Melanie's eye had been caught by something.

'Check out this guy, coming over. Hope he's a maniac,' Jody heard her say, as she turned to discreetly look.

Jody was shocked to see Adam Burscough walking towards her. Dressed in a long black overcoat, a deep blue patterned tie was just visible with his cream coloured shirt. Looking back at Melanie, she could see her friend was instantly smitten.

'I thought it was you as I passed the window,' he said, pointing toward the glass.

'Hello, Adam' Jody replied briefly then felt her leg being kicked under the table, as she introduced him to Melanie.

'I came over to say I hope I didn't appear rude at the airport the other day. I had so much on my mind at the time,' he told her.

241

'No, no, not at all,' Jody assured him. 'I should have contacted you by phone really.'

'That's okay. I wanted you to know I won't be taking my enquiries any further with Granton House. Maybe it's a bit too big for what I'm looking for.'

Jody felt relieved his interest had gone and, more importantly, that he seemed okay. They spoke for a while longer, mainly about his music, before he told her he had to leave.

'Are you keeping okay yourself?' she asked him, seeing Melanie look quizzically at her strange question. Ignoring this, she playfully kicked her back under the table.

'I am now, though I wasn't too good after my trip. I felt some pain in my right arm and shoulder for a day or so, but it seems fine now.'

Jody knew his words were significant, though she could not yet understand why. As he left, he added, 'I wouldn't want to lose the use of my hands, being a musician.'

With a final smile, he left them to their coffees. Jody found hers was almost cold by the time she tasted it again. Melanie had already stood up, telling her she would get them each a fresh drink.

'Then, lady,' she whispered in her ear, 'you can dish the dirt on Adam!'

Jody smiled to herself as she watched her friend head back to the counter. Looking out of the window, she watched people go by all going about their own lives. She wondered whether by going to the airport to meet Adam she had altered something. Had the pain Adam had felt in his arm been less than it might have been intended to be?

Her thoughts were disturbed as the intrigued Melanie returned.

Returning to Langdale Estates after her lunch, Jody had no reason to expect something waiting for her, especially not another letter. As she entered the office, she saw Mary was on the phone. She waved briefly at her boss, removed her coat then noticed a letter open on her desk. As she sat down, Mary finished her call.

'Thought that would interest you,' Mary said.

Holding the letter, she noticed the quality of the paper. The letter had been handwritten on headed paper. The name at the top of the first sheet read Joseph Westgarth – a name that was unknown to her – but she felt her mouth go dry as she read the letter through. It informed her that Joseph Westgarth was the owner of Granton House.

It also stated that a representative of the owner would like to meet with someone from Langdale Estates at the property, with regard to the recent viewings. A date was included towards the end of the short letter. Jody re-read it a couple of times, before Mary caught her attention.

'You want me to do that?' she asked.

'No!' Jody replied sharply, and then apologised for her bluntness. Mary let it go as she let Jody continue, 'I'd like to go, maybe to put my own mind at ease.'

'Well, let me know if you change your mind.'

She knew she wouldn't. It was as if she felt the place was calling her again. Trying not to make anything of it, she put the letter in the top drawer of her desk and returned to her current work.

For the rest of the day, Mary kept to herself but occasionally she looked across at Jody to see that she was okay. During the afternoon, Jody dealt with most of the customers who called, even arranging a couple of viewings for a couple of newlyweds who came in. They seemed to get on well with Jody and a couple of times they broke into laughter as they spoke. By the time the office closed, her mood seemed to have lifted.

'Look, if I could cancel, I would,' Barry Sedgwick almost shouted, continuing to collect files on the table as he spoke. 'But I'll be back before you know it.'

Behind him, his daughter still seemed less than impressed. Jody had returned home from work to find him preparing for a business trip. The thought of him being away for a few days only served to make her bad mood return. She listened as he tried to explain that although it was short notice, he had little choice or say in the matter.

'But can't someone else go?' Jody asked him.

Beside her, Melanie looked on awkwardly as the two of them continued their heated exchange. Melanie had called round to ask Jody if she wanted to go to a concert for which she had tickets, but had walked in on the two of them exchanging comments with each other. When she had tried to make her exit, Barry had asked if she would stay and try and talk some sense into Jody.

When he looked at his daughter, she suddenly looked as fragile as when she was a little girl. Then he had had her mother to support him and shoulder any hurt she felt. Even though she was now an adult, the job seemed just as hard at times. He held her by her arms and noticed how her eyes avoided his for a moment, until she finally looked at him. The smile she gave him was weaker than normal, the lost look lingering on her face.

'You know I work away a lot,' he told her. 'Remember, it keeps a roof over our heads.'

Jody smiled more warmly now, a smile that told him she accepted that he really had to go. She held him tight to her, then let him continue with his packing.

By the time he had finished, Melanie had made them both a cup of tea. Taking his drink from her, Barry noticed how dramatic Melanie's make-up was today. Her burgundy eyeshadow, edged with what looked like silver to him, seemed to make her eyes bulge from her face. Over the years Barry had got used to her looks and ways, knowing how important the girls' friendship was. He caught her looking at the two of them as silence fell.

'If you want company, why not ask the Bride of Frankenstein here to stay with you?' he pointed at Melanie in an attempt to install some humour.

Melanie looked up and smiled, surprised at being brought into the conversation. He often teased her, so was not surprised at his comment.

'Would you mind?' he asked her.

'You still got that single malt?' she asked, biting gently on her bottom lip. 'The one in the fancy box?'

Barry nodded his head as he laughed at her question. 'If it cheers up Grumpy here, yes, I have.'

'Then show me the spare room, Igor,' Melanie replied.

As it turned out, once her father had left, Jody talked Melanie out of staying. She loved her friend dearly, but she had just needed to be with her father. She had wanted to tell him about the new appointment at Granton House and the fears she felt rising within her. In her heart she was unsure whether she wanted him to go with her when she visited, or if she needed to know he was safely away from the house. Either way, she had let him go untold.

Her drink had gone cold and, while she poured it down the sink, she looked across at the kitchen noticeboard. On it, a yellow post-it note had been stuck. It read, "Back Tuesday, love you always".

An hour later, she finally got Melanie to leave, holding the boxed whisky close. Jody had no doubt that her friend would have gone with her to Granton. But now she believed she might be better going there alone.

The following day, Jody drove in silence to Granton House. On the first visit, her car had been full of music and her mind full of anticipation, as she had raced her way through the early morning sunshine. Now heavy clouds filled the sky. The overnight rain had at least cleared, but the light remained gloomy. Where the tree canopy covered the approaching roads, dark shadows gathered. She kept her speed down as she wondered what on earth she was doing returning to the house. Yet within her, she felt drawn to it, as if the house itself was again calling to her.

She had woken early from yet another dream. This time she had ended sitting upright in bed, a scream desperate to escape from her. She had lain back on her pillow and rubbed her face with her hands, her body coated in perspiration. When she had stepped out of her bed, her head was pounding, making her eyes wince. She had run the shower once she had made it to the bathroom, but the spray of the water only made her headache worse. In the bathroom cabinet she had found some painkillers and, taking out two, she drank from the cold water tap and swallowed them. Her reflection in the mirror had done little to lift her spirits. Her eyes looked swollen and red as if she had been crying. By the time she had stepped back under the spray of the shower, she almost felt like doing so.

In her dream she had been inside Granton House, but this time not alone. She had walked from room to room, noticing that all the doors had been removed, a strong breeze flowing freely throughout the house. As she walked, she became aware of another presence. When she had looked, she had seen Nathan Lyall alongside her. The side of his head had been crushed in and his hair was matted with blood, some of which continued to run down the side of his face. Ahead of her she could see another figure approaching. Again, the features of Darren Longton were severely damaged. He stood clutching his chest, his hands covered in blood. Jody had tried repeatedly to close her eyes from the images around her. When she felt safe to open them, she had found she was back in the hallway. At the bottom of the stairs two boys stood. Even if she hadn't recognized their school uniforms, she would have guessed who they were. She had found she could not look at their features and turned towards the front door. Panic had gripped her as she found the door failed to open, and she had clutched desperately at the door handle, terror now suffocating her. As she had screamed, she found herself upright in bed, grasping at the air in front of her. The echoing sound of thousands of birds' wings being flapped took a while to clear from her mind.

The road straightened out now as she remembered, and soon the outline of the house became visible through the trees. Slowing her speed even more, Jody could make out the stone pillars of the entrance approaching. She was far too early for her appointment – by as much as an hour – yet when she pulled up to the driveway, she found that both of the gates had been drawn back. Turning her car into the driveway, she wondered who could have opened them.

Her apprehension towards the house seemed to stifle the air inside the car. Desperate for some fresh air, she wound down the window. Although it felt cold, she welcomed the breeze as it blew around her. At the side of the flowerbed near the front of the house, a car was parked.

It was an old Mercedes; lovingly cared for, she thought, judging by its age. She pulled up behind it and turned off her engine. There was a heavy stillness in the air as she stepped out of the car. She could hear birdsong in the distance, and on one of the lawns she saw a blackbird pecking at a worm which stubbornly refused to leave the grass. The resistance was only brief as the bird pulled harder, finally capturing the unfortunate worm. Of the crows, there was no sign.

She noticed, as she neared the archway, that the front door was wide open. Jody could feel her heartbeat increasing, her mouth becoming dry. In the right hand pocket of her coat, she reached for her mobile. Whoever had a key for the gates also had a key for the house itself. In the doorway, she called out 'hello!' But no answer came.

A coldness seemed to have settled in the house. It made her feel as though the air inside the house had not been disturbed in years. Her footsteps sounded heavy as she walked into the hallway. At the bottom of the stairs, she called out again. She turned quickly around as she heard movement behind her.

'Hello, you must be from Langdales?'

The man who had spoken looked to be in his late seventies. Dressed in a long grey coat over a dark jacket and trousers, he wore no tie, but around his neck hung a crimson coloured scarf. His grey hair, which was still quite full for his age, was neatly swept back. When he had spoken, his blue eyes had seemed to sparkle as he smiled at her.

'Hello. Yes, I am,' Jody replied, before moving towards him. When she shook the hand he had offered her, she found his handshake was surprisingly firm. The grip seemed to calm her somehow.

'I hope you don't mind that I let myself in. I was keen to see the place again.'

She was still unsure of him and noticed he had said 'again'.

'I was supposed to be meeting someone with regard to the owner, Joseph Westgarth,' Jody told him, before introducing herself. 'Have you been here before? And how did you get in?'

'I have been here before many times,' he told her, seeing the concern on her face. 'There seems to be some confusion here,' he added, keen now to reassure her. 'The reason you found the gates open, as well as the front door, is that I have a full set of keys for the house.'

As if to confirm his statement, he then produced the set from his coat pocket. As with the keys in the house's doors, the keys he held – there must have been over forty – all carried a variety of coloured markings. 'The reason I have them is because I'm the owner. I am Joseph Westgarth.'

'Then it's me who should be apologizing for asking how you got in,' Jody told him.

Joseph smiled, putting up his hand to dismiss her comment.

'Not at all. I should have been clearer, but I didn't want you to come with the knowledge that I was the owner.'

'Why?' she asked.

Joseph put his hands in his coat pockets, and walked away from her. By the stairway, he looked down as if looking for words.

'You did the recent viewings here, I believe?' She nodded. He continued, 'How did you find the house?'

'How did I find it?' she questioned.

'During the time the house was being viewed, did you experience anything unusual?'

His statement completely surprised her. She had come, she believed, to show someone around the property. Instead, the man before her seemed to be confirming her very thoughts and fears about the house. She felt herself being scrutinized as she wondered how to respond to his question.

'I sense that you did,' Joseph added before she could reply. 'Just you, or the others that viewed the house?'

'Mr Westgarth, I'm not sure what you are driving at…' her words trailed off as he smiled at her again. His smile was warm and reassuring, yet she felt that there was more to him than she had first seen. His eyes had a depth that she honestly felt she could fall into; it was almost like she was being hypnotized.

'Please call me Joseph. I take it from your response that you witnessed something.'

She broke away from his stare, but still felt light-headed from his eye contact. By the doorway, she took in some fresh air.

'Do you mind if we talk outside? This place gives me the creeps.'

Before he could respond, Jody was heading outside.

When he followed her, he found her leaning against her car, arms crossed against herself.

'Tell me about the viewers,' he said.

'There were four,' she told him. 'The first were a couple of property developers, then a couple with a young child.' Joseph was quiet while she spoke. Clearly she felt happier talking out of the house. 'The others were a couple of sisters and a musician.'

'Have you heard from any of them since they viewed Granton?'

She went on to tell him about Darren Longton and Nathan Lyall. Joseph seemed unmoved by the events, almost as if she was just telling him about a holiday or something; even when she told him about Lily. He did, however, look up when she related the events around Adam Burscough.

'So you altered something then?' Joseph said quietly.

'Sorry?'

'Oh, I'll explain in time. The interesting thing is that the house hasn't changed.'

'Did you not hear me when I told you that people have died following their visits here?' she snapped at him. Again Joseph kept his calm, letting her sudden anger pass. In the moments that passed, neither spoke, then she appeared to settle.

'Maybe I should tell you a bit of the house's history before I answer that. Do you want to take a walk?'

Jody bit down on her bottom lip as she thought of his request. She wanted nothing more than to get in her car and see the back of the place, yet she had endless questions she wanted answering. When Joseph looked at her again, the deep look in his eyes had gone. In the daylight outside the house, he looked less sinister. When he held his arm out in a gesture for her to walk with him, she rolled her eyes and smiled weakly. She didn't answer, but began to walk with him. They headed past the side of the house, before walking onto the rear terrace. Jody kept her arms folded as he began to talk.

'I bought Granton House over thirty years ago. I was a much younger man then, filled with dreams and ambition. I moved here with my wife, Abigail, and our two sons. For a while we were happy here, the children loved the space and played endless hours in the grounds. It wasn't long, though, before we started to experience things within the house.'

'What sort of things?' Jody asked.

'All in good time, my dear,' he told her, before continuing. 'It was quite a struggle when we first came here; the upkeep of a house of this size was much greater than Abigail and I ever anticipated. Yet my work began to prosper. I was a struggling artist when we came here, but found the house gave me great inspiration. My work soon became highly sought after; my exhibitions became a huge success. I soon had more than enough money behind me to easily cope with the upkeep of the house. The first summer we were here, however, I lost my two sons.'

They took the short steps down onto the rear lawn. As they walked across, they left footprints across the moisture on the grass. Joseph noticed that Jody had lowered her arms, and now walked with her hands in her coat pockets.

'What happened to your sons?' she asked, noticing how the memory seemed etched on his face.

'Not far from here, there is a river. My sons were keen canoeists. They loved to go down there most weekends, but one particular weekend they failed to return. By nightfall my wife and I were worried sick so I went out there to see if I could find them, but it was too dark for me to see anything. The following day, we contacted the police and, later on the same day, the police found their bodies. They were both experienced and damned good swimmers, yet somehow they had both drowned.'

Joseph slowed his pace now almost to a stop. They had wandered to the edge of the garden where a fallen tree lay. Joseph sat down on it, his face looking tired as he took a handkerchief from his pocket. He blew his nose as she sat beside him.

'I believe the house was responsible for their deaths.'

'But how?' she asked.

'Because I lost my wife the following year. She had a bad fall from a horse while she was visiting her sister down south; a few days later she died of her injuries. All the time though, my work flourished. During my initial grief, I produced some of my finest work. In the time I lived here at Granton, I got everything I ever wished for with my career, but at the same time I lost all that was dear to me and everything I ever loved.'

'You lost all your family, because of the house? You realise how impossible that sounds, don't you? ' Jody told him.

They had reached the far rear terrace and now sat on the stone seat where Jody had talked with Georgina. The little dampness the seat held was unnoticeable to them. The air was beginning to cool. The earlier brightness was fading, as a fine drizzle fell.

'To be honest, I feel nothing is impossible in this house. I have seen many strange things within the house, so I'm curious to know what you experienced yourself.'

'I'm not sure what I saw, to be honest,' she told him. 'Mainly it was the doors. They seemed to open and close by themselves. At one point I took the keys out of the upstairs doors, and all hell seemed to break out. I heard a loud bang before finding the keys in a pile on the hallway floor.'

Joseph gave a slow nod and wagged a finger in front of himself before saying, 'Ah, so you did disturb the house then.'

'What do you mean, I disturbed the house?' she asked him. 'And what is it with all the keys?'

Joseph's blue eyes seemed to hold such sadness in them, she felt compassion for his losses and regretted snapping at him earlier.

'Some of the things I have witnessed in the rooms of this house,' Joseph told her, 'I wouldn't like you to know about. After a particularly strange experience in one of the bedrooms, I fitted a lock to the door of the room as I simply couldn't bear to enter it again. For a while, the house was quiet. When other incidents happened, I fitted more locks. Eventually I held keys to every room in the house. I felt by locking the doors, I began to regain a little control of the place.'

Jody looked back towards the house now, pulling her coat across herself.

'Now I know why you said I disturbed the house.'

The heavier clouds had cleared, allowing a pale sunlight to fall across the house and gardens. Shadow from the woodland was gradually edging across the lawns; in the area that caught the brightest sunlight, several crows began to land.

Jody watched as several others took flight from their nests high in the trees. While some joined those on the lawn, others circled up above. Their calls carried through the still air. As they walked back down the rear lawn, Jody could see the imprints their feet had left earlier. Looking at Joseph, she asked, 'What's with the crows? When I did the viewings, I got kind of spooked by them. One in particular came so close, I felt it was watching me.'

'They have always been here. From the moment we moved in, they seemed to focus on us. At each tragedy they were always there.'

'I've always associated them with death,' Jody told him.

Others now landed on the lawn. A couple broke away and began pecking at each other. A chase ensued, which led to them both taking flight back to the trees.

'Most people do,' Joseph replied. 'Though I think they get labelled wrongly somehow. Did you know that when the first reporters arrived at Hiroshima after it was bombed, they found that a plague of crows had descended on the ruined city? Wherever they went in what was left of the city, they encountered crows.'

'Would that not prove the theory then?' she asked.

'Possibly. But what if the crows signified something else? Particularly here,' Joseph suggested.

'How do you mean?'

'I mean, what if the crows came not to represent death, but to help avoid it?'

Jody could find no answer. She felt a connection with Joseph as they stood looking back at the house. Still the crows remained on the lawn; occasionally she caught the eyes of a few of them. None approached her, almost as if they were cautious of doing so. They held a confidence that, strangely, she could not help but admire.

Although the brightness remained, a fine drizzle began to fall; so light it appeared to hover in the air in parts. Before the light weakened, the fine raindrops seemed to shimmer as Jody looked across towards the house. Without a word between them, they headed back to the house.

They returned to the front of the building, where the archway offered welcome shelter. Joseph ran a hand over his hair and saw it was quite damp. Keen now to get out of the rain, he suggested they return to the house; again the building smelt stale as they stepped back inside.

'You were saying that the birds could be there to help avoid death, not beckon it,' Jody reminded him as they stood at the foot of the stairway.

'Oh yes,' Joseph acknowledged. 'Over time I feel that they are intrinsically linked to the house. There is a great power here at Granton that I still feel. I have always felt it, especially when I used to work so passionately here. It's as if the place opens your mind to what you really want. The things that I have always wanted, I got while I lived here; but, as you now know, at a high price.'

'As did the recent viewers. They have all lost something while gaining so much, even though they were only here a few moments really,' Jody suggested.

'There have been others in the past,' he told her.

Jody felt as though she should have been surprised by this revelation, yet she listened as Joseph told her of misfortunes that had fallen previous viewers. All the time he spoke, Jody felt he was holding back on the amount of detail he was telling her. Maybe he wanted to spare her more upset, or he was simply keeping the memories of his own losses at bay.

They sat on one of the lower steps of the stairs where a cool breeze could be felt from the open doorway. Joseph looked up, as if he was listening to the house itself. Jody remained seated as he stood, rubbing his thighs as though they had stiffened while he had sat. As they seemed to ease, he put his hands in his coat pockets and looked at her.

'So, what about you then?' he asked her. 'What makes you different?'

'Me? What makes you think that?'

'Because, with Adam Burscough you were able to prevent possible injury to him or those around him'

Now Jody stood. 'But we can only guess at that. Something could still happen to him,' she suggested.

'True, but I feel you took control of the events and I think I know why,' he told her.

'This is crazy. If I could control what happened to people, I would have saved everyone.'

'You weren't aware then, though.' Joseph stepped back outside; the rain had now cleared and the air felt invigorating after the confines of the house. A few moments later he sensed Jody behind him. Turning to her, he thought her face look tired. He knew the effect the house was having on her, the energy it was drawing from her. She seemed at a loss at what to say to him.

'You never asked for anything while you were here, did you?'

'How do you mean?' she asked.

'I think you are the only person to have come here and not wished for anything.'

Jody considered what Joseph had said. Maybe, amidst all this madness, there was some truth in what he had just told her. It was true that she hadn't wished for anything while inside, but she never had at any time in her life. Wishes couldn't come true, she knew that. In moving the keys that day, hadn't she felt as though she had disrespected the house? By returning them to their correct home, had she taken the first step towards gaining control? She could sense Joseph observing her as she thought about the house. The windows seemed darker than ever before as she looked up; never more uninviting. She walked over to Joseph and for a moment struggled to find the words that she wanted to say. Eventually she found them.

'If, and it is only an if, I have control,' she said, 'I want to find out by myself.'

She could see a confused look falling across Joseph's face as she continued.

'I don't want any harm to come to you, so I'd like to go back inside by myself. I need to know. Most of all, I guess, I want to put an end to all of this.'

As she headed for the doorway, the sky began to darken. The darkness of the archway seemed to consume her as she entered the building. He heard loud cries from above him now. When Joseph looked up, he could never remember a time when he had seen so many crows.

With the front door closed behind her, Jody stood in the hallway and listened. No sound came from anywhere in the house. As she tried to clear her mind, she felt her breathing become lighter. Occasionally she licked her lips, as her mouth felt dry. She stepped onto the spot where the keys had landed, almost expecting something to happen. Nothing did. Looking up the stairway, she almost turned around and walked straight out. Instead, she was drawn to the dining room beside her. She put her ear to the door and listened. There was a sound coming from inside the room. Trying to calm herself, she breathed out. As she concentrated her mind on the doorway, it slowly began to open.

The table drew her eye straight away. The length was well over ten feet; below the thick top she could see ornately carved legs supporting it. Two candelabras stood on the centre, the candles sending a warm light around the room. Only one chair was at the table, which could easily have sat twenty. When Jody stepped into the room, she saw the table had been set for just one person. The rest of the room seemed unchanged. No other furniture stood anywhere; the only difference to the room was the table and chair itself. When she looked back at it, she almost jumped. The whole table was full of food. There was so much of it that she failed to see any of the table top beneath. Several meats, some still on the bone, filled most of the plates. Around them were dishes filled with a whole variety of foods. She saw bowls and jugs filled with rich sauces; huge bowls of fruit seemed to spill down onto the surrounding dishes. Amidst it all, with several bottles of wine, were bottles of champagne. The beads of moisture on the bottles seemed to shimmer as Jody looked upon them. At the far end of the table, the only chair was now occupied. Jody felt her breath catch as she looked at the woman who sat there. She wore the same black clothes as in Jody's dream but the bodice seemed much tighter, her breasts fuller. The black hair was wild around her heavily made-up features. Jody noticed the deep red nails of her fingers as she clutched at the food around her.

The woman's teeth tore at the thick joints of meat before discarding the bones. No sooner was one mouthful finished than another began. The food was literally grabbed off the plates around her. In between mouthfuls, she drank heavily from a tall gold goblet. What appeared to be wine ran down the sides of her chin, so full was her mouth. Still eating, she wiped the excess food and wine from her mouth with the back of her hand. The sight began to repulse Jody; the eyes of the woman looked crazed, the mouth held almost a content sneer.

Jody looked on at what appeared to be herself, but felt appalled at how the woman gorged. The sound of eating became louder in her ears, she could hear the food being crunched beneath the woman's teeth, the gulping of the wine the only thing that silenced her heavy breathing.

Jody looked away, needing to be away from the scene she had witnessed. She pulled the door open quickly, almost falling out of the room. She was surprised to find herself standing at the top of the stairs; the passageway before her showed all the upper doors were open. She felt like she was dreaming, as if she needed to be awakened from the sights unfolding around her. Jody slapped the side of her face, hoping to restore herself to the present time. When she raised her hand again, her cheek stung, the skin feeling tender as she touched it. She remained standing where she was, but now heard the sound of running water coming from the bathroom at the end of the passage. When she looked she saw steam swirling and rising around the top of the door frame. Tentatively Jody walked towards the bathroom.

She became aware of several strong scents reaching her; there were so many that the smells, while subtle at first, became almost overpowering. On the floor, just inside the doorway, lay rose petals. As she looked into the bathroom she saw where they had come from. Bouquets of roses, interspersed with white lilies, stood all around the room. They mingled alongside masses of lit candles. Some of the flowers lay on the side of the bath, into which water poured from the now gleaming silver taps. The foam on the top of the water was beginning to spill down the sides of the bath; water would soon follow. Around the room, incense burned and a layer of smoke hung high in the room, the curling edges illuminated by the glow from the candles.

No-one occupied the bathroom, but Jody still felt someone was close. Laughter from the bedroom alongside soon confirmed this. She had been concentrating so much on the bathroom that she hadn't looked into any of the other rooms on her way down the passageway. The

257

adjoining bedroom door stood open, and Jody felt as though she was intruding as she started to enter. At home, her bedroom was an intimate place for her; a place of great privacy. She walked inside, already knowing who was occupying the room.

She was sitting up in the middle of a huge bed. The sheets she had slept on were of shimmering gold, around which was red trim and decoration. With one hand she clutched a silky sheet over the front of her naked body, while she ran her other hand through her wild hair. When she lay back, Jody saw her legs move under the bed covers. The woman laughed as she arched her back, the sheet falling from her hand. She moved rhythmically, as if unseen hands were caressing her entire body. Jody could hear the woman's heart rate increase as the passion within her rose. The laughter that came from her sounded almost corrupt.

From the dining room to the bedroom, Jody had seen glimpses of a woman completely indulging herself. Though she saw no-one else in the bedroom, she felt the presence of many others all around her. Jody became aware of another noise coming to her ears and, when she backed away from the bed, her back collided with the bedroom wall. Her ear could hear the sound clearer now; it seemed impossible to her, but she knew that nothing inside Granton House was beyond the realms of possibility. The sound was heavy breathing. It was coming from the walls themselves. When she stepped away to the doorway, she could almost feel the sensation float across the room towards her.

Jody now ran along the passageway. As she passed the other rooms, she caught glimpses of other scenes to which she tried to close her mind.

From one room her grandmother called to her. The sound of screaming came from another room, where bloodied handprints smeared the door frame; she could barely imagine the scene within. Another doorway showed her a group of unknown people, all celebrating something. She heard champagne corks being popped, glasses clinking together as they all toasted someone. Somehow she knew it was her they were all looking at. At the top of the stairs, desperately trying to clear her mind, she risked a look back just as all the doors slammed shut; the scenes within now lost. Only the breathing sound continued as she stumbled down the stairway, hearing her name being whispered over and over again.

'Stop it!' she screamed as she reached the bottom of the stairs, holding her hands over her ears. Almost in an instant the breathing noises ceased and the house became quiet once more. Her own breathing was now the only sound she could hear. She felt as though the air within the place was diminishing, as if the house itself was somehow smothering her. Jody concentrated hard on steadying herself, allowing her chest to rise and fall slowly. After a few moments her own breathing came under control. Around her, the noise of what had appeared to be the house itself breathing, remained at bay. Gaining control again, she felt her attention sharpen. Standing in the middle of the hallway, she looked all around her. There was a sensation running through her now, slight at first, but slowly it began to increase. Her vision became incredibly sharp, her hearing so sensitive she could hear the noise of her coat brush against her hand as she raised it. Around her all the ground floor doors were closed. She glanced across at the living room door and, using only her mind, ordered it to open. The door flew back on its hinges. She thought of the image in the bedroom and asked for the same feeling the woman had felt upon her neck. Her chin began to rise as all along the sides of her own neck she felt the soft sensation of being kissed. From above her, she could hear the bedroom doors open and close as she commanded them to. Even the lights in the hallway glowed on and off at her request. Jody had to stop this. She had to clear her mind. Closing her eyes, she thought of nothing other than a blank white space. The kissing sensation disappeared, the doors steadied themselves, and the house became still around her once more.

Jody had no doubt that the other rooms of Granton House contained every thought or desire that she could wish for. Her love of food had been overindulged, as had her constant need to cleanse herself of a world around her which she failed to grasp or understand at times. The constant immorality which she fought against in her own life, had been totally abused by the deep desire she had witnessed in the bedroom. She had yet to feel the true love of another person aside from her family; when that moment arrived, she wanted it to be so special. None of this in the house was her. None of this she wanted or hoped she ever would. Joseph had been right when he had said that she had an ability to control the house, and bring to it all she could wish for. Although she was a grown adult, the only thing she craved for now was her father – the one steadying aspect of her life. Her mother seemed lost to her; the love she had once shown her now seemed a distant memory. She needed to be out of this house before the place consumed her. In her mind, temptations came to her; some she felt she needed, others so frightening she couldn't bear to look at them. Voices whispered around her, all calling out her name. Again she focused on the white space in her mind as she reached agonizingly for the front door handle.

Jody had failed to notice how gloomy the inside of Granton House had become, so when she stepped outside, she was forced to shelter her eyes from the brightness of the sky, despite the cloud. She felt relieved to be out of the place, relieved she had found the strength within her to leave.

Her eyes now adjusted as she stepped onto the driveway, wondering where Joseph had got to. She was near to her parked car when she saw him appear from the side of the house. He looked concerned as he approached her, walking quickly. Jody knew he was aware of what the house could contain and wondered how her own visions differed from his own. By the time he joined her, she was standing at the top of the driveway looking towards the house.

She looked drained of all emotion. Her eyes held a distant look, as though things were still fresh in her mind. When she spoke, her voice sounded weak.

'Seems you were right.'

That was all she told him about what she had experienced while alone in Granton House. He didn't ask her, for he knew himself what could happen inside there.

From the nearby woodland, the noise of birds taking flight came to their ears. Many kept to the air; the sound of their calling seemed to echo around them both. Only a few of the crows landed nearby on the lawns. Jody stood watching the ones that flew above her. One called out louder than the others, before swooping down towards her. She realised it was the largest of the birds as it circled around her. Others began gathering on the lawn until only the bird, the one flying around her, was in flight. Joseph watched as Jody held out her right arm.

The crow eyed it cautiously, at one point climbing higher, until it splayed out its wings and landed gently on her arm. Joseph walked to the side of her, keen to see her expression. Neither Jody nor the bird showed any cautiousness with each other. Jody angled her arm as she drew the bird closer to her. It remained still, its eyes never losing contact with her own, so that it was now only inches from her face. Then the crow did move. It moved its head next to Jody's cheek, before softly brushing the side of her face with its beak. On the lawns the other birds looked on tentatively as Jody smiled at the bird, which remained silent on her arm. Now it hopped onto her hand as Jody held out her arm fully. Leaning back, the crow gave out a loud caw. Its wings flapped swiftly as it called out to the others, making them all take flight.

What communication she had with the crow in that moment, he could not imagine.

Joseph thought he saw Jody sway slightly as if composing herself. She let her breathing settle, adjusting the intense clarity her vision had been holding. The fluttering of countless wings drifted away in her ears as she faced him once more.

There had been almost an intimate moment between them that Joseph had found completely mesmerizing. A moment of complete understanding. For a while the sky seemed to blacken as the birds flew frantically around the house, before the numbers began to thin out as they returned to their nests in the woodland. Only the largest of the birds remained. Joseph stood alongside Jody as the bird itself flew off. It silently headed down the driveway, eventually disappearing into the woodland.

'I think it's time for me to leave here,' she told him, looking once more towards the house. Jody felt her hand where the bird had landed, remembering the scratches she had seen across her arms in her dreams. As she faced Granton House, light rain began to fall again. Tilting her head, she felt the drops fall gently against her face. The tiredness she had brought with her seemed to have left. There was even no trace of a headache.

'You know, Joseph, I came here full of fear for this place,' she told him. 'In the days between this and my initial visit, I sometimes felt I was losing my mind.' She tucked her arms deep in her coat pockets as if feeling a chill across her body. Joseph saw the trace of moisture in her eyes, then her gaze seemed to look right past him. 'Inside I saw what I could easily become...'

'But you would have the ability to control events that happen here,' he told her, his voice almost pleading.

'You could well be right,' she answered, 'but I want no part of it.'

'Even if it could give you all that you could ever want?'

'Even if that,' Jody answered quietly, as she began to walk now towards her car.

On the windscreen of the Mini drops of water were beginning to run down the glass. On her coat sleeve a fine mist of tiny drops gathered. Her senses were sharpening again, the breeze around her brought sounds which remained unclear. She closed her eyes and shook her head as she opened the car door. As Joseph approached, she slowly opened her eyes again. Turning to look at him, she found her eyesight was normal again.

'Joseph, I am sorry for your losses, I truly am.' She closed the door again and leant back against her car. 'But I want no part of this place.'

After shaking Joseph's hand, she sat in her car with the window open. Jody wished him well before she drove off. He looked a tiny figure beside the house as she looked at him in the rear view mirror. At the gates she looked across to the woodland. No birds came to her. The only thing she felt was the light rain that blew in from the open window. Silence fell around her as she closed the window. Moisture began to rise again in her eyes as she pulled onto the lane. The tears fell heavily as she drove away from Granton House.

Joseph stayed at Granton House until late afternoon, by which time the fine drizzle had developed into a steadier spell of rain; the light from the small windows failed to penetrate the shadows around the house. He spent time in each of the rooms where so many memories came back to him. Most of them were related to his wife, Abigail. Mainly the earlier days when they had first come to the house. Occasionally he heard whispers and saw movement in the darkest of the shadows, but he managed to keep his mind solely concentrated on his memories.

In the most central of the bedrooms, he looked out over the drive and down into the front garden.

To hear the news of the recent events brought a renewed sadness to him. Time had healed all but nothing. The power of the house still remained, yet someone had come who had been able to alter the course of planned events; a person who had the ability to control what the house had to offer. He wondered what she had seen or felt in her time alone in the house. If there was great reward for her here, why had she chosen not to take it? Was it as it had been with everyone else, the cost that came with the reward? Having the ability to control what was offered was surely worth the risk, wasn't it?

In another bedroom, the thought of Jody's choice stayed with him. Had something guided him to choose the estate agency where she worked? Had fate brought her here to him? Had she had to go through the experiences similar to each of the viewers to gain understanding about the house? There seemed so much to try to make sense of. He closed the upper doors, locking each one, before returning downstairs. His legs felt stiff and ached by the time he reached the bottom. Through the still open front door, a welcoming breeze blew. Walking through the doorway, he noticed the rain had stopped and puddles had gathered around his car. The water reminded him of how dry his mouth was, and he took a small bottle of water from the passenger seat of his car. As he drank, he could hear the crows in the woodlands, though none were in view across the gardens. He felt better for having a drink, and decided it was time to leave.

He took a final look around downstairs. All the time, he could hear the sound of doors being opened upstairs, along with more whispering. Again he ignored these. Leaving the dining room, he held one last memory of Abigail. One spent over a dinner they had held for several guests. She had looked so elegant that night, dressed in a sequined black dress. She had been the perfect hostess. They had sat apart from each other during that dinner, as they had been busy with conversation around the table. It had been a moment when they had caught sight of each other across the table, where she had looked at him and smiled. That was the moment he now remembered, when she raised her glass to him, and mouthed the words, 'Thank you.'

It was his favourite memory of her, the one that had even kept at bay the sadness he had brought on her. Joseph closed the door and the memory behind him and left the house. He stood looking up at the property, from the spot he had been with Jody. She would be the last person who would visit Granton House; he could no longer let people come here. Joseph had no idea what would become of the place once he informed Langdales to take if off the market. He would then be the sole key holder, the only person who would enter.

He doubted very much whether he would ever see Jody Sedgwick again. Maybe some time in the future, if he was still around and his ageing body allowed it, she would return. Somehow he doubted that day would come. As he climbed into his car, he realised that she had taught him a great lesson. He and others who had come to Granton House, had been wrong to choose their own destiny. Fate would simply not allow it. Jody was taking the greatest of journeys herself – one that each of us took, the journey of life itself. The outcome was meant to be unknown.

Along the way, she would be guided by experiences which would map out the way for her. Many she would never understand, others would give her great pleasure and happiness. Each and every day would be an adventure in itself. The opportunities that she would fail to take or see around her, would soon become regrets within her, ones which she would hold for ever. Yet these would be balanced out by so many blessings. Maybe, because she had chosen to let her life develop in its own way, she would get the greatest reward.

It took him a while to manage to close the gates. One in particular was stubborn to move in its rusting hinge. When he finally clasped the lock, he felt a great relief run through his body. Few leaves remained on the trees now, the recent wind and rain had brought most of them down; the ones that remained blew across the grass, disturbed only by the wind.

In the following years, with the grounds unattended, he presumed neglect would begin to take hold, both in the gardens and within the house itself. Further leaves would fall onto the ground with the coming of each autumn – the time of year which would always be remembered by him as when he closed up Granton House for good. Through failing daylight, only a solitary crow watched him leave.

Whatever happens to people in their lives, whether it be rewarding or tragic, it is always followed by the same thing. For each and every one of us time moves on, as it did for Jody Sedgwick. She left her job at Langdale Estates a week after she had last seen Granton House, feeling as though she needed to make a new start. More than once, Mary tried to get her to change her mind, but soon found that she was absolutely determined and so respected her decision.

Jody spent a couple of weeks simply resting her body. She had returned home from her time at Granton so physically and mentally drained that her father had ended up calling their local doctor out to see her. Though it was a worrying few days for them both, and some of the hardest nights Barry could remember, Jody checked out fine. All her doctor advised was that she needed to rest.

Barry kept a watchful eye on her for the next week, trying not to overdo the care he showed her. Since he had returned home, she had barely spoken about what had happened to her at Granton House. Occasionally she opened up and talked freely with him, but she kept the scenes she had witnessed to herself.

While she rested, the haunted look in her eyes began to fade, and after another week Barry could see a great improvement in her. Only occasionally did she venture outside and then she seemed affected by crowds around her. In a queue at a supermarket, she felt the air was beginning to stifle her; the people beside her looked on bemused as she walked out of the store, leaving her shopping at the till. Each time she tried to withdraw into the safety of her home, Barry put pressure on her to get back out. A few times they exchanged heated words, ones which she later regretted. Jody would always end up in her father's arms, always in tears, as the emotion of the past few weeks slowly began to leave her.

As Christmas approached, Barry toyed with the idea of them going away for a break, maybe until the New Year. He suggested instead that she should spend the time with some of her old friends but apart from Melanie who gave her a support that Barry found moving, Jody still knew few people. Over supper one night she said that she much preferred the idea of Christmas being just the two of them. Besides, she told him, he was her best friend.

During the week of Christmas, they walked for miles from the cottage they booked in the Yorkshire Dales. The weather was generally poor and rain fell most days, but they still managed out daily. By the time the New Year came, Jody seemed back to normal.

She rarely dreamed, especially the dark dreams she had experienced before. Any nightmares she had now were the normal ones experienced by other people. At the end of January there was a significant shift in her when she started work at a newly-opened hotel in the city centre. Being on the reception desk forced her to renew her contact with people.

Initially the work felt so demanding to her, the slightest bit of pressure threatening to engulf her. More than once she made her excuses and found herself being sick in the toilets. The extra make-up she wore helped to hide her pale face from those around her as she worked long shifts, gradually easing herself back into the routine of life.

Over the following month, she let her life continue the way it was meant to be. She had her good times, mainly with Melanie who continued to help her along the way, and faced the normal amount of everyday problems. She had to work some extra hours to keep her credit card company happy, she broke a finger in a fall while rushing up some stairs, and even dated a couple of people. But none of the dates led to anything; the clothes of the stranger who was to be the one person she wanted to truly love her, were still unknown. Yet all the time she kept a look out for him, as well as for any opportunities she could spot.

On the first Saturday of spring, she accompanied her father to the wedding of a family friend's daughter. Barry had been surprised that Jody wanted to attend, especially as her mother would be there. He sat watching his daughter in the church, thinking how beautiful she looked in the flowery dress she wore for the day. Occasionally during the service he saw her hat twitch slightly as she looked across at her mother. Barry kept them apart for most of the day, but at the small reception held afterwards, he felt relieved when he saw the two of them eventually speaking. He watched them talk briefly, the conversation no doubt polite. As her mother left, he saw her reach out and touch Jody's arm. Barry noticed she didn't pull back at her mother's touch. Maybe the hurt was finally beginning to leave her.

Towards the end of the afternoon, Jody left a present and card for the couple on a table in the dining room of the small hotel. To the side of the room, a door led to a sitting area where French-style doors offered views across the hotel grounds. Stepping into the room, Jody saw that the doors were open, allowing a gentle breeze to enter. Sunlight streamed into the room through the gap, the early spring warmth holding on as the day lengthened.

Along the breeze Jody heard the sound of flapping wings approaching. As they grew louder, a large crow flew into the room. She watched as it landed on the back of one of the tall chairs around the table. A smile began to spread across her face as the two of them locked stares. The crow cocked its head to the side as it studied her.

Jody wondered what had drawn the bird inside. Was it possible that it was the same bird she had held the previous year? She doubted that was possible, yet the way it looked at her seemed to convince her it was. From the open doorway the breeze caught the edge of the bird's feathers, as it still continued to watch her. On the breeze, Jody now caught the scent of spring blossom. It seemed to float around her, almost making her light-headed. The sound of the wedding reception in the room behind her seemed lost as other sounds became clearer. The scent of leaves and moss reached her. As the crow shifted its position, Jody could see tiny specks of moss within the bird's claws; along the edge of one wing, small pieces of dead leaves were caught in the bird's feathers. All her senses were caressed following the bird's arrival. Now her eyesight and hearing had again become enhanced.

Unlike the time at Granton House, she felt no fear or unease within her. As quickly as it had appeared, the crow flew out of the doorway. From behind her she heard the returning sound of music and laughter from the reception. Her senses returned to normal.

She walked out into the sunshine and looked to see if she could see where the bird had gone, but it was nowhere to be seen as she looked across the gardens. Jody raised her face towards the sunshine, closing her eyes; she stood still, enjoying the warmth the spring sunshine cast on her face.

She walked back inside knowing the crow had come for some reason; not to warn her, but to direct her in some way. She kissed her father's cheek as she rejoined the reception, enjoying the safety she felt from him as they danced together. On their journey home, as her father drove, she watched trees pass in a blur outside the window. Occasionally she drifted off to sleep, but each time she awoke the feeling remained within her. It seemed something was about to happen that would change the direction of her life. The wait would soon be over.

Ethan

Don

The steam momentarily caused his glasses to mist over as he took a sip from his hot drink. Enjoying the warmth that the transport café offered, Don Locke cradled his mug of tea firmly between his hands and looked out of the café window. Despite the moisture that had formed across the glass, he could still make out the shape of his Scandia truck parked close to where he sat, bathed in the pale yellow of the car park lighting. In another couple of hours he would be making his final delivery, and then he could think about getting himself home.

Don smiled to himself as he pictured his wife, Jean, asleep in bed, the duvet tucked up around her neck the way she liked it. In less than one hour, her bedside clock would go off, breaking the peace of her sleep.

Don had been away on the road for over a week now and, this being his last day on, he was looking forward to spending some time at home. Having started out at 3.30am, he had made good progress northwards on the M6 motorway until several complaints by his growling stomach had convinced him to take the next exit and get some breakfast. He took another mouthful of his drink, before he removed his glasses and rubbed his eyes.

He was two years away from his sixtieth birthday and unsure how much longer he would go on driving. At one time he had planned to continue as long as he could, but the industry had changed so much now. The competition and rising fuel costs had made it almost impossible for many companies to make a profit.

Several other drivers had recently been laid off, making the faces he knew on his stops slowly dwindle. For now though, the company Don worked for were busy and for that he was grateful. His increasing hunger needed satisfying and he eagerly awaited the meal he had ordered.

Although early, Madge's Café was quite busy. Don had been coming in here for almost five years and had never met anyone on the staff actually called Madge; he presumed the place got its name from a previous owner. The cafe was an old-fashioned place serving traditional meals, and the food was as good as the company the place usually offered. Similar places were becoming hard to find as the overpriced service stations provided ever more facilities. This morning the place was used mainly by truck drivers, though near to the counter a group of taxi drivers sat huddled around a table. Occasionally they burst into laughter as one of them passed around a mobile phone, no doubt showing an amusing message that deserved to be shared.

Don had always liked the sound of laughter and smiled briefly before turning his attention back to the newspaper he had brought with him from his cab. The back page was dominated by the latest witch hunt to try and remove a football manager who had only been in the job for five minutes. Don shook his head and turned the page over just as his food arrived. Tucking into the bacon, eggs and mushrooms, he began to read the story which had – days before – barely been worthy of a mention, but which now graced most of the front pages.

The brightness of the comet and how visible it had become over the past week had taken astronomers by surprise. Each was now of course falling over themselves to come up with an explanation, but at present not one could be made.

Don recalled the Hale-Bopp comet back in 1997 and how long that lasted in the sky, though, as he read on, this one was supposed to be moving by much quicker. Eating another piece of bacon, he became aware of a slight draught as the entrance door behind him opened. Paying no attention, he continued with his meal and felt the warmth of the café soon returning again.

From where Don sat, he could now see the person whom he presumed had entered the café a few moments ago. Towards the centre of the room, a man stood looking all around him. Even though nobody appeared to be watching him, there was something about the man's actions that caught Don's attention.

His hair was long, in places resting on his shoulders; the full stubble across his chin seemed to suit his features, somehow adding an amount of character to his face. Watching him look around the room, Don was unsure of the man's age, possibly due to his odd sense of dress. His grey trousers seemed almost a size too large for him and touched the floor generously, making it impossible to see his feet, and the long white coat he wore looked as if it had not been washed for quite a while. As the man began to move, Don looked back to his paper at the same time as the man reached the counter.

Having now finished his breakfast, Don enjoyed the full feeling in his stomach. When the waitress came back around, he ordered another mug of tea before she cleared his plate and walked away. Again Don saw the man he had been watching, and noticed how he walked around the room with a drink in his hand while looking at the people sitting at the various tables. Mostly, as before, he went unnoticed, but occasionally one of the customers looked up at him. All the time the man's eyes kept moving. It was almost, Don thought, as though he was looking for someone. Whether he sensed Don watching him or not, the man suddenly stopped in his tracks and looked across.

The other three seats at the table where Don sat were all unoccupied. The man stopped in front of him and looked down at the seat opposite.

'May I sit here?' he asked.

'Please do,' Don told him, folding his paper in half as his fresh drink arrived. With the man sitting opposite him, Don became aware of the blueness of the man's eyes which, despite their intensity, gave his face a peaceful, composed appearance. The man glanced down at the newspaper folded over on the table and seemed to smile briefly before turning back to face Don.

'Cold this morning,' Don said, as if to try and break the silence between them. The man nodded and drank from his mug.

'I'm travelling,' the man said quietly, before staring directly at Don. He blew gently on his drink to cool it, before looking out of the window as if distracted by something, then added, 'Always travelling.'

'Where you heading?' Don asked, intrigued by his manner and words.

When the man looked back at him, Don thought for a moment that he hadn't heard properly, but before he could repeat himself, the man felt in his pocket and eventually brought out a small book. The cover and pages were well worn; several elastic bands were wrapped around it, seemingly holding it together.

'I need to find someone,' he told Don, as he began to undo the bands.

Once open, the book seemed to contain several small pieces of paper; most were blank, but on some Don noticed small sketches, though they were too obscure for him to work out. He did, however, manage to see a series of what looked like astrological symbols, as well as a series of the moon in differing stages. The man flicked through the intact pages at a speed which took Don by surprise, before he stopped at a page which – from his expression – was the page he was looking for.

'I need to get to this place,' he said gently, before turning the book to face Don.

On the page was written the name of a place, with a date and time underneath it:

Parrin Street – Saturday 23rd February – 11.37pm

The handwriting was neat, though Don felt it had been written by some-body much older than the man opposite, due to the ornate style of some of the letters. There was no name of any town or city on the page of the book, nor was there any reason given for the exact time shown. When the man closed the small book, he began wrapping the elastic bands around it again. Only when he felt it was secure, did he return it to his pocket.

'That's tomorrow. Something important?' Don asked, his curiosity rising further.

'Very much so,' the man told him. 'More than you can imagine.'

Don had finished his drink and, after looking at his watch, knew he had to be making a move. He picked up his paper and stood, collecting his coat from the back of the seat. Across from where he stood, the man continued to sit peacefully at the table, his drink barely touched.

'I must be going,' Don told him, pulling on his coat. 'It was nice to talk with you. I hope you get to the place on time.'

As the man thanked him for his company, Don headed over to the counter and, catching the attention of one of the women, settled his bill. When he received his change, he noticed a collection box for a local hospice placed to the side of the till and dropped the coins in. Thanking the staff again for their service, he headed for the exit, noticing that the man no longer sat at the table. He looked a forlorn character when Don noticed him standing by the doorway. For someone who was allegedly travelling, he carried no bag with him and looked as if he could not walk any distance. As Don approached him, he noticed that one of the man's trouser legs was pushed back, revealing that he wore only sandals. He held the door open for Don, as he zipped up his coat.

'Which way are you heading?' Don asked.

The man seemed surprised by the question and smiled before he answered.

'East. I have been travelling East.'

'Well, I can take you as far as Manchester, if it helps? That's where my last drop is.'

'Then that is where I'm heading,' the man replied.

'You're in luck then, mate,' Don laughed, again struck by the man's odd ways.

He never gave strangers lifts, hadn't in over twenty years; it was a pact that he and Jean had agreed on for his own safety, as much as for her peace of mind. Yet here he was at nearly six o'clock in the morning, doing just that. Maybe it was that he felt a touch of sympathy for the man or that he felt like some company, but either way the two of them left the café, stepping out into the darkness. The cold air felt strong against Don's face as they walked over to where his truck was parked. While Don hunched his shoulders in an attempt to keep out the cold, the man seemed unconcerned by the temperature. He still had a contented look on his face, which now seemed illuminated by the lights of the car park.

Once the Scandia 420 was unlocked, and the two of them had climbed aboard, Don fired up the powerful engine and moved some paperwork from the passenger seat to give the man more room. While he waited for the engine and cab to warm, he watched as the man looked around the cab, his interest evident.

'It's very kind of you to help me,' he told Don.

'That's okay, but I have to confess that I rarely give strangers lifts.' He held out his hand to the man, before adding, 'My name is Don.'

The man looked at the hand for a moment before shaking it. Don was surprised at how soft his passenger's hand was, but was at the same time aware of the firm grip. Within the light of the truck's cab, the man's eyes seemed darker, the blue of earlier now lost. They seemed more peaceful though to Don, as the man smiled again

'I am Ethan,' he said.

Out of the darkness of the transport café car park, the 12-wheel truck pulled slowly away, joining the main roadway where its speed gradually increased. Inside the café, the waitress began clearing the table where the two men had sat. Wiping down the surface, her movement caused a small white feather to lift slightly off the floor, before gently drifting unseen under the table. When the waitress casually looked out of the window, she noticed the tail lights of the truck as it headed out of the parking area, quickly fading into the darkness.

7.05am

Carla Hall lay listening to the clicking sound of the central heating boiler as she began to wake up. For the first morning in a while, she had woken up to heat; a warm feeling that she was reluctant to leave. She stretched slightly on the pile of blankets she lay on, enabling her to reach inside the coat she wore and take out a bar of chocolate. Even though her watch told her it was just after seven o'clock in the morning, she broke off a piece, enjoying the taste and comfort it gave her. What Carla really needed was a decent meal and to move on, but for now she enjoyed the warmth that the boiler house gave her. Breaking off another piece of chocolate, she leant back close to the heating boiler and closed her eyes, welcoming the darkness once more.

Carla had hitched a lift to the outskirts of Manchester, where she had walked for nearly an hour, before eventually being forced to stop. Her back had ached, not helped by the rucksack she carried, and she had desperately wanted to soak in a hot bath. Whenever she removed her bag the ache eased slightly, but she had soon found the discomfort increased each time she resumed her walk. At a corner shop, she had bought herself a couple of sandwiches and a drink with what little money was left in her pocket, trying not to worry about what she was going to do when the money finally ran out. Carla had stood in the shop doorway for a moment, putting her food and drink into her bag, not wanting to lose the shelter from the cold wind which continued to sting her face. As an elderly couple approached, she had been forced to step aside to enable them to enter the shop, before she decided to continue on her way. At least she was now close to where she had to be.

Just after four o'clock a police car had passed her slowly, one of the occupiers eyeing her closely. And, for a moment, Carla had thought that the car was going to stop. Before the driver could decide, she had turned down a passageway and lost herself in the shadows Somehow she enjoyed the darkness that the winter brought, allowing her to go about her way unnoticed.

Being alone in a city that she had no knowledge of brought with it plenty of risk, especially as she was only just eighteen years old, yet Carla knew she had little choice but to continue. As she had turned the next corner she had hesitated slightly as if unsure of her direction and rested for a moment against a wall, rubbing her back once more.

Ahead of her, Carla had noticed a workman loading tools into the back of a van. She had watched as he walked down a pathway from the main road into the doorway of a poorly-lit building, for a moment losing sight of him in the shadows before he returned again, carrying more tools. With his arms full, the man had been forced to lift his leg in an attempt to kick the door shut. Although the door banged loudly, Carla realised that the door had failed to shut properly. Expecting the man to go back and check it had shut, she had been surprised when he climbed inside his van. When she had seen the red glow of a cigarette in the front of the vehicle, her hopes had risen at the sound of the engine starting and the man drove off. Once he had gone out of sight, Carla had walked over to the building – the sign on the front stated that the property was owned by the local council – which looked to be mainly unused at the moment. She had walked down the pathway which ran alongside, and tried the door the man had attempted to kick shut. It had been unlocked. The smile that had fallen across Carla's face was something almost alien to her nowadays. Looking over her shoulder, she had checked there was no-one about and quickly stepped inside the building.

From her coat pocket, Carla had taken out a small torch and clicked it on, nervous about putting the overhead light on in case she attracted attention. Though the beam from the torch was small, it gave off more than enough light for her to see the room around her. The boiler house was about fifteen feet square with the central boiler sitting in the far corner; the heat instantly warming her. She recalled how she had closed her eyes as she felt the heat run through her body, the comfort it gave her had almost made her cry.

A set of stepladders stood close to the main boiler, next to several boxes of light bulbs. In the opposite corner Carla had noticed several bags which, she discovered, contained old curtains and blankets. The name of a homeless charity was displayed on the side of the bags, and she reached inside and took out a couple of blankets. Carla had lain them on the ground and, after slipping off her rucksack, slowly sat down. Resting her torch beside her, she had opened one of the sandwiches she had bought, and bit greedily into it, keen to lose her hunger. Taking another mouthful of her sandwich, she had stood once more and pushed the door shut, checking first that she could open it again from the inside.

The safety she had felt while she had slept remained with her now as she opened her eyes again. The packaging from the previous night's sandwich still lay beside her and crunched noisily as she pushed it away with her foot. Carla wished that she had saved some for the morning, but consoled herself by finishing off the remainder of her chocolate bar. She removed her woollen hat and ran her fingers through her long dark hair, most of which was tucked inside her coat. She ran her other hand over her stomach. Holding it still, she felt a slight kick from the child she carried.

Ethan sat looking out of the side window, watching the daylight slowly appear. He relaxed his vision and allowed the passing lights to blur into a constant colour, before he slowly closed his eyes. For a while he slept, only stirring when he heard Don's voice beside him.

'You okay there?' he heard him ask.

'Yes, thank you,' Ethan replied. 'I was more tired than I realised.'

Don looked at him for a second, before turning his eyes back to the road. He felt much better being back on the road, with his breakfast warm inside him and knowing that Jean was getting closer. Though Ethan had hardly spoken since they had set off, Don found himself enjoying his company. He had an odd look about him and his words had been strange, especially at the table in the café, but there was a way about him and a manner which Don found quite relaxing.

As they approached the outskirts of Manchester, the early morning traffic began to increase, and they slowed as they joined a queue on a dual carriageway. It had been possible for Ethan to learn much sooner that he was heading for Manchester; in fact he could, if he had wanted to, have known every event that would unfold before he got to Parrin Street. However he preferred to let the places and events come to him gradually. So only when Don mentioned Manchester did he know that was to be his destination.

Don's Scandia gradually slowed as the traffic increased, eventually grinding to a halt. As it did, Ethan lifted himself off his seat and began to look around at the other vehicles. Don eyed him curiously, wondering what had suddenly interested him. The vehicles in the adjoining lane began to move off, only to slow down after a short distance as more traffic joined from a junction to the left. Ethan appeared to settle in his seat again, and to Don he simply appeared to be looking down from the cab at the traffic. Ethan was actually watching the car entering from the left, which was unseen to Don from his angle. A young girl of about six or seven was looking directly up at him, a hand placed against the glass. He gave a smile and gently nodded his head to her, at which the girl broke into an unheard laugh before waving back. When the traffic began to move again, the young girl disappeared into the darkness of the car once more. There were always those who sensed him whenever he travelled. Their ages varied most of the time but, like the young girl who had just waved, they were often the young whose hearts and minds were as yet untouched by the harshness which life often handed out.

'When I call at the industrial estate to make my last delivery, you'll be about four miles from the city centre,' Don told him. His words sounded loud after the silence of before. 'Then I have to get myself home.'

'That will be fine. I appreciate your help,' the man smiled at Don. 'I can make my own way from there.'

The daylight that spread across Manchester heralded, for most people, the start of a new day. Yet, while the vast majority awoke and set about starting their day, for others the time differed. There were those who had worked through the night, providing services that the sleeping people took for granted. In hospitals and care homes, staff had helped patients and loved ones to get through the night, knowing that someone was caring. Others were at home tending to the sick – young and old – frustrated as though they weren't doing enough somehow, as well as holding the fear of losing the person who meant everything to them.

There were those who used the night to commit crime, or used the darkness to cover themselves and their actions. People slept, dreamt, cried, prayed for health, love or companionship. Some still drank, gambled or had partied through the night. For the insomniacs, the troubled, the burdened, the homeless or lonely, the night finally passed.

For a chosen few, the next two days would start like any recently; they would continue with the plans they had made, even though certain objects around them would change things in so many ways.

A pink mobile phone lay on a kitchen table, an artificial Christmas tree remained in darkness within a box, a pair of heeled shoes stood waiting, a suitcase remained as yet unpacked, a nail slowly deflated a tyre, while a magazine was yet to be delivered. All of this was unknown to the people it concerned; except to the man whom Don Locke was bringing to the city.

8am

As Don Locke neared the industrial estate, he slowly manoeuvred his truck into the lay-by by the side of the busy road. Behind him traffic was forced to slow down almost to a halt, to enable him to park the large vehicle. With the vehicle now straightened, the following traffic finally got moving. Don looked across in the half-light to where his passenger sat.

'Seems the time has come for us to part,' Don said, before adding. 'Are you sure you'll be okay from here?'

'Yes, thank you,' Ethan replied, as he unclipped his seatbelt and stretched his back, raising his arms slightly.

'I hope you make your appointment on time,' Don told him, still curious about the odd arrangement even though he had not asked for any further details. He was sure Ethan understood this as he sat looking across at him. While he was thinking of what else to say, Ethan turned to face him.

'And you, Don? What plans have you got then?'

Don was taken aback by his question. Before he could even think of answering, Ethan continued.

'I have heard many times that the most important things in our lives are around us all the time, yet we are always searching for something better. How about you, Don?'

Don found himself gripping the steering wheel tightly now, as if Ethan had touched a nerve.

'That's what they say, whoever *they* are,' he replied, a slight laugh escaping him. At the same time it seemed to ease the tension that had risen in him. 'I have issues in mine,' he added.

'In what way?' Ethan asked.

'It will be just Jean, my wife, and myself when I get home.'

Ethan saw tension etch itself across Don's face as he spoke. He ran his tongue over his bottom lip as he continued, 'I have a daughter, but we don't see her any more. We don't even talk.'

Ethan reached for the door handle, acting as if he hadn't heard Don's words. With the door open, the cold air outside soon drifted in. When he held a hand out towards Don, he said, 'We are always talking, Don. At times only to ourselves. Sometimes, though, people hear what we have to say.'

Don shook Ethan's hand, again feeling the strength it held. The first strains of morning light only seemed to emphasize the man's features. It had been a strange few hours in his company; a few hours in which Don felt as though something had moved deep within him. He had heard the man's words with great clarity, yet he struggled to understand why he had just spoken so openly about his own thoughts.

'Thanks for your help,' Ethan said as he released Don's hand. He pushed the cab door open fully and climbed down onto the road. As he closed the door, he heard the air brakes disengage and felt the movement of the truck moving away reverberate through the ground beneath his feet.

Graham

11.07am

The three boxes remained in the same place Graham Curren had left them nearly two months before. They had been placed on the bed in the spare room of his house, each one bound securely by coloured tape bearing a pattern of snowflakes in varying sizes. Inside the boxes, the artificial Christmas tree and decorations remained undisturbed. It had been three years now since his wife, Margaret, had passed away, and this was the first time since then that he had brought the decorations down from the attic. He had been determined, as Christmas approached, to show that he was coping and moving on, but when he had sat in the attic looking at a lifetime of memories, his emotions had overcome him. The three boxes that remained in the spare room were the only things he could bear to move. He had closed the attic hatch behind him and locked away the memories once more.

Throughout his life, Graham had always liked company. His early retirement plans had been cut short by Margaret's sudden illness. The hustle and bustle of his days in the industry in which he had worked had soon been replaced by even longer hours caring for his wife. In the weeks and months that followed her death, the phone had rung constantly as people passed on their condolences. Now the silence his life knew seemed his only companion. Recently, days had passed without him even speaking to anyone, apart from a visitor earlier that morning; a meter reader had called at his house trying to gain entry to the nearby church hall. As church warden, he had a full set of keys for St. Andrew's Church and for the hall alongside. After grabbing his hat and coat, he had walked the short distance to the hall with the meter reader.

Even though Graham noticed how much cooler the air felt since the last time he had been outside, he found himself enjoying the fresh air. The meter reader had been a jovial man who had shown a keen interest in the church building. Graham had only partly listened to the man, even

285

though he reminded him of himself when he was younger. He still felt young in his mind, even though he would be sixty-five in the summer; but not as young as Margaret, who had not reached sixty. After the reader left, Graham had stayed in the church hall for a while, looking at the artwork on the wall which the scouts and cubs had recently done. The bold use of colour had impressed him, before he headed back outside. By the time he turned the key in the church hall door, the wind had increased causing some dead leaves taking refuge in a row of old yew trees, to blow across the church grounds. Several items of litter had also carried in the wind, causing several items of paper to get caught in the trees and bushes around the church. Graham noticed how some takeaway packaging had become caught against flowers recently left by a graveside. Once he had locked the main door, Graham had given it a firm push, checking it was firmly shut. From across the road, hidden amongst the shadows, Ethan had watched him turn his coat collar up against the keen wind and rub his hands together in an attempt to generate some warmth before finally heading home.

Carla was surprised to have slept for so long. Though rested, she awoke to the discomfort her pregnancy brought. Taking a sip of her remaining water, she looked at her watch. It was 2pm. She had planned to have left the boiler room by now, but the warmth it had given her felt too good to leave behind. Thankfully, with it being a Saturday, no-one had visited the building while she was there. But she had somewhere to be, somewhere that she knew was of great importance. Yet Carla was going by information that she had gained during a dream. She had been sleeping in a chair in the lounge of a care home, close to the outskirts of Birmingham, when she had drifted into the deepest dream she had ever known. In the dream she had found herself sitting in a railway station. There had been dozens of people moving around, so quickly that she had been unable to focus on any particular one. She had lifted her eyes from the rapid motion of the crowd and focused on the destination boards above her. No destinations showed, only numbers which changed at regular intervals. When Carla had looked away from the boards, she had found a gap had appeared in the crowd of people, through which she could see a figure approaching her. She had failed to see the stranger's face, as it had been covered by shadow, yet she had felt that somehow she knew the man. Carla suddenly wanted to ask the stranger a series of questions, ones which she had no idea about as she recalled her dream. When he sat beside her on the seat, Carla had tried to speak but the stranger had put out a hand as if telling her to stop. She guessed by the skin on his hand that he was in his mid-thirties, his nails were perfectly manicured, yet on the back of his hands there were what looked like traces of scars. While Carla continued to dream, the man had pointed up towards the destination boards. She recalled looking up at the same time that she heard a voice saying, 'all will be explained'. When her eyes had met the boards, the numbers had gone and had been replaced by the name of a street being repeated over and over again. Next to the name of the street, the time 11.37pm showed repeatedly. Sensing movement, Carla had looked back beside her, but found the man had gone, as had the rest of the crowd around her. The only other movement she could see was a couple of small white feathers which hung in the air, as if caught in a breeze.

At that point she had wakened from the dream, and found herself back in the chair in which she had fallen asleep. As dawn approached, she found herself awake and staring into the distance, thinking about the place and time that remained stuck in her head.

Whether it was the thought of that dream which had made her leave the relative safety of the shelter and hitchhike all the way to Manchester, or something else, she was unsure. But she knew that her dream had been the only time recently that she had not felt alone.

Jeanette Hall had left her daughter Carla alone one day, without reason or even a word of explanation. After three days she had failed to return home to their tiny flat and, unable to stand the silence around her any more, Carla had pulled on her coat and walked to a police station several miles from her home and told the women on the desk that her mum had gone. Carla had been eight years old at the time.

There had been no search party organised, no all-points bulletin to airports and ports; not even a mention on the local news. The social workers who had taken her into care soon learned of the frequent disappearances by Jeanette Hall. There had been several other occasions when her mother had left her to fend for herself while she led the life she wanted to pursue; the only difference this time had been that Jeanette never returned.

Over the next seven years, Carla had been passed around the care system like an unwanted present, only occasionally finding a sense of what she believed was called a family or home. She could have passed love and affection in the street and not recognized their appearance; such was the lack of interest in her. Each time she became used to a care worker, the staff seemed to change and the whole process of building up a trusting relationship would have to start again. The last home she had been placed in, close to her seventeenth birthday, was Beaumont House in the centre of Birmingham. It turned out to be the worst of all the places she had stayed in.

There Carla had had a series of arguments, and even fights, with some of the other girls staying there, one resulting in the police being called when Carla had held a bread knife against one of the staff after punching out three front teeth of one of the other girls. After a tense standoff, Carla had had to be restrained for over an hour until she eventually calmed down. After a caution and a dressing-down from everyone who wanted to stick an oar in – most of which she failed to remember – she had been allowed to stay, but then walked out two days later without a word. No-one had come after her, or attempted to trace her whereabouts, mainly, she suspected, because no-one really cared. The similarity between her choice to leave and her mother's actions years before nearly broke her there and then, but she had fallen back on a strength she barely noticed she had.

In one of the care homes she had stayed in, when she was around ten years old, there had been a small library where she had come across a book of short stories all about angels. With her poor standard of reading she had struggled to understand parts of the stories, but they had left her both enchanted and captivated. The wonder within them had given her a renewed sense of hope. Whenever she had found herself a moment of peace and quiet, she would gaze upon the angel image on the cover of the book and along the top of each story, and sometimes even talk to the images. However, in one of her exchanges of home, the book had got lost and she had been inconsolable for months in a way people had failed to understand. For a long while Carla feared she had lost that feeling within her, until she found somewhere where she could talk to them again. Around the city in which she now lived, she had discovered various churches which each contained carvings of angels, so ornate and beautiful that she would sit for hours enjoying the connection she felt with them. Even the ones that looked down on her from the old gravestones in the churchyards appeared to connect with her. Their weatherbeaten faces always appeared to smile at her. In springtime, Carla would gather fresh flowers and place them beside the headstones, as if presenting each of them with a gift. In the warmth of summertime, she would sit among the long grass and talk with the statues which always seemed to acknowledge her and bring the peace she craved.

Through one particular church she was introduced to a homeless charity who had offered her a room in a new housing shelter on the edge of the city; one which seemed to settle Carla for a while. The people there varied in ages and backgrounds and were kind and considerate to her, soon making her feel much stronger. As time had gradually passed and her confidence grown, she had started to venture further into the city which had once held fear for her, and mixed openly with other people. One night though, she had been taken in by attention and charm and mistook sex for love, waking up the following morning in a bed she didn't recognize.

In the months that followed Carla had begun to feel her body change and feel so different, only then realising what had happened. By that time, it was too late.

James

2.20pm

When he ran the back of his hand across his forehead, James Elland saw that his hand was coated in sweat. When he touched his upper lip with his tongue, he was able to actually taste the moisture that gathered there. Yet when James looked around at the other passengers on the 317 bus, he looked like the only person who still felt cold. Where he had a scarf wrapped around his neck and the collar of his coat turned up, the other passengers around him had adjusted their own clothing as though the temperature within the bus suited them. James thought he had lost the heavy cold from which he had recently been suffering, but today it seemed to have returned with a vengeance. It was rare for him to feel unwell, but today his whole body seemed to ache, each joint having had its own way of giving off pain and discomfort during the day.

Much earlier James had wished that he had spent the day at home instead of going to see his girlfriend, Natalie. Having had lunch listening to her endless complaining about the lack of time they spent together, James had wondered how much longer he himself actually wanted them to be together. In the seven months they had been an 'item', as Natalie put it, James had seen so many different sides to her that he wondered where the girl he had first been attracted to had gone. She had a temper now that she never appeared to have before, and her constant bitching about the people she classed as her friends was driving him mad. He had thought about ending the relationship a few weeks back and had gone round to see her to actually break the news, but had found her in tears when he arrived. She had told him that her grandmother had suffered a bad fall and been rushed into hospital. Natalie was closer to her grandmother than she actually was to either of her own parents and, while James sat next to her in the hospital, he had seen how shaken Natalie was by her grandmother's condition, making him change his mind.

Looking out of the bus window beside him, James saw the yellow sign of the Shell petrol station pass by and knew he had two stops to go. Just the stop by the old folk's home and then the next was his; he could get inside the familiar warmth of his flat and lose himself in a hot bath.

In the seat next to him a large woman, who had been trying to squash him up against the side of the bus for most of the journey, picked up her bag and leant forward to press the stop button. James felt instant relief as the bus began to slow and the woman waited to alight from the bus. There was now enough space for him to move across and stretch his legs out, although what he really wanted to do was keel over and fall asleep. Behind him, the dull thud of a teenager's headphones only added to the increasing headache that was now settling in.

James stood up as the bus neared his stop, but noticed it slowing rapidly as the traffic ahead ground to a halt about two hundred yards short. He sighed at the continued delay and lowered his head to look through the bus's front window to see what was delaying the traffic. He noticed there was no movement on the other side of the road and thought that it must be an accident or something which was holding them up. The voice of the bus driver broke through his thoughts, and he only realised what had been said to him when the bus doors opened. With the traffic going nowhere, the bus driver had suggested people could alight from the bus and make their way to the next stop if they preferred. James and two other passengers – one of them the teenager listening to the thumping music – stepped out onto the street and continued the remainder of their journey on foot.

Not far past James's intended stop, a crowd of people had gathered by the side of the road. Ahead of him in the distance a siren could be heard as an ambulance weaved its way slowly through the traffic.

Eager to see what had happened, James quickened his pace and soon came to the crowd of people. Making the excuse he was trying to pass by, he pushed gently through the people until he was quite close to the front. To the side of him a young woman was crying, tears running freely down her face. There were signs of shock and worry etched on the faces of other people who looked across to where a girl lay motionless in the roadway. On the road beside her a pink mobile phone, which she had been using seconds before the car collided with her, lay in pieces on the ground. James thought she looked about seven, maybe eight; her black hair lay across her face, obscuring a large part of it. Even so, James could see the bleeding from the wound to the side of her head, and below her face a small pool of blood had gathered on the road. However it was the shape of the girl's right leg that was shocking most of the crowd. It was bent back the opposite way to what it should have been, as was one of her wrists which protruded from the coloured jacket she wore. A Toyota Corolla was parked at a strange angle, close to a railing which ran down the side of the road. The front of the bonnet was dented from what had no doubt been the impact with the child.

James felt an increasing need to help. The child needed urgent attention, yet everyone close to her was arguing over what had happened. Two men were close to punching each other as they became increasingly annoyed; a woman, whom James presumed was with the taller of the men, seemed keen to join in the argument as well. Thankfully the ambulance had arrived and a paramedic was moving through the crowd. Directly ahead James noticed a man who, instead of looking at the accident scene, appeared to be looking directly across at him. The man twisted to the side as if sensing the paramedic trying to get through – soon followed by his colleague – but all the time he continued to look directly at James. Despite the cold weather, the man looked more dressed for early summer in his faded white coat and trousers. There was a release of emotion from the crowd as a cry of anguish came from the injured, but now conscious, girl. Though she sounded in great pain, James thought at least she was alive.

Now his mind began to wander back to a decision he had made three years ago, a decision he suddenly regretted. Under the scrutiny of the man's stare, James wondered why on earth he had pulled out of his medical studies. At the time he had felt that he couldn't cope with the amount of work the course required, as well as the constant pressure from his parents. So one day, without even considering what other options were available to him, he had simply walked away from the course. Since then he had never regretted it, not even when he had sat comforting Natalie in the hospital alongside her grandmother. Yet in the moment he stood looking down at the paramedics trying to keep hold of the young girl's life, he had a strong feeling that he could have done something to help her if he had continued with his training.

The man opposite was moving back now, his interest in James seeming to diminish.

James could see the young girl was being lifted gingerly into the back of the ambulance, an orange-coloured frame supporting her neck and head. There was something about the stranger that James felt drawn to, almost as if the man had caused him to recall his discarded course and to realise that he could actually do it if he put his mind to it.

The crowd was beginning to disperse, the sound of the ambulance's siren making people move quicker to let it through. For a moment James thought that he had lost sight of the man, but a glimpse of the white coat through a gap in the crowd renewed his confidence that he could catch up with him.

With the ambulance now departing, some of the traffic behind James began to move. Again in his haste he lost sight of the man; this time when he bumped into a woman pushing a double buggy. The impact of his leg against the pushchair started one of the children crying, making its mother turn on James, asking him to watch where he was going. After apologising and making numerous excuses, he finally managed to break free of the crowd of people. He found himself standing at a road junction with three choices of exit. There was no sign of the man, the only movement a pile of old newspapers that caught on the wind. James was too busy looking for the man to notice the white feather that landed at his feet as the gust of wind faded.

Nicky

7.10pm

The three-inch heels she wore were not only holding her back too much, but were becoming incredibly uncomfortable. At one point she even considered taking them off and simply running, but thought that would only take up even more time. When she reached the main road she was too late, the 192 bus was already pulling away despite her shouts for it to stop. Her breathing became heavy and her heart sank as she watched her bus home continue on its way.

Nicky Mallen cursed silently as she reached down to rub the back of her heel. Where the shoe had been rubbing, the skin felt tender to her touch and she was sure a blister was going to follow. Her best friend, Emma, had told her the shoes looked great on her and she would soon get used to the feel of them. She had even practised walking in them while she had got changed at Emma's house, enjoying the freedom that the two of them had with her friend's parents away. There was no way that she would ever get so much leeway at her home. But now she wished she had chosen another pair of shoes with a smaller, more comfortable heel.

Nicky loved the variety of clothes that her friend owned, the amazing colours and styles. And, like the shoes, she had tried on several items before finally choosing an outfit. In the warmth of Emma's bedroom, with Girls Aloud blaring out of the CD player, the short skirt felt perfect as had the cut-off top Emma suggested for her. Now standing alone at the bus stop watching her bus fade into the distance, she pulled nervously at the bottom of her skirt in an attempt to make it longer, her earlier confidence having now waned.

She also felt cold now, not having planned to be standing around. Reaching into her bag she took out her mobile phone and flicked through the numbers she had stored in the address book until she came to Emma's. Her phone beeped as she was about to dial her friend; the low battery warning flashing in the corner of the screen. Annoyed at herself for not remembering to charge it, she sighed heavily and wondered why the evening was suddenly going wrong. Despite the battery warning, Nicky still pressed "dial" as she looked down the road, hoping the battery would last long enough for her call. After a couple of rings the screen went blank and the battery finally died. Nicky closed her eyes as she felt her unease begin to increase. She had no idea whether any more buses were due, as she was on the opposite side of the city to where she lived and didn't know where any others which came would be heading. The security of familiar surroundings escaped her and she struggled to think of a number for a taxi company. She had at least five such numbers on her phone but, unable to access them, they may as well have been pinned to her bedroom wall at home. The realisation of her situation began to dawn on her as a vehicle approached on the opposite side of the road.

If it was a taxi she would flag it down and head back home, as she no longer wanted to go into town as planned. She should have gone out with Emma and her neighbours, as she had told her parents she was doing, instead of thinking she could go into town alone. Her plan to meet up with her friends, Kristen and Gemma, now seemed foolish. All week the two of them had been goading her about all the fabulous times they had whenever they were out, plus the endless list of boys that they always attracted. So this weekend Nicky had been determined to show them both that she could do the same. It seemed a stupid idea now, as she wondered how on earth she was going to get back. Worst of all, her parents thought that she was out with Emma and wouldn't expect her home. How she would explain the clothes she was wearing plus the large amount of make-up she had on her face, she didn't know. In Emma's bedroom she had felt like a grown woman but now, as the car approached her, she felt all of her sixteen young years.

The car she had seen slowed as it passed by her and Nicky stepped back slightly when a youth leant out of the rear seat window and shouted something. Although she failed to hear, his hand gesture made it clear to Nicky what he had been referring to. When she looked across again, the driver sounded the horn repeatedly and laughter could be heard from the other occupants of the car within the quietness of the street. Now two youths leaned out of the car and both gestured as it moved off. Nicky raised her hand and stuck up two fingers at the car, instantly regretting her action when the brake lights appeared and the vehicle stopped abruptly.

Nicky felt her stomach knot as she moved back against the frame of the bus shelter. Her eyes filled up with emotion as she hastily fastened the jacket she wore although, like her top, it did little to cover her waist.

Now the car reversed quickly towards her, making Nicky look around in the hope of seeing someone she could run to for safety, but there was nobody in sight.

As soon as the car stopped, the two youths who had been in the back of the car stepped out. They were both well over six feet, and dressed in jeans and T-shirts despite the cold weather. The beanie hat that one of them wore was being used more as a fashion statement than to keep him warm. The one who had been in the front passenger seat inhaled on his cigarette as he got out of the car, but stayed back leaning on the car and laughing as he spoke to the driver, who was still unseen. The other youths now approached her. The hatless youth also had a cigarette in his mouth, but his face didn't hold the humour his friend's expression showed. Nicky noticed a tattoo on the side of his shaven head as he bounded towards her.

'Who the hell do you think you are, you little slag?' he shouted as he pushed her hard against the bus shelter. Her small handbag slipped off her shoulder, spilling the contents across the floor. Nicky felt an excruciating pain in her right shoulder and neck with the impact, and cried out as fear quickly overcame her. She kept her eyes closed in an attempt to shield the pain she now felt, but felt her body jerk as one of the youths pulled on her jacket collar.

'You look like you're dressed for fun!' the youth shouted at her. The smell of the smoke on his breath made the short breaths she was taking much weaker. 'Maybe me and the boys would like some.'

Nicky felt her short top and jacket ride up her body as he grabbed at her clothing again, exposing more of her waist. Tears began to form in her eyes as she felt a rough hand against the side of her stomach. She felt paralysed by fear and couldn't even force out a scream, despite numerous attempts. At the side of her, she could hear laughter as the hand continued to touch her body. Only the force of the youth against her seemed to be keeping her upright now, and Nicky felt sure her legs would give way at any moment. A sob escaped her as she felt her jacket being pulled, the top below tearing slightly with the force, exposing her shoulder. Still she was unable to bear opening her eyes to see what was happening.

The loud bang which suddenly crashed against the bus shelter made her jump. Nicky heard the glass of the frame suddenly shatter and fall to the ground; parts of it bounced off her legs and feet. At the same time she seemed to regain control of her senses and was able to focus again. She felt the hands on her slacken as the youth appeared to back away. When she finally opened her eyes, she found that the one who had been pressed against her was now staggering about. His nose looked completely crushed. Blood flowed heavily from the wound as he raised his hands in an attempt to stop its flow. Nicky realised what had caused the loud crash beside her as she backed away from the youth, who had fallen to his knees. The one beside the car had dropped his cigarette and was looking over to his friends, wondering what had happened. One minute his friend had been up against the girl, while he had been laughing and egging him on, the next he had somehow been lifted off his feet and his face rammed against the bus shelter. Even the youth wearing the hat, who was standing much closer, was struggling to make sense of what he had just seen.

Nicky felt another hand and began to fear that another of them had grabbed her, but this time the grip that pulled on her arm was more out of guidance than of menace. The touch felt so much softer than the previous one, and when she looked around she saw a strangely dressed man smiling back at her. Given the circumstances, she felt as though she should be trying to escape and run as fast as her legs could carry her away from danger, but instead she found the look on the man's face so reassuring. The youth who had been standing by the car had also seen the man approach and now walked quickly across.

'You want something, eh?' he shouted at the newcomer, annoyed at his fun being disturbed and at the same time pulling something from his pocket.

'Yeah, you want some piece of me?' the now focused and much braver hat-wearer asked, while trying to understand not only the situation but also the ridiculous white coat which the man wore.

Nicky felt her legs weaken again as she saw the light from the bus shelter glint off the blade of the knife. She felt the grip of the stranger tighten around her arm as he pulled her sharply to the side, putting himself between the girl and the two youths. Nicky saw the intensity of the youth's hate, as he glared across at them both.

The brightest light which Nicky had ever seen suddenly appeared all around the stranger, forcing Nicky to raise a hand to shelter her eyes from the sudden glare. It became so bright that she was forced to close her eyes and look away. The youth who had stepped across was also blinded by the light, which forced him to take a couple of steps back, dropping the knife as the aching in his eyes increased. When the light faded, Nicky looked back to see one of the youths staggering around holding his eyes; the other youth, who was still holding his nose, had managed to get to his feet but had also been temporarily blinded. Blood still wept from his wound and Nicky could see where it had run down one of his arms. The stranger who had helped her turned to face all three of the youths. Nicky thought she heard him say something to two of them, but his words were too softly spoken for her to hear clearly. The youth behind the wheel of the car pressed urgently on the car's horn, calling to them loudly, eager to get away. It was the youth with the facial wound who now attempted to get the others – still blinded by the intense light – back to the car. Several times the three of them stumbled as they struggled to make the distance across to their waiting vehicle. Only when Nicky saw them climb quickly into the car did she really begin to cry; she felt her legs weakening under her, despite the grip the man still had on her. When the car was finally out of sight, her legs lost the little strength they had and she collapsed heavily to the ground.

Carla found the extra blankets and clothing which she took from the other charity bags in the boiler house helped greatly with her comfort as sleep began to find her. The central heating boiler stayed on continuously, keeping her warm. An hour before she had managed to walk to a nearby petrol station, where she had been able to refill her water bottle in the washroom. Several cars had been filling up with fuel and the small shop where people paid had been pretty crowded, enabling Carla to enter unnoticed. Her hunger was so great that she had grabbed a handful of bars of chocolate from a display as she leaned back to pass two customers in the queue as she left. She felt guilty at using her condition as a diversion and of the level she had fallen to by committing the theft. As she headed back, she worried that someone would come after her, as well as the prospect of not being able to get back into her makeshift home when she got there. Thankfully no-one had been inside the room and her rucksack lay undisturbed on the blankets where she now sat, rocking herself for comfort while eating the chocolate bars. Later in the darkness, she pulled the blankets over her, caring little for the smoke-sized dust particles that continued to escape from the comet nucleus high above her. The escaping gases helped to drive the comet forward, its tail ever-lengthening behind it as Carla finally slept.

As her tears finally ended, Nicky Mallen could feel a growing pain in her right knee. When she reached out to touch it, she winced as her fingers caught an open graze. She could feel small pieces of gravel stuck to the wound, following her fall, but trying to brush them off only inflamed the pain more. She felt someone lift her underneath her arm and, despite the weakness she still felt in her legs, she managed to stand. Nicky still struggled to see clearly, mainly due to the intense light which she had seen as she had been held against the bus stop. The only person now remaining with her was the man who had appeared suddenly to help. There was no sign of the youths, nor the car which she remembered driving off. And although she still felt a little bit scared, she could feel no fear towards the man who had come to her aid.

He began to let her go, but soon held tighter as her legs became unsteady again. Nicky brushed her hand across her nose, smudging further the make-up she wore. It felt uneven and uncomfortable on her face as she looked at the eyeliner and mascara on the back of her hand. When Ethan looked into her eyes, they appeared red and puffy from her tears.

'I think you should be getting back,' he told her, his voice barely more than a whisper. Nicky felt unable to answer him but didn't pull away from him even when he began to lead her off. They walked slowly, the cut on her leg protesting at the movement; the pain still throbbing in her shoulder and neck. Nicky wanted nothing more than to simply disappear and start her day all over again. Knowing that she couldn't only made her begin to cry again. She buried her face into Ethan's coat as if too ashamed of her tears, but still managed to continue to walk with him.

When they stopped, it felt as though they had only walked about fifty yards, yet Nicky found herself back at Emma's house. The outside light glowed weakly down on her, yet she found great comfort in it somehow. She rested her hand against the door frame and turned to the man to thank him, but could find no trace of him. It also suddenly dawned on her how quickly they had both managed to get back to Emma's without her giving any directions. The bus stop had been at least fifteen minutes' walk away, yet they had done it in what could only have been less than a couple of minutes. She had a great need to be inside now, to be within the warmth of her friend's house, away from the city she had earlier been so eager to take on.

300

Nicky still could not see the stranger and wondered what had happened to him. The battle between getting safely inside and wanting to thank him was momentarily lost as her mind drifted to her handbag which she remembered dropping. In a panic, she jerked her hand up to her shoulder and found it hanging where it had been earlier in the night. Reaching inside, she found the contents undisturbed and inside the inner pocket was the key Emma had given her. It took several attempts with her shaking hands to insert the key in the lock, and she closed her eyes in gratitude as the door finally opened. Before she stepped inside, her eyes were drawn to the thick ivy growing up alongside the doorway, and in which several white feathers had become entwined within the green leaves. Nicky could feel the warmth of the hallway as she drew her eyes away and stepped inside, slowly closing the door behind her. Again she slumped to the floor, but this time she knew she was safe. The tears fell from her young face as she buried it in her shaking hands.

Mark

Saturday 10.05am

The sound of the plate breaking on the floor caused several people in the Drop-In Café to look across to the counter. A few cheers and laughs rang out as one of the two women in the kitchen gave a slight bow and waved to the onlookers.

'You lot shouldn't laugh!' one of the women shouted out loudly. 'I serve your food, remember?'

More laughter could be heard as the woman wagged her finger at the onlookers. Irene Medlock smiled across to her sister-in-law, Edna, as the café began to settle again. For ten years the two of them had managed the busy café close to the main police station. The standard joke was that it was the only place where you ever saw a policeman. Mostly they came in for takeaway drinks, as had the two uniformed men who now stood at the counter with their helmets tucked under their arms.

As Edna handed them their drinks and thanked the two, she reached for a dustpan and brush and began to clear up the broken plate. The conversations at the various tables continued, only disturbed by the calling out of orders from people waiting to be served. There was a variety of ages in the café on this afternoon; all of them were being watched by Ethan sitting quietly in a corner next to a tall plant, which seemed to have outgrown its pot and threatened to fall over at any minute.

Ethan was on his second cup of tea and had been sitting at the table for nearly an hour. Irene and Edna both knew that a lot of people came into their cafe for the warmth as well as the varied company, so had left him to enjoy his drink in peace.

All the time Ethan had been listening. He placed his elbows on the table and rested his head on his hands, slowly allowing his mind to open; gradually his body relaxed and he began to hear the thoughts of the people around him.

A young mother sat stroking her young child's hair, thinking of the present she had bought for her in-laws' fortieth wedding anniversary, hoping that they would like her gift and it would help to bring her closer to them. An elderly woman wearing a bright red hat was remembering days spent waltzing with her husband; the music which she could still hear caused her head to move slightly in time to the music. At the table beside Ethan sat a couple in their twenties. The woman was stirring her drink while her boyfriend played incessantly with his mobile phone. She was thinking about how she was going to end their relationship, as she had become increasingly bored with the man beside her. Another young woman checked the time on her wristwatch; her train was leaving in fifty minutes and she had to get herself to the station. Two workmen sat reading newspapers, though one of them was only looking at his, his mind on money worries concerning his business. Each and every one of them had a thought or concern pressing on their minds, yet each was oblivious to any other thought than their own. All the voices faded into the back of Ethan's mind as he picked up the thought he was searching for.

He was sitting in the opposite corner from Ethan. On the wall behind him, posters of up-and-coming shows at the city's theatres were displayed. The man was thirty-four; Ethan knew that exactly. He also knew that the man's name was Mark Hatton and that he had plans for the rest of the day which he was currently thinking about. These were about to be drastically altered. Once he had finished his drink, Mark pulled on his thick jacket and stood up, tucking the chair under the table. He called a thank you across to Irene, who blew him a kiss as he left; the gesture made Ethan smile. There was no need for him to follow the young man as he left, for he would be seeing him later. For now Ethan returned to his drink and let the people around him keep their thoughts to themselves; the sound of their thoughts gradually faded from his mind.

When Mark stepped out onto the pavement, a cyclist nearly knocked him over as he weaved his way through the people walking by. He shook his head, wondering why the cyclist wasn't on the road where he should be. As he stood on the edge of the pavement, Mark heard a horn sound and raised a hand to acknowledge it. The silver Audi A3 waited a moment in the traffic before turning sharply round in the road and pulled up alongside Mark. The front wheel banged hard on the kerb at the same time as another motorist sounded his own horn and shouted towards the Audi, annoyed at the sudden movement in front of him. As Mark opened the passenger door of his partner's car, he understood why the cyclist had been on the pavement.

There was a greyness to Martin Welch which Mark noticed each time he saw him. Today it had been brought on by his latest meeting with his ex-wife, which was the reason Mark had been drinking coffee in the Drop-In Café, to give his friend a moment to try and sort out his latest problems. Mark was often puzzled why, as she was now an ex-wife, he spent more time there than he had when he was married. Martin had been due to pick him up an hour ago but he had phoned Mark to let him know he had to stop at a garage to have a slow puncture checked on one of his tyres. At seven years his senior, Martin showed no sign of envy that Mark had recently made Detective Sergeant – a rank above him – which Mark really appreciated.

'So, how did it go?' he asked as Martin pulled out into the traffic.

'Fine,' he answered briefly, but Mark knew it had gone badly. Later on, when the greyness lifted, he would let Martin talk. For now, however, it was another day as work colleagues.

'Come on, mate,' Mark said, adjusting his position in his seat. 'Let's go catch the bad guy.'

Laura

11.08am

Usually Laura McCormick enjoyed the winter, especially the days like today when the air was cold and crisp. The cold air always made her feel so alive and more energetic. This winter, though, she thought it would never end. As she straightened one of the curtains in her bedroom, she watched as the wind caused the branches of the newly-planted trees in her neighbour's garden to lean over, fighting to withstand the strength of the wind. Even though she was inside, she thought she could feel the cold in the air just by looking out. Earlier that morning the weather forecast on the radio had talked of the possibility of snow by the following week. Although this was something which usually excited her, Laura wondered why all of a sudden she had a longing for some warmth. She knew her small suitcase, sitting on the bed behind her, held the answer to that question; one she felt unable to face. Folding her arms, she hunched her shoulders in an attempt to warm herself while continuing to watch the trees struggle against the wind.

Her flight was still three hours away and she had planned to be well on her way to the airport by now. But she had been continually held up all morning. Numerous phone calls had taken up nearly half an hour, as had making the arrangements to enable her to be away from home for four days.

She really needed the break; a change of scene always worked wonders for her and the trip would give her time to think about her future. At first she had resisted Michael's invitation to Barcelona, making every excuse she could think of to avoid going. Yet, during another heated argument with her husband, Clive, she had decided to abandon her principles and go and have some fun. Nothing had actually happened between herself and Michael; he was strictly a work colleague, who she felt tended to understand her much better than Clive did these days. Michael didn't immediately judge whenever she had something to say, or when she dared to express an opinion.

Shaking her head as if it would instantly clear her thoughts, Laura turned and picked her case up off the bed, attempting at the same time to put on a smile as she headed downstairs. In the hallway mirror she checked her appearance, more than pleased with the way she looked. Now thirty-four, Laura still held onto the striking looks which she had always taken for granted. Turning up the collar of her jacket, she ran her hands lightly through her long brown hair and thought about Michael. Why shouldn't she? What the hell would Clive mind or care? It had been months now since he had even been civil with her, let alone intimate with her. He was so obsessed with his own work that her own equally important job barely got a mention. So, yeah, she would go on her business trip and he could go to hell, she thought, as she headed into the living room. She sat on the settee and began pulling on one of her boots. The picture on the sideboard caught her eye as she placed her foot inside the boot; Joshua and Calvin smiled back at her. Laura had taken the picture of her children herself – one of several they had taken on a day when, as a family, they had all seemed much stronger. Joshua in particular appeared to look directly at her as she gazed upon the photo. Though at six he was three years younger than his brother, there were times when he acted much older and wiser. The calm way he viewed things always moved her.

Laura felt an increased feeling of regret at leaving them for the four days, but she had told them that her business trip was important. Her eyes seemed transfixed on the picture now, finding it almost impossible to turn away. In her mind she could hear Joshua's voice saying, 'But it's not business, is it Mummy? It's not the reason you are going, is it? Does it mean you don't love us any more?'

Laura let out a gasp as the picture suddenly fell forward, hitting the sideboard hard. It broke her from her stare and caused her to drop her boot. When she quickly stood, her legs felt unsteady and for a moment she fought to get her breath. Still looking at the fallen picture frame, she reached down and found the boot she had dropped, her eyes never leaving it as she pulled it finally on. She breathed deeply and moved forwards, picking up the frame. There was a break in the glass more or less directly between the two boys, which made her close her eyes as she thought of the image of them being separated. Running her finger over the break, she hoped that it would somehow repair the glass and remove the image her mind was trying to suggest. Opening her eyes she glanced at her wristwatch which told her she had to get to the airport. When she placed the frame back on the sideboard, she did so with the image face down. After grabbing her keys, she picked up her case and closed the front door behind her.

Now the cold air felt good against her skin, helping her to focus. She unlocked her Peugeot 308 and placed her case in the boot, alongside her boxes of work files.

Laura made a conscious effort not to look at her home as she started her car and immediately reversed down the short driveway. As she reached the gateway, she felt something on her hand and braked to enable her to look. It was a line of blood which had run from her index finger onto her thumb. Knowing she had a tissue in her jacket pocket, she thought she would pull up on the road outside her house and clean herself up.

Again Laura looked over her shoulder as she reversed through the gateway, but her speed and urgency meant she had no chance of avoiding the figure who stepped out behind her car. There was a dull thud, which made her stomach churn, before she managed to bring the car to a stop. A hundred thoughts and fears went through her mind as she hastily got out of her car.

To her surprise Laura found the figure she had expected to see lying on the floor behind her car was instead standing on the pavement outside her gateway. His odd dress sense threw her mind slightly as she struggled to find words to say to him. Where she initially wanted to ask if he was okay, she then moved onto wanting to tell him to look where he was going. The man's smile, however, cleared all intention from her. Strands of his near shoulder-length hair partially covered one of his eyes, but Laura still felt the full force of his stare. The white coat that he wore looked as though it offered little warmth against the cold day and also appeared, she thought, to need throwing out.

'Are you okay?' she finally managed to say, as she ran her hand through her hair.

'I'm fine, thank you,' Ethan replied.

'But I thought I hit you... I felt the car hit something...'

'Simply brushed my jacket,' he told her, his smile widening further. 'It's you that looks hurt.'

Laura noticed that he was looking down at her hand by her side which still had the blood on it. When she removed the tissue held against it, she looked closer and found what appeared to be a deep cut from which blood still ran. Ethan passed her a white cloth which she pressed against her injured finger.

'Oh, it's nothing; I must have caught it on the glass,' she told him. 'I picked up a broken photo frame just as I was leaving. I didn't realise I had cut myself.'

'We are always leaving wounds behind us. Some we don't see, others could be avoided. Was the photo important?'

'Yes, very. It's of my two sons.'

'What age?'

'Six and nine,' she told him, her eyes becoming ever more distant.

'Ah well, the glass can be replaced,' Ethan suggested.

Laura failed to answer his last comment, his statement seeming so final. In that moment of silence between herself and the stranger, Laura wanted nothing more than to hold her sons; to feel their strengthening bodies next to hers and to feel the wonder and excitement that they always gave her. For some reason she pictured Clive's face with tears running down it, as they had when he had witnessed both births. They had washed away all the pain she had gone through, as if he had himself taken it on board; but then hadn't he always done that? Had he ever put himself before the boys? Even last week when she couldn't stand to talk to him, he had taken them both away with their football across to the nearby park, only returning when he knew she would be rested. Then, as they had changed for bed and she had dropped her barriers, had he not at least tried to communicate with her? He'd told her to go on her business trip and not to worry about the boys, as he was only too happy to have the time with them.Looking back to her house, Laura felt an urgent need to be back inside. The cold wind cut against her face and more than once she had to hold back her hair to prevent it obscuring her view. When she went to speak to the stranger again, she noticed a white feather had blown against her jacket. It fluttered gently as the wind continued to press it against her. Picking it off her clothing, she looked up but could find no trace of the man with whom she thought she had collided. Stepping onto the road, she couldn't see which way, if any, he could have gone.

Laura left her car halfway between the pavement and her driveway and hastily rushed back to her house. In her haste she had forgotten her keys, which were still in the ignition of her car. Discarding the feather, she clutched frantically at the car door, breaking a nail against the handle but not caring. A minute later she was at her front door and felt instant relief as she stepped inside. Nausea was overcoming her as she raced into the kitchen and vomited into the sink. She felt her body retch several times as she tried to clear her stomach. With one hand holding back her hair, she gripped the edge of the worktop as she struggled for support.

As the nausea passed, she rinsed her mouth with a glass of water then splashed water on her face. The teacloth on which she dried the tears which now fell, showed traces of her make-up when she put it back on the worktop.

She wondered what was happening, as she took another mouthful of water, this time directly from the tap. She was adamant that she had hit the man; she had even felt the weight of the impact. Yet he claimed the car had only brushed his jacket. So what had the weight been? When she looked at herself in the small mirror on the windowsill, she knew the answer. It had been the weight of her conscience.

Walking back into the living room, she picked up the face-down photo frame of her two sons and lay on the settee looking at the image. The bleeding on her finger had stopped, but she had an ache within her now that had nothing to do with her sudden sickness. Holding the frame up to her mouth, she kissed the edge of it as she closed her eyes and tried to shut everything else out. Laura was still there four hours later when she heard a key being inserted in the front door.

Lee

2.37pm

Lee Holden had been watching the property for nearly an hour. Several times he had crossed the street thinking it was an opportune moment, only for something to cause his plans to change. He had been counting people in and out of the off-licence for twenty minutes, and cursed as another car pulled up outside. Three men in their early twenties got out of the Ford Escort, two of them sharing a joke as they entered the shop. Lee noticed the other shaking his head at his two friends, before following them inside. By his reckoning there were now five people inside, enough to make him want to give up and go home; but just as he was about to leave, he looked across and saw the two original customers – a couple of pensioners – leaving. Hopefully that left just the three men behind. He took a final drag on his cigarette, hoping to calm himself, before throwing it down on the ground and putting the stub out with his foot while he waited for a car to pass. The cigarette stub lay beside the six others he had used in an effort to calm his nerves.

When the three men emerged from the shop, each carrying a case of lager, Lee began to cross the road. By the time he reached the other side, their car had pulled off. His mouth felt dry and he had to swallow hard to steady himself as he felt inside his jacket. His hand rested on the handle of the small handgun, the weight of which felt reassuring to him in his pocket as he entered the off-licence.

A high-pitched buzzer sounded above the door as Lee entered. Having rehearsed his plan several times, he knew exactly where the security cameras were and which area of the shop they covered. On his previous visits, he had watched the image in the screen above the counter while waiting in the queue. The main camera only seemed to cover the entrance and the right hand side of the till. Anyone who approached at speed from the left would surely be hidden. This was his intended direction. Having already disguised his appearance for the main camera with the baseball cap he wore, he felt sure his plan would work. He had found the gun two weeks ago by sheer chance, after witnessing a robbery in a similar style of shop nearby. One of the robbers had dropped the gun as he fled and Lee had carefully picked up the weapon with a plastic bag he found at the kerbside, intending to hand it in at a local police station. But when he had heard on the local news how much cash had been taken in that and similar raids, he had begun to make up a plan. If he was to carry out a similar robbery himself, then dump the gun, it could easily be linked to the other robberies and leave him in the clear. The weapon still had the prints of the original user on it, as Lee had been careful enough to use gloves each time he had handled it.

On an area of wasteland near his home, he had fired the gun a couple of times to get used to the feel of it. The recoil as it was fired had surprised him, as had the adrenalin rush that had filled his body. Using it in anger was never his intention, but he might be forced to use it by firing into the ceiling to make his demands clear. Once he had learned how to release the safety catch, he had grown in confidence, rehearsing his plan over and over again in the bedroom of his flat. He was adamant that his plan would be successful. The money would be used to win back his former girlfriend. She had no right to dump him, no right to say the disrespectful things she had said to him. With some money behind him, he could get the bloody job she had always been going on about.

God, he had been so confident the night before, almost swaggering around his flat pointing the weapon and quoting lines from his favourite films. But now in the shop's confined area, he face felt bathed in sweat and he could feel his stomach continually knotting. To try and calm himself, Lee casually browsed the magazine rack. Occasionally looking towards the counter, he noticed the owner – a tall Asian guy – was busy marking up some figures in a large book. Most likely a newspaper round, he thought, making him remember the round he had had himself as a child.

Lee could feel nausea coming over him as he made his way towards the left of the shop. As he passed the alcohol section, he picked up a bottle of red wine and headed towards the small grocery section of the shop. Lee had thought about picking up a couple of items from there to make his visit seem more genuine, but decided against it as he felt his nerve weakening. Knowing that he needed to be beside the alcohol to approach the counter from the left, he welcomed the tall aisles which gave him some shelter from observation as he tried to muster up some confidence. His mouth felt so dry, and he could feel his heart beating fast against his ribcage. In his ear the thud of his heart almost made him sick. At least his walk around the shop had confirmed his opinion that it was empty of customers. With a deep breath he moved down the aisle, knowing that a sharp turn at the bottom would bring him straight to the counter. In his mind he imagined himself pointing the handgun towards the owner, his shout echoing around the shop as he demanded the cash in the till. His mouth felt so dry it could have been full of sand, and his hand trembled badly as he reached into his coat pocket.

Behind the counter, the shop owner could feel his own heart pounding. Something was making him uneasy; the young man's movement around the shop had unnerved him. His actions were not in any way similar to those of other customers. If they couldn't find what they wanted, they simply asked; far too lazy to look, he thought. Underneath the counter he had a long stick of wood, but that would be of little use if a weapon was pointed at him. The shop owner tried to calm himself, but his imagination and fear were running riot.

Lee felt the coldness of the edge of the weapon as he reached for it, but his hand must have caught on his coat or something as his hand wouldn't fit into the pocket. He cursed silently as panic began to spread through him. Again he tried, but the pocket entrance seemed much smaller, his trembling fingers far too clumsy. He was about two feet from the end of the aisle when a figure came round the corner. Lee was so surprised that he almost screamed. Where the hell had this guy come from? Lee hadn't heard the buzzer sound or even the door open. Now his hand seemed stuck within his coat, as if he was being prevented from releasing it. His eyes locked onto those of the man who had appeared. The intensity of the man's blue eyes was almost hypnotic; they had even drawn Lee's eyes away from the man's long white coat, the overhead lights illuminating his slight beard as they looked at each other. This wasn't happening, he thought. He had prepared such a plan; it couldn't possibly go wrong now. In the time that the two of them exchanged stares, time seemed to stand still somehow. Lee felt his body become heavy, like an impossible weight. Only the strange man seemed to be able to move, slowly brushing past Lee. Although the eye contact was lost, the man somehow held his attention still. In the briefest of seconds Lee heard a voice in his head. It seemed to come from deep inside his mind. At the same time an image of his former girlfriend, Natalie, appeared in his mind. There were tears running down her face, tears which concerned him. Even though he appeared to be looking down at an image, he could feel her wrap her arms around him and hold him close, and realised then that the tears were those of happiness. In her touch he felt so much pride come from her towards him, as her body shook against him. He looked down at his own arms and found that they were dressed in a uniform he didn't recognize. As the image disappeared, a voice repeated over and over again in his mind, 'Don't do it, Lee…'

As the man passed, Lee bumped into the rack of bottles beside him, the chinking of the glass helping him to focus his mind. Lee carried on around the corner and as he did, he felt his hand free itself from his jacket pocket. From behind the counter he could see the shop owner reach down for something. Lee placed the wine bottle he still held down onto the counter.

A moment passed between the two of them, when their silence matched that within the shop. Each of them felt the uneasy silence lift, as the shop owner scanned the bottle of wine. Lee, having finally managed to remove his hand from his jacket, reached for his trouser pocket this time. As he felt for the ten pound note he had folded in there, he noticed a pile of magazines on the edge of the counter. The magazine closest to him was advertising jobs locally; on the cover were a group of people in various uniforms. The figure on the edge of the group wore the same coloured uniform which Lee had seen on himself in the image which had flashed before him. As he reached for a copy, his eye was drawn to a small white feather which hung in the air momentarily, then fell slowly to the floor close to the edge of the counter. Lee felt the tension being released in his mouth, enabling him to finally speak.

'This as well, please.' He handed over the copy of the paper.

As he handed Lee his change, the shop owner felt the tension in the air ease. Thankfully his heart rate had also lowered, but he felt shaken by the experience. As Lee left the shop, the owner rested his hands on the counter and bowed his head as he continued to control his breathing, only looking up as the other man approached. Ethan smiled gently at

313

him. The shop owner was surprised as he had only just noticed him. They exchanged stares for a second, before Ethan turned away and left.

The cold air felt gentle upon his face once away from the heat of the shop. Up above, Ethan could see breaks in the clouds where a pale sun attempted to appear. There was no sign of Lee or anyone else about on the street, only the noise of the occasional passing car disturbed the air. He took a look back towards the off-licence. Through the window he could see the shop owner placing some items on the shelves, as he obviously tried to regain control. Ethan knew he would be fine and continued on his way, glancing upwards occasionally as he walked, continuing to smile.

The line of Victorian houses that ran down the western side of Edwin Street had originally been prestigious family homes, making it one of the most sought after locations in this part of the city throughout that period. Sadly for the street, that prosperity had gone and over time the majority of the houses had been converted into separate flats. What had once been a well-respected row of houses, where deep foundations for family life were set, now housed mostly students. The gardens that once matched the upkeep of the properties were now largely overgrown and uncared for. Nearer to the road junction, which eventually led onto Parrin Street, the houses dropped from three storeys to two. It was here that only a few of the houses were occupied, mainly by elderly people who had been in the area for years. They had each seen all too well how the area had changed over the years, and how it had recently fallen into neglect.

The property that Ethan neared at 6.55pm stood at the far end of Edwin Street. As he approached, he saw that several of the upper windows were broken, the glass no doubt lying in the overgrown garden in front of it. The lower floor windows had long since been boarded up and, even in the glow of the street lights, Ethan could see most of the boards were covered in graffiti. The path that led to the front door of the property had long since disappeared under the overgrown bushes of the garden, and now held onto deep shadows throughout the day. Alongside the empty house, the gardens fared not much better, yet the houses themselves had so far managed to remain in relatively good condition. Multi-coloured signs stood close to the road, advertising the properties for sale. In one of the gardens, three different estate agents' boards all fought for any buyer's attention. It was the end property – the most neglected – which Ethan had specifically chosen and now stood before.

Ethan was forced to push back most of the overhanging bushes to enable him to reach the steps which led to the front door. By the time he reached it, several small branches and twigs had become entwined in his hair and coat. Now completely hidden from the road, he still waited a moment while a couple of cars passed by before he raised his hand and rested it against the door. There were several splits and blisters on the door's paintwork, parts of which flaked off as he placed his hand against it. Ethan closed his eyes and, without any pressure upon it, the door slowly opened. Its progress was only hindered by the pile of leaflets and unopened letters which had piled up behind. With the door half open, there was enough room for him to squeeze himself through and, after stepping over the unwanted post, Ethan stood silently in the hallway of the house.

Damp and decay hung heavily in the air as Ethan brushed the last of the remnants of the bushes off him, even though the room was in total darkness. As he often did, he used his mind and memory to help himself see. The house made a good choice, the location was perfect.

Making his way into what had once been the main living room, he walked into the centre of the room where he thought his footsteps sounded heavy on the bare floorboards. Close by something scurried across the floor unseen, and Ethan listened intently until the mouse, or some other small creature, was well clear of the building. Then, still unseen in the darkness, he stretched out his arms and turned the palms of his hands towards the walls of the room. The outline of his figure then became illuminated as patches of light began to appear on each of the facing walls. To begin with, it looked as though someone had pointed a torch beam at each of the two walls, but gradually the light intensified.

In the centre of each illuminated area, two sets of flames began to appear. Each flame soon licked greedily at the paper which, despite the dampness of the building, still remained quite dry. Within seconds the flames had reached the ceiling. Now Ethan lowered his arms and stood watching the fire travel down through the air, centering where he had just been standing. Ethan's eyes reflected the flames that spiralled before him. Boxes filled with long forgotten and abandoned belongings, stood awaiting the flames; their contents would soon add fuel to the fire. The heat began to intensify as he headed towards the front door, this time using his hand to pull it firmly shut behind him as he left.

7.13 pm

Everywhere Carla walked, there seemed to be crowds of people. She was about a mile from the city centre, on a main road which was home to several pubs and bars. Most of them seemed to cater for students who appeared more than keen to indulge. In the window of one of the bars, a gaudy yellow poster informed that a happy hour ran between 7 and 9pm. Even with her poor standard of mathematics, the poster seemed confusing.

Having finally made it across the busy main road, she was forced to step to the side to allow a group of men to spill out of a busy pub. One of them blew a kiss across to her as he passed by, before laughing out loudly as his friend playfully jumped on his back. Another group – this time women out on a hen night – quickly replaced them inside the entrance to the pub, their loud voices as they passed making Carla want to move on. As she walked away, one of the women entangled in balloons and plastic "L" plates tumbled to the ground; the blonde wig she wore slid down one side of her head, making the other women laugh out loudly again.

Wanting to leave this madness behind, Carla passed by several bus stops where more than once people pushed past her in their rush to board their appropriate bus. Everywhere she walked there seemed to be noises that combined to irritate and annoy her, making her wonder why she had come here at all. All she wanted now was to be far away from the city, somewhere quiet where she could hide herself away. Eventually though the crowds began to thin out and Carla found herself on a quieter road, close to the doorway of a closed furniture store, where she pulled her woollen hat down over her ears hoping to drown out the sounds of the city. Having lost the warmth that the boiler house had given her, Carla could feel the cold beginning to seep through her body.

For nearly an hour she walked around the city centre, trying to find an indication of which way to go, her previous awareness of direction now lost. During the afternoon she had walked around the large department stores keeping warm and trying to clear her mind of why she was really here. She had sat for long periods in clothes stores, holding items of clothing as if waiting for a friend in a changing room, only moving on when the assistant had asked if they could help her. In a Boots store she had looked at a large make-over display where a girl with perfect looks sat being made up. With a heavy heart Carla had turned away and left, wishing she had been in there to be pampered and made beautiful. In the many reflections she saw of herself around the store, her image looked almost alien, the long coat she wore failing to hide her swollen figure. Her back seemed to ache continuously and she had an increased hunger which she had no money to satisfy. More than once she considered stopping a passer-by and simply asking, but inside she knew she would eventually be able to find her way again. She still had over four hours before she had to be on Parrin Street and there was something else that concerned her now more than her hunger; her contractions were becoming closer.

7.45pm

The fire that had been burning in the end property of Edwin Street had been, until now, restricted to the single room; the hungry flames had continued to lick and taste the walls of the room but had not spread. Now something had moved within the property, something unseen which had been containing the fire to the single room. The heat had been intense in the centre of the room, but only now released the flames which were more than eager to spread to the rest of the house. It spread with speed, relishing the freedom it had been given, quickly devouring the discarded contents within the room and all that lay in its path.

A passing motorist slowed down as he passed the property, having spotted the flames illuminating the broken windows on the upper floor. On his mobile phone he dialled for the fire service, as did other people further down the street now that the property was well alight.

8.37pm

Graham Curren reached for his wife's hand and pulled her close to him. From up above leaves began to fall all around them, one landing on top of Margaret's hair; the leaf's auburn colour matched the strands of hair that had fallen across her face. As she brushed it back with her hand, Graham heard her laugh gently; the smile that appeared took his breath away, as it had always done.

This was one of their favourite places, a place which held a special meaning to them both. It had been thirty years ago in this very place that he had stumbled on his words as he asked her to spend the rest of her life with him. When she had embraced him and held on, he had not needed to know her answer.

The woodland offered several marked walkways, all of varying lengths, and over the years they had been together, the two of them had walked them all many times. The colours and the scents that autumn offered had always been special to them both.

She broke away from him now, and began walking through the fallen leaves. Underneath her feet the dry leaves gave off a crunching sound which brought another smile to her face; looking back, she teased him to chase her. As he did, the light seemed to flicker around him, his vision becoming distorted. The sunlight seemed to fade as the flickering increased, slowly turning a pale blue. Graham found himself lying in his bed, the bedside light still on and the book he had been reading still lying on his chest.

With his dream now lost, his eyes began to adjust to another blue light illuminating his bedroom, and he became aware of the banging sound coming to his ears. As he climbed out of bed, Graham felt a loss within him, of losing the dream he had been enjoying, as well as leaving the bed's warmth behind.

The banging sound came again, this time harder and much louder. Taking his dressing gown off the back of the bedroom door, he realised that he had no idea what time it was or who could be knocking at his door with such urgency. Making his way downstairs, he could see through the frosted glass of the front door and began to make sense of what the blue flashing lights had been.

10.22pm

Throughout her journey, Carla had wondered what Parrin Street would actually look like. Sometimes her mind imagined it as a busy main road with traffic moving by at great speeds. Other times she imagined it as a quiet residential street where generations of families had grown over the years. Maybe there would be a church there or some other similar kind of building, where she would feel at ease. Knowing she was quite close, doubt began to fill Carla's mind as she wondered what the reason was for her having to be there and – more worrying for her – what she would find there.

She led herself purely from instinct, which for some reason had returned to her. Whenever she came to a junction in the road she barely hesitated, always knowing deep within herself which was the correct direction. Often she rested. In her condition she thought it was madness to be walking around, but she knew the journey was nearly over and she could at least rest. But where and with whom? Her few possessions were in the small rucksack she carried, the only money that she had was some loose coins in her coat pocket. She was also becoming incredibly hungry and the cold wind continued to numb her face as she waited for traffic to pass before crossing the road.

At the next junction she almost collapsed as she felt another contraction, only steadying herself by clutching onto a set of railings beside her. Carla tried to control her breathing and focusing her mind on where she actually was. When she managed to look up, her eyes fell upon a road sign about thirty yards ahead of her, just visible beside a tall overgrown hedge. From where Carla looked, the entrance to the road seemed quite narrow, much smaller than she had imagined. Even so her hopes lifted slightly, even if her comfort didn't, as she approached, knowing that she had finally made it to Parrin Street.

The street was only about two hundred yards long; the left hand side from where Carla looked, edged what appeared to be a small park. She followed much taller railings than she had earlier used for support, until she came to a set of high gates held secure by a thick chain and padlock. Behind them the street lights illuminated a pathway which she presumed led into the park. Peering into the semi-darkness, she could just about make out the shape of a child's climbing frame and a set of swings, beyond which she could see nothing.

Turning to face the street again, she noticed the road contained few buildings. There were no houses, just a row of different sized properties, all of which – even though it was night time – appeared unused. A four-storey building gave the street its only height. Several refuse bags had been stacked against the building, probably dumped there by someone because the property looked unused. One of the lower bags was torn open, allowing some of the contents to spill onto the pavement. When the wind gusted, it picked up a discarded can from the rubbish bag and blew it noisily down the street until it finally came to rest against one of five cars parked in the road. Carla lifted her coat collar against the wind and pulled on her hat as she looked up at one of the buildings.

At one time it had obviously been a busy print shop. Several advertisements could still be seen sticking out from behind the boards which masked the windows, all offering amazing value. The print shop, like so many other businesses in the area, had fallen victim to hard times and what was considered to be progress. Alongside most of the other buildings were boarded up, making Carla think there must be some mistake with the location she had been told. Yet she hadn't been told, had she? She had got her message in a dream, from a person unseen. Carla suddenly felt incredibly stupid, as if she had somehow misinterpreted the message and made a huge mistake. Trying to control her breathing once more, as well as the discomfort she was feeling, she became aware of the smell of smoke in the air.

Mark Hatton had noticed her the moment she turned into Parrin Street. He had been waiting in his car – the last car in the row which Carla had seen – for nearly an hour, although his back felt it had been much longer. When he noticed movement at the end of the street, he had become alert and discarded the can of Red Bull he had been drinking. But the shape and movement of the figure approaching was wrong. Jimmy Gledson, for whom he had been waiting, not only looked like a rat but also scurried along like one as he walked. The shape of this person was wrong, making Mark hope the figure would soon move on. Jimmy was overdue and the last thing he wanted was for someone else to turn up and wreck his plans.

Now the figure stood close to the gates of the park and appeared to double over, almost as if they were going to be sick. 'Jesus!' muttered Mark to himself. 'Just what I want, someone all pissed up.' This idiot was going to ruin everything.

For two months Jimmy had been supplying him with information about the Kerrigan family; a family who occupied more police time than Mark cared to think about. Over the past few months Mark and his team had been able to pick up and press charges against most of the family, but they had been mainly light charges because his team had been forced to tread carefully around the main family members who were still out of reach. That was until yesterday, when Jimmy had got in touch with him and assured him he had the evidence and at least two witnesses who were willing to come forward and testify. This had been the break he had wished for; one which would make all his efforts seem worthwhile. Mark himself had suggested the location and time, but had gone alone, having kept the information to himself. He knew Martin was not going to be happy with him, nor would the rest of his team whom he intended to inform when Jimmy had squealed. Mark was more than aware of the dangerous game he was playing in going alone to meet Jimmy, yet he reminded himself that desperate times call for desperate measures. If the numerous connections that the Kerrigans had were aware of his meeting, he could easily be in trouble. There was also the option that Jimmy was setting him up. While Jimmy Gledson reminded him so much of a rat, he didn't want himself to end up at the bottom of the nearby canal where he imagined Jimmy living. Crossing the Kerrigans could put Mark there on a permanent basis. Trying to clear his mind, he became more concerned that the whole thing could go tits up if the figure he was watching didn't move on. Winding the side window down slightly for some air, he became aware of the smell of smoke in the air.

10.35pm

Jimmy Gledson was actually two streets away from Parrin Street when the first of the fire engines turned into Edwin Street. He had been keeping himself as close to the buildings as he could, stopping every so often in doorways to make sure that he wasn't being followed. More than once Jimmy had been forced to suppress an annoying cough – the remnants of a chest infection from which he had been suffering recently. The cold night was hardly helping, nor was the cigarette he held in his mouth as he walked. The information he had for Hatton was worth more than the usual fee he normally got, and it was worth coming out for even if it brought back his chest infection. Close to a pelican crossing Jimmy drew on the last of his cigarette and tossed it into the roadway as another cough escaped him, turning to look out of curiosity when the still lit stub failed to hit the ground. Slowing his pace slightly, he casually turned his head and noticed a figure standing in the street, a figure holding the cigarette stub he had thrown away. He had no time to waste as he was already late, and Hatton would be on his case soon enough if he didn't get moving. Ignoring the figure, he lowered his head and broke into a weak run, only to immediately collide with someone at the next corner which caused him to fall to the ground.

The streetlights that Jimmy had been keen to avoid glared down on him as he lay dazed on his back, thankful that his thick coat had taken the impact of his fall. As he tried to stand, he became aware of a figure looming over him, the same figure with whom he had obviously collided. Whether it was shock or just surprise, Jimmy felt unable to move. He had no recollection of banging his head, so was at a loss to explain why his vision seemed to be fading. Though he remained perfectly still, his head appeared to be rotating in a slow circle and the whiteness of the clothing worn by the figure standing over him became ever more significant for a reason he could not grasp. There was no concept of time or place for Jimmy Gledson as his vision faded and he passed out. He would wake eight hours later, asleep in a doorway, cold and uncomfortable but otherwise unharmed. The noise of a passing refuse truck would then sound louder than ever after the peace of his unexpected sleep.

Mark could hear sirens shattering the stillness of the night. Whatever was alight was close to where he had parked. At the far end of the road behind him, two police cars pulled up across the roadway, their blue lights illuminating the inside of his car. There was no way Jimmy was coming now, thanks not only to the figure still on the road ahead of him, but also to the commotion going on nearby. Mark started the engine of his car, banging his right hand hard against the wheel, annoyed that his plans had gone wrong. Only when he pulled out of the row of cars did he switch on his headlights, which seemed to make the illuminated figure in the roadway turn to face him. As she collapsed in front of his car, he saw her face and realised that it was a young woman.

11.05pm

'Oh God, please not now!' Carla thought as she attempted to stand. The bright light in front of her continued to partially blind her, but she soon became more concerned about someone approaching her. Carla was in too much discomfort to make sense of the words the person spoke, but did notice that the few words she managed to pick up were tinged with annoyance.

Mark tried to place his arm under her own in an attempt to help her stand, but failed to get a good enough grip. When he thought she was about to fall again, he attempted to get a more secure hold on her, only to become aware how her weight suddenly seemed to diminish as she was held as upright as she could manage. Where on earth the man now supporting her had come from, was unclear to Mark. He could work that one out later; for now his mind kept drifting back towards the young woman.

'We need to get her inside,' the stranger informed Mark, who was still unsure of what was happening. When Carla's coat opened slightly he became aware of her condition. Despite her protests they managed to move her back into the doorway of one of the disused buildings; one close to where Mark had been parked. He knew it had been empty for over a year since the youth centre had moved to a new purpose-built building nearby. But as they approached the doors, they appeared to open by themselves. As they entered, the lights above them flicked on from seemingly untouched light switches. While some of the lights lit instantly, others glowed weakly as if objecting to being disturbed.

Carla struggled to make sense of what was happening to her body. By her reckoning her child was not due yet, but her body was telling her otherwise. Focusing on her current surroundings, she tried desperately to work out where she had been brought, let alone who the two men were she was now with. Within the light of the room, which appeared to be a large hallway, she could see the man who had approached her from the car headlights that had blinded her. Dressed in black jeans and a fleece, he looked in his late thirties, his clothing failing to hide his well-built frame. Carla saw concern on his face which she imagined matched her own. But it was the other man, the one she had not seen appear and who still held her arm, that she felt she needed to face. The collar of his white coat brushed against her face as she sat, as did his long hair. Although her discomfort remained, she began to feel settled for some reason.

'My name is Ethan,' he told her. 'I am the reason you came here.'

'No!' Carla protested, wincing suddenly as the discomfort returned. Breathing heavily, she managed to say, 'I came here for something… for a reason…'

'It's okay, it's the same thing,' he said trying to reassure her by placing a hand on her shoulder. Removing her woollen hat, he brushed her hair away from her face. Carla felt a deep silence fall within her, which she suspected had been placed there by Ethan himself. When she watched him turn to face the other man, her breathing became easier and she began to take in her surroundings.

The wooden floorboards had long since seen no form of polish; discarded paper and empty cardboard boxes were dotted around the near empty room. At the far end of what she now realised was a hall of some sort, a stage stood with red plastic chairs stacked against it. Carla noticed there were drawings pinned to the wall, as there had been towards the back of the stage. Most of them looked to have been done by children. Voices now clouded her mind; one she felt as though she had always known, while the other she didn't recognize.

'Mark, I need you to listen to me.'

Still struggling to accept how the last few minutes had changed so dramatically, Mark Hatton barely had time to wonder how the man knew his name. In the light of the hallway, Mark could see the strange clothing which the man wore, and – more than anything – the intensity of his blue eyes.

'My name is Ethan, and this is Carla,' he told him, reaching out to hold her hand. 'She is going to give birth, and you are going to deliver it.'

'You're kidding me?' Mark shook his head. 'No way, she needs medical help.'

'She will soon get it, as they are close by. All that has already been arranged.'

'Well then, she should wait for them. I actually happen to be a police officer who…' Another contraction caused Carla to cry out and clutch Ethan's hand tighter, breaking Mark from his words.

'What you are is unimportant; it's who you are that matters now. All the medical attention that she needs will soon be given to her, but the child will have been born by then. This place and time have already been decided long ago, as was the choice of person to help with the birth. That was you, Mark.'

Mark held out his hands and backed away, continuing to shake his head as if pushing Ethan's words from his mind. When he stopped by the still open door, the cool air highlighted the perspiration which had gathered across his head. His car was still jutting out into the road, the headlights illuminating the park's railings. Mark ran his fingers through his hair and breathed out heavily, trying to compose himself.

'I can't do this!' he said out loud as he entered the hall once more. 'I have somewhere I need to be.'

'Jimmy is not coming, Mark, and the Kerrigans can wait for another day,' Ethan told him, still kneeling beside Carla.

Mark again ran one of his hands through his hair. He was about ask how the hell a man he had never met before knew what he was originally here for, but his mouth seemed to freeze. Try as he might, he couldn't get a single word to come out. Then something happened which surprised him even more. The sound of the wind and noise of the sirens nearby in Edwin Street faded in his ears, till he could hear nothing at all. Ethan stood slowly and faced Mark, his eyes looking more intense than ever. He held out a clenched hand, which stayed motionless for a moment before he opened it, allowing a small white feather to fall out. As it fell, the gentle noise of it caressing the air came to him. In an almost hypnotic gaze, he watched it spiral around, as if it had fallen from a much greater height, forever changing direction as it continued to fall. From the tips of the feathers a gentle sound came which soothed his mind and held his attention. When the feather eventually hit the floor it almost bounced, the edges of it shimmering, giving off a shower of what appeared to be tiny dust-like stars, which sprinkled onto the floor as it finally lay still. The feather stood out sharply against the discoloured wooden floor, but now lay alone as the shower of tiny stars had faded.

When Ethan spoke, his words came directly to Mark's mind. He looked at Ethan's face, but saw his lips remained motionless, held together in the smile he now wore.

'Mark, you know you can do this. You've done it before, haven't you? Sheltering from the rain that night by the motorway bridge?'

Although that had been six years ago, the memory came to him in an instant. It had been his last week in uniform. He had been leaving the city centre one night when his patrol car had been passed on the other side of the road by a car driving erratically at speed. Amidst the spray of the heavy rain that had been falling, Mark had turned his patrol car around and immediately followed. As the vehicle had approached a junction, it ignored the red light showing and had driven straight across, causing another motorist to brake suddenly to avoid a collision. The driver's horn had still been blaring as Mark and his colleague had raced through themselves. Approaching the inner city motorway, the car had begun to slow and careered to the side of the road where it struck a barrier protecting the bridge support, before finally coming to a halt. The falling rain had instantly soaked Mark as he stepped out of his car, the blue light of his patrol car illuminating the edge of the bridge as he had cautiously approached the car.

Expecting to find a drunken driver slumped over the wheel, Mark had been surprised to discover that a young boy of no more than twelve had been driving. The bridge above him had given the car shelter from the rain, but the tears that had fallen from the child's face looked as though the rain was still pouring across him. In the passenger's seat, the boy's heavily pregnant mother had cried out. The desperate measures the boy had taken to get his mother to hospital now seemed so fresh in Mark's memory as he recalled that night.

Then Ethan spoke again, his words still feeling soft in Mark's mind.

'That's why you were chosen, as you have helped in the past.'

The rainfall of that night now sounded in his mind, mixed with the sound of the baby's cry as he recalled the relief of the mother and her son as he had come to their aid.

As the noise of his surroundings returned once more, the cold air blew across his head and shoulders and he walked once more towards Ethan and Carla. There were no words exchanged between Ethan and Mark as he knelt beside Carla, who attempted to mouth the word 'thank you' through her tears. Holding onto Ethan's hand, she raised her head slightly to look up at the ceiling and, despite her condition, she felt a sense of reassurance flow through her. There were other drawings above her on the ceiling which she only now saw. In large parts of them the colours had faded badly; in places even the outline of the figures was unclear. But Carla didn't need to see the whole of any of the images; she could tell what they were by their clasped hands and the halos of light that shone around their heads. As a cry of joy left her, she noticed that the faces of the figures up above were all smiling.

At 11.37pm, the sound of a child being born into the world echoed around the hall.

11.42pm

Don Locke knew that Jean was going to cry; his wife always did whenever she watched one of her favourite films. She loved the old black and white ones the most, the days of the silver screen, believing that the way actors could hold your attention back then and the effortless timing from that era, couldn't be compared with nowadays. Tonight it was Gregory Peck who was holding onto her heart and bringing her emotion to the surface. Occasionally Don got caught up in the moment himself, but when it was a film he knew he often left her to it and went to make her a drink, blaming something in an eye making it water whenever he returned.

Deciding to make them both a coffee this time, Don headed to the kitchen, where he put a spoonful in both of their mugs and waited for the kettle to boil. On the worktop he lifted the lid of the dish which still contained the remaining portion of the dinner they had eaten earlier. The lamb casserole had been wonderful and the aroma still smelt good as he leant over the dish.

Across the room from him on the calendar on the kitchen wall, he could see the red circle that had been drawn around the end of the following month. It was the day he was thinking about finishing work. When he had returned home, Don had talked at length with Jean about retiring, and as ever she had listened to his words and thoughts quietly, letting him express all his views before she made comment. He felt that there had been too many nights apart from each other, especially in more recent years when working conditions had been tougher and the expectations of him had greatly increased. They led a simple life in many ways and felt the savings that they had, though not great, were more than enough to enable him to retire.

After making the drinks, Don opened the back door of their house just as he heard a banging sound. Knowing the noise was coming from the gate at the back of the rear yard, he stepped out into the cold wind which continued to blow strong. For months he had been planning to fit a new catch to the gate, as it continually blew open every time they had strong winds. Maybe he could start a list of jobs to do in the house when he had all that free time. He smiled to himself as he closed the gate, thinking about the limit he would have to put on Jean adding to the list.

Turning back towards the house, he could see the outline of the comet in the night sky partially obscured by the trees in neighbouring gardens. Don opened the gate again and walked out onto the rear road to enable a better view. The tail of the comet appeared longer now, the image much brighter. One of the reporters on the news had been saying that the increase in size and light was due to an increase of temperature, which had caused a sudden outburst of gas and dust. Don had failed to see what the excitement was about with this comet, even when the story became prevalent. The longer he watched it, the greater its significance became for some reason; one which he failed to understand. The cold wind gusted again, causing the trees alongside him to strain under the sudden force. Don, more than ever, needed the warmth of inside around him, and most of all to be with Jean again. The light of the comet sank behind the trees once more as he secured the gate and headed back inside.

11.44pm

Nicky Mallen ran a hand through her hair and was convinced it still felt slightly greasy. The new shampoo that she and her mother had chosen a week ago was failing to turn her hair into that of the standard of celebrities who lined her bedroom wall. In her heart Nicky doubted whether the product was going to make her hair shine endlessly as it had promised; she just wanted to lose the greasy feel which her fingers occasionally felt.

Turning her mind way from her never-ending battle with her hair, she flopped on her bed and looked at the silver photo frame on her bedside cabinet. The frame had been a Christmas gift from Stephen Langton – the best friend of her cousin, David – and was the most treasured of the gifts she had received. Stephen, though quiet, had a slow reassured way about him that Nicky really liked. It didn't bother her in the slightest that it wasn't Stephen's image filling the frame, as she loved the picture of herself and her mum which now looked back at her.

Running her finger around the frame, she imagined Stephen choosing it in the shop. How many did he look at before choosing this one? And how did he manage to pick the one she so loved? The fact that he had even thought about her was more than enough to make her smile and keep her content. Beside the frame, there were several Christmas cards bound together with ribbons, ones which she didn't want put in the loft when her dad had recently had one of his severe tidy-up spells throughout the house.

Moving across her bed on her stomach, she felt the dressing which still covered her knee catch on her pyjama bottoms. Sitting up, she pulled the legging over her knee, and touched it gently. It still felt tender to touch, even through the dressing, yet the sensation reassured her somehow. Nicky had told no-one about the events of the previous night, even Emma. She had made up an excuse to her friend about how she had cut her knee while out and had decided to cut her night short. After a night of sleep and reflection, she had gone home the following morning.

Around her home today, and especially when she was near to her parents, she wondered why she felt a renewed sense of security. She knew how lucky she had been to get home safely, yet strangely she had little recollection of how she had actually got back to her friend's house.

The room had become quiet around her now as the Britney Spears CD she had been listening to ended. Nicky slid off her bed with the intention of pressing the repeat button. Beside the curtains in her bedroom, her television set was still on with the sound muted, so Nicky couldn't hear the newsreader commenting about the comet story which her dad had been talking about earlier. She was sure that her father had been wrong when he had told her mother that the tail of the comet could be up to 8 million kilometres long. As Britney began to sing again, Nicky pulled back the curtain in her room. Looking up towards the east, her eyes were drawn to the brightness of the comet in the night sky, before it was covered once more by the curtain falling back.

At the same time, James Elland finished the last of his late night drink before looking out of his window. It had been the first time he had taken any real notice of it, as his mind had been elsewhere. Placing the cup on the windowsill, he turned back and continued unpacking the books he had stored years before.

Laura McCormick reached for the hallway light and switched it off, confident enough to climb the stairs in darkness. In the doorway of the bedroom where her sons slept, she paused and listened to the sound of them sleeping. A soft night-light reflected the glitter that made up the

331

outline of the comet's tail on the picture they had both been working on that afternoon.

When she finally climbed into bed, she lay close to her husband, enjoying the warmth his body radiated. Laura stayed awake for nearly an hour before sleep found her, all the time wondering why things seemed different somehow.

11.55pm

Given the size of the property, the fire crew attending the scene had been surprised at the intensity of the fire, especially on the lower floor. The majority of Edwin Street residents had earlier been evacuated for obvious safety reasons and had largely gathered in the community hall of St. Andrew's Church, where Graham Curren busied himself organising help and comfort for the people gathered there. Within half an hour he had several students handing out blankets and warm drinks and, when he heard a mixture of conversation interlaced with laughter spread around the hall, it made him feel content inside. When Graham walked through the gathered residents, he saw a student with streaked hair making an elderly couple laugh with a story he was telling them; the woman dried her eyes with her handkerchief, at the same time smiling at Graham as he passed. A group of small children played a game of Twister they had found in the Sunday School room, which Graham had opened up. As he looked around him, Graham could feel no trace of the tiredness that had been weighing him down recently.

For the fire crew the biggest concern was not the other residents, but containing and dowsing the fire while making the building safe. Chief Fire Officer Alan Howden was considering another approach at tackling the fire. Standing close to one of the three appliances attending the scene, he ran his hand across his face to clear some of the perspiration that had gathered across his eyebrows and looked across to the burning building. At that moment the flames began to fade, far too quickly to have been a result of his team's actions. Alan stepped from beside the vehicle and raised his helmet slightly to get a better view.

The flames were nowhere to be seen and, more strangely, there was no trace of the intense heat the building had held. Around him other fire officers gathered, and Alan could see the bemused look upon their faces which he knew mirrored his own. Even in the centre of the house where the fire had originally started, there was no sign of it; darkness had returned to cover the building. The charred timbers and ashes gave off little if any heat, only disturbed by the water that still rained down from above.

Something else caught Alan's attention as he remained looking up at the house on Edwin Street. It was a figure approaching from the nearby cordoned-off street. He appeared to be dressed in grey or white; it was hard to tell in the street lights and the artificial light around him. It must have been the effects of the heat of the fire, or the fact that he was so tired, but the approaching figure appeared to glide through the barrier which had been placed across the road, as if it wasn't there. One of his crew came across and spoke to Alan, making him turn away.

'That's okay,' he answered his colleague's question. 'Oh, and see if you can make sure the scene is sealed off properly. I don't want anyone wandering around here.'

When Alan looked back to where he had seen the figure, he was surprised to find the man standing directly at his side. His peculiar, unkempt appearance matched his unruly hair, which he pushed back with one of his hands.

'Sorry, sir,' Alan told him, holding out one of his arms. 'But you can't…'

'There is a woman who has just given birth in the open building around the corner. She needs help,' Ethan interrupted him, before walking past. Alan continued to look towards Parrin Street as if only just registering the man's words. Within minutes he had an ambulance crew, which had been on the scene, heading towards Parrin Street. Alan needed to turn his concentration back to the fire scene. He answered a call on his radio before turning to ensure that the man who had spoken to him had moved back safely behind the cordoned barrier. He could see several members of his team going about their duties, but there was no trace of the man in the white coat.

With Carla now holding her child, Mark only noticed how tired he was himself when he attempted to stand. He was surprised at how settled Carla looked, failing to even comprehend what thoughts and emotion ran through a new mother at these moments.

After telling her he would check at the doorway to see if Ethan had got the help he had gone for, Mark found two paramedics quickly approaching the building He gulped in the cold night air for a moment then walked back in with them, grateful for some reason that one of the paramedics was a woman. He gave brief details of the birth as Carla gripped his hand tightly, thanking him through her tear-filled eyes. When he returned to the doorway the air tasted even sweeter than before. Stepping into the narrow road, he intended to move his car to a safer place, but noticed what looked like pieces of ash in the air, presumably from the nearby fire scene. Noticing the smell of smoke had now dissipated, he realised that they weren't pieces of ash. Raising his eyes to the glow of the street lights, he noticed that the number of small objects that floated in the air had increased, so much so that in the pale glow of the streetlights they could easily have been mistaken for snowflakes. Mark watched as one gently landed on the palm of his outstretched hand; the whiteness along its spine so striking, as were the soft edges it held. Mark smiled as he looked up and watched them spiralling in the air all around him. From within the hall came the sound of a baby's cry once more, while outside the air was full of feathers.

Carla sensed him long before he appeared by her bedside. Though she felt incredibly tired, sleep failed to find her, resulting in her trying to convince herself that she was at least resting. From the light etching its way across the small hospital ward in which she found herself, Carla knew a new day was dawning. It was as she rested the side of her head against the pillow that she knew he had approached. Still dressed in the clothing he had worn the night before, she found his smile instantly reassuring.

'I knew you were here,' she told him as he stepped closer to her. A nurse passing by paid little attention to them, almost as if she hadn't seen them.

'Can she...?' Carla asked, somehow knowing the answer to her question.

'No,' he told her. 'She only sees you.'

The nurse collected a pile of papers and looked at the watch hanging on the breast of her uniform, before she left the ward and the other patients continued to sleep. Carla looked back at Ethan.

'In my dream, that was you at the railway station sat beside me, wasn't it?'

'It was, though it wasn't a dream.'

'But how...?'

'It was just how I chose to tell you, Carla. The time and place were already determined. I just needed to get you to believe enough to be there. I appreciate that you have many questions, but there are many that I couldn't answer as of yet if I wanted to. Your child is special, Carla, not in a way that you could instantly recognize but time will show him to be of great worth.'

'In what way?'

'That I can't tell you, mostly as that hasn't been fully decided on yet. Your child will live a predominantly normal life, he will feel the losses and hurts that all people suffer, but there is great protection out there for him and he will always be touched by the grace of love. In the time I was travelling to meet you, I reshaped the lives of seven people who will play a significant part in your son's life. Some of them will be totally unaware of the importance of their actions, while one or two will feel that something special has happened to them, yet they will all be unable to fully understand what they have done.'

'I don't understand,' Carla told him, shaking her head, struggling to take in everything he was saying.

Ethan shook his own head slightly. 'You don't have to,' he told her. 'That's part of the beauty of it.'

Ethan could have gone into greater detail and given her dates and times of some of the major events she and her son were going to have to face, but knew that the burden would be too great for her to carry. In any person's life – not just Carla's – to have no expectation, surprise or sense of wonder would be to destroy the whole beauty of living a life unknown. Ethan had seen over time how it usually took a major event such as an illness, or the loss of a loved one, to really make people appreciate the amazing significance of the dawn of each new day where the control and destiny of it becomes our own.

As he looked down on the young woman, he stroked back a strand of hair that had fallen across her face. He knew that so many of those days of wonder had already been taken from her, but also knew that the stunning result of her son being born would more than make up for them.

Ethan closed his eyes and allowed his mind to wander, finding himself rising up and drifting over towns and cities. At great speeds he travelled, through days and months where the sun rose and set within seconds. He travelled over expanses of open country where the terrain varied so much, and seasons came and went in an instant. When he selected a time and place, he viewed scenes already determined, but which had not yet happened.

He walked another hospital corridor where he found Carla crying, frantic with worry. This time the hospital staff tended to the injuries that her three-year-old son had suffered. While the sight of her hunched up in the emergency ward brought a sadness to him, he knew that the blood transfusion her son would soon be given would be considered to have saved his life. Ethan knew otherwise.

At the same time that Carla would feel the joy of her recovered son in her arms, a young woman nervously crunched the gearbox of the car she was learning to drive. Beside her, Nicky Mallen's father winced at the treatment of his car as his daughter continued on her way. Nicky had thought little of where the blood she regularly donated would go, her life and mind so busy now as the doors of her life opened around her.

Ethan drifted again, much further, to where he found Carla arguing with two members of staff in a railway station. Standing still on the main concourse, the people busily going on their way either glided through him or hurried by. He listened to an older but frantic Carla retell details to the security staff, as well as to a police officer, who had now intervened in the scene between them. Unseen to Carla, her son's hand was being held and led elsewhere in the station. Only when the staff moved Carla towards one of the security officers did she manage a glimpse of him. Through a gap in the crowd of people jostling for position to board the train she was due to catch, she saw a man walking her son away from her as she agonizingly looked on. Carla broke away from the policewoman trying to calm her down, calling out as she pushed her way past people in her attempt to get to her son. An overweight businessman shouted at her as she knocked him sideways, spilling the contents of his briefcase across the floor. Carla ignored him as she ran frantically across the station, her son her only concern. By the time she caught up with them, she found her son was still holding the hand of Lee Holden. Sweeping him up in her arms, she cried out a torrent of abuse at Lee, asking what on earth he was doing. She had failed to see that the uniform he wore matched that of the other staff she had been talking to moments before, as time passed by on the large clock above her.

Over a hot drink and more tears, Carla would eventually thank Lee and the rest of the staff for finding her son, who was again scolded about wandering off.

The train that they had missed or, as Ethan liked to think, were prevented from boarding, would later feature tragically across numerous television stations and newspapers.

Back across to the same city to which Carla had journeyed, Ethan glided with great speed to where the smell of fresh paint hung in the air. Laughter was also carried across the air; one of the few emotions that sound carried – a sound which always brought Ethan joy. He found himself standing on a newly-laid carpet where once a car had often been parked. The former garage was now joined by an extended section, which would soon all be part of the same self-contained flat. The subtle pastel colours were soothing to Ethan as he walked through the rooms of the flat. The unmade beds would soon feel the caress of fresh sheets, hangers which stood motionless would strain under the weight of clothing, yet it would be another month before Carla Hall would sit in a bus shelter drinking a cup of coffee and circle the advert for the flat in a newspaper. Another week would pass before she would view and eventually move in there. For now though, Jean Locke flicked another off-cut of wallpaper at her husband, Don, as they continued with the decorating, laughing again as it landed in the drink that Don had been trying to enjoy.

While Ethan had wandered within scenes yet to happen, it had been barely seconds to Carla; about the time it had taken her to watch him smile. The significant events which would include James Elland, Laura McCormick and Graham Curren, were far off, and in part not yet determined fully. Mark Hatton also thought that his involvement with Carla and her son was over; but time would show him otherwise, in ways neither he nor Carla could think possible at this moment.

'Why was I chosen?' she asked, as Ethan sat on the edge of her bed. She was still unsure even now why she felt so at peace with the scene unfolding around her.

'Because you have never lost belief, or hope. It is what you have passed down to your son.'

Carla felt as though she could have gone on asking him questions yet never have found an end to them. She felt a rise of emotion as he reached across and held his hand against the cheek of her face, feeling a slight tingle across the surface of her skin.

'I just checked on your son, he is sleeping contentedly,' he told her as he stood up once more. Since Carla had been admitted to hospital, the baby had been cared for in an adjoining ward where his weak condition still caused the staff concern. Though her child was out of sight, she could feel his young heart beating softly and the presence of his tiny body being emitted towards her through Ethan. Without needing to ask him, she knew her son would soon be well enough for her to hold in her arms again.

As she watched Ethan walk to the end of her bed, she knew that he was leaving. Not just for now, but for good. She gingerly propped herself up in her bed, biting gently on her bottom lip as she felt a slight discomfort, while attempting to make herself see clearer. As if sensing her thoughts, Ethan stopped and turned to look back at her.

'How will I know?' she asked, surprised when he failed to answer. 'These events you have spoken of, how will I know when they are happening?'

Ethan smiled once more and breathed in deeply, as if building up to his answer. He turned as he spoke, his image blurring slightly as the strengthening sunlight broke across the floor of the hospital ward.

'Oh, you'll know. His birth was signalled by the arrival of the comet. As for the other events, you just have to see the signs…' she heard as his voice carried to her as if caught on a summer breeze.

Along the edge of what had once been his shape, a row of white feathers held in the air for a moment before they started to move and fall silently to the floor across the empty space where Ethan had once stood.

The birds gathered in large numbers as they fed on the scattered pieces of bread that had been thrown for them. Occasionally a few flew off when a noise or movement nearby disturbed them, but for now they eagerly fed on the unexpected meal.

Elsewhere across the park, people continued to enjoy the late summer weather. The day was warm again, like the past week, and the warmth of the sunshine felt nice across the face of Carla Hall as she held her face up towards it. With her eyes closed, she let her mind wander so that she imagined she was sitting on a deserted beach with clear blue water lapping at her feet. When she opened her eyes once more, instead of white sands she saw the greenery of the park around her with the outline of the city centre buildings in the distance.

Across the nearby trees she noticed the first changes in colour on the tips of some of the leaves; on the large sycamore tree where a group of boys played football, the change was more evident. Today though the temperature was warm and she was enjoying the moment. A slight giggle beside her made her turn and smile. She reached out and felt the tiny fingers of one of her son's hands. They felt so delicate and soft against her own and as gentle as the smile which he wore on his face. The parasol above his pushchair, which protected him from the direct sunlight, cast an orange glow across his small form, adding extra cover as Carla looked lovingly upon him.

While Carla folded up the blanket she had been sitting on, she smiled as she watched him kick his legs out, giggling again. He seemed to be growing stronger each day and her early worries had now faded. She placed the blanket beside her bag on the back of the pushchair and headed back onto the pathway. The last of the birds flew away and disappeared, lost against the bright blue sky above. Carla sang a gentle lullaby as she walked, hoping her son would hear.

Close to a small pond, she approached a bench where two elderly women sat; both smiled at the figure in the pushchair as they got closer. A soft toy fell to the ground as they neared, and one of the women bent down to pick it up for Carla.

'He's a happy looking boy,' the woman told her as she handed Carla the toy.

'He is most of the time, thank you,' Carla replied, before kneeling down herself to replace the toy in the pushchair.

'How old now?' the other woman asked.

'Nearly six months,' Carla told them both, surprised herself for a moment at where the time had gone. Now both the women made a fuss of him, making Carla feel special in a strange way. When one of them asked his name, she answered clearly and precisely, knowing that all during her pregnancy she had never considered what her baby was going to be called.

'Ethan,' she told them. 'I named him Ethan.'

Carla thanked them for their words and for handing back the soft toy, then walked on. The two women resumed their own conversation as they enjoyed the warmth of the day. A gentle breeze blew across the park, feeling refreshingly cool against Carla's skin as she walked slowly along the path. Not far away, masked by the branches of the beech trees which dominated the park entrance, a white feather blew by, landing for a moment on the grass where several others had earlier gathered.